PRETENDING TO BE ALIVE

Author, Richard Jan

ISBN
Hardback: 978-1-964289-70-0
Paperback: 978-1-964289-69-4

Pretending to be Alive is the title of the third book in a series titled **Dying to Succeed**.

The books in this series include:
Book 1, Winds of Success
Book 2, Living with Death
Book 4, Presumption of Sanity
Book 5, Running with Regret
Book 6, Longing to go Home
Book 7, Afraid to Hope
Book 8, Waiting in Infinity
Book 9, Chasing after Time
Book 10, Casualties of Words
Book 11, Traveling into Chaos
Book 12, Snows of Fear

This book is dedicated to Gary Jaarda, a good friend and business partner.

Note: My books do not have chapters. Instead, they have episodes like journal entries which are identified by place, date, and time. The speaker is also identified. Where only the time has changed from a previous episode, the date and place may not be repeated, but the speaker is always known. Please forgive me if this is initially confusing. I am confident it will become easier to understand once you have read a few pages.

Richard Jan

Music may best exemplify the internal workings of the mind. Not logic as is commonly thought. If logic ruled the world, we would live in a different world. Perhaps the problem is that we believe we live by logic when in fact our minds are governed by an operating system far more elusive. As I wrote these books, I often played music. May I suggest that as you read these books, you listen to music in the background. I cannot pretend to instruct you concerning what music to play. We all come to music, as we do to words, from different backgrounds. Play the music you love, something that moves you deeply in your soul.

RJ

Deep calls to deep.
I hear your voice in the roar of a waterfall.
And in the rush of breaking waves washing over my soul.
You send your love with the light of a new day.
And in the dark night, your song is still with me,
Like a prayer on my lips to you, the God of my life.

Contents

ACKNOWLEDGMENTS

It is only fair that I acknowledge the help and encouragement which I received from New York Book Publishers. I went to them initially looking for guidance in editing, cover design, marketing, and distribution. They promised me that they could fulfill my needs. I accepted their proposal and began working with them virtually while living in the Midwest with their company's resources located in New York City. Our journey together has been an adventure; one not taken lightly, but traveled with some trepidation and concerns. Special thanks goes to Victor Hughes, who guaranteed me they would not let me down. And thanks to my daily contact, Serena Hoffman for understanding my concerns and assuring me that everything was progressing as it should. And to Jim Bannister who took the time to talk to me when I needed a conversation. And to the many editors and artists who have contributed greatly to the final product. Thanks to them all for helping me achieve what I had hoped for when I first contacted this New York Book Publishers.

AUTHOR'S NOTE

Although I am familiar with the colored gemstone industry from having worked in it for ten years, I don't pretend to be an expert on any level. My knowledge can best be described as that of a man traveling through a city without ever stopping for an extended period of time to experience the living conditions up close. And yet, as I contemplated my journey after it came to an end, I thought it was interesting and perhaps worthy of being a wonderful subject for a book.

But what I discovered as I wrote was that the real story was not the gemstone industry, but how the cast of characters reacted to the challenges they faced, challenges similar to what we daily endure. And it is my hope that knowledge gained from existing for a time in their shoes as you read this book; may encourage you to live a fuller, more purposeful life.

- Richard Jan

Page Left Blank Intentionally

AMBERGRIS ISLAND, BELIZE, FRIDAY, APRIL 24, 1998, 2:30 A.M. JOHN VAN LAAN

Lifting her head, I look into her still, quiet eyes.

I am lost, somewhere in a vast walled canyon filled with crescendoing, violent noise. The echoes of sporadic gunfire constantly reverberate through my ears. Tracer beams hover overhead, painting passionate red lines across the room, searching for targets of pain, darting through the smoke-filled air like the vapor trails of tiny red ghosts dancing anxious, jerky dances of despair. Yet, I see nothing of their killing desires. Only her... I only see her face.

Her body is resting on me where we have fallen on the floor in one last pathetic embrace. Soft, moist blood drips from her cheeks like warm tears onto my lips, sweet to taste. I wait...hoping for some faint signs of life, but her eyes are vacant, her lips silent. Holding her body close, I begin to slowly rock... rock back and forth until gradually I wake up in a dark night.

My throat feels parched and dry, as if I have been screaming for hours. And I am afraid, afraid because I know I have been dreaming and my dream is quickly fading like a dying flower petal falling through a void in time. I don't want my dream to end. I want to remain in my dream, live my dream. I want to be with her again, even in death... I want to stay with her forever.

But dreams are not real, and I know that she is dead from a bullet to her brain. My only regret is my dream, a nightmarish reproduction from my past, has ended, as have other similar dreams. And I am once again alone.

Softly breaking waves on a seashore outside my bedroom window remind me where I am. The sounds of their rhythmic lapping wash through my mind like music and help me slowly calm down.

My pillow is damp and sweat-soaked. I lift my head to turn it over, lying down again as warm breezes glide through the trees and in through my bedroom windows. Insects and tree frogs fill the silence of night with their chorus of cries. I am thankful for their voices. I don't like silence. Silence is lifeless.

I lie awake in the dark as I do most nights, thinking of her, feeling an emptiness as only it can be felt in the middle of the night.

8:10 A.M. ILANA

Ilana released the shoulder straps of her summer dress, permitting a warm breeze to gather the soft folds of cloth and help remove the offending garment guilty of obscuring the beautiful curves of her lovely tan body.

Disguised now by only a rather skimpy white bikini, she laid face down on a towel near the far end of a wooden dock jutting into the Caribbean Sea. The morning sun quickly warmed her tanned skin. She was very grateful for a breeze because, without it, she would have quickly become too hot. As it was, she was perfectly comfortable as she rested some distance from shore at the end of a dock. Even though she was nearly naked, she did not care if someone saw her. She knew she was beautiful. Let them look.

The morning was hers, free to do as she pleased, as were most mornings, just as she wished it.

Her meeting with that unpleasant man who was paying her to watch an American was not until shortly before noon.

8:24 A.M. JOHN

For me, the best time to be on my dock is early morning.

By midday the sun beats down from directly overhead out of a clear blue sky with torrid heat. But in the morning, the sun lays low over the water, casting a warm glow over the Caribbean Sea. More importantly, Ilana is usually on my dock in the morning, as was true this morning. The sight of her beautiful tan body sunbathing at the end of my dock made me smile as another dark night filled with nightmarish memories of Monica's death evaporated under the warm rays of bright morning sunshine and the natural allure of a gorgeous island girl.

The Caribbean Sea stretched out in front of me as far as I could see in all its rippled blue-glass splendor. On the edges of the horizon, large sea swells driven by the wind over miles of open ocean could be seen curling over a reef in a rush of cascading white water. Once their strength was dissipated by the reef, the waves floated harmlessly toward shore as only weak replicas of their former grandeur, creating a gently rolling, blue-green aquatic sanctuary between the reef and the shore.

After placing a folding chair next to Ilana, intentionally covering her body with my shadow; I pretended to be completely unaware of her lovely existence. I took a sip of hot coffee from a mug and waited quietly for her expected response. Eventually she opened her eyes and frowned when she saw I had taken her sun. But instead of complaining, she simply slipped over the edge of the dock into the warm water. I watched as she gracefully stroked through the calm waters, swimming as a creature who naturally belongs in the sea.

In a way, it was true. The sea was her home. A native of Belize, she lived on the island of Ambergris near the sea. She told me she had left her island only once to visit Belize City on the mainland. This was as far as she had ever traveled. Her mother and father were dead. Her brother was a fisherman. He is her only family and she lives with him in their family house. Occasionally, she works as a waitress during the busy tourist season, but this seems to be the extent of her ambition.

I often find her on my dock in the morning. I don't mind. She is a very attractive woman with big brown eyes and jet-black hair typical of her Spanish heritage. But truth is, ever since Monica died, I have spent very little time thinking about Ilana or any other woman. The memory of my late girlfriend is still too close. The night she died continues to plague my thoughts during the day and occupy my dreams at night. This makes my life difficult. But I try, I try to live, one hour, one day at a time.

Last year, when I couldn't stay in Charlottesville, Virginia, anymore, I left town. Just needed to get away. Too many memories existed in that town, too many of my dead girlfriend, Monica Sorensen.

I packed a small bag with no idea of where I was going and said goodbye to Arny, my African American housekeeper and best friend. Written instructions were given to my secretary, Helen, stating no one could evict him. Arny was free to live in an apartment I had built for him as long as he desired. Both my apartment and Arny's are housed in an office building in the hills near Charlottesville owned by me. It is also the international headquarters for a company I founded named Gemstones International, Inc. Its business is an international supplier of the gemstone sapphire. The business has been extremely profitable, and as a result, I am a very wealthy man.

When I first considered leaving Charlottesville, my initial thought was to return to the place where I was born and raised, Grand Haven, Michigan. Although this seemed logical, I had no place to stay there. The cottage I owned on the shores of Lake Michigan had been destroyed, burned to the ground. It is my belief that this was the work of some friends of a former business associate named Phillip Palmer. At least, this is what I thought happened. But in fact, the crime has never been solved. So, I don't really know for certain.

Without having anywhere to go but knowing I needed to get away, I stopped at my bank as I drove out of town and bought some traveler's checks. I assumed the checks, along with an assortment of credit cards and a passport, would allow me to travel wherever I wished. As I drove to the airport, I remembered a short visit I had made to Belize after a business trip to Columbia, South America.

Columbia was a frightening place. I traveled there initially to investigate the possibility of marketing some of the beautiful emeralds mined in Columbia through my company. In order to become a dealer in these gemstones, I needed to find a partner in Columbia. However, after several days, I learned just how difficult this might be. My contact in Columbia did nothing to ease my discomfort. Manuel Ortega was his name. He operated one of the largest emerald mining companies in this country. Truth is, I didn't like him from the beginning. Even though he appeared to be very congenial, something was missing. Maybe it was trust. I never felt he was being completely honest with me, always hiding something.

Or maybe it was simply being in Columbia. Nothing felt secure there. I was very happy to leave that country without being killed or kidnapped.

I had read about Belize before traveling to South America and always wanted to visit. I decided to stop there as a reward for surviving my trip to Columbia. The small island of Ambergris off the coast of Belize had danced in my head ever since that visit, filled with memories of sea breezes, rustling palm trees, pelicans, and frigate birds floating in the blue sky. The clear emerald green sea required only a mask and fins to lazily enjoy. Free diving among the rich marine life below the surface was a joy.

After arriving at the Charlottesville airport, I inquired about flights to Belize and learned that a flight to Belize City in Central America from Miami could be booked. From Belize City, a short single-engine prop plane took me to Ambergris Island. After a few nights staying in a hotel on the island, I rented a house with a dock. A real estate agent said I could probably stay there as long as I liked. The owner had died. He was American, very wealthy or at least this is what the agent said. The house was tied up in estate litigation, something which was likely to take a long time.

From my lounge chair on the dock belonging to the house, I lazily watched Ilana turn over and dive, her strong tan legs propelling her into the clear blue sea. Holding her breath, she swam with the fish before resurfacing.

'Come in,' she yelled as she paddled near my dock.

I waved her off, content to gaze out over the vast rolling surface of the glassy blue-green sea. It was all too easy to become completely mesmerized by the constantly changing vista of flowing white clouds passing over this living ocean, content to rest and allow the sun to warm my tired body after another exhausting night of anxious dreams.

I am mostly okay during the day. But my nights are hell. Too many times, Monica returns to me at night in vivid, wonderful dreams, her image filled with grace and love. I hold her in my arms, her kisses soft on my lips, her smile in my heart. But when I am finally happy again, she always slips away. Death takes her. I never know how or when she will leave. I only know it will happen.

Sometimes, we talk first. She reassures me everything is fine, but I know better. I know she will go away. Other times it is like the first time, the real time in a hotel room, like the dream I had last night.

Some of the dreams are surreal, filled with strange places that are illusionary... Like I am standing on a shore watching her ghost glide across rolling waters. She is a beautiful solitary figure flying on the wind, dressed in a flowing white gown. A fog rolls in, and her image dissolves into the mist, and I am alone again.

It doesn't matter how my dreams end. The result is always the same. She is gone, and I am alone. This is hard. My nights are very hard. The memory of the night she was accidentally killed lingers in my mind like it was yesterday. I guess this is why these dreams keep coming.

I closed my eyes and let the sea breeze cool my restive mind, trying to relax, trying to think about something other than my dead girlfriend.

'How are you today, Mr. John,' Ilana asked after climbing a ladder onto the dock. She always calls me Mr. John. Even though I have often asked her to call me John, she ignores my request.

'I'm very fine,' I lied.

'What are we doing today,' she looked at me with her big, beautiful brown eyes as she toweled off after her swim.

'What would you like to do?' I replied, observing the soft, subtle curves of her body.

'I think I would like to go for a sail today, Mr. John,' she answered after a pause.

I considered her request, but only briefly. A sail was as good as anything else. And having Ilana with me... well... she would make my afternoon very pleasant. I nodded in agreement.

'Okay, Mr. John. I will see you after lunch. I have an errand to do first.'

11:45 A.M. ILANA

After leaving John on his dock, Ilana returned to her family home to do some chores. Completing her work quickly, she changed into a fresh, lightly colored street dress, which complimented the deep tan of her smooth skin. Locking the front door, she headed down a dirt road towards the main street of her hometown, San Pedro.

The town was originally a fishing village. However, in recent years, it has become a resort destination. It now passed as the closest example of modern civilization on her island. Newly painted houses and tourist-trap shops line both sides of its dusty-dirt main street, which runs parallel to the beach. The imposing structure of a Catholic Church dominates the town's main square. The church is old and tired looking; its faded pink stucco exterior is now only a pale, washed-out replica of how it must have looked in the grandeur of its original deep red color.

Ilana hurried by the church, ignoring a strong urge to go inside. Maybe, she thought. Maybe it would be good to say a few prayers at the altar. Maybe this would be better than meeting with the ugly man at the jewelry shop. But she was already late for her meeting, and she needed money. Ignoring her good intentions, she quickly passed the church.

A few male laggards leaning against the wall of a nearby corner t-shirt shop intently followed the simple ballet movements of her slim body. Street dust rose from her leather sandals as she hurried by their staring eyes. The only building in town taller than the Catholic Church was the three-story Ruby Hotel. Its name is spelled RUBY on the street side of the building and RUBIE on the beachside. Nobody seems to care. The misspelled name is simply another casualty of the prevailing winds of procrastination, which seem to waffle lazily through the trees on this island. Common wisdom is to put off until tomorrow anything which does not need to be done today.

Interspersed along the buildings on the main street were a few dive shops and a usual assortment of service businesses, such as a storefront that sells insurance. And, of course, there is an ever-present real estate office. This is a resort town, after all. On the north side of town, worn gray, sun-decayed wooden docks jutting into the sea, serving as a marina. The safe harbor is used mostly by local fishermen. Native islanders occupy a majority of the houses near the marina. Ilana's family house is no exception, situated only a few blocks from the docks. Although it is old, the house is in reasonably good shape. Her brother inherited it from his parents. It is Ilana has lived since she was a small child. Even though her brother tries to make it nice for her, she spends very little time there, using the house more as a place to store her belongings than as a home. Her lifestyle is not appreciated by her brother.

A number of privately owned resorts have recently been built along the beach on the south side of town. The lodgings of one of these resorts are covered with fake thatched roofs meant to look like native huts. And they could pass for native except for ugly protruding metal air conditioners, which can be seen poking from their windows. Other resort accommodations are clean, modern condos, similar to what you might see in Florida. A few old relics left over from the happy hippy sixties are scattered along the beach, rusting travel trailers and busses marring the natural beauty of the seashore. Most have been abandoned and should have been hauled away. A few rotting old boats lay half buried in the sands, deposited on the shore by past hurricanes or storms. No one seems to mind these old rust buckets. They are simply allowed to rest in peace until they rot and eventually wash away. Interspersed among the resorts and the clutter are several stately private homes, including the house John was renting.

Ilana's destination that morning was a Mayan silver jewelry shop situated near the center of town past the Rubie Hotel. Stopping briefly once she was inside the door of the shop, she pretended to look at displays of local jewelry on shelves under a glass top case. Seeing no one inside, she quickly slipped behind a dark blue, floor-length cloth curtain which hid a private back room.

He was waiting patiently for her there, sitting on a bench at a badly scratched old wooden table. A plate of half-eaten enchiladas rested in front of him. Occasionally, he took a bite of food to pass the time.

The man was old, but not so old. Truth was, it was difficult to determine just how old he was because he had a deeply tanned, badly wrinkled face from too many days in the hot sun. This made him look old, but it was possible he wasn't old at all. A full head of curly black hair touched with a hint of gray at his temples did nothing to indicate his age. Thick black eyebrows matched a bushy mustache above thinly drawn lips. If it wasn't for his wrinkled skin, he could have almost looked attractive. Except, something unpleasant seemed to inhabit this man's body, something which spoiled a good impression and made him appear to be ugly. It was as if a sense of contained violence emanated from his strongly built torso. You immediately sensed you did not want to make this man mad.

'Would you like something to eat?' he asked in a low voice, pointing at some enchiladas slowly cooking on a black wrought iron pan over an old metal stove.

'Yes,' Ilana replied without hesitation. She was hungry. Taking a fork from a drawer, she carefully lifted the food from the pan on the stove and placed it on a handmade ceramic dish. Sitting on a chair at a scratched table across from the man, she began to eat. Neither of them spoke for long minutes, eating in silence.

Finally, the man asked her, 'How is our friend, the American?'

Ilana looked up from her enchilada as if she had forgotten this man was in the room.

'Oh, he is fine,' she answered nonchalantly. 'We are going sailing this afternoon.'

'So, nothing has changed,' he asked.

'No, nothing has changed.'

'You would tell me if it had.'

'I would tell you, signor.'

The man spoke English with a heavy Spanish accent, not one Ilana recognized. She could speak Spanish. Most Belizeans can. Although Spanish was not the official language of Belize, English is. Ilana preferred to speak English, and the man spoke simple English to accommodate her, but it was obviously not his native tongue. This much Ilana knew, but she didn't know where he came from and she didn't ask.

'My phone number, do you remember it?' he asked.

'I do,' she replied.

'Repeat it for me.'

Ilana repeated the number from memory without hesitation.

'And your friend, does he give you money?' the man inquired.

'No, Signor. We eat together sometimes.'

'But you refuse his money if he offers?'

'Yes. He has sometimes asked me if I need anything, but I have always said no.'

'Good,' the man said. Taking a small roll of bills out of his pants pocket, he slid the money across the table to Ilana. Then he stood without finishing his enchilada and walked out a back door.

Ilana put the money in her purse.

2:25 P.M. JOHN

The gleaming, dark blue, fiberglass hull of the sailboat cut effortlessly through a choppy emerald green sea.

A gentle but steady breeze filled the boat's billowing sails into great swooping curves of cloth, perfect arcs spread across a clear blue sky. The power of the wind pushed the hull through the living sea as if the water existed for no other purpose than to carry the boat on its shoulders.

I leaned against the cockpit in a moment of quiet contentment. My friend, the wind had appeared magically out of nowhere, doing its work before disappearing into the distance. Like a great invisible hand in the sky, God's ethereal wind spirit drove us at a good and steady pace. After years of hectic living out of suitcases, I found much joy could be had in traveling in no need to be in a hurry; no jet planes, no fast cars, no traffic or airport delays to worry about; nothing more than a steady pace dictated by wind and water with no need to be anywhere, anytime soon.

I purchased a sailboat about six months after arriving on the island. Beginning to feel a little better at the time, I decided a boat might be useful. I lived on an island, after all, and the best method of travel from one place to another was on the water in a boat.

After giving it some thought, I christened my forty-four-foot sailboat, 'The Retreat.' The name seemed appropriate. Because retreat was what I did after Monica died. I walked away from it all.

I guess you could say I retreated from the horror and the memories. More than anything, I traveled to this island to get away and forget. But unfortunately, I have not been very successful at forgetting. I often wake up at night in a panic. In dreams, I again feel Monica's warm blood running down my face from the wound in her head. I look into her eyes. No life exists in those eyes, only a deathly blank stare. A bullet through the back of her skull killed her instantly, leaving me no goodbye kiss, no chance to say I loved her, loved her since the first day I met her in my office in Charlottesville, Virginia.

Did she love me?

I have often wondered. Our relationship was rocky. We were forced apart several times by the violent events which engulfed our lives. Even so, before she died, we had decided to be together, to brave the risks. This was why one tragic night found us together one time too many. Agents from the CIA stormed a hotel room in an effort to rescue us. A firefight erupted. She was shot dead before she hit the floor, killed by a single bullet, which was probably meant for me.

In the first months after arriving in Belize I spent my time walking its beaches thinking about her. I wondered if she had tried to protect me from the bullets that flew across the room that horrible night. She pulled me to the floor, and I think she did this because she loved me. But maybe I believe this because I want it to be true. Truth is, I don't really know, even though it would be nice to know. It would be great to hear her say that was the reason she pushed me to the floor because she loved me. But life doesn't always give us the Shakespearian moment that we so desperately desire.

A slight flutter disturbed the jib sail. Leaning over, I pulled a quarter turn on a chrome winch handle, watching the big white sail smooth into a perfect curve of power. 'The Retreat' leaned into the sea, spray splashing over its fore deck. A frothy white wake trailed behind the stern, marring the clear blue waters. After an adjustment to our course with a gentle turn of the wheel, I sat back, once again content to simply enjoy the ride.

Ilana rested on seat cushions opposite me in the cockpit. Her eyes were closed under the glare of the sun, her body already a perfect shade of tan. We had decided to sail to one of our favorite diving spots on a reef. It was about five nautical miles south of my rented beach house.

After Ilana left me in the morning, I sat for a long time on the dock, sipping coffee as a sea breeze blew and pelicans flew in thermals. I have discovered I can sit for hours, watching these big birds fly. I wonder how I ever was a man who ran a multi-national company, working intently for ten to twelve hours or more a day, flying to every corner of the globe. Now, I want nothing to do with my former life.

Eventually, I went into town to do a few errands in the morning. Food from a local grocery store was needed for our dinner on the boat. Some fresh fruit, vegetables, cheese and Belikin beer were now packed below in the galley.

Ilana helped me prepare the boat for sailing. I could have done it by myself, but it was easier with her help. Plus, her slim body, only vaguely obscured by a white bikini, improved an already wonderful view.

I'm not quite sure how she has come to be my friend. But it doesn't make me unhappy. My first few months on the island were a lonely time. After renting the house on the beach, I did almost nothing except exist on a bare subsistence diet. Trips to a grocery store for food and booze were all that was required, nothing else. The house came fully furnished with everything I needed. My days were spent mostly walking the beach, reading, and sleeping. And drinking, I drank gallons of whiskey and beer. It didn't help. Even though I thought booze would help me forget Monica, I discovered that I did more drinking and remembering than I did drinking and forgetting. And the hangovers were horrible. After a while, I gave up booze. And eventually I stopped worrying someone would come down to this island to finish the work they started up north.

No attempts have been made to kill me while living in Belize, nothing like the months before the shooting in New York when Monica was killed.

3:30 P.M. JOHN

I gently brushed back Ilana's jet-black hair as she rested on a cushion next to me.

She opened her eyes and smiled.

'We're almost to the reef,' I said. 'Would you mind helping make anchor?'

'Of course, Mr. John.'

Her quick, athletic movements on a rocking boat were a source of wonder for a land-lover like me. As she waited for my signal to lower the jib, I briefly wondered again how she had come to be my friend. I really didn't know and didn't care. I was just grateful. She, more than anyone or anything else, was helping me recover from a self-induced coma of regret which I had fallen into after my arrival in Belize. As beautiful as was this island, filled with bougainvillea, palm trees, and constant warm sea breezes, none of its natural wonders seemed to lift me out of my depression as much as she did.

I don't remember when my relationship with Ilana began. She simply appeared one morning on my dock, sunbathing and swimming. I had not invited her. I did not know her. I was still drinking heavily at the time, and it was as if her lovely body had stepped out of one of my booze-induced daydreams.

At first, I simply let her happen without saying a word. I didn't talk to her. Didn't send her away. Didn't say this was private property. I just let her be. Some days, I said hi. Other days, I said nothing. One day she asked me if I would like to go for a swim with her. I said yes. I'm a good swimmer, high school swim team. No world records, no records, period, but I do okay in water.

She was amazed. 'You swim like a native,' she observed.

We began to swim together almost daily, which was good because I badly needed exercise. One morning she arrived in an old outboard boat, said it would be fun to snorkel off a reef. She was right. We began to go often. And then we started to spend time talking after our swims. Not much in the beginning, but eventually, we had long, involved conversations. It seemed she could talk for hours. She had endless questions about the world outside her island of Ambergris. In this respect, she was a lot like Monica, always full of questions.

I told Ilana the outside world beyond her island was not important. I said she had everything she needed where she lived. But she was naturally curious. She pestered me with questions about places and things which existed in my world, the world I left behind. I answered her questions even though sometimes I found it difficult to talk about my world.

One day, I invited her to my house for lunch. We had been talking on my dock. It was a nice day, not too hot, comfortable. I was getting hungry and she was busy asking me her many questions. I decided inviting her for lunch was necessary if I wanted to satisfy my appetite. Besides, it seemed the polite thing to do. I couldn't exactly walk away in the middle of a conversation. Besides, I was enjoying her company.

She agreed.

Sadly, my refrigerator was mostly empty with nothing much in my pantry that day. I think we shared a can of soup and a sandwich, some luncheon meat smothered with mustard, my usual bachelor fair. She said she didn't like my food, just looked at the sandwich warily at first and then nibbled a little, trying to be polite, finally ignoring the sandwich completely.

That's how it began, our relationship if you could call it a relationship. Occasionally, we ate together, not all the time, only once in a while. Mostly, I ate while she watched. As I said, she didn't like my food. My meals were not to her taste, canned soup, and sandwiches. Eventually, she'd had enough of my diet. She made a list of foods she wanted me to buy at a store. And then she started to cook after explaining I wasn't a very good host.

I didn't argue.

One day, while we were resting outside on a deck after lunch, she asked if I would like to make love to her.

The second-story deck of the rented house where we were sitting overlooked the sea. The house, architecturally, was like a southern-style mansion, painted white wood exterior with four big pillars on the ocean side supporting a roof deck over a long porch. The interior walls were covered with ugly flowered wallpaper. I had a local handyman rip out the wallpaper and paint the walls an off-white color. I couldn't stand the busyness of the wallpaper. I knew the house didn't belong to me, but I didn't care. I had rented it for a year. I wasn't going to live with this wallpaper for a year. I would compensate the owner for the wallpaper if he didn't like my paint job. The resort-style furniture also had to go. It was covered with busy, pink and yellow patterned cloth. I couldn't stand to look at it, made me nauseous. I stored it in a back bedroom on the first floor. New wood tables, cushioned chairs, and couches were purchased. Simple local furniture with tan cloth cushions now inhabited the rented house.

The day she asked me her wonderful question, I was busy staring over the sea, lost in thought. A glass of wine was in my hand. I was probably thinking about Monica. I don't remember. Naturally, her question surprised me. I turned to her, wondering if I had heard her correctly.

She smiled and clearly restated her question. 'Would you like to make love to me?' she asked in a manner which seemed so easy, so natural.

After turning into the wind, I signaled Ilana to lower the jib. The breeze was steady, not very strong. Only one anchor line was required that afternoon. Ilana brought up our swim gear from below deck: fins, masks and a spear, while I finished lowering the main sail down. Electric winches did most of the work. Once the sail was secured, I relaxed for a moment as the boat gently rocked in an almost nonexistent sea. I was tempted to lie down on the deck and take a nap in the sun.

'Come on, Mr. John,' Ilana said as she fastened fins to her small brown feet. 'The fish, they are waiting for us.'

'Okay, okay,' I replied, grabbing my mask.

Ilana dove smoothly off the side of the boat, disappearing into the water. I put on my fins and waddled awkwardly to the stern, more falling than diving into the warm blue waters. Leveling off on the surface, I swam easily to where Ilana waited. Without a word, we both flipped over into the waters by the reef.

A school of steel gray barracuda flashed by as we swam near the surface. A vee-shaped gray blanket, evidence of a manta ray, floated slowly across the light brown sands below us. I stopped kicking when my lungs began to rebel from lack of oxygen and floated to the surface. Ilana was able to remain underwater longer than me. In time, she surfaced and quickly flipped over again. I followed her down towards a large outcropping of coral. Swimming under the coral's outstretched wings of lace, we were careful not to hit its brittle surface. We did not want to break what the sea had taken years to build.

Beneath the sheltering surface of light brown coral, schools of orange and red fish darted for safety when we approached. I swam easily to conserve oxygen as my lungs began to tighten in my chest. Exhaling spent air bubbling to the surface, I was able to ignore a growing need for oxygen for a short time as I breathed in the life forces which surrounded me in this colorful sea. I was beginning to feel more alive in the sea than on land. The multi-colored fish reminded me of the sparkling blue sapphires and green emeralds from my previous life. When my lungs began to scream for air, it was time to surface. Slowly, my body drifted up as I watched Ilana swim effortlessly below me.

Breaking the surface, I lay on my back and paddled easily to maintain my balance in the water while deeply filling my lungs with precious oxygen.

4:55 P.M. JOHN

While resting on the deck of my boat, a sea breeze cooled my wet skin under a warm sun.

Ilana continued swimming in the sea, fishing for our dinner. Life was good. It was time for a nap. I relaxed, leaning against the mast, allowing my eyes to close momentarily, but no more than a few seconds before my satellite phone began to ring.

I purchased the phone because telephone service in Belize was less than perfect—in fact, it is downright terrible. However, this didn't bother me too much because I almost never called anyone, and no one called me. Still, I assumed it was good to have a phone in case of an emergency. But the truth was, I almost never turned on the dumb thing, and I had no idea why the phone was on duty that day.

Caller ID indicated a familiar number I recognized. Clarence was calling from Australia. He was one of only a few friends from my old life who still communicated with me. I briefly considered taking his call but decided to let it go to voicemail while making a mental note to return his call later. A nap before Ilana finished fishing seemed far more important.

I closed my eyes and dozed briefly before the incessant ringing of the phone again startled me. Silently cursed myself for not turning off the stupid thing, I answered it this time without first looking at the caller ID for reasons I can't remember. If I had known who was on the line for even for a second, I probably never would have accepted his call.

'Hi,' I said hesitantly, no longer accustomed to speaking on a phone a hundred times a day like when I was working.

'John?'

'Bob?' I recognized his voice. Bob was the guy who took my job, CEO of my company after I resigned.

'John, how are you?' he asked.

'I'm fine. Why are you calling?' I answered curtly. I really didn't want to talk to Bob, and I was mad at myself for answering my phone.

'Nothing special, just thought I would call,' he answered. 'You know, see how you are doing.'

'I wish you had shown the same concern for me when I needed you most,' I replied, with no thought of hiding my sarcasm. He knew what I was talking about. I was referring to the time when Bob had unwittingly allied with the men who tried to kill me and take over my company. However, when it was over, I was convinced he didn't know what they were planning. He had simply been an innocent dupe. I forgave Bob for his part in the affair. There was no point in punishing him. Instead, I nominated him to succeed me as the CEO of the company. Now, this may seem an unlikely reward for a man who had caused me numerous problems. But in reality, I had no choice. No one except Bob had the experience necessary to run the company.

Bob was once one of my most trusted partners. He was the head of our New York Distribution House. One of three Distribution Houses: New York, London, and Hong Kong, businesses that sold gemstones supplied by my company to different regions of the world. The London House was managed by a man named Arthur Wilson. He was killed in a hail of gunfire on the streets of New York. Lin, my other partner, managed our Hong Kong Distribution House. Lin died the same night and in the same gun battle which killed Monica. The result was that of my three senior partners; Bob was the only one still standing when the smoke cleared. As a result, he was the logical choice to succeed me. I'm not sure he wanted the job, but like a good soldier, he accepted it anyway.

'Sorry, John,' he said. 'I guess I shouldn't have called.'

'No, it's fine, Bob,' I interrupted, thinking it served no purpose to be antagonistic towards him. 'Let's bury the past, okay?

'You sure?'

'I'm sure. So, what's on your mind?'

'Oh, nothing special; I was just remembering some of the good times we had.'

'Are you telling me you called to chat, nothing else on your mind?' I asked, somewhat confused. Bob was never one for small talk.

'Yes, that's right.'

'Okay, what do you want to chat about?'

I adjusted my sitting position against the side of the mast. From where I was sitting, I could see Ilana surface occasionally, flip over and dive into the glassy blue water. Once, she stopped and looked at me quizzically as if wondering what I was doing. She had every right to be curious. I almost never talked on my phone. I was not surprised she thought it odd I was sitting in my boat having a conversation.

'How you are doing?' he asked. 'I assume you've had some rough times given everything which happened,' Bob inquired.

I was not surprised by Bob's question. He was normally blunt in conversation, sometimes painfully so. I was never sure why. Maybe because he never understood the nuances of conversation, the multiple levels of subtle communication that can invade a simple sentence. Everything was black and white for Bob.

'I'm fine.' I replied.

'Look, John, you know I feel responsible for what happened. And I want you to know I'm sorry.'

Now, this surprised me. It was his first attempt at an apology. 'Thanks, Bob. That's really touching,' I replied. 'But look, let me put your mind at ease. I'm sitting on my boat near a reef in the Caribbean. The air temperature is about eighty-five degrees, and the water temperature is about the same. A gentle breeze is blowing, and my drop-dead gorgeous girlfriend is in the water, spearing a fish for our dinner. So, I'll let you answer your question. How do you think I'm doing?'

He laughed heartily. 'Sounds like you are doing a hell of a lot better than me.'

'Okay, so now you can stop worrying about me. I'm over it. Okay?' I lied.

'I'm glad. That makes me feel better.'

'Tell me about you.'

'Nothing really to report, John.'

'Sales still good?' I asked, immediately regretting my question. I really didn't want to know. It just seemed an obvious question to ask the CEO of my former company.

He hesitated briefly as if he was reluctant to answer. 'Oh,' he finally answered. 'We are not doing as well as when you were in charge. But it's okay. The company is operating at a comfortable level.'

His answer sounded rather evasive. So, I asked him one more question, one I regretted later. 'Are sales up or down?'

He answered my question like he was reading from a well-rehearsed script. The words came quickly as if he had been asked this question many times.

'Well,' he began. 'We have not been able to sustain the kind of growth we experienced before the catastrophe in New York. Everyone in the industry heard about what happened to you. Something like this has an effect, you know. We couldn't just go on doing business like before.'

Bob was talking about the night Monica was killed. She and I were in a meeting with a man who I since learned was the head of an old family dynasty from Thailand. Actually, it would be more accurate to describe it as a forced kidnapping. The man and his goons forced their way into our hotel room and demanded a meeting.

At the time, my company had a stranglehold on a worldwide market in sapphire gemstones. In a few short years we had gained control of a product which for hundreds of years had been almost exclusively controlled by this man's family in Thailand. It had been the source of their power and wealth. They understood better than anyone what we had accomplished. And they wanted it returned. They wanted to own my company. They made this very clear. When the head of the Thai family asked me if I would sell my stock to him, he informed me in the same breath I had no real choice. Without saying it in so many words, he told me I was a dead man if I refused his generous offer.

Unfortunately, or fortunately, depending on how you view what happened next, the CIA was monitoring our conversation through Monica's cell phone. The man's thinly disguised threat to kill me caused the CIA to break into our room. The conclusion to our meeting was a confusion of suffocating gas and deadly gunfire.

The Thai businessman somehow avoided injury in the gun battle. His name is Mr. Nue. The Immigration Office kicked him out of the country. He returned to Thailand. No charges were brought against him because he was traveling under a diplomatic passport. He was immune from prosecution. I was told he had high level diplomatic connections within the Thai government. However, when directly challenged, these connections were very vague. Mr. Nue, it seems, had certain diplomatic responsibilities in a shadow government. Apparently historic positions of power in third world countries often blend in with their modern governments in mysterious ways. But I guess this is also true in our government, where big money interests have hidden influence over a seemingly democratic system. Nothing is ever as it appears.

'I guess you're right, Bob,' I continued. 'Something like what happened has an effect. But how about now, is business beginning to return to normal?'

'I'm fine, and the company is fine. You need not be concerned, John.'

'So, sales are good?' I asked.

'Well... not exactly. We are down approximately thirty-five percent for the current fiscal year.'

I was shocked. 'Do you see sales returning?' I asked, hoping for a positive answer.

'Well, John,' he replied. 'We are mostly holding our own. Profits are still fine. We cut the advertising budget to reflect slower sales. Our percentage of profit, although not as good as before, is healthy.'

He paused as if waiting for me to acknowledge his efforts. When I didn't respond, he continued defensively. 'Of course, we also had to cut some overhead. You know, some employees have been let go to improve the bottom line.'

Typical reaction of a number-cruncher, I thought. Cut advertising. Cut overhead. Don't respond to the root of the problem. Just look at the bottom line.

'Where have the sales gone?' I asked, getting deeper into our conversation than I desired.

'Well, that's hard to say,' he replied deliberately, as if speaking with emphasis would somehow make his words sound less pathetic.

'Are you talking to our clients? Are you asking them where they are buying their gemstones if not from us?' I asked, knowing this was a market research question in its simplest form. I wondered if he understood how frustrated I was becoming.

'Oh, you know our customers,' he replied evasively. 'They tell us what we want to hear. They never really answer our questions.'

'So, you don't know.'

'Not really.'

Bob finally gave me a straight answer. I guess because he felt it was his duty. He had a military background. He had been in the

Army. Someone once told me he had been a Colonel. He was a big man, broad shoulders and perfect posture, cut his hair real short like he was a retired general. Acted like one most of the time.

'Who is buying the rough sapphire from the mines, the stones our company previously purchased? Is it the Thai? Are they getting back into the market?'

I had to ask, but at the same time, this conversation was beginning to assume all the symptoms of a dreaded disease. I could feel an oozing, mushrooming sorrow creeping in. Our conversation was beginning to cloud my mind with an invading gray mist of stone-cold ugly. I suddenly wanted out in the worst way. And I knew why. Thoughts of a certain man were beginning to surface in my brain. It was like a bubbling mud hole rising up from the deep recesses of my subconscious into a geyser. Mr. Nue, the man I held responsible for all the violence in New York. He, more than anyone, had created the situation which caused Monica's death. He may not have pulled the trigger, but if it wasn't for him, it would never have happened. Problem was that I wanted to forget him, and I had been trying to put him out of my mind, but I could not. Not completely. Not ever.

'I think so,' Bob finally responded. 'But you know there's nothing I can do to stop them. And even if I wanted to, I don't think it would be prudent to try after what happened.'

I guess I couldn't fault him for saying that. He certainly didn't want to experience similar disasters to what I had lived through. He was telling me he had made a conscious decision to avoid challenging the Thai. He didn't want them to try to kill him like they had tried to kill me.

Still, two competing companies cannot control a market at the same time. Either my old company had control. Or a competitor would eventually take over, someone like the Thai family dynasty of Mr. Nue. To make matters worse, this disturbing set of circumstances was not isolated. It not only affected the health and well-being of my old company, it also affected everyone in the colored gemstone business, from the miners to the retailers. If what Bob said was true, then certain events were bound to begin happening. And it would start with the miners. They would be first to feel the effect. The prices they received for their hard work would decrease. They would be forced to return to the near poverty conditions they had endured for centuries.

I asked, 'Are our miners still willing to sell to you exclusively? That is if you wanted to buy their entire production. Would the miners sell it to you?'

'Well, as I explained. Our sales are down. So, I don't need as much rough as I did before.'

'So, you don't know.'

'That's right. I don't know.'

'Tell me about prices for rough sapphire from the mines,' I probed deeper. 'Are the prices same as before?'

'No, prices have decreased.'

'Because they are no longer under your control?'

'That's correct.'

'I see. But you are fine.'

This conversation needed to come to a quick conclusion. I had learned far more than I wanted to know. Besides, Ilana was swimming towards my boat. A fish was wiggling on the end of her spear. It was time to forget Bob Anderson and return to thinking about something far more pleasant, like Ilana.

'I'm fine,' Bob replied.

'Good, thanks for calling. It has been great talking to you. Let's talk again sometime.'

'Okay...but,' he seemed to want to continue.

'Goodbye, Bob,' I said quickly.

He started to say something more, but I had no desire to hear it.

I had already hit the end button on my phone and leaned over the side of the boat to help Ilana with her fish.

SATURDAY, APRIL 25, 1:30 A.M. JOHN

Like most nights, she got out of bed and slipped away silently.

I was never sure where she went after she left. I assumed it was to her brother's house on the other side of town where she lived. But it was none of my business.

Ilana knew I liked her to sleep with me at night, at least for a little while.

During one of our afternoon talks, I told her Monica's story. How M died. I also told her about my nightmares. Ilana knew I had trouble falling to sleep. So, she would often lie beside me in bed until I closed my eyes. I was grateful because the presence of her warm body helped to keep the images of smashing bullets and black shadows from occupying my mind as I fell asleep. And she probably assumed I didn't hear her leave later in the night, and sometimes I didn't. But most of the time, I did because I am a light sleeper; like last night, I heard her go.

After she was gone, I lay awake trying to focus on something good, anything other than thinking about Monica. I thought about our afternoon of sailing and diving. She had speared a red snapper while I sat in my boat talking on my phone. We cleaned and fried the fish together. Cooked it lightly breaded in a small galley on the boat while drinking a couple of bottles of cold Belikin Beer. Along with some fresh fruit, cheese, and vegetables I had purchased earlier, we had a great meal. After dinner, we went for a swim, floating lazily on the surface, simply immersing our bodies in the refreshing coolness of the ocean.

As usual, I got out of the water first. She continued to swim as I toweled off below deck and put on some dry swim trucks. Afterward, I relaxed on the boat, watching wildly angular frigate birds float lazily in thermals and black-headed seagulls glide over the gently lapping water. Eventually, Ilana climbed into the boat, dripping wet. I waited with a fresh towel. When she turned her back to me, I suggested it would be easier to dry her body if she would allow me to remove her wet bikini.

She knew this was an excuse to see her naked, but she didn't resist. I gently undid the back of her top and let it slip off as I dried her round shoulders and firm young breasts before sliding the skimpy bottom of her bikini down her long tan legs. When I had finished drying her, she sat down naked on the cockpit seat cushions, covered only with a towel, and asked me to sit by her. I did as she suggested while feeling my excitement grow.

We made love with the wind as our companion and afterward rested without speaking, simply allowing the gentle roll of the boat and warm breezes to wash over our heated bodies.

Then it was time to return. Sails were raised as the sun set over the island. By the time we arrived at my dock, it was dark. I tied up the boat, deciding to clean it in the morning.

Talk was sparse that evening. Unusual for Ilana, who normally badgered me with questions about my former life or the places I had been. She was an intensely curious person and it was becoming increasingly obvious that she was very intelligent. However, that night, something was different. She was silently subdued, perhaps intuitively understanding something was bothering me. It was. I was depressed despite having spent a great day with her. I shouldn't have been. But I couldn't stop thinking about Bob. His call was bothering me. As much as I was trying to ignore what he said, I couldn't. So much about our conversation was wrong.

As I lay in bed, my afternoon conversation with Bob kept replaying in my head, keeping me awake, messing with my mind like a bad dream. But this bad dream was real, and it was not from the past. Because if what Bob said was true, and I had no reason to think otherwise, then my former company was in real trouble.

It was simple. Bob told me he was no longer purchasing most of the rough sapphire on the open market. And if he was not buying the gemstones, then miners were selling to someone else. They didn't have a choice. Their livelihood depended on selling their stones. And by deduction this meant Bob and my former company no longer had a stranglehold on the market. Our control of the market had been broken. And without control, we would eventually lose all rights to influence prices for cut and polished sapphires. The simple fact was Bob had let our competition back into the market, and eventually, they would take control and drive down prices because this is what competition does; it fosters lower prices.

The purpose of controlling the market is to maintain high prices because high prices mean high profits. Conversely, lower prices mean lower profits. It is a house of cards. Once my company lost control, it would not take long for everything to crumble. We would soon become insolvent simply because our cost of operation was higher than our foreign competitors.

But, so what, I wondered. I knew Bob would fail when I nominated him for my job. He didn't have the drive or vision necessary to sustain the company. He was a number-cruncher and an order-taker. He was simply doing what he was capable of doing and nothing more. He was staying the course. And maintaining status quo for most companies almost always results in a backwards plunge. A company must constantly grow if it is to survive over the long term.

So okay. I knew this about Bob before I nominated him. So why was I letting it bother me now? I guessed because I had hoped it wouldn't happen. But his call confirmed my worst fears. Now I knew it was happening. The company I had built from scratch was slowly disintegrating. In fact, as I thought about it, I wondered if Bob's call was really a call for help. His transparent show of concern for me was probably nothing more than an excuse to tell me how bad the company was doing. This seemed more like something he would do. He had never shown any concern for my well-being in the past. But he was smart enough to know he needed help. So, he had called under a pretense of asking how I was doing; when all he really wanted to tell me was; you need to become involved with the company again or it is going down the drain.

So what? I asked again. The company wasn't my life anymore. I didn't need to be involved. I had enough money. I didn't need a job. What I needed was to think about something else, something I could control. And I could not control Bob.

As I lay in bed listening to night sounds outside my windows, I made a concerted effort to concentrate on something more pleasant, something like the high-pitched songs of the tree frogs over the gently lapping rhythm of waves washing up on the beach.

Most nights, I sleep with the windows open unless it is too hot. I don't like noisy air conditioners and don't use them unless it is oppressively hot. Besides, Ilana hates air conditioners and usually leaves my house if I turn them on. They seem unnatural to her. But I am a boy from a cold Midwestern state in the U.S.A.

I don't do well when the temperature rises above ninety.

MONDAY, APRIL 27, 7:05 A.M. JOHN

'Clarence... Yes, it's John. You called yesterday?'

Last night had been no fun. I didn't sleep well. Even though I had tried not to think about it, the conversation I had with Bob ran through my troubled brain all night like a noisy runaway freight train. In the morning I remembered Clarence had also called, but I hadn't taken his call. I decided I should have talked to Clarence instead of Bob. I assumed it would have been a far more pleasant conversation. Clarence usually calls just to talk about old times, nothing serious like Bob.

I badly wanted to stop thinking about Bob or anything related to the company as quickly as possible, hoping to enjoy the rest of the day without having to wade around in a smelly sewer of unhappy memories. My hope was that Clarence would help me do just that.

It was early Monday morning in Belize when I called Clarence, but it was evening in Australia on the other side of the globe. I thought I could catch him before he went to bed and fortunately, he answered after the first ring.

'Hey mate, thanks for returning my call,' he said.

The sun began to rise in the east over the ocean as we talked. Streaks of red light emanated from below the wide ocean horizon to touch misty, early morning clouds, turning them into God's brush strokes of luminous pink across a canvas of blue sky. I was born on the western shores of Lake Michigan, where the sun rises behind the dunes and sets in the west over the lake. In Belize, it is just the opposite. The sun rises over the ocean and sets over the land. This was one of only a few things about this island I didn't like. I miss the sunsets over the water.

I had brought a folding chair out onto my dock in order to be comfortable while talking to Clarence. Normally, I wait until later when Ilana is on the dock, but this morning, I went out early to talk to Clarence.

'So how are you matey?' I asked, attempting to mimic his Australian accent.

He chuckled. 'As good as a cold glass of beer.'

Clarence is the CEO of Nullamana Sapphire Mines and Laboratory. He lives in the small town of Inverell in the mountains of eastern Australia. He is a big man like Bob. But unlike Bob, Clarence had a genuine sincerity about him. I don't think Clarence would ever deceive me, but I'm never completely sure this is true with Bob. An old, tattered red hat is Clarence's trademark. He always wears it when working at the mines. It covers a tangled mess of thinning, curly blonde hair. I always suspected the real purpose of his hat was to disguise his balding head. I pictured him wearing his hat as we talked.

'Want to share a beer?' he asked.

'No, it's too early for me,' I replied with a chuckle.

'Right, well then, I'll come right to the point,' he said quickly before I could speak another word. 'Your company is in a lot of trouble and well... you need to come back to work, mate... now, not later. You've had your vacation, one you richly deserved. I truly understand why you needed to get away. I know it must have been hard. But I trust your head is now properly screwed on again. So, look here; it's time to get back to work. Because, well... because we need you, understand... There... It's that simple... I said it. I know it is a bit harsh, but someone had to tell you.'

The directness of his statement was a shock. Obviously, he had rehearsed his speech. And his shotgun approach to our discussion was not typical for him. Normally Clarence never gets around to doing anything real fast. He lets things take their normal course, kind of eases into fixing problems. But not this time. This time, it felt like he had to hit me over the head with a baseball bat to make his point.

Now, this was not the conversation I had hoped for when I called him. Instead of taking my mind off the troubling conversation I had yesterday with Bob, Clarence shoved it right back in my face. Normally, I enjoy talking to him. In fact, he was about the only person from my former business life I have talked to with any regularity during the last year. He always made a point of not bringing up specific details about the company. I think he knew I didn't want to talk about it. But not today... today was obviously different.

'Clarence,' I replied slowly and deliberately so he was sure to get my meaning. 'I do not ever want to be part of that company ag-'

'I know, mate, and I'm sorry,' he interrupted.

'Stop, you're not listening to me.

'I am, but you must...'

'I know what you are going to say, Clarence. Bob called yesterday. He painted a rather negative picture I didn't want to hear. So, save your breath. I don't want to hear the same bad news from you.'

'John, you have to hear it!' followed by a rapid-fire series of statements spieling from his mouth before I could stop him. He must have assumed if he said the words real loud and real fast, I would have to listen. And he was right. I listened even though I didn't like hearing what he was saying.

'My sales are down twenty-five percent,' he continued. 'And to make matters worse, yesterday I had a visit from a representative of a Thai sapphire company. He offered to buy any and all gemstones I would sell to him. Of course, the price he offered was less than the company's price. But he must have known my inventory was high and my sales were down. He acted like a vulture circling a dying carcass. I didn't like the man.'

'Clarence, I don't want to...'

'No, John, you need to listen. I told him to get lost. I told him I would never sell to him. Do you know what he did? He just smiled and said he would be back. When I was ready to sell, he would come back... The little bastard,' Clarence paused and took a breath as if it felt good to get all this off his chest.

'Clarence, I appreciate what you are telling me, and I wish I could help you. But you know I can't do it.'

He didn't respond immediately. Perhaps because he wasn't sure he should say what he was about to say. Or maybe he just needed time to get up a new head of steam so he could blast me one more time. And blast away is what he did.

'John, you built this company. You put everything you had into it. It was your life as much as anything. Remember, I watched you do it. Now, I know what you have gone through, mate, and I know it still hurts. But maybe this is how to make it right again. Maybe the way to even the score is to come back to work.'

He and I both knew he had struck a real nerve... Still, I wasn't ready to give in.

'Clarence, I don't think I can.'

'Yes, you can.'

'Maybe I don't want to.'

'John, your company needs you... I need you. And blimey, mate, I think this is something you need to do for yourself.'

Clarence could not have been more direct. To deny him would have been a slap in his face. As I sat wondering what to say, I noticed Ilana sitting on the edge of the dock, flipping her feet in the water. I didn't know how much of the conversation she had heard. It didn't seem to matter. I think I heard Clarence take a swig of beer as I hesitated. He had given me his best shot. Now, he waited for what he hoped would be the proper reaction on my part.

'I talked to Bob yesterday,' I began. 'I know what is happening. And I know it hurts you and your operations. But I am not sure I'm capable of returning to work, even if I wanted to. Can you understand that?'

'I can, John, and I know it will probably be the hardest thing you ever do. But, mate, there are things we all have to do. God gives us no other option.'

'Okay Clarence. Thanks for your advice,' I replied, wanting badly to put an end to this conversation. 'It must be getting late in your part of the world. Enjoy the rest of your beer. Let's talk again soon.'

'You will think about it then,' he persisted.

'I'll think about it, but I promise nothing.'

'Just think about it, John... Okay?'

'Okay.'

'G' night'

'Good night, Clarence.'

Ilana sat on the dock as I steamed.

I had a sudden urge to toss my satellite phone as far into the ocean as possible. The last two calls had put me in a lousy mood. On top of this, I suddenly felt guilty about living in a tropical paradise when my company badly needed me. My Dutch work ethic was beginning to filter into my subconscious. I felt like I needed to walk through the hidden door built into the bookcase of my Charlottesville apartment, go into my office, and get to work now, not later. Things needed to be done, people to talk to, and places to go.

But I wasn't in Charlottesville. I was in Belize with Ilana, sitting on the dock, looking strangely at me in her skimpy blue bikini. A towel was over her shoulder, and the sun was beginning to make me feel hot.

I suddenly didn't care. It was time to forget the calls and go for my morning swim. Hopefully, a brisk workout would exorcise all the ugly shit from my troubled brain.

'Good Morning, Mr. John. Was that a pleasant phone call?' Ilana asked innocently.

'No, it wasn't,' I snapped. 'A former business associate...' I began to explain, then hesitated, 'I don't want to talk about it... Want to go for a swim?'

Surprisingly, she declined my invitation, 'No. I think I have some errands to do in town, Mr. John,' she casually replied.

'I think I will do them now before it gets too hot. Then I will return.'

9:45 A.M. ILANA

She walked the beach, returning to the house she shared with her brother, the one he inherited from their parents, the house where she kept her clothes.

The house was located not far from the fishermen's marina. By this time in the morning, her brother was usually gone, on his boat fishing. Good because it meant she would not be bothered by him.

Her brother had a new boat. It wasn't new, really, but it was better than the one he had before. She had helped him buy it with money she received from the man in the jewelry shop. She hoped her brother would be safer in his new boat. Sudden storms off the coast of Belize could be deadly for fishermen. She was happy she could help her brother buy the boat. But when he had asked her where she received her money, he had all but accused her of selling her body for it. She told him he was wrong and swore on Mary's statute she was innocent of his accusations. When she said this, he did not continue to argue with her. Without asking her any more questions he had used the money to make a down payment on the boat.

Ilana took some bread and cheese from a small refrigerator in the kitchen, enough for a quick snack. As she ate, she tried not to think about what she was going to do. She procrastinated, cleaning the kitchen, hoping this would make her feel like a good person. After all, didn't her brother need her? Wasn't she helping him more that helping herself? Hadn't she looked after him when their parents died? He was never one to clean up after himself. This was her job, and she was happy to do it. Finally satisfied the kitchen looked better, she locked the back door and set out at a brisk pace.

The main road into town was dry that day. It had not rained for a week. Dust swirled up around her driven by hot winds blowing her dress. She did not like this hot wind. It was a scorching wind. And it meant Mr. John would probably turn on his noisy cold air conditioner. She wondered briefly if she should return to his house after she had completed her task.

Passing the large, faded pink Catholic Church dominating the main square of town, she thought about walking inside to say a prayer, ask for forgiveness for what she was about to do. It is what she did most days. She said a few prayers at the altar. But today she walked past the church without a glance, as if her religion meant nothing to her. This was not true. She just didn't want to think about what she going to do.

She passed a few tourists who were combing the shops along the main road of San Pedro looking for trinkets, mementoes of their trip. Entering the Mayan silver jewelry shop in the center of town, she asked the owner if she could please use his telephone.

He said yes.

She knew he would agree. It had been prearranged for her to use the phone whenever she needed. Going behind a dark blue curtain, she lifted the phone from the wall and dialed a memorized long-distance number.

A man whose voice Ilana recognized answered his phone.

'Signor,' she said, still feeling uneasy about what she was about to do. Truth was she did not want to talk to this man, but she knew she must. The man had paid her. She had taken the man's money. She was obligated to make the call.

'Yes.'

'I thought I should call you, Signor. I think it is not important, but Mr. John had two phone calls recently. I think they were from men in his company. The second man asked him to do something. I don't know what he asked. You understand, I could only hear what my friend was saying, not what he was being asked to do.'

'Yes, I understand.'

'I thought I should tell you. That is all.'

'You did well, Ilana. Thank you for calling. Let me ask you one question. Did your Mr. John promise this man anything? Did he say he would return to work in the States?'

'No, no, signor. He did not promise anything. I think he said he would think about it.'

'Thank you, Ilana. You did well. You will call me if you learn anything new.'

'I promise, Signor.'

10:05, AM, BOGATA, COLUMBIA, MANUEL ORTEGA

Far away from where Ilana listened to an empty click, ending her telephone conversation, Manuel Ortega put down his phone and thought for a moment, wondering if the information he had received required further attention. But then, he had obligations, as did Ilana, and obligations needed to be met.

A marriage of convenience had developed over time between two men who were both employed in the gemstone businesses. They had met years ago and found a common ground, one which could prove to be potentially important for both of them. In addition, they shared a similar perspective when it came to accomplishing their work. Objectives were more important than methods. One needed to do what was necessary, no matter how illegal or cruel.

Months before, this acquaintance from the other side of the world had asked Manuel if he would be willing to offer assistance with a problem which existed in Central America, an area where Manuel had influence. A substantial amount of money was offered to Manual for agreeing to help with this difficult situation.

Manuel had been only too happy to be of service.

Rummaging through his desk, Manuel found the information he had saved for when it was needed. Dialing a long-distance number, he listened as a female voice on the other end of the line spoke a language he could not understand. Ignoring the foreign words, Manuel stated his name and waited. As expected, his friend came on the line and spoke to him in clipped English.

'So, he has been asked to return to work?' his friend asked slowly after Manual explained why he had called.

'It seems this is true. My source told me he received two calls from former partners. He promised them nothing.'

'It doesn't matter. I know this man, and he will return now.'

'So, it needs to be done.'

'Yes, please do it now.'

'It is all planned,' Manuel explained.

'Good. You will call me after it is done.'

'I will.'

Manuel Ortega hung up.

Then, he dialed a long-distance number connecting him to an associate who lived on an island off the coast of Belize.

WEDNESDAY, APRIL 29, 6:35 P.M. JOHN

Her sails bent the power of the wind to her will, driving her dark blue hull through a choppy, emerald green sea.

It was as if the boat was laughing at the wind, mocking the wind, using the wind. But the wind knew better. The wind knew it would have its day with her. And that day could be terrible.

It had been hot, too hot for me. I knew Ilana hated air conditioners. I suggested a sail to Cay Key in the afternoon. After anchoring, we went for a swim to cool off. An early meal at a local restaurant with an air conditioner was next on our agenda, despite Ilana's objections. Then it was time to return.

I adjusted the main sheet once we got underway, cranking a chrome handle a couple of clicks, taking some luff out of the sail. The boat leaned over appropriately and its knot meter rose to eight knots steady. A natural freedom stems from having wind drive a boat through the water. I relaxed with Ilana sitting comfortably next to me. Hot wind flowed through her black hair. She seemed content. Although... she had been oddly quiet all afternoon. I didn't press her. I had enough on my mind without having to worry about what was bothering her.

Most days, I didn't need much more than having Ilana near to stop thinking about my problems. Her beauty alone could make me forget about my past and enjoy long hours filled with the simple wonder of being in the presence of a beautiful woman. She looked especially good in her tight blue bikini, her slim tan body sculpted by a life near the sea. She moved with a natural grace on a boat that could not be taught, smiling at me often during our afternoon sail. But today, it seemed I needed more than her beauty to put my past behind me. I was having difficulty ignoring a growing urge to consider Clarence's request to return to the States.

The wind was holding steady at around twenty to twenty-five knots as we continued. It was getting toward evening, and usually, the wind slows in the late afternoon, but not today. This was unusual. A weather front could be headed in our direction because it also wasn't getting any cooler. Fortunately, we were sailing inside the reef. The waves were no problem, only a gentle chop.

My dock soon came into sight, and I was grateful to have Ilana help me tie up the boat. Doing it alone would have been difficult in the wind. She prepared to lower the main sail as I released tension from the jib and started the motor, having decided it would be easier to dock under power. Heading into the wind, I released pressure off the jib. Hitting a switch, the sail began to wind down. Then, the main sail slowly settled with Ilana's help. The boat slowed, now under power, turned and headed towards my dock, where we tied up. After securing the sails, we went directly up to the house. I was too tired to clean up the boat that evening. I hadn't slept much the previous night; too much to think about. A glass of wine on the main deck seemed more appropriate. It was time to relax.

During my first year in the rented house, I purchased a wood-framed couch covered with canvas cushions for sitting on the main outside deck. The cushions were waterproof and could be taken in if the weather looked like rain. The house had two stories. The ground level was devoted to utilitarian purposes such as laundry and storage. The main living areas, kitchen, bedrooms, and great room were on the second floor, with a big covered deck across the entire front. This was where I put the couch, specifically for viewing the ocean in the evening when the sun was setting behind the house.

The dock in front of the house could accommodate as many as six sailboats. But from where I sat slowly sipping a glass of wine on the second-story deck, my sailboat and a small rubber runabout were the only boats bobbing lazily in choppy seas, tied to the dock,

I gradually began to relax as wine soothed my troubled brain. It was time to decide, and I did. Although I truly wanted to help Clarence, I personally could not fix all the troubles of the world. I had done my part for my company and I had almost paid for it with my life. Monica had paid with hers. It was time for someone else to do their part. I had done enough.

Besides, I didn't need the money. I had more than I could ever spend. In fact, if the e-mails from my broker were correct, I was earning money at a rate which far exceeded my current ability to spend it. I knew I would have to address this problem sometime in the future. Perhaps a foundation could be established dedicated to giving a portion the money to good causes. This was as much work as I wished to contemplate in the future.

Ilana eventually joined me, carrying a glass of wine, wearing the same blue bikini she had on when the day began. She looked great, her firm young breasts hidden only by a veil of a thin blue cloth. She smiled at me as if reading my mind and came over and gave me a kiss on my cheek. She seemed unusually affectionate. Something was different. I didn't know what it was, and I didn't ask. We had never discussed our relationship; just let it happen. It seemed more natural this way, and this was fine with me. I wasn't ready to be in love again, not after Monica's death. I didn't want to be hurt again, not like the last time. My current relationship with Ilana suited me perfectly. We were casual friends with benefits and no commitments.

A black-headed seagull floated past the deck, flying into the wind. Evenings in Belize were my favorite time. I took a sip of wine and rested, knowing this was home for me now. Perhaps I would return to the U.S. someday, but only as a visitor.

'Mr. John,' Ilana interrupted my thoughts.

'Yes,'

'You seem troubled today. Are you okay, Mr. John?'

'I'm fine. And stop calling me Mr. John.'

'The phone calls, did the phone calls trouble you?' she asked, ignoring my request.

'Yes.'

'Were the calls from friends in your company?'

'Yes.'

Like Monica, she had days when she constantly asked questions. Normally, this was fine with me because, in return for answering her questions, she entertained me with stories from her life. She lived in a simple world. The worst thing that ever happened to her was the early death of her parents. Ilana was just a child at the time. A few weeks after her mother died, her father was killed in a fishing accident. Or maybe from a broken heart. Ilana was not sure. He simply did not return one day, lost at sea. Fortunately, her brother was old enough to raise her. It didn't really affect her much. She simply went on with her life, free and easy, without parental supervision, just a brother to care for her. In a way, I envied her and I told her so.

'What did they want, Mr. John? Your friends, what do they want from you when they call?'

'They wanted me to return to the United States to work at my old job.'

'Do you want to do that?' she asked with a hint of sadness in her voice.

'No, Ilana. I want to stay here with you. This is my life now.'

'I am happy, Mr. John. I was hoping you did not want to leave.'

'Why would I want to leave?'

She smiled and slid over next to me. She was not a big woman. She easily fit under my arm on the cushions of the couch. I gave her a kiss on her forehead.

'I like it here with you, Ilana,' I said. 'I hope you like being with me.'

'I like to be with you Mr. John. I think you know this.'

'I know,' I replied. 'Say, maybe someday we could take a trip north. I would like to show you where I grew up. Would you like to go with me? You could meet my friends.'

My comment made me think about my friend, David. He and I had become buddies during our high school years in my hometown of Grand Haven, Michigan. He was also my attorney and he was supervising the rebuilding of my cottage on the shores of Lake Michigan. I had called David months earlier and suggested he have my cottage rebuilt. After sketching some crude floor plans, I mailed them to him. He had my sketches converted into blueprints and returned to me for approval. Construction was well underway. I assumed the house was almost done. David called recently to tell me construction was ahead of schedule.

'Oh, I would like to go with you very much,' Ilana replied.

Perhaps because it was so hot, perhaps this is why the idea of returning home during the summer sounded good. Summer is a great time to be visiting the shores of Lake Michigan. A plan began to take shape in my mind. I assumed Ilana would enjoy seeing some of the places we had talked about. Maybe even some places we had not talked about. We could travel. I had money. Why not use it. I would show her the world. It would be fun.

'Okay, we will go in a few months when it's warm,' I said. 'In the meantime, we can do some planning.'

'But you are not returning to your company, are you?' she asked innocently.

Her question seemed odd to me, especially coming from her. Why should she care about my working at my old company? Made no sense. In my mind I had already moved beyond this decision. Still, it seemed to concern her. Maybe because of all the violent stories I had told her, all related to the company. I wondered if she was worried about her safety if she came with me. I decided to put her mind at ease.

'No, I'm not returning to Charlottesville, where my company is located. We will go to Grand Haven, Michigan, and visit my cottage on a big lake.'

'How big is your lake?'

'It looks just like your sea. Only the water is greener and colder. And it does not taste salty.'

This seemed to satisfy her. She stopped asking questions and became quiet.

I took the opportunity to sip some wine and dream of summer sunsets over Lake Michigan.

THURSDAY, APRIL 30, 2:15 A.M. JOHN

It was hot, too damned hot to sleep.

Air temperature was still in the upper eighties with a steady breeze blowing through my bedroom windows doing nothing to cool the room. I simply could not sleep. I tried rolling over, but the sheets stuck to my sweaty body and got tangled. Finally, when I couldn't stand it anymore, I got up out of bed. I could have turned on the air conditioner, but I really didn't like the noisy thing, especially at night. Besides, I was already awake.

Slipping on a pair of shorts, I wandered to the kitchen for a glass of cold water from the fridge. Ilana was gone as usual by this time of the night. As I said before, I had no idea where she went, and I never asked. It was her business.

Thinking a swim would feel good and cool my overheated body; I headed outside in the moonlight. Reaching the end of the dock, I dropped my towel, stepped out of my shorts, and slipped noiselessly into the water, feeling the cool sea refresh my naked, sweaty body. Moonlight sparked off the choppy water when I raised my head above the surface of the water. A steady, hot wind was blowing from the southeast. The sky was filled with silky gray clouds racing overhead, occasionally obscuring a half-moon. A storm was brewing. The front was still too far away to be seen. I swam lazily for a while, simply relishing the cool water caressing my body. Eventually, I got tired, climbed wooden stairs attached to the end of the dock, and retrieved my shorts and a towel.

I had no desire to return to my sweaty bed; it was too hot to sleep. Only troubled dreams waited for me there. Instead, I folded my towel for a headrest and lay down on the hard dock on my back. The dark sky, an immense spectacle of bright stars greeted my sleepy gaze. It felt good to simply lie on the hardwood and let the night breezes wash over my tired body. Waves lapping up against the side of my boat tied to the dock produced a calming rhythm, music to my ears. Refreshed and relaxed from my swim, my eyelids soon became heavy, and I slept.

After a few hours, the hard dock became uncomfortable, and I had to sit up. Off to the southeast, lightning flashed across the horizon, giving ethereal definition to distant black clouds from a coming storm. It seemed prudent to get off the dock and wait out the storm in the shelter of my house. I threw my towel over my shoulder and began to walk up the dock.

A shadow, a black outline of a person, moved near my house.

It was getting close to morning by this time. The sky behind me had begun to lighten in the east over the ocean. Still, it was difficult in the dim light to see. The shadow could have been the product of my overactive imagination. I wasn't really sure. But when two dark figures emerged from the house, I clearly saw two men carrying something out of my house.

Very little criminal activity plagues the island of Ambergris. But petty thievery is not uncommon. I assumed the shadows were cat burglars looking for anything they could easily carry away in the night. I had often considered installing a burglar alarm in the house, but I had very few valuables: nothing more than a stereo, a TV and a DVD player for watching an occasional movie, and, of course, my books. The thieves could have this stuff if they wanted it. Everything could be replaced. It wasn't worth a confrontation. I waited on the dock, hoping the thieves would simply take what they wanted and leave. And to my relief, they quickly disappeared into the night.

After waiting a few minutes to be certain they were gone, I continued up the dock towards the house.

A white flash brightened the night sky, followed by an extremely abrasive boom that penetrated my brain like hard pieces of metal shrapnel were being driven into my ears by a hammer. Instinctively, I dropped off the dock into the water as flames exploded out of a first-story bedroom window, sending black debris high into the night sky. A second explosion shattered an area directly below my second-story bedroom. I watched in horror, too shocked to believe what was happening. The house slowly began to burn, red flames spewing dusty soot high into the black night sky.

My response was to run. They, the people who had tried to kill me before, they were after me again. The nightmares which I thought I had left behind; these same nightmares had followed me to Belize. I had been a fool, thinking I could escape their reach. I cried inwardly as I climbed cautiously into my sailboat, water dripping from my body. Staying low, hoping no one saw me, I loosened the lines which held the boat to the dock as echoes from the explosions reverberated through my hard skull. In a highly disturbed frame of mind, I concluded my boat was my only way out. I was afraid to walk into town, afraid someone might be waiting for me on the road in case I survived the fire. My only option was to slip away silently on my boat before anyone knew I had survived the fire.

Flames were rising high into the night sky when I glanced back at my rented house for one last time. The roof sagged and collapsed into the fire. I said a short goodbye and released the last line, shoving the boat away from the dock.

This place had been good to me.

I was very sorry to leave.

8:05 A.M. JOHN

Not more than half an hour ago, the golden sun had risen lazily out of the sea, spreading a glow of streaking red high into a clear blue morning sky.

What is the saying? 'Red sky at night, sailors delight. Red sky in the morning, sailors take warning.' And it certainly looked like I had every reason to be warned. A bank of billowing gray storm clouds could clearly be seen on the horizon, racing towards me. The clouds eventually covered the sun, blocking its warming rays and casting a dark shadow over the sea.

I had escaped the island by turning on the motor of my sailboat and silently cruising out to sea while my rented house burned to the ground in intense red flames, lighting a portion of the solemn black night sky. I was fairly confident no one had seen me leave, assuming or perhaps hoping that anyone near the house at the time was probably more interested in watching the house burn than observing a boat slipping quietly out to sea.

Normally, I never sail beyond the safety of the reef. But after the sky began to lighten, I became increasingly concerned about being spotted from shore. The men who firebombed my house could be looking for me once they discovered the boat was gone. I knew I was being paranoid, but I couldn't help it after what happened. So, as a precaution, I decided to sail out beyond the safety of the reef, where it would be difficult to identify my boat from land. And this was where I was now struggling through large sea swells pushed by a steady thirty-five-knot wind ahead of what I was soon to learn was an approaching tropical depression of some consequence.

Problem was, I had no contingency plan for sailing in a storm. My panicked reaction to the burning house had driven me out to sea, nothing else. The shock and noise of the explosions were still clearly resonating through my shattered brain, and I was having difficulty concentrating. Avoidance is what I think the experts call it. But eventually, I had to face the fact that a line of dark storm clouds was flying across the sky, coming to get me. The wind was after me, desired me. It was payback time for services rendered in the past, for scorned ignorance. A day of reckoning had come. Already tell-tail signs of the storm's escalating winds were clearly evident in dull, rippled wind shifts racing across the glassy sea.

My sailboat was a capable boat, reputed to be able to withstand almost anything the wind could throw at her. Still, I had never sailed her in a really big storm before. It was clearly time to think about what needed to done if I wanted to survive. After lowering the jib, I reefed in the main sail to about a third of its normal height for stability and started the engine because when the storm hit, I would need to turn the bow into the approaching wind and waves to survive. As part of my preparation, I closed the cabin door to prevent seawater from spilling below. So, it was something of a surprise to see the door seemingly open by itself, and Ilana poke her head up through the opening.

'Good morning,' she said as if this was the place and the time she always appeared on my boat.

'Go below and get some storm gear on,' I instructed.

I didn't have time to quiz her about why she was on the boat. The storm was almost on top of us, and I knew I might need some help.

'Okay, Mr. John.' She quickly disappeared below and came back up in a few minutes wearing a yellow storm suit and deck shoes.

The boat heeled over dangerously when the first real blast of wind leaned hard on the main sail. Crouching in the cockpit to maintain balance, I held on to the wheel with difficulty. The boat was quickly becoming little more than the storm's plaything, tossed around like a child's toy in the storm's increasingly vicious grip. Growing rapidly in strength, the wind sliced past wire mainstays with such velocity that the stays literally hummed as they vibrated.

Fighting the wheel to keep the boat headed into the waves, I feared the boat could go over if I lost control, pushed upside-down by approaching walls of water. Each new wave larger, bigger, and higher than the last one. Mounds of water viciously rising up, one after another in repetitious onslaughts of white-water fury. I became increasingly afraid. I was losing the battle. The reefed mainsail helped, steadied the boat, but I was having a great difficulty keeping her pointed into the waves which seemed determined to push us precariously sideways before we slid down the back sides of the giant waves. Increasing the motor speed helped gain some control, but I wasn't sure it would be enough.

'Hold on,' I yelled to Ilana, as a crashing white water monster broke over the bow, sending a torrent of splashing liquid mass rushing over the deck, hitting me square in the chest with a hard, wet blow.

Ilana lost her balance as the wave washed over her, falling and sliding down and against the sides of the cockpit. The boat heeled over, its mast swinging down perilously close to the sea as another cresting wall of blue-green water rose up to assault us, pouring over the boat. There was nothing I could do. I was convinced we were going over, upside down. Somehow, the boat fought back, finding a reserve of strength, an inner resolve to climb the wave's swirling, glassy face, rising upright to my relief. Eerily balanced on the crest of a wave before sliding down its backside, my forty-four-foot sailboat is not a small boat, but we were nothing more than an insignificant speck of life in these turbulent seas, bobbing and weaving and fighting to avoid giving in to the absolute will of the wind.

Ilana managed to crawl into a corner of the cockpit, where she sat beside me, dripping wet, attempting to hold on as the storm's fury increased. A look of absolute determination was glued to her face. I could see her out of the corner of my eye as she fought to keep from being bounced overboard as the boat twisted and turned against incessant walls of rushing, flowing water. She looked scared, but I could do nothing for her. I had my hands full, working the wheel, which was becoming increasingly difficult, my arms aching from the constant exertion.

A huge swell suddenly appeared, rising up, looking like a ten-story building. A rouge wave was on top of us, a bully of the sea, the storm's ultimate enforcer. The boat tilted almost straight up into the face of this angry mass of white water cresting high above us, rushing down, blasting us in pounding surf of stinging water. I grabbed for Ilana and the wheel at the same time, holding on to her life jacket with one hand, wrapping my elbow around the wheel with my other arm. White water rushed over us as I held her, blinded in a fury of wet force. My elbow screamed in pain, locked to the wheel with all my strength. Ilana pulled on my other arm, dragged by surging water towards the back of the boat. My grip on her slick, wet jacket began to slip as she swept past me, sliding towards the stern. I could not hold her, my fingers too wet to maintain grip. She slipped away in the watery confusion.

The moment I lost grip, I knew she was dead. I watched in horror as she rushed toward the sea off the back of the boat. Once in the water, she would have no help. She would eventfully drown. Even if, by some miracle, I was able to turn the boat around in the storm, it would be almost impossible to find a small bobbing head in mountainous seas. Thankfully, she managed to catch a backstay with her hand as she dropped over the stern of the boat, her legs dangling precariously in the furious white water. Somehow, she was able to hold on as the ferocious wave washed over us, and the boat began to slip down the other side of the giant swell. She scrambled back into the cockpit as soon as the wave released its hold. I screamed at her to go down below where it was safe. She hesitated with sad eyes as if she thought she would see me no more. Opening the cabin door, she obediently disappeared below.

Each new wave now loomed up over me in all its fury as if challenging me for the right to be in this ocean. Breathing became difficult. The wind drove the sea into a fine spray of rising swells, making it all but impossible to distinguish between air and water. I coughed and fought to breathe, my arms a mass of aching pain, muscles rebelling from the constant exertion of hauling on the wheel, trying to keep the boat pointed into the wind.

The malevolent sea was determined, continuing to challenge the boat's right to exist. The boat fought back with all its strength, staying upright even when it seemed physically impossible, fighting defiantly as it rose up and rushed down the backside of the waves, surviving each wave only to see the next wave rise up, another white-water monster, a wind-driven, foaming, churning, crashing demon intent on breaking our will. I twisted and turned the wheel, leaning into the wind and waves, knowing if the boat got turned sideways to the wind and waves, it would go over, and I would die.

Time stood still in this wet, raging fight. Seconds, minutes, hours; each moment, a miracle of life staring into the face of a watery grave, death ready to take me, caress me with its watery fingers. There were times I wanted to give in, thoughts I could continue no longer, my body aching, strength gone, fighting each new passing monstrous liquid horror, trying to survive one more cresting hill of white water bearing down on me; the wind so strong I could not see through the crashing surf, eyes stinging, filled with salt water, constantly pushing, leaning against me, no rest. Blindly pressing against the wind, I fought, I cried, I screamed in anger, exhausted, in a place where no one heard me, no one cared, where even God seemed to have deserted me. Still, something in me would not give in. And just when a fleeting hope I could maybe survive this monster storm grazed through my exhausted brain, the boat suddenly deserted me and leaned over after finally being overpowered by one too many towering giant walls of water. Too late; nothing I could do this time; the boat was going over, its mast dipping into the sea. I held onto the wheel to keep from being swept overboard as I stared into the sea's watery grave.

With all hope now gone, the churning seas reached up for me, and I prepared to dive in after releasing my death grip on the wheel. But at that moment, the boat's descent into the sea began to slow as I watched, wide-eyed in wonder, sure I was a dead man only seconds before. Watched as the mast slowly rose, dripping wet out of the sea, and salt water poured off its decks.

And then, as if by some miracle, the storm began to ease almost imperceptibly at first. After what seemed a lifetime of agony, the wind lessened, and the waves decreased. A blue patch of sky opened overhead, and the sun glistened off the tired, wet surfaces of the boat. Ilana poked her head out of the cabin and smiled weakly.

I relaxed, turned the engine down. We were alive. The reefed mainsail pushed us forward as we cruised in a thirty-knot breeze, which felt like a gentle zephyr compared to the heavy gales we had just survived.

4:45 P.M. JOHN

White billowing sails set to perfect, gentle curves, drove us ever steadily towards our destination.

Four to four and a half knots registered on the gauge. The compass indicated we were on course. I wasn't worried. As long as I could see some trees on the shore off the port side, I figured we were in no danger of getting lost.

Ilana was resting on the deck, once more adorned in nothing more significant than a skimpy string bikini. Moderate breezes and bright sunlight warmed her tender skin. The storm had passed and the sea had returned to its normal, tranquil state, almost as if nothing ever happened. With the exception of several ugly black and blue marks which were clearly visible on Ilana's body where she had been battered and bruised during the storm, and the injuries I knew existed on my body because of the pain I felt every time I moved, we were okay, lucky to have escaped.

Conversation was sparse.

It was as if we both needed time to exorcise the dreadful demons of the furious storm from our conscious minds. Something ugly from a different time and place had stalked us. Talking about it might bring it back to life. It was easier to avoid the subject and simply enjoy being alive.

We stopped at an island in the afternoon for clothing and food. Our trip had been unplanned. We had almost nothing with us when we left. Fortunately, my wallet was in my shorts when I went outside the morning of the fire. As a result, we had money and credit cards available to buy supplies. But I began to worry about the men who had come to kill me, thought they might be looking for me now. Or it was possible they were still under the assumption I was dead from the explosions. However, sooner or later, they would be told no one had died in the burnt house, no bodies were found. Then they would notice my boat was gone, and it wouldn't take them long to come to the proper conclusion.

I sent Ilana alone into the fishing village to buy shirts, shorts, a dress, food, and water for our journey. I personally stayed behind, out of sight, thinking no one would notice a native girl who could speak Spanish. I gave Ilana the cash from my wallet because credit cards could be traced. Cash left no trail.

We sailed from the island as soon as she returned. The old anxious feelings of always needing to be somewhere soon had begun to creep into my consciousness again. I had lived for many months without this noxious need to always be in a hurry, and I didn't like feeling my nervous anxiety return. But I sensed it might be required if I was to survive.

The port of Cancun was our destination. Life, as I knew it in the past, would resume there, meaning the resumption of apprehensive days of travel and worry, constantly searching for an elusive peace. Days when just surviving to live another day was its own reward, combined with days filled with pulsating terror.

I leaned back and allowed the wind to blow through my hair, wondering if I closed my eyes, could I hold this moment inside. Could I make it live forever in my mind? Could I just exist in this one place and time forever. Never again needing anything more from life than the vision of her trim brown body lying on the deck of my boat under white sails set to a warm wind blowing in a clear blue sky. Never again having to face decisions about the future... nothing more to life than a few simple pleasures.

It was tempting to consider sailing across the Atlantic, searching for ambiguous ports over watery horizons.

Ilana sat up to adjust her bikini top while smiling at me. It was time to face reality. The moment had passed. I motioned for her to sit by me.

Seeming to know what was coming, she obediently sat down and kissed me on my cheek, 'Is there something you want, Mr. John?'

I sighed. 'First, please stop calling me Mr. John. I would prefer you call me John. Okay?'

'Okay, John. I think I like your name. I will call you, John.'

'Good, now maybe you can tell me how you happened to be on my boat last night.'

She looked down without immediately answering my question.

'Ilana, we are on a journey together. If we are to continue, we need to be honest with each other.'

I hesitated.

Perhaps this wasn't true. Perhaps it wasn't really necessary for her to continue with me. In which case, she didn't need to explain anything because she would soon be gone.

A plan had been forming in my mind ever since my forced departure from Belize. First, sail to Cancun. Direct flights were available from the resort town of Cancun to Miami, Miami to Chicago, Chicago to Muskegon near Grand Haven, Michigan, my hometown. After Ilana unexpectedly appeared out of the galley, I automatically included her in my plans without thinking, assuming she would want to come with me. Mostly, I guess, because I wanted her to come. Now I realized, as I thought about her, she didn't have to go with me, or perhaps she didn't want to be with me, or more appropriately, it probably wasn't a good idea in the first place for her to go with me. Because it was all too obvious, I was in danger again, and anyone traveling with me would share this danger. Therefore, it would be better to send her home from Cancun.

'Okay, look,' I said, making a quick decision. 'Forget it.'

She turned her big brown, inquisitive eyes up to look at me as if trying to read my mind. 'No, Mr. John, I mean John. I think we need to talk... And I will answer all your questions,' she spoke with determination in her voice, more determination than I had ever heard from her before. Truth was, we had existed for so long in a playful, almost whimsical relationship without commitments; I was not accustomed to hearing this tone in her voice.

'First, let me tell you why I was in your boat last night,' she began.

'Okay.'

'I promised my brother I would not sleep with you at night. You must understand, he is very protective of me. Even though I have told him you are a good man, and you treat me well, he is still worried. He knows you are a rich American. And he does not like rich Americans. He does like me to be with you. So, I promise him I do not sleep with you at night. To fulfill my promise to my brother, I leave your bed. Sometimes, I do not like walking home when it is dark. Sometimes, I go to your boat and sleep in the cabin. This makes it easy to see you in the morning on your dock. I didn't think you would care.'

I was shocked. Exposed might be a better word. I had not considered this girl's reputation. I had only thought about what I wanted, what I needed.

'I understand your brother's concern,' I replied. 'You should have told me about him.'

'But you have so many things to think about, Mr. John. I mean John. I didn't want to bother you about this problem with my brother.'

'You should have told me.'

'I am sorry.'

'No, I am the one who should be sorry.'

'You have done nothing wrong.'

'Yes, I did.'

'No, you did not,' she said forcefully. 'You have done nothing except what I asked.'

I looked at her, wondering what I was missing.

'Okay,' I replied. We needed to move on. We could talk about our relationship later. We had more immediate concerns which needed to be addressed first.

'That explains why you were on my boat,' I continued. 'But why did you wait to come up until the storm hit?'

'When I heard big noises, I came up to look. I saw a fire in your house, and I saw you. I was afraid. I hid in your boat and waited, hoping you would leave so I could go home. But after a while, I knew you had taken the boat out to sea. Then I thought you would soon go to a port, and I could leave without you knowing I was on your boat. But when it became stormy, I wanted to help you.'

I took a moment to think about what she said. It seemed logical.

I asked her, 'You said you saw my house burning?'

'Yes.'

'Some men put bombs in my house. I was not in the house because it was too hot to sleep and I had decided to take a swim to cool off. I was on the dock when the bombs blew up the house. Otherwise, I would be dead now.'

'Oh...' she looked suddenly frightened.

'It's okay,' I said. 'As you can see, I'm alive.'

'Is this like the stories which happened to you and Miss Monica, the bad stories you have told me?'

'Yes, it is like those stories.'

'I am sorry.'

We were both silent for a moment. Then she said something I did not expect.

'If this is true, then I think you need to ask me more questions.'

'I don't understand; questions about what?'

She hesitated. 'Questions about those men who blew up your house.'

'How would you possibly know anything about them?'

She moved to the other side of the cockpit. I waited for her to speak. She hesitated. It was obvious that whatever was on her mind was something she was reluctant to tell me.

I waited.

'I do not know who blew up your house,' she finally continued. 'But I do know other things, things which might explain why it happened.'

'Ilana, what are you talking about?'

She sighed before telling me all about a man in the Mayan jewelry shop and his money and what she had to do to earn his money. At first it seemed like a harmless job, she explained. And she needed the money. Besides, she did not like me in the beginning. I was just another ugly, rich American tourist.

I thought about what she said, and she was right about the ugly American part. When I first met her, I was not very attractive. I was drunk most of the time.

After a while, she said she started to like me, liked being with me. This only made it easier for her to do her job. The man in the Mayan jewelry shop thought it was a good idea for her to be my friend. He gave her more money, which made her happy. And her job—it was fun.

It all seemed harmless to her in the beginning. But after I told her stories about Monica, she began to understand why the man wanted to know about me. She said she was so sorry she told the man about the phone calls. But she had taken the man's money, so she had to do her job.

'What phone calls?' I asked, still trying to digest what she was saying.

'The phone calls from your business friends. I told him about the calls.'

She was smart, smart enough to understand the connection between the calls and the bombs. And this meant she also understood that she was partly responsible for what happened. She began to cry. Turning so I could not see her face, she went down into the cabin, where I heard her whimpering softly.

Of course, it all made sense as I thought about what she told me. They had kept an eye on me from the beginning of my stay in Belize. My past had never gone away as I had hoped. It had simply stepped back, watched, and waited for the right time to return. And now it had affected an innocent woman from Belize. Everything became quiet below after a few minutes. I put the boat on autopilot and went down to find her curled in a corner of the galley. Bending down, I gave her a kiss.

'It's all right, Ilana,' I said sympathetically. 'I'm the one who should be apologizing to you. I'm the one who is responsible for this mess. Not you. I had hoped it was behind me, but I was stupid. And now it has involved you.'

She looked up at me.

'Please don't be sad,' I said. 'We have had enough trouble for one day.'

'Are you not mad, John?'

'No. Now come up topside and bring some food, please. We need to eat.'

Her eyes were still puffy when she returned, but she put on a happy face, placing a plate of fruit and cheese on a seat cushion between us.

As we ate in silence, the wind drove us onward.

My plan was to sail to Cancun without stopping. I didn't want to chance being spotted. This might seem extreme, but I knew it wouldn't be long before my pursuers started looking for me again and I wanted to be in Cancun when this happened. I figured an American would be difficult to locate in this resort town. American tourists were obnoxiously numerous in Cancun. I could blend in with the rest of the rowdy crowd. And I needed to get back to the States in a hurry. It was obvious I was no longer safe in Central America. But I had one big problem. I didn't have my passport with me. It was not in my wallet. It was in the house. My hope was that money could solve my problem, especially in Mexico, where money was king. So, I wasn't overly concerned.

Ilana was another matter, however. She was a problem not so easily solved. Getting her into the States would be difficult.

The solution, however, was obvious. She needed to go back to Belize. Because even if I managed to get her into the States, it wouldn't be fair to involve her in my problems, in the danger. I knew what I had to do. I had to buy her a boat or a plane ticket so she could go home. And I didn't blame her for her part in the mess. In fact, I could easily understand how it had happened. My fantasy world in Belize was just that, a fantasy. No more days in paradise for me. I was disappointed, but it had to be done. She had to go home.

As I considered my current situation, I remembered a past conversation with a former business partner from Sri Lanka. He told me the success of our company had come too easy. He said we would have to pay someday. He had been right. He had paid with his life. He had been poisoned. And I was paying now. I just didn't know how much. But I was learning.

Sunlight played off her face as we sailed. The wind freely blew through her flowing black hair. I looked at her small round shoulders and the gentle curve of her neck. She was a very beautiful woman and I had grown to enjoy her company. I realized now I had become very attached to her without ever thinking about it. It had come too easy. It just happened.

I checked the sails and compass. I had fallen slightly off course. We were slowly drifting away from shore. I adjusted the direction of the boat, moving to the northwest, towards where I could see the shore.

'Mr. John,' Ilana said.

'John,' I corrected her. It was obvious this name change would take some time. But why bother, I wondered. Soon, she would be gone.

'John,' she said. 'Yes, I will call you John. I will not make this mistake again. I am sorry.'

'It's okay. You can call me Mr. John if it makes you happy.'

'No, now it is John,' she said with determination. 'John, I cannot go home. You need to know this.'

'Why?' I asked, surprised.

'The man in the jewelry store told me he would kill me if I told you about him. He made this very clear. He is not a nice man. He will do it.'

'But I'm gone. It won't make any difference now.'

'No, he will do it. I know he will. He will come to my village and kill me or worse.'

'That's nonsense.'

'No, it is not, John. He will wonder why you were not in your bed the night your house was bombed.'

'He will think I warned you about him. And he will blame me.'

CANCUN MEXICO, TUESDAY, MAY 5, 11:00 A.M. JOHN

The resort town of Cancun, Mexico is an artificial playground on the shores of the blue Caribbean Sea.

New restaurants and fancy modern hotels have been built along its beaches in great numbers. And although the town has gone to considerable expense to look eager and new, a fine brown dust riding on the hot dry winds from the interior of the peninsula, coats all things new with old and brown. The town is never completely able to escape the world of poverty which surrounds it. The dust is a constant reminder of its origins.

However, the average tourist is completely unaware; the dust made to disappear daily, wiped away by legions of diligent, smiling natives. Hidden from view, the past is relegated to the old section of town, far from where tourists eat, drink and play games; blind to the poverty which surrounds them, confident their manifest destiny has entitled them to consume extravagant quantities of food washed down by more alcohol than they can reasonably consume.

I never liked the place.

Only a few yards from the pristine blue sea, beyond the irrigated green resort lawns and gardens; clumps of scrub grass can be found barely surviving in the dry brown dirt, surrounded by an arid landscape.

However, the native Mayans are friendly people. Short in stature with big brown eyes and wonderful smiles, they are naturally helpful and kind. I have often wondered for how long they will tolerate the demanding tourists before they can stomach their arrogance no more.

This, however, was not my problem. My problem was I needed to leave this place quickly before the guys who wanted to kill me, found me and finished what they began in Belize. To escape I needed money. All my cash had been spent on sailing supplies. Credit cards were all I had left and I knew the cards would leave a digital trail. If the bad guys could find me on a small island off the coast of Belize, they could find me anywhere in the world.

And it was probably my trail of credit cards which had been giving me away. But now I was in Cancun and I didn't have a choice. I had to use my credit cards to pay for a hotel room. Staying on my boat was not a logical choice. I feared my enemies were looking for my boat.

It felt good to return to dry land. Although I love to sail, I am a landlubber at heart. Days of cruising on the boat under the hot sun without a break had quickly became more work than play. Plus, taking turns sailing the boat at night left us both sleep-deprived.

I had a bad case of sunburn. Fortunately, Ilana was in better shape than I. The sea and sun were in her blood. Her beautiful brown skin seemed to glow in the sunshine. While I was spending most of my time trying to cover every inch of my body, she wandered around in a bikini.

We stopped a few times for a swim, to cool off and move around, but I was always anxious to get going again, to get to Cancun and out of Central America as fast as possible. I suddenly felt very vulnerable. We were alone with no one to help us. If my enemies found us, I assumed the odds of my staying alive were not good. So, we kept moving, always keeping the shoreline in view.

I ate sparingly on the boat. Not because I was seasick, but because I wasn't hungry. After several days of sailing, my stomach felt queasy. I assumed it was a case of nerves. Life in Belize had been easy. The tension of the storm and the shock of seeing my house go up in flames had given my nervous system a serious wake-up call. It had been a long time since I had lived with stress and I wasn't adjusting to it well.

Walking off the dock at a marina in Cancun after days of living on a boat was an amusing experience. It took a few steps before I could walk a straight line. My sea legs did not immediately adjust to standing on something solid.

My first task after setting foot on dry land was to find a hotel room for the night. I needed a shower and a shave in the worst way. The two of us must have looked oddly out of place entering the fancy lobby of a resort hotel, sunburned and slightly unkempt with almost nothing in the way of luggage. But the hotel management was only too happy to accept my credit card when I asked for one of their more expensive suites, no questions asked.

As soon as we had settled into our room, I used the hotel phone to call a long-distance number.

'David...,' I said as soon as he answered. 'Yes, I know we haven't talked in a while.'

David was my best friend from my hometown of Grand Haven, Michigan. He was also my lawyer. He had my power of attorney in case something happened to me and he also had access to one of my bank accounts which he used for my benefit.

'Okay, just shut up please,' I interrupted him. 'We can catch up later when I return to the States. Right now, I need your help. I have a situation here.'

I explained in as few words as possible why I was in Cancun and why I needed to get out fast. I asked him to charter a jet and send it to Mexico to get me. And yes, I knew commercial flights were available almost every hour of every day, but I had a problem. I didn't have a passport.

Ilana sat near me as I talked. Ever since we had arrived in Cancun, she had stayed close. I assumed this was because she was scared. Or maybe she thought I would leave her if I had an opportunity. This was not true. I believed her when she told me she was in danger. She was coming with me. We would face our problems together.

The blue Caribbean Sea could clearly visible through a window in our high-rise hotel room. The interior of the room was over-decorated for my taste, too many brightly colored floral patterns on the walls and furniture, but the colors seemed to make Ilana happy. She had never been in a big hotel like this before. When I ordered some room service food, Ilana thought that was a marvelous idea. Out of the corner of my eye, I could see her happily munching some fruit and watching television while I talked to David.

'Yes David, I know it will be expensive, but it needs to be done. I'll call you later... Yes, I know this is going to mess up your day, but if you want to see your old buddy alive again... well...I think you get my point.'

David listened without comment. He seemed to understand. He didn't ask many questions. We disconnected after I told him that I would call him again in a few hours.

I got up to give Ilana a kiss to reassure her. Told her she need not worry. I would take care of her.

After a welcome shower, shave, and nap, there wasn't much else to do, except maybe buy some new clothes. Arriving in Charlottesville, Virginia, dressed in ragged shorts and a tee shirt did not seem appropriate attire. Besides, it was early May and the weather could be cool in Virginia. I had changed my mind, decided to return to my apartment and office before flying to Michigan. There were a few things I needed to do which could only be accomplished from my office.

In the morning I planned to move to a different hotel. I didn't want to stay in any one hotel for more than one night. I hoped this would make it harder for someone to track me even if they were able to trace me through my credit cards, always staying one step ahead of my pursuers. We would move as many times as necessary. But first, we had to shop for clothes and luggage. Then get a good night's sleep.

The rest was in David's hands.

WEDNESDAY, MAY 6, 2:30 P.M. LAWYER

The security guard at the gate to the marina took the two new crisp twenty-dollar bills given to him by the lawyer and shoved the money into his pocket while waving the man through.

This was more money than the short, slightly overweight, balding Mexican lawyer had planned to give the guard. He had hoped to keep most of the money for himself. But everyone wanted money in this town, lots of money, American money. It was not like the old days. Still, he was happy his money achieved its purpose. He was allowed to enter the marina.

Wandering up and down the docks, he searched as he had been instructed. Personally, he was convinced this was a fool's mission, but he had been paid well, so he dutifully looked for a forty-four-foot sailboat with a dark blue hull and a single mast. The name of the boat was 'Retreat'.

It became immediately apparent to him that the boat would not be easy to find. The marina was large and filled with many big boats, mostly foreign-owned boats of all sizes and descriptions. Foreigners were filthy rich. This made the lawyer mad. Plus, it was midafternoon and it was hot. He didn't want to wander around this large marina for hours looking for a boat. He had asked his new client if he could wait until evening to do his job. It would be cooler in the evening, he had suggested. But his client, who wired him his generous fee, said it had to be done now, as soon as possible. Take the job or someone else would be called.

Sweating under the hot sun, his wrinkled suit quickly became very uncomfortable. He was a professional lawyer. He always wore a suit, even on hot days. It made him feel important. However, today, it just made him sweat.

A young girl in an almost nothing bikini lay on the deck of a big white motor yacht getting a suntan. She was very pretty, with long legs and a deep brown tan. The balding lawyer stopped to wipe his hairless head while he eyed her. As a result, he almost missed seeing a sailboat tied to the dock next to the yacht occupied by the sunbathing woman. Only by chance, only out of the corner of his eye did he happen to notice the boat was about the right size and the right color. He doubled back to look for the name of the boat's stern. A small dingy had been tied over the back covering the name. Checking to see if anyone was watching, no one was near, except the girl in the bikini and she was sunbathing with her eyes closed; he stepped carefully onto the sailboat and leaned over the stern to lift the dingy. Underneath he could clearly read the word 'Retreat'.

The lawyer tried the cabin door after calling a weak, 'Hello.'

No one answered and the door was locked.

Almost done now, he would be finished after reporting to his client; his money earned. Stepping off the boat, he looked up to see the girl and didn't notice that the dock was wet. His smooth leather shoes slipped, causing him to lean precariously over the edge of the dock before... thankfully... regaining his balance before falling into the water. The pretty girl who had been sunbathing on the yacht was sitting up now with a smile on her face, obviously enjoying his amusing antics. Embarrassed, he made a hasty retreat, trying to ignore the girl's grin. Wiping sweat from his forehead with the sleeve of his jacket, he took out his cell phone from his pocket. It occurred to him as he dialed a long-distance number, that perhaps his client might request he stay to watch the boat and report any activity. Spending an afternoon in the hot sun in his wrinkled lawyer's suit was not the sort of task he had contemplated as his life's work when he graduated from law school. He made his call anyway. It was a living. Besides, a bar was located nearby in the marina. He could sip a cool drink while sitting at the bar in the shade of a canvas awning.

From there, he could clearly see if anyone returned to the boat.

THURSDAY, MAY 7, 10:00 A.M.
JOHN

Ilana sipped a cold soft drink while we waited in the main lobby of the airport.

She looked very pretty in her bright yellow blouse and white skirt, new clothes which came from a local store in Cancun; a tourist trap with high prices. I didn't mind. It had been fun watching her buy clothes.

She owned only very few dresses. Her wardrobe in Belize consisted mostly of shorts, tee-shirts, and of course, tiny bikinis. That was the extent of what she needed in the way of clothes. Her bikinis were my favorite. I had suggested she wear nothing else, but this was about to change. I had warned her it would be much cooler in the States. She would need warmer clothes.

She had a great time shopping.

Brightly colored dresses and blouses were her favorites. I suggested she buy some more conservatively colored outfits, but most of the time, I let her do as she pleased. A limit of one suitcase of clothes was the only restriction I placed on her buying spree. I suggested she could buy more clothes when we arrived in the States. Unfortunately, this didn't slow her much. She probably bought more clothes in that one afternoon than she had purchased in a lifetime. I also bought a few items, a couple of pairs of pants, shirts, a sweater, and a jacket; only what I needed for the trip.

Two new carry-on luggage bags now rested next to us in the main lounge of the airport terminal building. We had arrived at the Cancun airport earlier than necessary. Our plane was not due for another hour, but I was sick of waiting in a hotel room. It was time to be gone, the sooner the better.

Sleep had been elusive the last night of our stay in Cancun. I wandered the suite's sitting room, and didn't want to bother Ilana with my tossing and turning in bed. I was anxious, desperate to be gone. The wait was driving me crazy. Ilana didn't seem to mind. She liked living in a hotel. I knew she was in for a big adjustment when we arrived in Virginia. I wondered how she would handle it.

David had called yesterday afternoon. The earliest he could schedule a chartered jet to Cancun was late morning today. I thanked him and told him I was looking forward to seeing him and Mary his wife. I said I would find time to visit them in Michigan once I accomplished a few necessary tasks at my office in Virginia. He informed me my cottage on Lake Michigan had been finished for several weeks. It was ready for occupancy. I thanked him and told him I would compensate him for his time. He said he expected nothing. My friendship was enough.

Ilana and I had ventured outside our hotel rooms only a couple of times during our stay in Cancun, mostly to shop. The rest of the time we hid in our hotel. Room service provided meals. All this was fine with Ilana. She was quite content, wondering if some people lived in hotel rooms exclusively, their food catered in daily. I told her some did, but not many. It was very expensive.

My major worry was getting Ilana into the US without a visa or passport. I assumed I could talk my way in. I still had my wallet. My driver's license was my identification. I could say I had lost my passport. Ilana was a different matter. She had nothing and she didn't exactly look typical American. Questions were bound to be asked.

We were scheduled to fly directly to Charlottesville. My hope was that U.S. Immigration didn't normally search private planes for illegal aliens, not in an airport like Charlottesville. I hoped to sneak her in, but the details were fuzzy. She was comfortable with the idea. Probably because she didn't understand the complications.

The closer it got to the time to go, the more nervous I became. By the time we arrived at the airport, I was not doing too well.

Ilana poked me in the ribs as I was trying to calm down.

A recent copy of the New York Times had been abandoned on the seat next to me by a departing tourist. I was reading it at the time to occupy my mind. I hadn't read a U.S. newspaper for almost a year. The world outside of my island paradise was of little concern. If something really important happened, I assumed I would learn about it sooner or later. However, this was about to change. I was reentering the land of the hurried and the worried. It was time to discover what was happening in the world.

Ilana poked me again.

'Yes,' I answered casually annoyed with her. The newspaper article I was reading was interesting.

'John,' she said.

She had, by this time, mastered the short version of my name. No more 'Mr. John'.

'John, a man keeps looking at me.'

'Maybe he thinks you're pretty.'

'I don't like how he looks at me,' she persisted. 'I don't think he is a nice man.'

Women have an uncanny knack for understanding human nature far better than men. They seem to have an innate ability that allows them to look directly into the soul of a person. Experience has taught me to never ignore their ability. I have always regretted it when I did.

'Where's the man,' I asked. 'Tell me without pointing or looking at him.'

'He is two rows straight ahead of us, sitting on the end of the row dressed in a light brown wrinkled suit. He is a short fat man with a bald head and bushy eyebrows.'

This was a pretty good description. The part about the bushy eyebrows wasn't particularly important, but it was helpful. I looked up casually from my newspaper and slowly scanned the rows of waiting passengers to avoid appearing like I was looking only at him. Ilana was right. He was looking directly at us and his balding head looked down quickly when I spotted him.

Body language is normally a clear indicator of a person's intentions and it was obvious he was either enthralled with Ilana's beauty or he had another reason for staring in our direction. I decided I needed to know his intentions and there was only one way to find out. Casually reaching for my suitcase handle, I told Ilana it was time to move. I tucked the New York Times under my arm and prepared to go to another section of the airport. Ilana followed my lead. We walked slowly as if we were not in a hurry.

I had decided earlier to avoid going immediately to the terminal building which serviced private planes. I assumed it would be better to wait until just before our departure time. Getting Ilana on the plane might be a problem. She was probably already in violation of some Mexican immigration laws. I assumed it was not a big deal for her to sail from Belize to Mexico, but it was a completely different matter entirely for an alien to fly from Mexico to the United States. I assumed the best way to get over this hurdle was to arrive at the gate at the last minute and rush through the process, no time for a lot of questions, just another rich jet-setting couple traveling the globe. Hopefully, Mexican authorities weren't in the habit of harassing rich Americans. Tourism depended on their neighbors to the north. But just in case we ran into trouble, I had gone to a bank in the morning for cash, enough to bribe my way out of Mexico, or so I hoped.

It was only a short distance down a crowded hall between lounges designated for different airlines. Brightly dressed tourists seemed to be everywhere. We fit in. Rich men with foreign-looking mistresses were not an uncommon sight in Cancun. I stopped at a drinking fountain and casually looked back in the direction we had come. The man with the bushy eyebrows was an unwelcome complication. I hoped I would not see his face again, but there he was, leaning against a wall in his wrinkled suit as if he was resting for a minute. It wasn't completely obvious he was following us, but it sure looked like he was.

We continued walking until we arrived at a lounge designated for American Airlines passengers. Navigating through milling passengers and suitcases, dragging wheeled carry-on luggage was not easy. A couple of seats near a window overlooking the runway seemed a good place to rest. If the jerk was tailing us, he would be forced to enter the lounge to find us. And unfortunately, this is exactly what he did. It took almost no time for him to show up. He came in, looked around, hesitated when he didn't see us right away, looking confused like he didn't know exactly what to do. Then when he finally spotted us, he turned away immediately, standing very still before wandering over to a seat near the entrance.

'I'm right,' Ilana said. 'The fat man with the bushy eyebrows is following us.'

'Unfortunately, I agree with you.'

'He is not a good man.'

'No.'

The short fat man took a cell phone out of his pocket as he waited. Oddly, he didn't look dangerous. In fact, he looked kind of pathetic in his wrinkled suit.

I held Ilana's hand to assure her everything was all right, but it wasn't. The short fat man was a new complication. As he talked on his cell phone, he moved his head up and down slightly as if agreeing with someone. He then looked at us, I assume to be sure we were still in the room. I stared back at him this time, now unafraid to acknowledge I knew he was tailing us. His response was to quickly stand up and leave.

'He is going away,' Ilana said. 'Good, I do not like him.'

'I think we need to get out of here,' I said to her.

We exited the American Airlines lounge, turned down a hall, and immediately headed for the private plane terminal. We had one chance to leave Mexico today. If the short fat man thought we were taking a commercial flight, he would return with whomever or whatever it was he went to find and he would search for us in the main terminal building. We wouldn't be there and hopefully, this would throw him off our trail and buy us some time, enough time to get on the plane and in the air.

With no guarantee this would work, our challenge now was to leave before he discovered we were using a private plane to travel. If we were successful, we might just be able to get out without too many questions. If not... well... that could be a problem, a big problem.

I wondered what he was doing. Was he meeting with an assassin hired to kill us? This didn't seem too plausible. He would never have left us if this was his plan. He would simply have waited and watched us, telling his killer where we were by cell phone, not letting us out of his sight. No, he had gone to solicit some other kind of help, maybe official help.

Ilana was having trouble keeping up with me. I was in a hurry now and her overstuffed suitcase was much heavier than mine. She had bought too many clothes at the store. When it came time to pack, she had a difficult time trying to stuff all her new clothes into the suitcase. I suggested she put some of her clothes in my suitcase. And to help her now, I gave her my suitcase which was considerably lighter and I took hers so she could keep up with me.

'Thank you...John.' I heard her hesitate and almost call me Mr. John. 'Why are we in a hurry?'

'Because I don't think the man with the bushy eyebrows is a friend.'

My mind was racing. Looking at my watch, it was still a half hour until our plane was due to land. I knew it was flying in from Miami. It wasn't a long flight. I hoped the plane would not need to refuel in Cancun and could, hopefully, take off again immediately.

Walking at a fast pace, trying to blend in with the other passengers, I searched, but the fat man was nowhere in sight. However, I sensed he would be looking for us soon. I couldn't help but wonder why he had let us out of his sight. Did he go for the police? Did he assume we had entered the country illegally? Did someone tell him? Was he a cop from Belize? Did he want to detain me to be questioned about a fire at my rented house? Could a warrant for my arrest be in the system? I didn't know. A hundred possibilities raced through my head, all of them a problem. Because nothing positive might come from an encounter with the local police. I had heard too many stories about Mexican jails. I didn't want to go to jail. Cops in Mexico could be bribed, inmates killed. I might not get out alive.

We were near the exit of the commercial passenger building.

'Paging Mr. John Van Laan,' a voice came through a loudspeaker.

'Mr. John Van Laan. Please report to the American Airlines ticket counter. Mr. John Van Laan.'

Ilana tugged at my arm. 'They are asking for you.'

'Yes, but I don't want to talk to them.'

I held the door for her as she dragged my suitcase behind her. A sidewalk connected the two passenger terminal buildings.

The sun was hot. I began to sweat immediately as we walked. Arriving at the entrance to the building which serviced private planes, a guard stood waiting at the door. He asked for ID. I presented my Virginia driver's license, showed him the picture. He looked at his clipboard.

'Your passport please, Signor,' the guard said.

'Stolen and I haven't had the time to get another one.' I replied and slipped a hundred-dollar bill under the license.

He looked at me and at the driver's license again, took the money, and shrugged. I motioned for Ilana to go through the door in front of me. The guard started to ask her something.

'She's with me,' I said, practically pushing her through the door past the guard.

We were in. I whispered to Ilana to take a seat inside and talk to no one. I went up to a woman sitting at the reception desk and asked her if she had information on my plane. She looked intently at her computer screen for a moment before replying. 'Your flight was on time, sir,' she said.

I thanked her politely and took a seat next to Ilana in the waiting room.

'Why don't you take your suitcase into the restroom and change into something else.' I said quietly to Ilana.

She seemed to understand the reason for my request and got up immediately. I decided to do the same. It was a small precaution, I knew, but we had time to kill and it was something which might help us get out of here alive. If someone came in, looking for us, a change in clothes might throw them off; especially Ilana, her colorful outfit would be her description.

When I exited the restroom, I saw Ilana had dressed in an off-white suit I urged her to buy. She had not liked it, did not like the color, but she bought it anyway to please me. The fact she wore it now told me she understood our predicament.

As we waited, I gave her a section of the New York Times, told her to hold it in front of her face. She didn't often read newspapers, at least not to my knowledge. It wasn't because she couldn't read. She could read very well. She had demonstrated the ability more than once in Belize. She simply wasn't interested in the news.

To pass the time, I buried my head in an article about the latest hit show on Broadway, reading but not really comprehending, mostly holding the newspaper so I was partially hidden behind it.

'Mr. Van Laan.' The young woman at the desk startled me, immediately afraid we had been found. I hesitantly went up to the desk, fearing the worst.

'Your plane will arrive early,' she said with a smile. 'It is in its landing pattern now and should be outside the building in about ten minutes.'

I breathed a sigh of relief and thanked her, happy for a minor miracle. Planes are never ahead of schedule. Maybe this was an omen. Maybe it meant we were getting out of Mexico after all. Still, the man in the wrinkled suit could be looking for us and I didn't think it would take him forever to find us.

I informed Ilana our plane was landing. Instead of looking happy, she began to act nervous. I knew why. She was apprehensive about flying. We had talked about her problem last night. It didn't come out at first, but when she suggested taking a boat home. I asked her why, why now. Wasn't she afraid of the man from the jewelry shop?

She didn't answer immediately.

I told her it was okay. If she really wanted to go home, I would buy her a ticket on a boat.

She finally admitted the reason for her change of mind. She said she was afraid of airplanes. Could we sail to America instead, she asked. I said, we could, but it would take a long time and be very dangerous.

She thought about my answer. 'No,' she finally concluded with defiance in her voice. 'The man from the jewelry shop will surely come and kill me. No, I want to go with you, John.' She had put her arms around me and I had held her until I felt her finally begin to relax.

'You don't have to do this,' I suggested. 'It's me they want, not you.'

She had smiled. 'Don't you not know by now I want to be with you Mr. John?' she said with a playful grin, hiding her apprehension.

Apparently, we had arrived at an arrangement without ever saying it.

She had called a bartender on Ambergris Island who was a friend of her brother. She told the man to tell her brother she was alright and she would contact him later. She asked the man to tell her brother not to worry. The call seemed to make her feel better. Still, the thought of getting on an airplane seemed to terrify her. I knew she was very nervous. I held her hand as we waited.

I occasionally glanced around my newspaper to check the door to the outside, hoping it would stay closed. Because each time the door opened, I held my breath, fearful the short bushy-eyed man in a wrinkled suit would walk in with a policeman or someone worse like a killer with a gun. But only passengers or an employee appeared through the open door, no one looking for us.

Minutes passed slowly.

'Mr. Van Laan,' the woman at the desk said. 'Your plane has arrived.'

'Thank you.'

The outside door opened. My heart hit the panic button. I expected to see Mr. bushy eyes walk through the door cutting off our escape. But instead, a man dressed in an expensive black suit arrived followed by a lady wearing too much make-up, red lips, lots of gold jewelry, and a white jumpsuit. I smiled. They were comic relief. I grabbed the handle of my suitcase with a sweaty hand and motioned to Ilana, telling her it was time to go.

Sunshine reflected off the polished metal surface of the plane and dust blew in a swirl as we watched it come to a stop. I don't think I had ever been so happy to see an airplane in my life. Looking like a big silver angel sent to rescue us from this artificial world of dust and lights; the mechanical bird's engines wound down to idle. Locks on its smooth round fuselage clicked and I watched in wonder as a door to another world from my former life opened. Stairs descended to the tarmac. A young, sandy-haired copilot poked his head out of the door and signaled for us to approach. I knew wonder waited inside for Ilana as we ascended the steps. I had flown many times, but the experience would be new for her, filled with energy and speed.

Ilana went up the stairs ahead of me and waited inside the door.

'Mr. Van Laan?' the copilot inquired at the top of the stairs.

'Yes,' I pulled out my driver's license and showed it to him.

'My name is John Van Laan. David Dykstra, my attorney in Grand Haven, Michigan, arranged for this flight. This lady and I will be your only passengers today. It is very important that we leave immediately.'

'Very good, sir,' he replied. 'May I see your passports, please?'

'No, you may not. It was stolen. I will have to apply for a new one when I return home.' I said with little patience.

He looked at me suspiciously as he eyed my driver's license again. Apparently, this was enough for him. 'Very good sir.'

'Do you need to refuel?' I asked.

'No, we had not planned to refuel. We can leave immediately,' he said.

I was relieved, thinking we were home free.

'May I see her passport?' the copilot asked.

'No.'

'Was hers also stolen?' he asked with a hint of sarcasm in his voice.

'No, she has never needed one before.'

'That is a problem,' he replied. 'As you know she will need a passport when we arrive in the United States.'

'I know, but more importantly, we need to get out of here fast. I will explain when we are in the air,' I said the words as emphatically as possible.

He hesitated.

'We need to go now,' my voice rose with more intensity than the situation required. I shoved past him and into the plane's interior. Ilana was standing inside listening to the conversation. The copilot remained standing by the door.

'I said I would explain. Now, let's go.'

The co-pilot went into the cockpit to talk to the pilot. We waited in the hall outside.

The pilot came and offered me his hand. 'Mr. Van Laan. It is good to see you again, sir,' he smiled.

I remembered him from one of the many times I had flown with his company. I wasn't sure what his name was, but I knew his face.

'Look, I know this is a little usual,' I began. 'But we need to get off the ground and into the air fast. Come back once we are airborne and I will explain everything.'

He looked at Ilana. It was obvious she was not an American. He must have thought my motives were less than altruistic. She was much too pretty.

'Very good Mr. Van Laan, we will get underway immediately.' he smiled, instructing the copilot to shut the door.

I breathed a sigh of relief.

Ilana was looking around. I'm sure she had never seen so much leather before. The passenger area of the jet contained several rows of thick leather seating and a couple of couches which could be opened into beds. I stowed our luggage under one of the seats and sat down, motioning for her to take a seat next to me. When she did, I leaned over and secured her seatbelt.

The plane vibrated as it taxied to the runway. With every turn of the wheels, the short fat man with bushy eyebrows was farther away. I was beginning to relax. Ilana on the other hand was looking anything but relaxed. In fact, she was starting to look as if I had tied her into an electric chair and was about to pull the switch. I leaned over and took her hand as the plane bumped and bounced along the uneven taxiway toward the end of the runway where it could take off.

'It's going to be alright,' I said, trying to help her to relax even though I knew there was very little I could do to comfort her.

Her face assumed a determined look, tight-lipped, color all but gone. I knew this would be one experience she would remember for the rest of her life.

The plane remained stationary once it arrived at the head of the runway. I assumed we were waiting for the runway to clear.

Either another plane was landing or someone in front of us was waiting to take off. Hopefully, the line was not too long. I looked through a window, but I couldn't see any planes ahead of us.

Seconds ticked like hours as we waited. We were still on Mexican soil and I assumed the the man with bushy eyebrows was still looking for us. The cabin door opened and the Captain emerged. He sat down across the aisle from me with a grim look on his face.

'The tower is asking us to return to the terminal. They say there is a problem. They won't give me any explanation except to say it has something to do with immigration. They want us to go back and fill out some paperwork. Shall I return?' he asked.

I spotted the pilot's nameplate on his uniform.

'Al, if you return to the gate, I and surely this woman may not get out of Mexico alive. It's very important we take off now. Promise them anything, but please get us out of here. I will explain when we are in the air.'

The captain looked at me for a moment, considering his options. 'Okay, Mr. Van Laan,' he finally agreed. 'I hope this doesn't get me into too much trouble, but you seem like a straight shooter. I will tell them we are late for an appointment in the States. We don't have the time, need to be in the air. We'll promise to send the required paperwork to them in the mail. Let's just hope they don't have the firepower to keep us on the ground.'

The captain returned to cockpit where I heard him arguing with the tower, persuasive in a calm way. Eventually, it sounded like they came to an agreement. The plane's engines revved, the brake released, accelerating quickly down the runway. I held Ilana's hand and for the second time in an hour, I took a deep breath and slowly exhaled. The plane's powerful engines pushed us into our seats as it climbed almost vertically into a clear blue sky.

Ilana had a big smile on her face when we finally leveled off at a cruising altitude. As did I.

We were headed home, my home.

GRAND HAVEN, MICHIGAN, THURSDAY, MAY 7, 2:35 P.M.
PHILLIP

Phillip Palmer took the call in a confined three-room office located in an old brick building on the main street of Grand Haven, Michigan.

'Yes, I understand,' he replied into his phone as he unconsciously twirled his ponytail. Playing with his hair was a bad habit. Normally, he wore his long, curly brown hair pulled back in a ponytail to keep himself from messing with it, but on occasion or just because he felt like it, he wore his hair down for dramatic effect, like an actor.

'Of course... If he shows up here, I promise to call.'

He listened as they gave him instructions over the phone while casually writing notes on a pad. The handwritten notes were, in fact, totally unnecessary because he knew he would remember. The information was too important to forget. This was the call he had been waiting for. He knew it would come eventually. It was just a matter of time.

Smiling to himself as he unconsciously adjusted his hair to fall lazily over his shoulder, he said, 'Yes, my clients were very satisfied with the latest shipment of stones. The color and quality exceeded their expectations.' After listening some more, he explained, 'I can't tell you how important it is for the cutting to meet exact specifications. No variations, please, within specified sizes... Yes, yes, I know you understand. Yes, and the colors must match. If not, my clients will return the stones.'

He knew they listened, but he wondered if they really understood. In their world, they did not need to be so exact. But this was not their world. This was America, and if they wanted to sell gems here, they would have to do it his way, and it was his job to explain this to them.

He knew John never had these problems. John's cutters and sorters were rigorously trained. He envied John, but he was making progress. Phillip's sales to U.S. jewelry manufacturers were increasing every month. Sure, he had some initial problems, but it was getting better. He could almost taste success now. It was happening. Too slow for him, but at least it was happening. Money was beginning to flow in as he had been promised. Only one problem remained to be solved, and this problem had apparently returned to the U.S.A. It was finally time to deal with him.

'Thank you... Yes. I'll fax new orders this evening.' He hung up his phone.

Soon he would be able to move out of his old office into a bigger, newer building, one better suited to his station in life.

CHARLOTTESVILLE, VIRGINIA, 8:50 P.M. JOHN

The overhanging fluorescent lights designed to spread light over the main parking lot of my Virginia office building were dark when we drove in.

The building looked to be completely deserted, lifeless behind the large, plate glass windows in the lobby. I had been telling Ilana about how we would need to go through security when we arrived. But not to worry, I explained. I was sure one of the security guards would recognize me. If not, if they were all new to their job, I could instruct them to call my secretary, who would verify my identity. So, it didn't matter; I was certain I could talk my way inside. But after surveying the deserted scene outside the windshield of our rented car, it occurred to me that getting through security might not be our biggest problem. I didn't like what I saw. Perhaps it was my heightened sense of paranoia, but nothing appeared to be as it should be. Just when I thought we were home free, when I could finally begin to relax, a new problem reared its ugly head.

Fortunately, everything had gone smoothly up to this time.

After clearing Customs, I drove to a restaurant in town to meet Al, our pilot. He had been very helpful after I explained our predicament to him during the flight. He taxied the plane to a private hangar after landing at the airport and turned off the engines. Searching for a spare stewardess uniform in a locker in the hangar, he gave it to Ilana, who changed into the uniform on the plane. The uniform allowed her to enter the United States by simply walking out with Al as one of his employees, a flight attendant. I thanked Al at the restaurant where Ilana was waiting for me. I told him I would ask for him next time I needed a plane. I owed him one. He waved me off. All part of the job, he said.

I actually had more problems getting into the country than she did. Seems Customs was not happy with me. They had received a complaint from their Mexican counterparts, something about a passport and an illegal female. I explained to them I had lost my passport in a fire. As for a female, I didn't know who they were talking about. They didn't like my answers, but there was nothing they could do. Ilana and her luggage were long gone by this time, except for a few of her clothes, which were in my bag when customs checked it. They had looked at me rather oddly when they saw the dresses and asked why some women's clothes were in my bag. I said the clothes were presents for my twin nieces. I'm not sure they bought my excuse, but eventually, they let me pass.

Getting Ilana a visa was something that would require attention in the near future. Hopefully, a case could be made for asylum. I had met my U.S. Congressman on a couple of occasions. I hoped he would help. Or I could call my friend Charlie at the CIA, if necessary. Not that I wanted to, I didn't. Mostly because we had some difficult issues that still needed to be resolved, but neither of us had made a point of initiating a discussion. I had not called Charlie since Monica's funeral in Ohio, and he had not called me. However, Charlie was not a bad option. He was well-informed about the man who was tracking me again. He knew this man was capable of murder. If I could convince Charlie that Ilana was in danger, perhaps he would help arrange asylum for her.

As Ilana and I drove through town under a dark night sky, I described the glass and brick office building, which would be her new home. I wasn't sure she was listening. She was looking anxious, trying to calm down from her recent adventures, the latest being her slightly criminal entrance into the United States. As of now, she was officially an illegal alien. But all this was a matter for another day. We had experienced enough excitement for one day. All I really wanted as I drove into the deserted parking lot was to lay my weary head on the soft pillow of my bed and sleep. I had not slept well since the house on the beach in Belize burned. I badly needed rest. Days and nights sailing on the boat had been exhausting and our time in Cancun uneasy. The last thing I needed or wanted was one more crisis. But as we sat in the rental car viewing a forbidding, dark office building, my first instinct was to cut and run.

It looked like a trap, but I almost didn't care... I was tired, exhausted, too tired to care. I wanted my bed. My nerves were shot. If this was my time to die... right here in this parking lot... well... I was almost willing to let it happen. As I sat in the car in tired suspense, wondering what to do, expecting the worst, I imagined red tracer lines disturbing the night air, followed by sounds of splintering glass and thuds from lead bullets hitting our car... Thinking this would be a fitting end to an exhausting day.

'John. What are you doing?' Ilana asked, forcing me back into reality.

'Something isn't right, Ilana. The parking lot and the building are always lighted. See those windows in the building. Lights should be on inside those windows,' I explained.

'We should leave,' she echoed my instincts.

'You stay here. I'm going to check.'

'Please, John, let's go,' she pleaded.

I knew she was right, but I got out of the car anyway and slowly proceeded towards the building. Nothing moved. If killers were hiding in the dark to kill me, it would happen now. I continued, half anticipating a bullet hitting my body any second.

My only excuse for taking a big chance was I didn't really think anyone was here, not yet anyway. I thought I had a few days head start, a few days before I had to worry. Still, this didn't look right. I almost turned around several times. But everything was quiet, so I proceeded to the front door of the building. It was difficult to see anything inside. The windows of the lobby were dark. I tried the glass entrance door. It was locked. I knocked and waited. No one appeared. Stepping back, hoping, I half expected the building to suddenly light and look as I imagined it should, as it was when I left. Tall lamps on the four corners of the parking lots illuminated our car. Soft night lights shone inside the lobby, the main security desk was manned by a guard sitting behind a desk monitoring an in-house video system. Everything was silent and dark: no alarm, no security guards, nothing.

I returned the car.

'Are we going now?' Ilana nervously asked.

'No, I want to check one other possibility.'

A driveway around the side of the building led to a back parking lot, guarded by a heavy wrought iron security gate at the entrance. Fortunately, it was not locked as it should be. The lot was on the same level as the basement of the building, one floor below the main lobby. It led to a garage under the main floor office complex. Automatic doors opened to a garage. This was where my cars were kept. Above the garage was my apartment. It had been added to the building when I got tired of sleeping on the couch in my office after too many late nights of work. Rather than fight the traffic in Charlottesville, I would often sleep on a couch in my office without bothering to return home. One day it dawned on me it would be easier to build an apartment attached to my office building. This way, I wouldn't need to drive back and forth to work. Plus, I could go to my office anytime I wanted, day or night.

I turned off the car's motor and waited, listening for trouble.

'John, can we please go now,' Ilana pleaded again.

The scene was eerily quiet, dark, no movement. I couldn't blame her for wanting to leave. Still, I was not ready to give up the idea of sleeping in my own bed, not yet. This was my home, after all, and I was tired, tired of running. After everything that had happened, I did not want to spend one more night in a hotel room.

Beyond the parking lot was a tree-covered hillside that fell steeply down to a valley below. When picking a site for the building, I chose this place because I liked the isolation and privacy it offered. But mostly, I chose it for the view of the valley.

A few overhead clouds momentarily covered the moon, darkening the dimly lit scene. I knew the way by heart. I decided to try to enter my apartment through a back door. To get inside, I had to climb emergency exit stairs on the outside of the building, which led to a small balcony where I usually kept a spare key on a hook under the railing. If the key was there, I could unlock the door to my apartment. After climbing the stairs, I peeked through a window in the back door. No lights, but this did not surprise me. There was no reason for lights to be on in my apartment. I had given strict instructions for no one to use it in my absence.

After some searching in the dark, I found the hook, but the key was gone. Big disappointment, but nothing I could do. I could break in, I supposed. But this might set off an alarm, and I was in no mood to deal with police while harboring an illegal alien. I took a moment while standing on the balcony to look at the lights in the valley below. In the past, I would occasionally sit on this balcony at night with a glass of wine and try to relax after a long day of work. It was a small comfort that the view had not changed. That's when I heard the faint sounds of an old blues jazz piece traveling the wind, interrupting the silence. At first, I thought I was imagining it, but eventually, I decided the music was real. Carefully walking down the stairs in the dark, I followed the sweet sounds of a saxophone drifting through the night air. Lights from inside Arny's apartment lit my way. I was surprised. All the other lights in the building were off. I assumed Arny was gone as well, but apparently, this was not true.

Originally, my friend Arny had been hired to work in maintenance at the office. But after finding him working late too many nights, I would bring a couple of beers from my office, and we would sit on boxes in the loading dock, talking. We had a good time telling stories of past glories and future dreams. That's when I learned his life story. And that's how he discovered his boss was just an ordinary guy. Eventually, we became good friends even though I was white and he was black. When I decided to build an apartment for myself, I also built one for him as a favor. Of course, he had other ideas. He claimed I did it so he would take care of me. Said I couldn't take care of myself. I eventually gave in and agreed with him. In a way, he was right. I think I needed him more than he needed me.

My friend Arny had originally been hired to work in maintenance but over time, we built a friendship, resulting from catching him in the office after hours. We bonded over beers and storytelling sessions. Eventually, when I built my office apartment, I built one for Arny as well, keeping him as my personal home assistant, Arny thought I needed taking care of and I didn't disagree. He became a constant, reliable, often sarcastic element of my daily work life.

Dead twigs snapped under my shoes as I neared the emergency stairs up to Arny's apartment balcony. Climbing the stairs quietly, I did not want to scare him. Fortunately, the emergency door to his apartment was open. He enjoyed the fresh air. I could see him through the screened door working in his kitchen, apparently unaware I was outside, too absorbed in listening to a jazz record playing from another room, whistling to the tune.

I knocked softly on his screen door. He almost fainted when he saw me. I must have looked like a ghost in the shadows outside his door.

'Arny, it's me, John. Take it easy,' I said through the screen.

'John, is that really you, man?' he sounded relieved.

'It's really me. Now, come here and open the door. I'm hungry, and I need some dinner.'

It didn't take him any time to adjust and return to the Arny I knew.

'I'm sorry,' he said. 'Y'all are too late. I'm not making anyone dinner at this hour. Just go away,' he smiled.

'Open the door, you old dog. And come out here. I want to give you a kiss,' I laughed.

After he opened his door, I wrapped my arms around him in a bear hug and gave him a kiss on his cheek. 'Man, is it good to see you.'

I looked him over. He had not changed since I left Charlottesville over a year age. Arny was one of those old men who never seemed to age. He still had the strong body of an athlete. His smile and his sense of humor were his welcome card. His way with ladies was legendary. I was privileged to call him my friend.

'You scared me half to death,' he said. 'Why didn't you call ahead?'

'I didn't think I had to.'

'Oh ya, well... things have changed around here.'

'Yes, I noticed. You can tell me all about it later. Right now, I need you to turn on the lights in the back parking lot and open the garage door. I want to park my car inside, and I have someone for you to meet.'

'Not a problem,' he replied.

In no time, he had the stove sizzling in the kitchen of my apartment, cooking up a storm. Steaks from his freezer were defrosting in the microwave. It was just like old times. Arny was his usual self, grumbling about having to cook a late-night meal while at the same time working his personal magic to win Ilana's heart.

She was smiling and laughing as he told her stories about fishing as a kid.

'This beer, it is not very good beer.' Ilana said to him after she had taken a few sips of a beer from Arny's refrigerator.

'What's wrong with my beer?' he asked her indignantly.

'Have you ever had a Belican beer?' she asked innocently, referring to a brand of beer brewed only in Belize.

'No.'

'Well then, you could not possibly know what is wrong with this beer. This beer does not taste good.'

'Then don't drink it.' He smiled and continued to work.

'Do you have any Belican Beer?' she asked.

'No.'

'Then I will have to drink your bad beer.'

'Nobody asked you to drink my bad beer.' Arny grumbled.

I could tell right away Ilana would have no trouble dealing with Arny. Good, because he could be relentless if he thought he had an edge.

Ilana watched, fascinated with Arnie's ability to make food appear as if out of thin air. He only needed a can of soup, some fresh vegetables, and a few mushrooms, onions, potatoes, and steaks. Pans were sizzling, and a meal meant for people far more important than us was about to be served. I casually mentioned that we would be happy to eat in his kitchen. Then, he didn't need to bring everything to my apartment, but he had declined emphatically.

'Not going to make a big mess in my kitchen at this time of night,' he responded. 'I already cleaned it once today. Not going to do it again.'

While they talked, I wandered around my apartment. It had not changed much except for being covered with dust and cobwebs everywhere.

'I'll clean it in the morning.' I heard Arny yell from the kitchen, apparently reading my mind.

'It's okay. I'm just glad to be home.'

I cleaned the bathroom while Arny cooked, mostly by wiping a layer of dust from the surfaces with paper towels and finding some clean towels and fresh sheets for the bed. Domestic duty was something I seldom performed in the past when I lived in this apartment, but I had grown accustomed to taking care of myself while I was in Belize. I could have hired a housekeeper while living on the island, but I liked my privacy. Besides, I had so little to do in Belize. Domestic work helped occupy my day. Now, it felt good to be doing these same tasks in my apartment, working to make this place my home again. As I smoothed the sheets, I couldn't help but think about the nights Monica spent in this bed. Not many, but now they all seemed so precious.

'Come on, boss. Your dinner is ready,' Arny yelled from the kitchen.

I knew he didn't like me working in my apartment. He feared I was taking his job from him. I guess we will have a talk about this in the morning. Things were going to be different now.

Our meal was placed on a table in the dinette. Plates and silverware had been washed, and the table cleaned. A bottle of wine sat open next to two clear, clean glasses. Steak and mushrooms, some kind of wonderful potato casserole, and a fresh salad were the course for the night. I don't think a meal ever looked as good as this meal, at least not since I left Charlottesville.

'Please sit down with us,' I begged. 'I know it's late, but I want to catch up with you.'

'No boss. I'll see you in the morning,' Arny said as he wiped down the kitchen, preparing to leave.

'Okay, but let me warn you. It's going to be different around here now that I'm back. By the way, have you been paid?'

'Yes, Helen takes care of me. She and I ...well, we kind of look after this place.'

'Thank you, Arny. It's good to see you again.'

'Not as good as it is to meet this pretty lady,' he smiled at Ilana.

'It is nice to meet you too, Mr. Arny,' Ilana replied.

After he left, we ate our meal in relative silence. We were both exhausted. After dinner, I briefly showed Ilana my apartment, the high windows in the great room overlooking the valley, a fieldstone fireplace built up to the ceiling, the wood floors, and oriental rugs covering the floor. The furniture was leather and cloth over simple varnished wood frames, very elegant in simplicity and very comfortable. I then showed her my bedroom. It had a king-size bed with the mattress resting on a simple, thick wood frame built low to the wood floor. I also gave her a tour of the guest bedroom because it seemed right.

'You can sleep here,' I explained.

The guest bedroom had a queen-sized bed with its own private tile bathroom connected.

She looked at me as if she was hurt. 'I want to sleep with you now, all night. Do you not want me?' she added.

'Of course, I want you.'

FRIDAY, MAY 8, 5:15 A.M. JOHN

Despite the fact I was in my own bed, sleep was elusive.

Too many memories lingered in my apartment, too many ghosts intent on visiting me from my past. Like lightning bolts, these memories kept igniting the frayed nerve endings in my restive brain. Bad dreams stalked me when I was able to sleep, wouldn't leave me alone for long. One dream forced me to relive the time I was attacked in this place. That dream woke me up in a cold sweat as smashing bullets and screaming tires filled my brain.

I had no desire to risk a repeat experience like that again, even if it was only in a dream. Although I was very tired, I got out of bed.

Ilana was stretched out sideways on my big bed when I looked back to check on her in the dim nighttime light. I don't think she had ever slept on a king-size mattress before. She seemed to be trying to occupy every square inch of the bed. And somehow, she had managed to confiscate my comforter, all of it. She had the warm blanket wrapped around her small body like a cocoon. Apparently, she was not accustomed to sleeping in a cold room, needed the comforter to stay warm. Thankfully, she appeared to be sleeping peacefully when I left.

I roamed the dark and empty office building in the early morning hours, a place filled with memories I had abandoned to the damp and dusty corners of my mind. It was very strange to be home again with no time to mentally prepare for the experience. Everything was happening too fast. Just being in this place again came with mental baggage: sights and sounds from my past, feeling and images, all rushing at me, some good and some filled with sheer terror.

The only light in my office I ever used when I worked at night was a desk lamp. After hitting the switch, it cast eerie gray shadows over soft dust and silky cobwebs that had invaded my workspace. The computer screens on my desk were dark. I imagined seeing them blinking with incoming data as in the past. But this morning, they displayed no such images, just dull, dusty, blank glass. After hand brushing some of the dust off the leather chair in front of my chrome and glass executive desk, I sat down. The phone on the desk was silent, no green lights blinking incessantly, indicating incoming calls from around the world. No dial tone when I picked it up. I opened my personal laptop computer and pushed the start button. It came on, but with no internet connection, it was useless.

Leaning back in my chair, I saw Monica, my dead girlfriend in my mind's eye, I imagined her sitting at the slate conference table to one side of my desk. That's where she spent most of her time when she was working for me. I originally hired her as an executive secretary. After admitting she was also an excellent lawyer, she volunteered her skills to help me with my problems. We came to an understanding eventually. I assigned her to an office near mine, but she wormed her way into my office, ostensibly to ask questions, continuous questions. She justified her intrusion by saying it was easier than having to come into my office every time she needed to ask a question. I couldn't argue with her logic since it seemed she always had a question on her sweet lips.

In the dim light of the desk lamp, I tried to imagine her asking one more of her incessant questions, but the chairs around the conference table were empty. No papers covered every inch of the table as when she used it. No beautiful redhead with flowing hair tied up in a bun sat there. No inquisitive look on her face, as if I was telling her a half-truth every time I attempted to answer one of her many questions. No Monica was in my office except the beautiful woman who still lived in my mind. Finally, I turned my chair around away from the conference table, hoping this would make her memory fade away.

Beyond the high windows behind my office desk, the gray glow of a new morning was beginning to seep into the dark night sky. Warm lights rose up from windows in houses in the valley below. A work day was beginning. If this had been a normal day for me, I would have already been working at my desk. I was always an early riser. Incoming sales data or reviewing a new advertising campaign were my normal morning tasks. But this morning, I had nothing I really needed to do.

Glass panels covered one of the walls in my office, concealing a small wet bar that was used occasionally, a coffee pot, a refrigerator containing soft drinks, and a TV. I decided to open the panels and turn on the TV. To my surprise, the TV actually worked. I guessed Arny was responsible for this minor miracle. He probably kept the cable to the building alive so he could watch his beloved New Jersey Nets.

I found the remote control and selected one of the 24-hour news channels. It seemed good to have some background noise to cover the unnatural silence that lingered in my office. After brushing dust off a couch facing the TV, I sat down. Leaning back on the cushions, I rested, watching but not really listening to the talking heads on the big screen.

Eventually, my eyelids became heavy, and I slept.

9:10 A.M. JOHN

The sound of a noisy vacuum cleaner slowly entered my conscious brain, forcing me to retreat from whatever reality had been occupying my restless sleep.

I blinked once, opened my eyes, and for one brief second, thought I was in Belize. Bright sunshine streamed through the tall dusty windows of my office, but the air was too cool, too cold for Belize. And everything inside my office was so still. No gentle breeze drifted through an open window; no melodically lapping waves played from the seashore, just a noisy vacuum cleaner in another room.

I was home again, but not the home I desired.

I had slept for several hours. It was morning.

The sound of a noisy vacuum cleaner came through the open door I had used to enter my office from my apartment. The door was disguised to look like the bookshelf on the wall. Activated by a palm reader, it mechanically opened and closed. Earlier when I had entered the office last night, I had pushed the door open and didn't bother to close it.

Arny smiled when I found him vacuuming in my apartment's living room. Ilana was working with him, dusting furniture in the same room. The aroma of coffee brewing in the kitchen smelled pleasant. I poured a cup and took a couple of hot sips before grabbing a roll of paper towels along with glass cleaner and headed for the den, allowing the two of them to work together in the living room without interference.

The ceilings in my apartment were high. Each room, with the exception of the bathrooms and the guest bedroom, had a wall of solid glass windows overlooking the valley. In the middle of the living room was a fieldstone fireplace, which was the only visual obstruction to the outside. Artwork, pieces I had collected from all over the world, covered the interior white walls. It felt good to see their images in the light of day again.

I moved quickly through the den, spraying and wiping furniture, using paper towels in rapid succession. This was not a method my Dutch mother would have approved. Just moving dust around, that's what she would say. But it was efficient, got the job done quickly.

'Hey, boss.' Arny poked his head in the den. 'Take a break. Have some breakfast.'

FRIDAY, MAY 8, 2:45 P.M. JOHN

She drove in the parking lot in the same car she had when I left town: an old, late-model Chevy. My office secretary, Helen, was, if anything, a very prudent and fiscally responsible person.

I held the lobby door open for her. Tall and stately, her figure was just as trim at fifty-five as when she was twenty. She must have been a very pretty young woman before age began to play with her good looks. Worries probably had something to do with it. The loss of a husband to an early death didn't help. She returned to work to keep her house in order. She had a daughter to raise. It could not have been an easy life. When I hired her, I knew she would do well and I have not been disappointed.

Her dull brown hair was combed into a tightly wound, beauty-salon style bun, similar to her personality: uptight, prim, and proper. She smiled and offered her hand after entering the lobby. But instead of shaking her hand, I gave her a hug and a kiss on the cheek. She looked embarrassed, but I didn't care. It was good to see her again.

'Let's go into my office,' I suggested, noticing her face was flushed.

Our dusty footprints across the marble floors in the silent lobby were the only evidence of recent human activity. The tall oak doors into my office were open, not like in the past.

Arny had asked me earlier if I intended to return to work, assume my old job. I sensed he would be happy to see things as they were before I left, but I wasn't sure I was ready.

Helen had come to the office because I called her. She was my in-house executive secretary when I was CEO of the company. The job occupied most of her time. She had a couple of grandchildren now who lived with her only daughter in Atlanta. They were her only other obsession. Occasionally, she visited them for a long weekend, but only as often as her son-in-law would tolerate her presence in his house, which wasn't that often. Other than her daughter and her grandchildren, her life was her job. Sometimes, I had to demand she go home. 'Your job will still be waiting for you in the morning,' I would reassure her.

I directed her towards one of the leather couches, which surrounded a glass-top coffee table in my office. The base of the table was an old, weathered brown log sculpted by the waters of Lake Michigan. I had taken the log from the beach after a storm. It had moved with me to Charlottesville. It always gave me a good feeling, bringing back memories of the big lake.

She hesitated, probably because I had seldom suggested she sit in this area of my office in the past. It was normally used only by important guests. She was more accustomed to sitting in a chair at my desk. She on one side of the desk and me on the other, very proper, very formal business, just the way she liked it. But today, I sat down on one of the couches and motioned for her to do the same.

She did, but only reluctantly.

'Arny will join us in a minute,' I began.

This was to be another first. I rarely, if ever, had the two of them in the same room at the same time. It wasn't because they weren't friends. They were, but their friendship existed in an atmosphere of constant verbal barrages of the mildly adversarial variety. It would be fair to say that they tolerated each other as much as anything. So, in the past, I dealt with them separately simply because it was easier.

'I want both of you to tell me what has been going on since I have been gone,' I said to Helen. 'Why don't you start while we're waiting for Arny?'

'The company moved its headquarters to New York. Didn't Bob Anderson tell you?' she began.

'No, but then I haven't talked to him much in the past year.'

'Well,' she said disgustingly, 'He came here one day and rounded us all into the lobby, where he announced he was moving the head office to New York. He told us he was CEO now, and he didn't want to move to Charlottesville to run this company. Besides, he explained, it would be cheaper to have it in one place, New York.'

'Really.'

'Yes, he brought job counselors with him. They set up shop, and we were herded in to see them one at a time. Each employee was given the option of moving to New York or taking a settlement package. Help was offered in finding a new job if they didn't want to move. Everyone had to be out of the building by the end of the day. Security guards were everywhere, making sure nothing of value was taken.'

'That's it?' I asked, finding it difficult to believe something I had spent years building could be dismantled in a day.

'That's it, John. Arny and I were the only exceptions. We were given the opportunity to be caretakers here at the office. Bob told us he would continue to pay us our regular salary because we had been loyal employees in the past. I informed him I had strict instructions from you. No one could push Arny out of his apartment. I reminded Mr. Bob Anderson that this building was owned by you and not the company. You had the final say.

He agreed, said Arny could stay as long as he wanted.'

'And he has continued to pay you as promised?' I asked

'He has without fail.'

'Good.'

'I have kept a complete record of everything. I can show you.'

'That won't be necessary. I'm sure you have done a fine job.'

Arny strolled in. 'Hey lover,' he said, eyeing Helen. 'Where have you been all my life? I've been waiting for so long with open arms.'

'You will just have to wait a little longer,' Helen sneered.

'It's not nice to keep a lover waiting, baby. You know I long to make beautiful music together.' He grinned broadly, knowing Helen did not appreciate his trash talk.

'Okay, I see nothing has changed between you two,' I attempted to get our conversation back on track.

Arny smiled at Helen, ignoring me. 'I'm like a little chirping bird sitting on a branch waiting for the love of my life.'

'The chirping part, I believe, your mouth is always moving,' she said without looking at him. 'As for the second part, not going to happen,'

'Oh, come on baby, time is a wasting.' He threw himself on the couch next to her, giving her a little shove.

I waited.

When she said nothing, just sat stiffly ignoring Arny, I asked, 'How is it possible you two have managed to keep this place together without killing each other?'

Helen answered, scowling at Arny. 'Actually, we have worked very well together. Arny calls me when he needs something. The big items, I request directly from New York. That's how Bob Anderson wants it handled. The other stuff, the day-to-day stuff, I have a checkbook to cover expenses for those items from a bank in Charlottesville. New York funds the account.'

'I see.'

'Of course, they refused to pay for items they thought were unnecessary, like security and internet service,' ... pausing before continuing when I didn't say anything. 'One thing has bothered Mr. Anderson from the beginning. He can't get into the vault. When he asked me about it, I told him you have the combination, nobody else.'

'So, the gems are still there?' I asked, vaguely remembering I had received several e-mails from Bob about the vault. I had ignored them. Didn't even bother to read them, just didn't care.

'Yes, they are still in the vault,' Helen replied. 'I told Mr. Anderson they were reason enough to continue using a security service to protect the gemstones in the vault. But he said if he couldn't get into the vault, then no one else could either. It wasn't worth the money. He said he would continue to ensure the stones, but that was as much as he was willing to do.'

I made a mental note to check the vault when I had time.

I turned to Arny. 'You've been taking care of this place?'

'Yes, boss. I did what I could.'

SATURDAY, MAY 9, 11:15 A.M. JOHN

The solid steel handle on the heavy metal door of the vault was covered with a thick coat of dust.

It was clear evidence the vault had not been tampered with for a long time. Still, I had to be sure. Earlier in the day I had searched my office for the combination to the vault. Although... I wasn't really sure I needed it. I was quite confident I could remember the combination. But still, it had been a year and I wanted to be certain to do it right.

It took a while to find where I had hidden the combination. Finally, after several minutes of searching, I checked the pages of a book titled, 'The Count of Monte Cristo' by Alexander Dumas. I had read the book as a young boy. It was the first really long book I ever read. And it was still one of my favorites. Inside, I found the envelope containing the combination.

Using a paper towel, I wiped the handle and dusted the anodized panel of the vault. The combination, numbers, and letters needed to be entered in proper sequence. Any mistake in the process and I would have to start over. After reviewing it one more time, I began, only to find it all returned to me easily, as if it was only yesterday and not over a year since I had last opened the heavy metal door. After the last number was entered, an audible click sounded, and the steel handle turned down a notch. Gears spun, and steel pins dropped; the door opened with a turn and a pull.

A stale odor immediately assaulted my nostrils from inside the vault. Ignoring the smell, I flicked the interior light switch, and the airtight room behind the heavy metal door instantly came alive, gleaming under full spectrum lights. It was an impressive sight, rows of stainless steel cabinets with drawers filled with gemstones. Inside each drawer were hundreds of parcel papers containing one or more gemstones. The parcel papers were neatly folded around the gems in a traditional manner, preventing the stones from being lost. Placing gemstones in folded paper is a method used for hundreds of years. On the outside of each paper is a brief description of the gem inside, including its origin, size, cut, color, and sometimes quality. Only the most unusual and expensive stones were kept in our Charlottesville office vault. These were sold individually to buyers who appreciated their rare beauty and value. However, some of the best gemstones were withheld from the market and only used for display purposes.

Opening the drawers at random, I began to inspect their contents. One paper in particular caught my eye. The description read: five and half-carat sapphire, gold with blue center, Montana. Wondering if this gemstone was still inside, not simply empty paper left behind to conceal a crime, I took the parcel paper to a small, brightly lit glass table situated in the center of the vault used exclusively for viewing the gems.

This particular gemstone was familiar to me. It had been originally mined in Montana. Thankfully, it was still inside the paper, undisturbed. Under the light, its clear gold crystal sparkled. Holding it in tweezers, the stone refracted light through its faceted surfaces. A round spot of transparent blue color could be easily seen inside the center of the gem, blending with its gold exterior. So-called experts did not value this gemstone highly. It was not considered valuable because the dominant color of the gem was gold. Gold is not a desirable color for a sapphire. Blues or reds are more highly prized. Still, beauty is in the mind of the beholder. I always thought the experts were wrong about this particular stone. That's the reason I had withdrawn it from sale. I thought the multi-colored stone was extremely beautiful, worth far more than the market would pay.

Ilana poked her head into the vault.

For the last few days, she had stayed close, still insecure in her new surroundings. The brightly lit room filled with shiny metal cabinets must have looked almost surreal to her. I motioned for her to come to the table. Taking her hand, I placed the gold sapphire in her palm.

She stared at the stone as if wondering if it was real. 'Why does it have two colors?' she asked.

'That's how it was formed in the earth. It is called a bicolor. Isn't it beautiful?'

'It's very nice,' she said simply and placed it back on its parcel paper.

I carefully refolded the paper and returned the bicolor to its numbered drawer.

'Would you like to see some more gemstones?'

She nodded.

When Helen originally told me, the vault had not been opened for over a year, I was glad, actually looking forward to seeing these stones again. It's difficult to explain why these small marvels of nature hold such allure. In truth they are nothing more than hard crystals formed deep in the earth. All they do is reflect light in different shades of color; very simple, nothing complex. And yet, gemstones are so much more. I like to believe it's because of the way they seem to play with light. It makes them irresistible. Without light, the stones are nothing more than inert rocks. But put them in light, and they come alive, transformed into a myriad of colors, flashing light teasingly into our eyes until we are almost mesmerized by the experience. It is as if the power of light takes control of our souls. Such as the star sapphire I held in my hand. Thin, shimmering lines of white iridescent brilliance buried deep in its shiny black core seemed to rise lifelike out of the stone, taking control of my eye. It was hard to look away.

I opened more drawers, examining their contents. Burma was written on one of the papers from a drawer, indicating the gemstone's place of origin. Ilana almost gasped when I showed her this stone. The six-and-a-half carat 'pigeon's blood' red ruby seemed to actually jump off the unfolded paper, its color brilliant under light.

'Can I hold it?' she asked.

'Sure.'

She viewed it in awe. And why not? Good rubies are rare. Ones with great color and size are extremely rare. This gemstone had both size and color.

As I watched her admire the gem, it occurred to me I was probably taking parcel papers from the reserved section of the vault, the gems that I had taken off the market because of their size and beauty. I remembered one particularly big, clear green emerald I purchased at a mine while visiting Columbia. I thought it was in this section. After returning the ruby, I searched for the emerald. After unfolding its parcel paper, I placed the stone in Ilana's hand.

Emeralds are not as hard as sapphires. They are 7.5 on the Mohs scale of hardness. Sapphires are a 9, and diamonds are 10. Emeralds are still very hard, but it is not uncommon for them to fracture. They contain small cracks or fissures which can break if the gem is not treated with care. Some fissures can be seen with the naked eye. It is not uncommon for dealers to fill these with oils or resins, making the stone look more appealing, but this doesn't fix the flaw. The stones are still prone to cracking. However, emeralds are simply too beautiful to discount because of their naturally occurring flaws. Any emerald of good color and size and considered eye-clean, meaning it does not have flaws that can be seen without a microscope, is very valuable. Emeralds, such as the one Ilana held, are worth far more than diamonds.

'Oh John, it is so beautiful,' she said.

While she danced around the vault, holding the stone in her hand with light passing through the bluish-green facets, I made a mental note to remember she liked this particular stone before placing it back in the vault. Thinking perhaps I would give it to her one day.

Methodically working my way through the vault, I opened drawers, examining several parcel papers from each of them, sometimes showing Ilana the gemstones if they were particularly beautiful. When I was satisfied the vault had not been opened in my absence, I turned out the lights and closed the thick metal door. The big iron handle clicked, and an internal mechanism locked down the vault.

The sound of our shoes walking the stone floors echoed across halls as we returned to my office. Only silence emitted from rows of unoccupied offices. Not like in the past when the rooms were filled with busy employees. When the company was under my leadership, this building was our headquarters. Everything was different then, filled with noise and constant activity. I had to admit I missed the turmoil. I missed the faces and the smiles of the employees. I missed hearing their stories. I suddenly missed it all.

Ilana followed a half step behind me as we continued down the empty halls. Time was just after twelve noon, time to go to my apartment and harass Arny for some food; see what he was cooking for lunch. He had been working very hard. I sensed he wanted everything to go back to how it was before I left town. I don't think he liked silence any more than I did.

I had promised him nothing. He was simply working under the assumption I returned to take control of the company again. However, I wasn't sure I wanted my old job again. I had been thinking about it. And the more I thought, the more I knew it was in the wrong. I was not the same man I had been before Monica died. I knew too much now. I could never return to the business with the same naiveté and enthusiasm I had before. I knew now my decisions had consequences that I had not considered in the past. And these consequences affected far more than simply me and my partners. They affected many people in far-off corners of the world. And this knowledge would make my job far more difficult. Not impossible, but a lot more problematic.

This had not been true seven and a half years ago. I was a different man then. I started the business because I thought the world of colored gemstones needed a unified marketing strategy. The stones were being sold for far less than what I thought they were worth. So, I did what no one else thought was possible. I created a marketing organization to promote the gemstones. I began by concentrating on sapphires. My company took control of a majority of the world's supply of these stones by paying higher prices for them from the mines, higher than our competitors were willing to pay. They thought we would go broke paying such high prices. But a worldwide advertising campaign increased market demand. That and the natural scarcity of the gemstones drove up their prices, richly compensating us for our efforts. The result of all our hard work was a modern market-driven organization, a business with a future.

But I had not done my homework. I saw only a small part of the picture. I did not see the whole. I now knew that changing a thousand years of traditional business did not occur without consequences. Displaced power and wealth would eventually fight back. Resistance was inevitable. Violence was probable.

My mistake was not taking the time to fully research my competition. I did not study the history and the culture of the people who would be greatly affected by my decisions in Charlottesville, Virginia. It was stupid to think I could do as I pleased, and they would simply accept my judgment without complaint. I had ignorantly decided they needed to change. And this change, I assumed, would be accepted as predictable and proper.

I was wrong.

And I paid dearly for my lack of understanding. But others paid a far higher price, like Monica. As did Vidu and Arthur, my business partners. They, like me, got caught in a vortex of violence. I paid a high price for my assumptions, but they paid the ultimate price. It cost them their life.

Problem was, nothing had changed since they died. If I returned to the business now, I knew it would be dangerous. And yet... a sense of unfinished business lingered in the air, the scales of justice tipped out of balance, needing to be righted. I felt responsible for the deaths that occurred, my soul was deeply consumed with guilt.

That was one of the main reasons I retreated to Belize, to a place where telephones did not ring. Where no one would accuse me of past mistakes. But now I was back in Charlottesville, and all my past sins came rushing back into focus, forcing me to face the reality of my mistakes again. And the most difficult problem of all was my sense of guilt. The truth was I had not understood the world I had entered. And as a consequence, I had put people in harm's way. In my naiveté, I thought the world would naturally accept what I assumed would make it better.

And that, I learned, was incredibly stupid.

But I couldn't stop thinking that this story was not over. I couldn't just let it end. My feeble brain kept wanting revenge. Someone needed to pay.

But was this possible? Was revenge possible? Or was revenge simply a word without substance, a concept void of meaning or execution? Because can there ever be an act which will completely satisfy the need for revenge. The only real revenge would be to turn back the hands of time, Monica rising out of her grave. Her murders denied their satisfaction. This was the only reality that would bring true revenge. And this, I knew, was not going to happen.

Yet, as I walked past the empty offices, listening to my footsteps echo across silent halls, I couldn't escape the feeling that something needed to be done.

SUNDAY, MAY 31, 5:15 P.M. JOHN

'I have some work to do in my office.' I said to Ilana, pausing near the double oak doors to my office. 'Why don't you find Arny and see if he needs help with dinner?'

Days and weeks had passed in relative calm since we arrived in Charlottesville. Life had begun to assume a pattern of normalcy. I wasn't completely comfortable, but after the tightly wound stress of the recent past, a few weeks of peace was refreshing. That Sunday had been exceptionally slow, nothing much to do. Ilana and I went for an afternoon walk in the sunshine. She had been with me most of the day. I suggested she find Arny because I thought she might be getting sick of hanging around with just old me.

My office was slowly taking shape. All it really needed now was a reason to function. But I had no intention of returning to work. Still, a certain satisfaction came with putting things in order. Perhaps it was simply being physically occupied. The activity allowed me avoid thinking about what was really bothering me; the important decisions I had been studiously avoiding, but knew I should be considering.

Telephone lines were reconnected. Computer internet service restored. Helen was responsible for most of this work, and she did it without telling Bob Anderson. I had specifically asked her not to call him. I told her I would pay for everything. There was no reason to talk to New York. So, Bob had no idea what was happening in Charlottesville. In fact, I had not talked to him since Belize. He probably thought I was still on the island. Only Arny, Helen, and David, my lawyer in Grand Haven, knew where I was. And this was how I wanted it. I hoped that maintaining some semblance of anonymity would buy a degree of security and sanity for now. Perhaps I wondered; if I stayed silent, maybe my enemies would assume I was no longer a threat and leave me alone. I didn't think of much beyond that because the next level of decisions was far more complex.

'Okay,' Ilana agreed.

She had begun to use the word 'okay,' picking up the habit from me. I didn't mind. I was happy she was agreeable. She was a woman, after all. I knew her blind acceptance of me wouldn't last very long. Eventually, she would begin to doubt me. But for now, we were living on a kind of new lover's honeymoon.

She skipped off, her footsteps echoing over the marble floors leading to my apartment. In the past, a security door would have slowed her progress. A palm reader attached to the wall near the door would have to be activated, the reader identifying a hand print before mechanically opening a heavy metal security door. But today, the metal door was open. No time-consuming procedure was required. And the tall, stained-oak doors at the entrance to my office were also open. Their shiny silver door handles clicked in my hand when I closed the doors behind me.

In the past, I almost never closed the doors because Helen did it for me. She didn't like seeing the doors open. If I didn't close them, she would automatically get up from her desk, muttering something incomprehensible under her breath, and close the doors. She wasn't happy with the doors open. Anyone could walk in, she would say, walk in without asking her. She didn't like that. She wanted to be in control. No one was admitted into my office without going through her first. That was her rule.

'You need to keep the doors closed, John,' she would scold.

'Yes, Helen,' I could hear myself answer.

But today, I closed the doors myself. I don't know why, really. I guess I closed them because it made my office feel like it was my office again, like in the past.

Arny had done a good job of making the place inhabitable. He had cleaned everything. The black glass panels covering the appliances built into the wall were shining in a late afternoon sun filtering through the trees into the office. And the half-inch thick plate of glass resting on the Lake Michigan driftwood was spotlessly clean. Soft leather couches had been vacuumed. Chairs were neatly arranged around a slate conference table. Even the books on the bookshelf had been dusted. At Arny's insistence our old window washing crew had cleaned the tall windows overlooking the valley. I always liked having the windows clean in the past. I was very grateful to Arny for all his suggestions and hard work. The only thing missing this afternoon to make me feel completely at home was the sight of my computer screens actively operating. They were still silent, dark glass without life. Not like in the past when computers were constantly updating the information, the lifeblood of the company.

I walked behind my desk and picked up the phone to test it. A dial tone indicated it was operational again. But no green lights flashed on the console, no incoming calls. Good, because I didn't know what I would say if someone did call. I sat down in the chair behind my desk and turned to look out of the windows. It was almost June, and the valley below was alive with a rich, vibrant green color of new leaves. Patches of wildflowers could be seen interspersed among stands of tall pines and hardwoods. The sun was setting in the west. A gentle breeze rustled through the leaves of a nearby oak.

I briefly considered calling one of my buddies to ask if he would like to play a round of golf at the club in the next few days. I was running out of things to do. Arny and Ilana could get along without me for an afternoon. They had become friends in the short time we were home.

But thinking about playing golf only made me feel guilty. I felt like I should be working. I assumed Helen and Arny expected me to retake control of the company. This was the reason they had worked so diligently. They didn't need to say it. I saw it in their faces. And Clarence's conversation from Australia was still running through my head. I knew I owed him a call, but I also knew it would be a difficult call. I had been putting it off.

A neat round hole suddenly appeared in one of the windows of my office, followed by an explosion containing hundreds of razor-thin shards of flying glass. One of the stinging missiles embedded cleanly in my cheek. As if in a dream, I raised my hand to my face, touching the warm blood that was running down my face, pulling it back to examine the blood, temporarily incapable of comprehending what just happened.

A second hole in the glass quickly followed the first, only this time closer.

Instinctively falling away from a rush of disturbed air made by the bullet which missed my ear by fractions of an inch, I crawled on my hands and knees under my desk seconds before the windows of my office were destroyed into a cascade of flying glass, scattering across the floor in a million facets of sparkling diamonds reflecting in the afternoon sun. Rolling under the desk while listening to the sounds of hard lead thudding into a far wall, I watched in horror as the dark panels of glass covering the entertainment wall of my office shattered and fell off the wall in large slabs of glass with razor-sharp edges, cutting the soft leather of couches below. The computers on my desk literally seemed to evaporate into a mass of loose wires; hardware junk. Disintegrating bits of furniture flew lazily across the room in every direction as I lay on my stomach behind one of the couches, mesmerized by the constant dull drumbeat of hard lead burying into the cushions.

Stunned pinned down in my office as it was fragmenting around me; the noise was deafening. Waiting...hoping...praying for it to stop. I hadn't been hit by a bullet; not yet, but that had to be pure luck. I expected to feel pain any torturous second.

I turned towards the big oak doors, anticipating them to open, and a stranger with a gun in his hand entered. Expecting him to raise his weapon to administer a fatal bullet. But the doors remained closed as I lay on the floor, paralyzed by fear, immobilized by the scale of the carnage around me, no hope, no reprieve. This time, I thought I was dead. Nowhere to run.

Telltale clouds of destruction seemed to float across the room for untold minutes of absolute terror: exploding plaster walls, bullets searching, annihilating, books shredded, pages falling like forgotten memories, wood splinters stinging my back like miniature missiles. It was so surreal, like watching a movie that was not happening to me, not me. This was my cherished office, my place to plan, execute, work; decomposing around me as I held my breath.

Conference table chairs were propelled into the air, falling in all angles. Finally, I covered my head when I couldn't look anymore, listening to the sounds of carnage, breaking glass, and ripping leather. Wondering, waiting for pain, for death, would it be fast, or would I die slowly? I was convinced death was coming. I thought I should get up and run... but I could not, could not stand.

I was paralyzed by the living hell all around me. Ilana, where was my Ilana, and Arny? I needed to do something. But I assumed I was the target. I had to stay down, had to hope a hard, fast bullet wouldn't find me. Hot lead split the air all around me as I lay paralyzed on the floor, wondering why I was still alive, waiting to die, waiting.

Then silence, an eerie silence, an unnatural silence... as suddenly as it started, it became quiet. Only the sounds of leaves rustling in the trees wandered peacefully through the air outside my shattered windows. Just the soothing sounds of leaves in the wind wandered into my office from some forgotten time.

Still, I waited, immobilized by the shattering noise of desolation still echoing through my brain. My mind was paralyzed by the broken destruction and anticipated death that surrounded me. I hesitated, frozen on the floor, anticipating the devastation to resume. Footsteps, I expected death to walk through the tall oak doors any second, thinking the silence was only a brief reprieve, time to say a prayer before the final act, a violent death coming for me.

But no one came.

Only an eerie silence entered my world. And in the still silence, I hear her crying somewhere close but far from where I had been only minutes before.

Had to get up, now. I was not dead. I still had time, time to play the game. But I wasn't sure I wanted to play. I thought I should be dead, but I was not. Instead, it was as if I had been propelled back into life against my will. I reluctantly got up on my hands and knees. Still unsure, the carnage was over. Crawling across the floor, staying low, I crawled to the door in my bookshelf, which had been left open, half expecting bullets to begin flying again, searching for me. But nothing, hearing only the sound of Ilana crying. I ran down the hall in my apartment, listening to the sound of her bitter tears, afraid, still fearing someone was coming to kill us.

Ilana was kneeling in a pool of red blood covering the tile floor of the kitchen when I found her. I feared she was bleeding to death, slowly dying. Anguish twisted in my gut, thinking I was going to lose her as I lost Monica. But then I saw Arny. She was kneeling over him, and it was his blood, not hers, which covered the floor. She was holding his head, trying to comfort him.

Arny lay on his back in a liquid crimson casket of blood, looking oddly happy even in death, as if even death could not stop this man from smiling. I bent over him, feeling for a pulse in his neck, looking for any signs of life, some movement, his chest rising to breathe... but I observed nothing, no movement, no pulse. He was dead. I closed his eyes in tight, hurt, inconsolable hurt.

'We need to get out of here.' I said to Ilana through acid, stinging tears.

'But Mr. Arny?'

'He's dead. We can't do anything for him.'

She looked suddenly terrified as if seeing the carnage around her for the first time. My apartment, like my office, was a mass of broken glass and bullet holes. I gently took her by her shoulders and helped her stand.

'Are you okay?' I asked.

'I'm okay,' She muttered, her small body shaking, her legs almost unable to bear the burden of what she just endured. Blood dripped from her pants, Arny's blood. I unbuttoned her pants and helped her take them off, using her pants to wipe the blood off her legs.

My shoes were soaked in blood. I took them off and threw them angrily in a corner of the kitchen. Told her to go to the bathroom and get cleaned up, get dressed, put some clothes in a suitcase. We needed to leave. Or should we just run? Was it already too late? Were they coming for us outside the door? It all seemed so futile, so unreal. I glanced momentarily at Arny, tears streaming down my face.

'It has been great knowing you, buddy. I'm sorry. God bless you, my friend.' I looked at him once more and turned away to follow Ilana into the bedroom.

No one came for us.

I didn't know why, didn't seem to matter at the time. I threw a few clothes, a razor, a toothbrush, deodorant, quickly into a duffle bag. Ilana tried to vainly stuff all her new clothes from Cancun into one suitcase. They were her clothes, more new clothes than she ever had. She didn't want to leave them behind.

'We can buy you more clothes,' I said to her as gently as possible. 'We have to get out of here.'

'But John...'

'No.' I took her suitcase and somehow managed to close it on the clothes she had already put inside.

WEST VIRGINIA, 10:05 P.M.
JOHN

Patches of dense fog descended into the valleys, whispering through the mountain passes.

Illuminated by a full moon, these misty apparitions appeared suddenly out of nowhere like ghosts in the headlights of my car. I had no choice. I had to slow down. I simply could not see through the fog.

I had been driving ten to twenty miles an hour over the speed limit for hours as if speeding could somehow erase the vivid memories from clouding my fearful brain, speeding to escape the pain that existed somewhere behind me in another place and time, a place filled with panic. The fog forced me to reduce my speed. Good because we had been driving for hours, stopping only once for gas. I was wearing down, concentration eroding, eyes wandering.

Few words had been spoken since leaving Charlottesville. Only to ask Ilana a few times to look behind us to see if we were being followed. So far, nothing unusual aroused her suspicion. Fortunately, my Mercedes 500 SL was performing flawlessly through the twisty mountain roads. Even so, I couldn't stop worrying, thinking tragedy was following close behind, destruction bound to appear suddenly around the next curve. I had been driving as a madman possessed, my desire to escape overpowering. Arny's lifeless smiling face was still too vivid a memory.

Ilana was curled up in the leather seat beside me as if she were still ducking incoming gunfire. It occurred to me as I drove that I may have thrown a cell phone in my duffle bag when I packed. Helen had given me the phone only a few days earlier, said I needed one again. Was it in my bag? I couldn't remember. Only one way to find out. I would have to stop. I didn't want to stop, but then, stopping was probably a good idea. I was getting tired and hungry. It was time to pull off the road for a while. I had just experienced a very lucky escape from death. It didn't make any sense to die in an accident on this cement ribbon weaving through the mountains simply because I was too scared to be cautious.

A sign along the highway showed a restaurant and gas station were at the next exit.

I had been planning to drive straight through the night to Grand Haven, Michigan. Beyond this mental exercise, I had no rational thoughts. Sights and sounds of crashing glass and blood were still clouding my judgment. Ilana didn't appear to be in any better shape than me, probably still in shock. Some coffee and food would be good for both of us.

The small town off the expressway was tucked in a valley between the hills of West Virginia. A few streetlights cast soft light on the trees along a road which were hiding old, run down houses. A Shell gas station was the only establishment in town with lights in the windows, indicating it was open. I pulled in and braked to stop.

Ilana opened her door to stretch her legs.

'Open the trunk,' I asked her. 'See if you can find a cell phone in my duffel bag.'

She did as I asked without comment. I was beginning to worry about her. She was too quiet. As I was filling the tank and cleaning the windshield, a gray Ford Taurus drove into the gas station and parked beside us. A man dressed in a suit and a white shirt opened the car door. A loose tie hung lazily around his neck, looking like a traveling salesman. Placing a gas nozzle into the back of his car without taking any notice of us, he seemed harmless enough. Even so, I watched his movements carefully as I impatiently waited for my gas tank to fill. In my current state of paranoia, everyone was suspicious. I half expected to see the man reach under his suit coat for a gun, raise it, take aim, and shoot to kill. Right here in this isolated mountain town in the middle of nowhere, my body lying dead on the cold cement of a lonesome Shell gas station tucked into the hills of West Virginia. It seemed an odd place to die. But then, I guess it doesn't much matter where you die. There's no dignity in death.

I shook my head, trying to clear the cobwebs, realizing I needed to stop being so paranoid. I couldn't live in constant fear. Life would become intolerable.

I turned to check the gas gauge on the pump.

'I found it, John,' Ilana appeared from the back of the car, handing me the cell phone.

'Thank you.'

A small restaurant attached to the gas station was open. It was warm inside, and the coffee tasted good. We ordered nothing special; good Southern home cooking was on the menu. Through the windows next to our booth, a few dimly lit houses could be seen nestled in the dark hillsides.

'Helen...' I said into my cell phone

'Yes.'

'It's me, John.'

My cell phone immediately exploded with a torrent of uninterrupted questions. Roughly translated, Helen was simultaneously asking me why I had not called her and was all right. It seemed she had, for some yet to be fully explained reason, decided she needed to drive to the office; something about something she forgot to do yesterday. What she discovered was a mess of unfathomable proportions, including Arny's dead corpse. She was scared Ilana, and I had been dragged off and killed somewhere. Or worse, kidnapped, tortured, screaming in pain. She had just returned home after spending her evening in the company of the police, who had been completely unable to help her.

The salesman, the guy who had been driving the gray Taurus, was eating in a booth not far from us as I talked to Helen. We were the only customers in the place. It was late, and the restaurant was mostly empty, close to quitting time. Only one waitress and a cook were working at the time.

I listened without interrupting Helen as she fired off another quick series of questions in no apparent logical order. Where was I? What was I doing anyway? What the hell happened to the office? And what...?

'Yes, I know.' I said to Helen as quietly as possible, not wanting the salesman to overhear my conversation. 'I'm sorry... Yes, you really liked him... Yes, we will miss him. Do what you have to. I'm sure he has many friends in Charlottesville. Give him a good funeral. I'll pay for it.'

Regrettably, this did nothing to satisfy her. I was once again obligated to listen patiently, allowing her to empty both barrels on me. She let me know, in no uncertain terms, why I needed to return, and now.

'Look, Helen, calm down. I think it's best I stay away for a few days. I'll call you soon. Please take care of things. Call Bob if you have to. Explain what happened. And don't worry about the expense. I'll take care of it.'

She let me know she was not too happy with this arrangement. Eventually, she calmed down some, enough to give me a chance to explain in between her nervous, rambling complaints and questions. 'I ran, okay? You saw the mess.' I half apologized in a whisper. 'Yes, Helen... Just listen... But I am...And Ilana is fine also. I will call you... I promise, but for now, please try to understand.'

'Yes,' I agreed to call the police. 'Yes, don't worry. Now, get some rest. I will call you again when I can...Yes...Yes, and thank you.'

I hung up with an empty feeling in my gut. It wasn't fair to leave her in the middle of the mess. But in my defense, I hadn't anticipated she would go to the office on a Sunday afternoon. I thought I had time to call and warn her. But this had obviously not happened. I was sorry, but she would just have to handle it. She was a tough old woman. Besides, I couldn't stay there and help even if I wanted to. It was obviously not safe. We had to leave. Or at least this was how I justified my panicked flight.

Our food came: steaming potatoes and home-fried steak. I was hungry, having nothing to eat since lunch.

Ilana didn't know what to order. The food on the menu was not to her liking. She didn't understand the concept of home-fried cooking. I tried to order something for her, hoping she would like it. I got her some chicken dumplings. Fact was, she didn't look too good, but then I probably didn't look very good either. I took a sip of coffee and ate quickly. Ilana ate almost nothing. She said she didn't like the food, and coffee was not her thing. I told her to try the grits with butter and brown sugar as I dialed another number on my cell phone while watching her pick at her food with a scowl on her face.

'David, sorry to call you so late, but I have a situation...Yes, I know this is getting to be a habit... Yes...Just listen. I'm on the road, had to leave my office in a hurry. I'm headed to Grand Haven... Yes, good... cottage is done. That's what I wanted to know. The key is under the mat. Thanks...ETA early tomorrow morning. I'll call you when I'm settled. Maybe we can have dinner with you and Mary... I will explain then... Yes, maybe tomorrow... Thanks, buddy. See you soon... No, don't worry. We're fine,' I lied.

The entrance ramp to the highway was easy to find, but the fog was thick. The night air had cooled. Hopefully, soon we would be through the hills and heading into Ohio. With any luck, the fog would dissipate when we drove out of the mountains. Just needed to take it easy now, I told myself. It was going to be a long night. My rear-view mirror showed no one following us into the entrance ramp. I took a deep breath and tried to calm down. Ilana was curled up in the leather bucket seat next to me, slouched down so low she couldn't see outside into the scary night. Hopefully, she would be asleep soon.

I turned on the radio, needed something to stay awake. Country and western music hijacked the radio's sound system in this area as I repeatedly clicked the search button, finally settling on a station playing country bluegrass.

White lines of the highway reached out to guide me through the fog while the down-home music connected somewhere in my brain, calming my jangled nerves.

10:55 P.M. SALESMAN

The loose-tie salesman placed a call on his cell phone as he waited in the Shell gas station parking lot next to his rented gray Ford Taurus.

After listening carefully to the instructions he was given over the phone, he took off his coat and threw the unnecessary garments in the back seat of his car. A steaming, big plastic cup of coffee sat on his roof. He took one final sip before placing a cover on the cup and climbing into his car with the coffee in his hand, attempting to get comfortable in the driver's seat. It was going to be a long night.

The Taurus proceeded to drive towards the entrance to the highway, not far behind a silver Mercedes.

GRAND HAVEN MICHIGAN, MONDAY, JUNE 1, 8:40 P.M.
JOHN

A cold northwest wind blew relentlessly off the dark green waters of Lake Michigan under a dense black night sky filled with thousands of stars.

My cottage was built on a sand dune covered with waving beach grass overlooking the lake. The pale sands of the shoreline at night below its deck appeared to be little more than gray shadows resting easy on the dark waters of the lake. Alone, wearing in a winter jacket against the cool night air, I rested on a lounge chair. The deck was a great place to view the lake and the stars. When I was a kid, I used to lie on the beach and look up for shooting stars in the night sky. I saw no shooting stars that night, and I was no longer a young boy.

As I rested, an endless cascade of tragic images... wide awake nightmares spun through the memories in my feeble brain. Like the night when a bright streak of light crossed this horizon, a rocket shot from the back of a boat over these same dark waters, exploding into a fireball of destruction, burning my cottage to the ground. No matter how hard I tried to think about something else, this memory kept resurfacing as if it was happening all over again. I began to worry the boat would return now to finish the job it had failed to accomplish before. I searched the lake waters for a boat, listening for the low rumble of its engine rolling across the cold water. I had escaped the previous time, escaped death only by chance. Monica and I had gone for a late evening walk on the beach. This was the only reason we were not killed. We were not inside the cottage when it exploded and burned to the ground.

My mind continued to work through a whole series of near-death experiences, rotating through my brain in endless circles of mental mayhem. Even though I badly wanted to think about something more pleasant, these terrible memories just kept coming: my burning house in Belize, my office destroyed in a torrent of lead, Arny's face a smiling black mask of death.

Ilana and I arrived from Charlottesville at my cottage on Lake Michigan near Grand Haven in the early morning. We went straight to bed, badly needing sleep. I was dead tired, having driven through the night on an adrenalin high. I slept okay for a while, dozed off and on. I'm not sure how long. Eventually, I woke up, and no matter how hard I tried, I could not go back to sleep. The sound of speeding bullets kept whispering through my brain, silent messengers of mayhem ripping through the air, intent on destroying any hope of my falling back to sleep. Finally, I got out of bed and roamed around my recently rebuilt cottage.

In the evening, I called my friend David as I promised. I waited until it was too late for a visit. I needed time to think. Maybe tomorrow, I confessed to him. I was in no shape to see anyone, not even him. He objected at first but finally agreed after I promised to come into town the next day.

Ilana and I watched the sunset from my deck, filled with beautiful blues, reds, and pinks spreading across a panoramic sky over the lake. Unfortunately, this momentary, eye feast of color disappeared all too quickly, a too-brief reprieve from the pain that seemed to be everywhere I looked. It disappeared even as I wished it would last forever because it alone allowed me to think about something other than death.

As I feared, the black night sky brought with it all the deadly memories in a rush. And it got cold, as soon as the sun set, it became very cold, too cold to be outside on the deck. But something about the clear, cold night wind was refreshing. It was as if the bitter cold air could freeze the bloody images that were plaguing me and crystallize these wide-awake nightmares into an inert ice storm. Send the clouds of frozen tragedies flying far away on a night wind washing endlessly over the white-capped waves of the lake to a place far beyond the horizon where they wouldn't bother me anymore.

Ilana was inside. As soon as the air-cooled, she went inside. She wondered how anyone could live in such a cold place as this Michigan. I told her it was not really that cold. I said it could be much worse. I described winter to her. Told her how the water in the lake would freeze, and wild winter winds would push great masses of ice over hidden sand bars, creating a series of icy, arctic hills in the water.

She didn't believe me, looked at me like I was a crazy man, and said she could not understand a cold thing like winter.

Still, I was happy she was with me, even when she was complaining. She seemed to be rebounding from the violence of the previous day, better than me. Although I was still worried about her, I was not as worried about her as I was worried about myself. I wished I could see the world through her eyes, which appeared to be far happier eyes than mine. I wasn't having much success. I wondered how long it would be before my mind stopped being traumatized by the memories of falling glass and Arny's dead eyes.

She had probably turned the thermostat up to eighty degrees like the weather in Belize. I lingered outside, searching the sky for the Big Dipper and the North Star. I knew where to look. I was familiar with this place. It was where I grew up. This was why I bought a cottage on the lake. And I was glad I did because it had been a good place filled with pleasant memories. And I wanted it to be good again, and I hoped it would be someday. But not tonight. The place was filled with too many past tragedies, including the ones I shared with Monica.

I couldn't let this continue. I knew it was not good for my mental health. It was time to think about something else... Someone else, like the dark-haired woman who now inhabited my cottage. She was not a tall redhead with warmth in her eyes. Ilana was not Monica, and she would never be Monica. But Ilana was just as wonderful and bright and beautiful in her own way. And she was the lady in my life now. I was very thankful for her. I needed to be with her now, not dwell on my memories of Monica.

I began by trying to think about what to do next. What happened in Charlottesville made it perfectly clear that the peaceful alternatives that I had once thought were a possibility... were not possible. And Arny, thinking about Arny made me angry. He did not have to die. In a way, his death marked an end to my previous life. That life was over. I could not go back to Charlottesville now and have it the way it was before. I had lost my future when Monica died. And I lost my past with the death of Arny.

He was my friend and companion for all the years I was building a company. He had given me a sense of light-hearted happiness, which balanced the long hours of hard work. He was my reprieve at the end of the day. I always suspected he understood his role. He knew how important it was. He had played his part well, and now he was gone.

Without Arny I could never return to my past.

I said a prayer for him while wiping my moist eyes. It was time to move on. I had decisions to make. But I was not ready, not yet.

I was getting cold despite wearing a thick, down-filled winter jacket. Still, I stayed outside a few minutes more, searching the sky, hoping to see a shooting star, hoping it would be a sign. Telling me tomorrow would be better than today. But only a black night sky full of shining stars shone down on me. Finally, cold and getting colder, I gave up and went inside, hoping Ilana's eyes could help me see a different world through her eyes, different than the torn memories that existed in my eyes.

The TV was on when I closed the slider. Ilana was sitting on a couch in the great room, mesmerized by American television, devouring knowledge from a twenty-four-hour news channel. She had told me in Charlottesville how much she enjoyed watching TV. The news channels offered her an instant education. But at the same time, they also created a thousand questions in her mind, questions she asked me. Most of the time, I was happy to answer her questions. But there were times when she would wear me down with all her questions. Occasionally, I had to leave the room to find some peace.

She smiled when she saw me and I knew I didn't have the energy or the patience to answer her questions. So, before she could formulate one sentence, I clicked the remote off-button for the TV and lifted her off the couch. Carrying her to my bedroom, I unceremoniously dropped her on my bed. After turning down the thermostat, I closed the bedroom door and opened a window.

Cool night air immediately began to whisper into the room, along with the persistent, gentle sounds of waves lapping on the beach. Ilana didn't move, sat on the edge of the bed, stubborn, mentally questioning my motives like I was a wild dog of a man.

'It is going to get cold in here,' I explained as I undressed. 'Only one place in this house will be warm, and it's in this bed with me.' I smiled.

'John, why are you so mean to me? You know I do not like the cold.'

'It's not cold in bed.' I laughed after pulling the blankets up over my shoulders.

Ilana had no choice, quickly removing her clothes, she jumped into bed.

'John, it is cold in this bed,' she instantly complained, the cool sheets chilling her small body. 'You lied to me.'

'It will be warm soon.' I snuggled closer to her, slowly caressed her naked body, bringing it to me in pleasure. We touched each other in places where tears and smiles live together. She came to me as gently as a summer wind and wrapped her body around and through mine until I could see only her smile in my mind.

After we made love, I drifted off to much-needed sleep filled with dreams of a young boy playing in the gentle waves of the lake, summer on a sandy, warm beach.

WEDNESDAY, JUNE 3, 6:45 P.M. JOHN

'I'll have a Coors. The lady here will have a Corona,' I said to the waitress. 'One pepperoni and mushroom pizza, please.'

The waitress nodded a silent approval and turned to my friends, David and Mary. They ordered their pizza and drinks while Ilana sat next to me like a hunting dog with her nose in the air, busy sniffing the strange smells emanating from the restaurant's open-air kitchen with a slight frown crossing her face.

'It's burning olive oil. Makes for good pizza.' I whispered to her.

'I'm not sure I like this smell,' she said.

'Yes, and you are going to hate the beer.'

Before sitting down in the restaurant, we had to wait while the waitress cleaned our table by ritually shaking the red and white checkered tablecloth over the floor to separate crumbs from the cloth before turning it over and placing it along with new paper plates on the table. The restaurant's many customers never complained about this less than perfectly hygienic practice. Fact was, especially during the summer months, customers had to stand in line to get a table in this restaurant; a torturous act which involved waiting, standing, while smelling the cooking pizza, their saliva juices flowing, jealously watching contented customers fill their empty stomachs with as much pizza as they could cram into their mouths as they quenched their thirst with a cold beer. The wait could be downright agonizing.

This night, however, we were lucky. It was still early spring and the town was not yet filled with summer tourists. We did not have to wait for a table.

Fricano's Pizzeria is located in an old painted blue wood house on the far side of town, has been for a long time. I remembered bringing new friends to the restaurant. They were a couple from out East who professed to love pizza. However, the first thing they did when arriving inside the restaurant was to turn up their noses, just like Ilana. It seemed they did not associate the pungent odor of burning olive oil, thinly cut pepperoni, tomato sauce, and cheese as a proper smell for a pizzeria. Of course, I had grown up with this smell. To me, it was the only real smell of pizza. Anyway, my Eastern friends thought pizza should have thick crusts and lots of toppings. They were not too happy with the oily, thin-crust pizza served to them. I just laughed and told them they needed to eat Fricano's pizza real fast. Because at some point, their gall bladder would rebel from all the oil, and they would not be able to eat one more bite. As it turned out, I had no need to warn them. They didn't eat enough to have a problem.

David called earlier in the day and suggested we have dinner together. Ilana talked me into going. I didn't want to, but she said it would be good to get out and visit friends. Besides, she said she wanted to see my town. I think she sensed I wasn't doing well, and she was right. I only agreed reluctantly. Now, I wasn't so sure she thought this was such a good idea after all.

'Aren't you concerned about your safety?' David asked while we waited for our pizza to arrive. He had earlier admitted to calling and talking to Helen after I called him. He was fully aware of my situation.

The cold beer in my glass tasted good, and the last thing I wanted to talk about was my dire situation. I just wanted to relax and enjoy the pizza. But David, it seemed, had other ideas, and he was right. I needed to face reality, return to a life of constantly looking over my shoulder, something I had done before and really didn't like.

'I've only been home one day,' I complained. 'It's going to take the bad guys a least a few days to figure out where I am.' I took a sip of beer.

Ilana was absorbed in a separate conversation with Mary, which I assumed was good; she needed someone to talk to besides me. And Mary, David's wife, was an excellent choice. She was a kind and gentle person, tall with dark brown hair. David and I grew up with her in the same high school. Mary was very pretty, and all the boys, myself included, had a crush on her at one time or another. I managed one date, but nothing came of it, nothing special between us. Because once David started dating her, no one else had a chance. I was happy for him. They belonged together.

'You're not safe,' David said. 'You know they must be looking for you.'

'Okay, but can't we just have fun tonight? I'll come to your office tomorrow, I promise. We can talk then.'

I could see him mentally reviewing his calendar in his head. David was a handsome man with sandy blond hair cut relatively short. A popular and busy lawyer in Grand Haven, Michigan, he occasionally took out-of-state court cases. He had a well-established reputation as a trial lawyer, one which had spread beyond the borders of his hometown. He could have worked anywhere. But Mary didn't want to move. So, David worked out of a small office with only a few partners. I think he was very content and happy with his career despite the fact he could have made far more money if he moved to a big city like Chicago.

'I have an opening at eleven,' he replied. 'Why don't you come in then? We can go to the club for lunch afterward.'

'Sounds good. Now tell me about your kids.'

'One more thing.'

'What?'

'The money, you have to give me some idea of what to do with your money. Think about it before our meeting, will you? That money has been driving me crazy. I'm glad you're here so I can finally get some direction from you.'

He was talking about the money I had received prior to the shooting in New York when Monica was killed. It was payment for my stock in the company. It came from a man from Thailand, Mr. Nue. He made it perfectly clear I should take the money in exchange for selling him my stock. The alternative, he intimated, was to be killed. He didn't say that in so many words. But the implication was obvious. And since he was convinced I would not choose the latter, he had the funds placed in a blind trust in my name. It was a done deal in his mind. The money was mine whether I wanted it or not, payment for my stock. That's what he thought would happen. It did not. The CIA had intervened. As a result, I never signed over my stock to him. It was still mine. And I had Nue's money in a bank account in Switzerland. David, who had my power of attorney, was the only one who could administer the account besides me. Before going to Belize, I left him a voicemail explaining the situation and asking him to look after the account. Ever since he had been bugging me to give him some direction about what to do with the money.

I always put him off.

The account held approximately $5.4 million before I left for Belize. I assumed it was worth more now, earning interest daily. Plus, Nue deposited a million-dollar-per-year annuity into the account.

9:45 P.M. JOHN

Tall oaks spread a sheltering canopy of leaves over the two-lane road.

Lake Shore Avenue is a gently curving ribbon of asphalt that runs parallel to the shoreline of Lake Michigan. It is a delight to drive when not crowded with summer tourists and it was not too busy as we headed back to my cottage. Only one set of headlights stared at me in my rear-view mirror.

My Mercedes 500 SL was performing effortlessly as I rounded a curve, enjoying the sensation of speed again. I had not driven during the year I lived in Belize. A car on the island was a useless waste. I never traveled far enough to need one. Most of the time, I walked. Or if I was in a hurry, I took a rubber dingy with a small outboard motor. You could get almost anywhere you wanted to go in a boat.

'John, this car is going too fast.' Ilana complained.

'Relax, you will get used to it,' I said, knowing Ilana had never been in a fast car before coming to the States. It made her uncomfortable. But it was time for her to become accustomed to speed. I couldn't drive slow, It was wasn't in my nature. I told her this, but what I didn't tell her was that not many drivers drove as fast as I did. It was a habit. I had driven fast from the time I used to race down these roads as a teenager.

I remembered one time in particular. David was in the back seat of my father's Ford convertible, traveling a curvy dirt road through a forest. We came over a hill at speed. A recent wind storm had deposited fine-grained beach sand across a dip in the road at the bottom of the hill. When my car hit the sand, it immediately fishtailed out of control and stopped suddenly, tires buried in the sand. David apparently had not been holding on because he was thrown out of the rear seat of the spinning car, landing harmlessly on his back in the soft beach sand with a surprised look on his face. He sat up and moved around gently, trying to determine if anything was broken. Satisfied he had not lost the use of any limbs, he casually stood up as if nothing had happened. We had a good laugh, pushed the car out of the sand, and went on our merry way.

Ilana had not grown up with cars.

She was more at ease on rough seas than she was in the soft leather seats of a sports car. I had to explain to her how to put on a seatbelt the first time she rode with me. She did not understand why she needed such a thing, but I think she understood now. Mostly, she played with the radio when she was in the car to take her mind off her fears. The radio was another thing she didn't understand. Why were there so many stations, all playing different music? She asked. Occasionally, she listened to a radio in Belize, but her island did not have many stations, and all the music sounded the same. I told her each station on my radio was trying to make money. She wondered how they made money playing music. The concept of advertising was not easy to explain, but I think she eventually got it.

After a few miles, it became apparent the car behind us was content to continue at a constant distance from our taillights, a couple of hundred yards behind, locked into my mirror. I decided to see if I could lose it. I knew this road by heart. A series of tight curves ahead would test the Mercedes' excellent suspension. It would be fun.

I braked hard for the first turn, leaning into the curve, floating smoothly through the corner, accelerating, braking for the next corner, floating, accelerating, anticipating the next curve, setting up the car so it flowed effortlessly through the corners like a choreographed ballet. Driving at speed is a joy when it is done right. I was having a good time. Ilana, on the other hand, was not. She was watching the road ahead as if she expected the trees on the side of the road to jump out and grab her with their low-hanging branches.

'Mr. John,' she regressed nervously to the name she used to call me. 'I...'

'Okay, I'll slow down,' I smiled, anticipating her complaint.

'I'm sorry. I don't mean to be scared, but I am not happy when we go so fast.'

'I know. You will get used to it. Don't be afraid. I'm a good driver.'

'Okay,' she responded bravely.

I slowed down which was fine because we were getting close to the driveway to my cottage.

Oddly, the headlights behind me again appeared in my mirror. It's not as close as before, but still behind. It should have been out of sight. No one purposely drives as fast as I just did through those corners. It suddenly occurred to me it might be a cop. But if it was a cop, I would be seeing flashing lights now. I had clearly been speeding. I waited, expecting to see him turn on his lights. But no flashing lights appeared, just two staring white headlights. Then, to make matters worse, the car slowed when I slowed for my driveway. It should have caught up. But no, it stayed back.

The entrance to my cottage came up fast on the right. I made a quick decision, hit the accelerator instead of the brake, and kept going.

'Do you have the cell phone in your purse?' I asked Ilana calmly, not wanting to alarm her.

'Yes,' she dug around in her purse.

'Good.' I told her David's number and waited while she dialed and handed me the phone. It rang in my ear as I glanced at the lights in my mirror.

'David, it seems you may have been right. I think I'm being tailed,' I said as soon as he answered.

'Okay, this is what we are going to do,' David replied immediately. He was a very decisive person. That was one of the reasons he was a good lawyer. 'First, tell me where you are. I'm going to call the State Police.'

'On Lake Shore just past my cottage.'

'Get over to 31. There's more traffic on that road. You won't be so exposed. Turn back towards town when you are on the highway. I'll get the police to meet you on the road.'

A quick look in my mirror revealed the car behind was suddenly closing the gap. I gave the phone to Ilana. A side road approached. I hit the brakes hard, turning left onto the road, tires sliding around the corner. One more glance in my mirror, hoping the car had not followed. But there it was, still glaring into my mirror.

I hit the gas.

'Tell David the car is closing in.' I said to Ilana. 'We need help fast.'

Trees alongside the narrow road flashed in my headlights. Even I was not comfortable at this speed on the dark road at night. Only an occasional light from a nearby house shed some warmth.

The driver did not come to a complete stop to look. A neighborhood car slowly poked its nose out from behind a tree at the entrance to a driveway and turned onto the road without taking time to estimate my speed. I hit my brakes, unsure which way the car intended to turn: right into my lane or left into the oncoming lane. It turned left in front of me, and I was on its bumper in a heartbeat. I swerved, missing by inches, sliding across the road, heading dangerously out of control toward some trees. Gravel and weeds, tires throwing up dust and stones, fighting for traction, bouncing across the dirt with the rear end fishtailing; I resisted an urge to turn quickly back onto the road, afraid the front wheels would dig into the gravel, causing the car to flip.

The startled neighbor now behind me must have wondered what flashed past him. While the car on my tail saw it all and never slowed for the neighbor, easily avoiding the slow-moving car and, in the process, made up a considerable distance, closing in; bright lights all over my mirror, inches from hitting me in the rear end. I punched the accelerator, drawing away.

Interstate 31 is a four-lane, unlimited-access, divided highway. I slowed only briefly at an intersection, looking for traffic, sliding, turning left across all four lanes, tires screeching for traction on the cement. A quick glance in the mirror revealed nothing. The car was gone; it must have turned right and headed in the opposite direction. I slowed to a normal speed.

The emergency was over as fast as it began.

THURSDAY, JUNE 4, 10:45 A.M. JOHN

'David... Yes. It's John.'

I had to convince David's secretary to let me talk to him. Now, not later.

She had informed me, saying she would not put me through. I guessed she was new and didn't know who I was. And her boss, my good friend David, was a very important man in her mind. She said she was not in the habit of interrupting him. Her boss was in a meeting, she explained. I could leave a message, or I could call back. It was my choice.

I told her to put me through to him immediately, or I would be forced to come to his office and walk in on him with or without her permission. And oh, by the way, just for future reference, I told her she should know I was a friend of her boss, a good friend... and a client. And I didn't think her boss would be very happy when he discovered she had not allowed me to talk to him.

Only then did she finally relent and connect my call.

'Yes,' I said to David. 'Sorry to interrupt, but I'm not going to be able to make our meeting this morning... Yes, I will explain when I see you... No, I'm not sure I will be at lunch either. Something has come up. But we need to talk. Try to clear some time in your calendar for me this afternoon.'

I listened to him even though my mind was already on to other things.

'Look, got to go. I'll call later.' I interrupted and hung up quickly.

David was still talking when my phone clicked off. That was rude, but I didn't want him to ask me where I was going. He would probably have tried to talk me out of it if I told him what I was doing.

The main street of Grand Haven was mostly deserted, even though it was almost eleven AM. Only a few lonely shoppers aimlessly wandered the pre-summer streets.

I had not slept well even though the State Police promised to watch my cottage through the night. The trooper we met on the road remembered me. The story of the firebombing of my cottage had been in all the papers. All the cops knew about it. I explained that I was in town for a short visit and was a little concerned after what happened the last time. I thought a car was following me, but after a while, it had turned the other way. Maybe I was mistaken. Still, it had me concerned.

The cop seemed to understand.

Fortunately, he wasn't aware of what had happened in Charlottesville a couple of days earlier because he didn't ask me any questions about that. However, he did ask me about Ilana. I simply told him she was a friend, and I was glad he didn't probe any further and didn't ask her for identification. Still, the episode made me realize again I needed to address her situation soon with the immigration authorities. It was only a matter of time before having her in the States without a visa could be a problem. She was one of the reasons I needed to talk to David.

That was going to have to wait because Phillip had called my cell phone.

How he got the number, I did not know. The phone had only recently been activated in Charlottesville. But he had called, sounding just as I remembered him, like he was a leading dramatic actor in a play about his life. He spoke with a resonant voice like he was working with an entranced audience. And in a way, his life was a drama. Mostly because he made it that way. Even when his life was simple, he found ways to make it complex. And when it was a comedy, he found ways to make it a tragedy.

It occurred to me he was making my life a tragedy as well. But I didn't really blame him. I had made choices, as had he. I was responsible, not him.

'Did you have fun returning to your cottage from Fricano's Pizza last night?' Phillip asked me after I answered my cell phone. 'It was a nice night for a drive, don't you think?'

I could visualize the smirk on his face as he was talking. 'What do you want?' I responded, obviously annoyed. 'I'm headed for an appointment. I don't have time for your bullshit this morning.'

'I thought we should get together,' he said, emphasizing each word distinctly, speaking slowly and carefully like an actor who didn't want his audience to miss one syllable of his exhortation. 'It could be just like old times,' he explained. 'You do remember the last time we met?'

I remembered.

The last time was the night when Monica was killed. Phillip was in the hotel room. Somehow, he had escaped unharmed. No one saw him leave. And he had never been charged with a crime. Charlie explained why. Except for my testimony, no one could verify he was in the room. Everyone who had seen him that night was either dead or gone. It would be my word against his. And my testimony could be seen as prejudiced, not enough to implicate him. So, Phillip had escaped unscathed.

I had no idea what he had been doing in my absence. I assumed he had been busy doing his usual dirty little deeds. But I really didn't know, nor did I want to know. He was just another memory I had been trying to forget. But apparently, this was one memory that wasn't willing to go away.

'I'm not sure I want to meet with you,' I answered. 'It's probably a trap, like the last time.'

He assured me this wasn't the case, and somehow, I didn't think he was lying. He told me he had something to tell me. He said I would want to know, and he would only tell me in person. In a way, he left me no choice. I had to go. But still, I wondered if it was important. Because the truth was, I didn't want to spend even a single minute talking to the jerk. Even so, I agreed to meet him.

'Now,' he informed me. 'Come now or don't bother coming.'

When I arrived at the restaurant, I looked for a place to park my car, still unsure if I should be seeing him. But I was curious. He had this effect on me. He always made everything sound bigger than life. It was like I had to know, I had to listen to his lies.

Regardless of my determination to avoid him like the plague, I couldn't help myself.

11:15 A.M. JOHN

I spotted his curly brown ponytail immediately after entering the dining establishment on Washington Street.

It was a popular spot, modern, light, and airy, with warm colors, fifties music in the background, friendly waitresses, and good local food. Phillip was sitting at his favorite table with his back to me. I couldn't see his long, straight nose or beady black eyes which dominated his thin, cleanly-shaven face, but I knew it was him. I could feel his dark presence in the room.

Of course, he wasn't that bad in reality. It was just that ugly repercussions seemed to follow in his wake like you knew something terrible would eventually happen if you got too close to him... If not today, then probably tomorrow.

He always ate at the same restaurant; this restaurant had breakfast and lunch. He was a fixture. Everyone knew him. Most people liked him, the town's people, that is. The locals sympathized with him when stories were written in the newspapers about him and me. David told me about it. I said I didn't care. I didn't live in Grand Haven any longer. I wasn't concerned about what the simple minds in this town thought.

A few people must have recognized me when I sat down opposite him in a booth. I could feel their narrow eyes staring.

'Hi Phillip, so nice to see you again.'

He didn't immediately respond to my greeting, didn't even look up; he just continued to eat his late breakfast: scrambled eggs and some sandwich I couldn't identify. Or maybe it was an early lunch. Like everything else about him, his biological clock was slightly off.

A waitress came over and asked if I wanted anything.

'Yes,' I replied. 'Coffee and a cinnamon roll, please.'

'I hope our demonstration of your vulnerability didn't upset you too much,' he eventually stated without bothering to look up.

I assumed he was talking about the car that had followed me down Lake Shore Drive as I drove home from the restaurant last night. And when he used the word 'our,' I guessed he meant himself and Mr. Nue, his friend from Thailand.

Everything had become agonizingly clear after seeing the two of them together in New York the night Monica died. I assumed it was Phillip who brought Nue's Thai family into play. He saw an opportunity and decided to capitalize on it. He, as much as anyone, understood what the Thai lost as a result of my company. No doubt he contacted them, and they agreed to work with him. With Phillip's help, they put a plan in play to return the international market of sapphires to Thailand. Or should I say return it to a certain family dynasty in Thailand, the family who had controlled it for hundreds of years, Nue's family. Thousands of jobs cutting the stones and hundreds of millions of dollars marketing the gems were at stake. Their decision to use violence was, most likely, never a question. They wanted the business returned and they were willing to use whatever means necessary to achieve their goal.

And this was when my problems began.

Of course, all of this fits nicely into Phillip's plans because he hated me, hated me for accomplishing what he had failed to do.

'Were you and your friend also responsible for trying to kill me at my office in Charlottesville a few days ago?' I asked, even though I assumed it was futile to question him. He never ever gave me a straight answer.

'Don't know anything about that,' he replied as expected.

'A friend died in the attack.'

'I told you I don't know what you're talking about.'

The waitress brought my coffee and a sweet roll.

'Okay, you made your point. Now what?' I stared at him.

He didn't immediately reply; he just took a sip of coffee.

I always thought coffee was a big part of his problem. It was his drug of choice. He drank the stuff all day long. If I ever drank that much coffee, I would be so wired I couldn't function. But not him. He just kept drinking the brew as if caffeine was the source of life.

'You have received millions of dollars from us, but you have not repaid us in kind,' he finally replied.

Of course, Phillip was referring to the five hundred million plus dollars that had been placed in a blind trust in a Swiss bank in my name, the same money David asked me about last night. I assumed the subject of this money would surface sometime during our conversation.

'I haven't touched it,' I replied. 'And I haven't decided what to do about it. Maybe I should put it in a charitable trust in the name of Monica Sorensen.'

'Ah yes, the girl who died in New York. Did you know her well?' he asked without emotion.

'I was planning to marry her.'

'I didn't think you were the marrying type.'

'You're missing the point,' I replied angrily.

He looked at me as if he was trying to understand my meaning.

'She died, Phillip. I loved her, and she died. Can you understand that?'

'Certainly, you don't blame me for her death?' he countered. 'If you had just signed the papers, you could have walked away. And your girlfriend would be alive today.'

'Maybe.' I replied, not completely convinced I wouldn't have been killed as soon as I signed. The papers he was referring to was a document which would have transferred my company stock over to Nue. Together with my stock, Nue held enough stock in my company to take control.

'How about all the other times you almost had me killed?' I asked him, getting angrier than I intended.

'Perhaps you have forgotten that it was me who set up a meeting with you in New York to stop the violence,' Phillip countered. 'That was your idea and I made it happen, but you didn't bother to show.'

He was right. I had asked him to help me put an end to the violence that was affecting me and my company. He had promised nothing at that time, but later, he called and asked if we could meet. He said he wanted to discuss a solution. I had agreed to meet with him, but when I told Monica and Charlie, her CIA friend, about the meeting, they refused to let me go. They said it was too dangerous. So, he was right. I didn't go as I had promised. However, later that evening, Phillip and his Thai accomplice, Mr. Nue, came uninvited into a hotel room where I was meeting with a business associate. Monica was with me at the time. They held us hostage, demanding that I sign over my stock or be killed.

'Okay,' I said to Phillip, knowing that arguing with him was a waste of time. 'You asked for this meeting and I'm here this morning as promised. So, what's on your mind?'

Phillip paused before replying. Finally, he leaned over the table and spoke in a whisper so only I could hear what he was saying. 'I have convinced my partners to give you one more opportunity to conclude the agreement which was offered to you in New York. Sign the papers, and you will be allowed to go on with your life without further interference. I assume this is what you want.'

I did not immediately respond; I just let him talk.

He continued, speaking slowly so I wouldn't miss a word. 'You do understand what I am offering you?' he asked. 'You can walk away after signing. No one will follow you ever again. You will be free to go on with your life. Do whatever you want with more money than you can ever spend.'

Silence settled over the restaurant. It was like everyone inside was waiting for my answer. That was nonsense, of course. No one heard what he said; it was just my imagination. I looked at him, trying to suppress a growing urge to wrap my fingers around his throat.

'You mean you promise not to shoot up my apartment again.' I replied while attempting to determine the depth of his deceit, the deep hole of duplicity which lay behind his beady black eyes. 'And you won't bomb my house like in Belize. Or follow me all over the world looking for an opportunity to put a bullet in my head,' I could feel my temper getting out of control. His offer was almost comical in a way, outrageous except for the grim reality of the situation.

'I think you get it, and I'm sorry about that stuff,' he said quietly, looking unconcerned. 'That was not my doing. I hope you understand.'

'Understand... Sure, I understand. But I wonder if you do? The woman I wanted to marry and my best friend were dead. Can you understand that?' I demanded.

People in the restaurant were beginning to stare at us, some probably aware of the animosity harbored between us. I didn't care. 'Do you really think for a moment that I can simply excuse your complicity in these murders and just walk away because you say you're sorry?'

I paused to let him think about what I said for a minute... Then I continued, trying to keep my voice low even though I wanted to scream at him. 'And now let me get this straight... You want me to forget about the whole mess. Forget about all the deaths. Forget about my dead girlfriend. Just take your money, go away, and be happy? Is that what you think I should do?'

He said nothing.

'Who do you think I am?' I demanded.

I let my question simmer in the air for a moment, thinking he would understand. But of course, he didn't. He just ignored me. His aberrant ability to ignore reality so dominated his ability to think clearly that rational thought was somehow prevented from filtering through his thick skull. More than anything else, this made me mad. The fact I could never get through to him.

'So that's your suggestion?' I asked him in amazement. 'Just forget it all?'

'What choice do you have, John?' he replied calmly without looking up. 'It's simple really. It always was. You have just made it more difficult than it needed to be. You do understand you are nothing more than a pawn in a game that is being played on a global board. And, in a way, so am I. Our fates are already known. We have very few real choices in the end. The outcome of the game has already been decided.' He smiled.

This was the kind of theatrical nonsense he always liked to dispense. But oddly, this time, it was possible he was right.

'Okay, what if I agree? What's next?' I asked, resigned to the fact his Thai colleagues were not going away. One way or the other, they were determined to be involved, and obviously, they had chosen Phillip to be their spokesman. I had to deal with him whether I liked it or not.

He paused before answering, obviously enjoying the drama of the situation. 'We meet one more time,' he stated emphatically. 'You sign the papers you did not sign in New York. Then you are free to go on with your life.'

'That's it?'

'That's it...There's one condition, of course. You must come alone. If I see or suspect you have invited anyone to our meeting, either electronically or in person, I will leave immediately, and our offer will be withdrawn forever.' He paused before adding. 'And you will, no doubt, eventually suffer the consequences you have luckily avoided to date.'

He said all this very slowly and carefully, as if every word was a matter of life and death.

I assumed it was.

12:35 P.M. JOHN

'He said he would give me a day.'

'Give you a day for what?' David asked me.

'I told him I wanted time to think about it.'

'Think about what? What's there to think about?' David countered.

I sat, resigned to listening to David harangue me even though I knew what he would say before he said it.

'Haven't you seen enough?' David scolded me. 'What chance do you have against these guys?' He paused, looking at me like I had lost all ability to reason before continuing.

A massive mahogany desk occupied his office, a big lawyer's desk that separated us. I was relegated to the guest chair on one side of his desk. He occupied a bigger, more comfortable chair on the other side. I knew I should be concentrating on what he was saying, but instead, I let my eyes wander around his office as he rattled on. Books lined the walls. File folders were stacked everywhere: on his desk, on his conference table, even on the floor. The folders represented open cases. I wondered how he kept them all straight. To me, his office was a mess. And the mess made me uncomfortable. I had once asked him about the folders. He said the piles of files were organized in an order only he knew where everything was. He said his secretary had tried to clean them up once while he was away on vacation. When he returned, he couldn't find anything. She was told never to do that again and threatened with being fired if she did.

David stopped talking when he noticed I wasn't listening and stared at me across his desk, his confident brown eyes daring me to disagree with his inevitable logic. I assumed he was waiting for me to agree with him, but instead, I was thinking about how he was just making me mad. I wondered how people like David could always be so confident. How could they take something as complex as my response to Phillip and reduce it to a yes or no question?

'Okay,' I finally replied. I know you're right, but maybe I don't like being told what to do even when I know I have no choice.'

'Yea, I remember your mother complaining about you're not liking to be told what to do,' he smiled.

He and I first met in high school. We used to joke that our mothers always tried to blame the other guys in our group for their son's bad behavior. It was never their son's fault. Their sons were good boys. In our mother's eyes, it was always the bad influence of our friends that was the problem. And in truth, our mothers were mostly right. We were a bad influence on each other. But despite our mother's dire predictions to the contrary, we all turned out alright. Well,...mostly alright.

'Look, David,' I said, feeling my emotions getting the best of me even as I was trying to act cool. 'Phillip's complicity in the murder of three of my friends is not something I take lightly... What am I supposed to do? Say, thank you, Phillip. Thanks for the money. And isn't it great your partners have promised not to kill me anymore... So sorry your friends didn't kill me when they had the chance, but as long as I have survived, isn't it wonderful they are now willing to call a truce? Thanks guys. Sure, bring the papers. I'll be happy to sign. Why don't we all get together for a drink afterward?' I rattled on.

David stared at me like an attorney analyzing a hostile witness on the stand.

'It's all too civil, David. Too cut and dried,' I continued. 'Too much legal language where dead bodies and dry blood are everywhere you look...You know what I really want to do? I want to wrap my hands around Philip's neck and squeeze until I don't have to listen to that lying piece of garbage anymore.'

David waited until I was done. He didn't argue with me. He just waited for me to calm down. Truth was, I wanted him to argue with me. I needed someone to be the brunt of my anger. He was too smart for that.

'Okay, you know I'm going to sign the papers,' I finally conceded. 'And I know I'm going to sign. I just didn't want to give Phillip the satisfaction of giving in without taking at least a day to consider my options.'

'Alright, John, I understand,' David sighed. 'Let's take a moment to talk about your options. For instance, you could get the police involved.'

'What can they do?' I asked. 'Will they be able to keep me safe? What do you think? What are the odds? Not good, right? So, it's not worth the risk. Is it?'

I knew David was manipulating me, forcing me to agree with his logic and there was nothing I could do but resign myself to being manipulated by him.

'Right. It's not worth the risk, and you know it... So that's that,' he concluded. 'You will sign over your stock, and hopefully, they will leave you alone.'

He paused before asking, 'So... are you going to return to Belize after you sign, or will you stay here?'

'I haven't thought that far ahead. It's barely been an hour since I met with Phillip. Do you mind if we discuss a few other things first before I go down that path?'

'Okay.' He sat back in his padded leather armchair and waited patiently.

I took a breath. 'I got a call from Clarence in Australia shortly before my house blew up in Belize. I can't prove it, but I think his call had something to do with the firebombing. I think someone told Nue I would be returning to my old job with the company. And that's why they tried to kill me.'

As soon as I told this to David, I instantly regretted it. Personally, I knew what I was saying was true. I knew it because Ilana had told me about the call she made before the house burned, the call to her South American contact. But I wasn't ready to tell David about her involvement in the affair, at least not yet. I didn't want him to know her slightly criminal involvement in my mess.

'Can you prove it?'

'No,' I lied. 'I just think it was too coincidental. First, the call. Then my house is firebombed. But more importantly, Clarence's call made me painfully aware of the problems the company is facing,' I said, trying to maneuver our conversation away from why I thought the call and the burning beach house were related. 'To put it bluntly, the company is unraveling fast. I guess I always knew it would. But it's happening faster than I thought possible. And Phillip's Thai friends are major contributors... From what Clarence told me, they are attempting to take over the sapphire market. And I have to assume as soon as they get control of my shares in the company, they will place their puppets on the board. And that's when you can kiss my old company goodbye. But here's the real problem and the reason why Clarence called. Clarence's company will be gravely affected when that happens, and maybe a few others, like the Montana operation. So, you see, this is not just about me.'

David listened attentively, 'Not your problem, John. Your problem is staying alive. You are in no position to help anyone.'

He was right, of course.

I was using him as a sounding board in my frustration. I desperately wanted to find another solution even though I knew none existed. Still, I persisted.

'I'm not sure you completely understand,' I argued. 'Many people in many places around the world have come to rely on our company. We have changed their lives. In most cases, we have made their lives considerably better, especially miners. Their standard of living has been raised from desperation to comfortable. So... can I simply abandon them now?'

David appeared unimpressed by my argument. He sat quietly listening, allowing me my day in his court. He knew the jury's ultimate verdict. Still, he allowed me to speak, to get it all out. Then it would be time to move on to a final judgment.

'So, what do you think? Can I do it; can I sign the papers and walk away from all the people who have come to rely on me?' I asked him again.

'Can you help anyone after you are dead?' he asked stoically.

'But I'm not dead, David. Not yet. And as long as I am alive, can I walk away from these people without trying to help them?'

He sat tapping his pencil on his desk, something I have seen him do many times when he was trying to be patient with people of lesser intelligence.

'Do you have a choice?' he finally asked.

6:10 P.M. JOHN

Beach grass waved in a gentle breeze below the deck of my cottage as I looked out over the lake.

It was evening. Time to rest, have a cocktail. Ilana and I were sitting on a deck chair listening to the sound of waves lapping on shore, washing easily through our minds.

Earlier, we had driven into town. She wanted to go to a grocery store to buy food for our dinner, good food like she had on her island. No more funny pizza, please, she dictated. We searched the store aisles long and hard to find the ingredients she desired for our evening meal. Now, the sweet smell of spices simmering on the stove in the kitchen waffled out through the open sliders.

Beautiful Ilana was being unusually quiet. She knew I had a lot on my mind. During our drive to the grocery store, I told her about my meetings with Phillip and David.

Phillip had been called. I told him I would sign the papers. A meeting was scheduled in his office. As a result, I was not concerned. Ilana and I were not in any imminent danger. I could relax. And yet, a discomforting anxiety complicated my day. I was not completely content with my decision. David knew this. He had agreed to meet with me. I had one more day before I was scheduled to sign over my stock.

The big lake, which is what West Michigan natives call Lake Michigan, constantly changes. This evening, it was a gentle rolling sea of murky blue water, still cold from the ice storms of winter. The late afternoon sun reflecting off the lake felt warm. Soon, it would be dark, and the evening air would cool as it passed over its icy waters. I took a sip of wine and tried to picture the warm lime-green waters of the Caribbean Sea. At that moment, I badly wanted to be in Belize.

Ilana went into the cottage to attend to our dinner on the stove.

A piece of paper was in my pocket. It was on my mind. David had written a message on it and stuffed it in the pocket of my shirt as I walked out of his office. Said he had forgotten to give it to me earlier.

I wondered if this was true. Somehow, I couldn't get the idea out of my head that David was playing me like a violin. He was saying all the right words, the ones I expected him to say. But there was more to his act than his words, like him giving me the paper just before I left his office. That was not like David. If David was anything, he was organized. Nothing was ever done as an afterthought by my friend David.

I played with the paper with my fingers, folding and unfolding it while searching the waters of the lake for peace, trying to relax.

A flock of merganser ducks could be seen swimming freely on the water near the beach. Occasionally, they dove underwater to fish. They migrated through these waters each spring. They were beautiful birds, flew like F-15 fighter jets. I always marveled at how long they could remain underwater. Some animals have multiple talents, like these ducks, who could fly, swim, and dive. I envied their talents and wondered what it would be like to fly like they do with speed and endurance.

They made me think about my grandfather, who was a naturalist in the style of Walt Whitman. A self-educated man, he had only a fourth-grade education. But he showed me more wonder in an ordinary field of waving grass than I ever knew existed. His gift to me was a love of nature.

Charlie's name and a cell phone number were written on the paper David gave me. Call the number day or night, the note said. I knew Charlie. He was the CIA agent Monica had asked for help the last time I was in trouble. It was his agents who had crashed into the hotel room the night she was killed. In fact, it could have been one of their bullets that killed her. I didn't know. I didn't want to know. What difference would it make? She was dead. That's all that mattered.

I thought Charlie might be able to help me with Ilana's immigration problem. He would instantly understand why I had to get her out of Belize. He knew how dangerous the Thai were. I assumed he had contacts who could get her a temporary visa. This was reason enough for me to call him. But what I didn't know was why Charlie wanted to talk to me.

And oh, by the way, David had reminded me as I left his office; I still had not contacted the police in Charlottesville. He knew I left that mess with Helen. So, I owed the cops a call. However, David suggested I call Charlie first. He said he had talked to Charlie earlier in the day. Charlie had asked several pointed questions. David patiently explained to Charlie that client confidentiality prevented him from answering the questions. Said Charlie needed to talk to me. That's why Charlie gave David his number. So I could call him.

It was time. I couldn't avoid talking to Charlie forever. I dialed his number on my cell phone.

'Charlie, it's John.'

'Mr. John Van Laan, I presume,' he replied slowly as if he was trying to remember my name. 'So good of you to call,' he said with a hint of sarcasm.

Charlie is an African American male who graduated with Monica from the University of Virginia Law School. This was their connection from the past. They also had another connection, a personal one from when they both worked in Washington, DC. I never knew if it was a romantic one or just as friends. Charlie is a very handsome and articulate man. We've had our differences in the past, but when the chips were down, he helped me. However, I was never sure if he was doing it for Monica or for me. Either way, I was grateful.

'David told me I owe you a call,' I began.

'You owe more than me a call, but that can wait. Where are you now?'

'Grand Haven, Michigan,' I replied simply.

'Okay, let's begin by you telling what happened in Charlottesville a few days ago and why you aren't there?'

'I guess I could.'

'That would be nice.'

'Please try to understand, Charlie. I needed time to think before I talked to anyone. You, of all people, should understand.'

'I understand,' he replied. 'But I also understand you have a responsibility to report to the police. You can't just run off and leave your secretary to clean up your mess. Who, I might add, is doing a great job of covering for you. But now it's time for you to get involved.'

'Okay, okay, you have made your point. I'm ready.'

'Good, get your ass back to Virginia.'

'I don't think I can do that.'

'Okay, let's go over this one more time. You asked me what to do, and I told you. And now you say no. You don't want to do what I suggested.' He paused, 'Can you tell me what part of this conversation makes sense?'

'It's not that easy.'

'It is that easy. And you don't have a choice. You have a legal obligation to report to the police.'

'What's your interest in my mess?' I asked, ignoring his suggestion for the moment.

'John, the CIA has an open case file on you. I have an alert on my computer which sends me info whenever something interesting happens in Charlottesville. When I read about a shooting in your area, I was naturally curious. I called the police chief. He told me what happened. He said your secretary was being very coy about some of the details. Well, as you might expect, I guessed this affair involved you. And I have been trying to locate you ever since. So, am I right? Were you involved?'

'Involved in what?' I asked.

'You don't really know?'

'Let's say I'd like to know what you know first.'

'Okay,' he said. 'Here's the deal. I will tell you what I know if you tell me what you know. Sound familiar?' He was referring to some problems we had in the past, which related to a serious lack of communication between Charlie and me.

'Deal,' I responded, thinking there was no point in not being completely upfront with Charlie. He had decided to get involved whether I liked it or not. And I didn't have Monica to intercede with Charlie this time. This time, I would have to deal with Charlie myself. It was time to come clean.

'You sure?' Charlie asked. 'Because if you want my help, you have to trust me.'

'I trust you, Charlie. Do you trust me?'

Charlie let my comment slide. He began by explaining that evidence from the site of the shooting pointed to a lone gunman or a couple of gunmen who fired on my office and apartment with automatic rifles. They were in the trees outside and spent cartridges littered the forest floor. Afterwards, they simply disappeared. The cops lost their trail at some point. It looked like a professional job. Charlie explained, Arny, my housekeeper, was dead. He assumed I knew this. He said he was sorry. Evidence indicated that someone had been with Arny, a woman from all appearances. She must have been staying in the apartment; clothes and makeup were found. The cops were checking her finger prints, but they found nothing in the computer so far. A man was also staying in the apartment at the time of the shooting. Bloody shoes were found. One pair about my size and a few other things like bloody finger prints. Charlie said he assumed the prints were mine.

'Okay, now it's your turn,' he said smugly.

'Charlie, I think I should first tell you what has happened to me since I last saw you.'

I described in as few words as possible the reasons for my retreating to Belize, then the circumstances surrounding the fire at my house on the beach, and finally, the shooting at my office. He listened attentively without comment as I finished by telling him about my meeting with Phillip. He groaned audibly several times during my recitation. The case was as personal to him as it was to me. Monica was his friend as well as mine. We both attended her funeral. That was the last time I saw Charlie. He took her death pretty hard. I didn't know if he felt personally responsible. I assumed he did. Although... I didn't want him to think I blamed him. I didn't. I finished by telling him I had an appointment with Phillip to sign the papers, turning my company stock over to the

Thai group. I hoped my signing over the stock would end my problems once and for all.

'You can't do that,' he said with absolute authority.

'Can't do what?'

'Can't sign those papers.'

'What choice do I have?'

'You have a choice.'

'Charlie, maybe you haven't been paying attention. These guys are serious and deadly. And they appear to have the resources to back up their threats. If I don't sign, I might as well put a bull's eye on my back and wait for the sound of a gunshot.'

'I can help you,' he responded.

'No offense, but that didn't exactly happen the last time.'

'Maybe if you had been more cooperative, things would have gone differently,' he countered with anger in his voice.

'Look, Charlie,' I responded, surprised at how easy it was for us to get upset in almost no time. 'I don't blame you for Monica's death, and I want you to know that. But I also don't think it's fair for you to blame me either.'

He didn't immediately respond, so I continued. 'It happened, Charlie. I don't think either of us could have anticipated what happened and certainly neither of us wanted it. I have replayed the night when she died over and over in my mind. If I could do it differently, I would. But I can't, and neither can you. We can't change what happened. She's dead, and we are alive. It should be different, I know... She was the good one. She should have lived.'

My last sentence came out of nowhere. It was not something I had planned to say. I felt a tear form in the corner of my eye after I said it... Suddenly, I didn't want to talk to Charlie anymore.

'Sorry, John. Of course, you're right. Let's bury it.'

'Sure, Charlie. Can we talk later?'

'No, we need to talk now. I meant what I said. You can't sign those papers. It will give them the victory.'

'What's the point? They are going to get it anyway. My company is half dead already. In a way, I'm not signing over anything which won't be theirs soon. It's inevitable whether I like it or not.'

'You can't quit without a fight, John,' he stated emphatically.

'I have no defenses against them, Charlie.'

'I told you. I will help.'

'Charlie, I don't know if I have any more fight in me. Can you understand that?'

He then said something I did not anticipate: 'That it doesn't sound like the man Monica loved.'

'What did you say?'

Monica and I had struggled with our relationship before her death. I thought most of our problems were due to the pressure of our circumstances. And this was certainly true, but it wasn't completely true. Some of our problems were due to my stupidity. For a while I thought she was having a relationship with Charlie. But that was just my dumb, naturally jealous nature getting in the way. Before she died, I knew it wasn't true because we connected in many non-verbal ways. But we never totally clarified our relationship. And since her death I have been assuming that certain things were true because I want to believe they are true. I want to believe she loved me. But I don't really know for sure because she never said it. Never said the words.

'Didn't you know, John?' Charlie stated as I struggled with my emotions. 'Didn't you understand why she did what she did for you? She didn't have to do those things, John,' he continued, shoving a guilty dagger deep into my gut. 'I always wondered how you could have been so blind, but it was not my business to tell you. But believe me now when I tell you she loved you deeply.'

I didn't know what to say.

The words I longed to hear from Monica were finally spoken out loud. But not by her, but by a man instead, a man who had made me jealous when, apparently, I had no reason to feel that way. And to hear the words now when she had been dead for over a year... this only made it worse; my loss deeper, my sense of regret harder to bear. I should have told her what was in my heart before she died... But I didn't. I was stupid.

'So now... Are you prepared to do what is right?' he asked, ignoring the fact he had just laid an emotional bombshell on my mental doorstep.

'What?'

'You can't walk away. You owe her, John. You aren't really going to let these bastards get away with murder, are you? Especially not now, not after they killed your friend Arny? How much do they have to do to you before you say, enough is enough?'

'So, getting myself killed, you think this will teach them?'

'I said, I will help.'

'I'm not sure you can.'

'I didn't say it wouldn't be without risk,' Charlie responded

Ilana was standing by the sliding glass doors, listening to my conversation with a strange look on her face. I didn't want to ignore her, but I had to finish with Charlie first.

'Okay, Charlie. I understand. But let me ask you one question first and I want a truthful answer.'

'Ask.'

'Let's say we do get these guys. Let's say we even kill a few of them. Will their deaths bring back Monica?'

He didn't answer.

I continued. 'Do you really think we can even the score? Will there ever be a day when we will feel good about what happened?'

'No, I guess not,' Charlie responded softly.

'So, why do it? What real satisfaction can be gained?'

'Because it is the right thing to do. You know it, and I know it.'

FRIDAY, JUNE 5, 6:35 A.M. JOHN

The sound of a storm's distant low rumble registered somewhere in my tortured dreams, waking me in the early morning even though I was still very tired.

Knowing it was useless to try to fall back to sleep; I slipped quietly out of bed, didn't want to wake Ilana. Her long black hair framed her beautiful face in a picture of contentment as she lay on her pillow in the pale morning light. I left her a note so she wouldn't worry. Opening a sliding glass door to the deck overlooking the lake, I hesitated for a moment before throwing my jacket inside. Didn't need a jacket this morning. A warm wind was blowing in from the southwest.

Low gray clouds near the horizon lay over the murky dark waters of the big lake, the first evidence of an approaching storm moving towards shore, pushed by an intensifying wind. Dashing whitecaps crested on the water, rising up in escalating waves. The sun rose very briefly in the east behind my cottage before being blocked by moisture-laden clouds.

Something intense was riding on the wind. Anticipation hung in the air. It was as if I could feel the distant hollow thunderclaps and white lighting in my bones.

From the edge of the deck, I watched sheets of gray rain begin to fall from the distant dark clouds near the horizon. Intermittently shafts of soft sunlight shone through openings in the racing clouds nearer to the shore, creating patches of sparkling glass water on the dull green, rolling surface of the lake. The beach below the deck had been wiped free of man's imprints by the escalating wind, creating gentle brush strokes across the stirring sands into softly curving lines of abstract art.

I could not linger long. I knew it would not be good to be on the beach when the storm hit. But as I stood on my deck mesmerized by waves rising up over sunken sandbars near the shore, watching their smooth leading surfaces ride high before crashing over finally in a tangle of white-water confusion; I badly wanted to join forces with the storm.

Occasional lighting near the horizon illuminated shades of the churning gray, furious clouds marking the storm front. Still, I hesitated. I needed to be inside the shelter of the cottage when the storm hit. I couldn't let the storm catch me on the beach dodging lightning and wind-driven rain. This was a familiar game; one I had played since I was a kid. There was a risk to this game, but there was also a reward. The risk was to be caught outside by the storm, drenched and cold. The reward was to exist for a time as a companion to the storm, experiencing the world of wind and waves for as long as possible. As beautiful as it was to watch the storm from the shelter of the cottage, it is far better to be outside in the elements; feel the wind's fury, taste the rain, see the churning clouds race overhead.

And it was certainly better than being in bed. I had not slept well; mostly tossing and turning, my mind a torment of thoughts. I had a decision to make.

Putting my problems momentarily aside, I went down the steps to the beach, setting out at a fast pace, walking near the water's edge with the wind at my back. But even with the wind and water pressing around me, I found it difficult to ignore my problems. My meetings with David and Phillip kept running rampant through my weary brain. And then there was Charlie's call. No matter how hard I tried, I could not dismiss what Charlie said to me. It was as if he was my conscience, my unnerving conscience. I had put off talking to him for as long as possible because somewhere deep inside I knew he would force me to rethink everything. He would want me to see the situation from his perspective. And that was exactly what he did. And it made my decision far more difficult.

It was time to make up my mind.

Not deciding was driving me crazy.

At that moment for some reason I did not understand, the pilot who had rescued me the last time I was in trouble came into my mind. What was his name, the guy who flew us out of Mexico? Al, I thought his name was Al. And I had his business card in my wallet, didn't I? He had given it to me, explaining I could call him anytime, twenty-four hours a day. I checked my jeans for my wallet and as I suspected, his card was inside.

I stared at it as the wind increased in strength, but only for a few seconds before making up my mind. I had my cell phone with me, having grabbed it off the counter as I headed outside. I could place a call now, didn't have to wait one minute longer. Good, because I didn't want to think about what to do for one more second. I only hoped I could be heard over the noise of crashing waves rushing up on the shore.

'Hello, Al, yes... John Van Laan. Can you hear me, okay?'

'Yes, Mr. Van Laan. I'm getting some interference, but I can understand you. Go ahead, sir.'

'Al, sorry to call so early, but I need another favor. I know this is getting to be a habit, but I was wondering if you or one of the other pilots in your company could pick me up in Muskegon, Michigan this afternoon. I know it's short notice, but it seems I need to get out of town quickly again.'

'No problem Mr. Van Laan. I'm up early, and I was planning to go into the office to do some long-overdue paperwork. But you know; I would rather go flying. So sure, I can come. What time?'

'Make it two this afternoon and don't turn off the engines.'

'Sounds familiar,' he chuckled. 'Where we going this time?'

'Going to Copper, Montana.'

'See you at two.'

'Thanks'

It was done. I had made my choice. God help me now.

Wind ripples could be seen flying across the glassy surface of the lake near the shore, signaling the leading edge of the storm. The storm was coming in sooner than I anticipated. The sky was already inky black overhead, illuminated by occasional brilliant flashes of white cloud lightning, followed closely by long peals of rolling thunder. An overhead mass of swirling dark gray clouds forming a perfect storm front rode across the entire length of the horizon. It brought back memories of the tropical storm Ilana and I had endured in the Caribbean. Only that day we had nowhere to escape.

I turned back immediately and headed towards my cottage, picking up my pace with the wind in my face. I had walked farther than I intended while talking on the phone. I had not been paying attention. My cottage was some distance away and it was not an easy walking on the loose, Lake Michigan beach sand, worse if I tried to run. Still, I hurried as fast as I could, head down, struggling against the wind, looking up occasionally to see the approaching storm clouds close in overhead.

The first real blast of storm wind leaned against me with all its strength, making it difficult to walk, much less run. A lightning bolt struck somewhere close, followed instantly by a thunderclap rattling my bones. I began to run on the solid wet sand at the edge of the water. This was easier and faster than walking in the loose sand on the beach, but it meant I had to dodge incoming waves which were now racing high up the shore pushed by the wind. Rain pelted down in large cold drops along with tiny hail stones slicing out of the black clouds, stinging my face. I pulled my hat over my forehead, seeing only waves breaking on the beach, dodging their rushing waters, my shoes soaked wet as I ran along the shoreline for the stairs and the shelter of the cottage. The cold heavy rain soaked me to the skin before I could reach the stairs to the deck. One last thunder clap shook the cottage before I got inside as if the storm was talking to me, telling me, 'I got you; I won our game this time...'

Ilana was waiting inside, standing by the windows still dressed in her bright yellow pajama top and panties. The look on her face told me she thought I had lost my mind. I smiled and kissed her on the cheek as if nothing was out of the ordinary. Like I always take morning walks in thunderstorms, don't I?

My clothes were cold and soaking wet. I took them off where I was standing, thinking it made no sense to drip water all over the rug. Naked, drenched wet, and shivering cold, I reached to embrace her warm body. She tried to get away, but not quick enough. I caught her and hugged her, felt her soft breasts under her pajama top, laughing as she attempted to wiggle away.

'Oh, I got you all wet. I'm so sorry,' I apologized. 'Only one thing to do now.'

'What?' she asked, trying to pull back from my cold wet body.

'Well, we need to get these wet pajamas off and get you warm,' I laughed.

I lifted her damp pajama top up over her head. Then, before she could protest, I picked her up and carried her to the bathroom, where I enjoyed the pleasures of a hot shower with a beautiful woman.

SATURDAY, JUNE 6, 1:17 P.M. JOHN

I explained our situation to Ilana while we drove into town after lunch.

Prior to leaving, she had been told nothing about where we were going or why before leaving the cottage, except to wear something warm and bring a coat. I didn't tell her because I knew what she would do once she found out. She would want to pack all her clothes and who knew what else. And I didn't have the time or patience to stop her. More importantly, I assumed we were being watched. A big suitcase dragged to our car would be a dead giveaway.

Intermittent cold rain fell on the windshield as I drove easily down Lake Shore Road toward town. Ilana was pouting, upset I had not let her pack a few things. I didn't argue with her and I couldn't blame her. When you have nothing most of your life, it is not easy to leave behind the few items you own. I assured her I would take care of her, buy her more new clothes where we were going.

A silver, four-door Ford remained stuck in my rear-view mirror during our drive. It was obvious we were being followed. The car stayed a reasonable distance behind, never getting too close. I was not surprised. I assumed I would be constantly tracked until I signed the bloody papers. My meeting with Phillip to sign the papers was scheduled for tomorrow. If we wanted to get out of town, it had to be today.

My morning had been spent on the phone in the bedroom. Ilana was watching television in the other bedroom. I closed the door to her room after saying I didn't want to disturb her.

Tim was my second call.

I told him we were coming to Montana for a visit. Please prepare the company-owned apartment in town.

He is the manager of a Montana sapphire mine. The offices for the mine are in Copper, Montana, a former mining town on the west side of the state. He sounded surprised to hear from me but pleased when I told him I was coming. He said he would make all the arrangements. I instructed him to keep it confidential. Tell no one.

I had earlier placed a call to Clarence in Australia. The time difference was fourteen hours. He was awake at the time. I asked him if he was serious about wanting me to return to run the company. He said he was. I asked him how serious; serious enough to make a last-minute unscheduled trip to Montana to meet with me. He didn't hesitate, said he would make travel plans as soon as we hung up. I told him to contact Tim when he knew his schedule.

Then I called Charlie at the CIA and told him what I was doing. He listened attentively and informed me he would be in Copper tomorrow. I didn't have to ask him to come. He volunteered. He said he would bring some fellow agents with him for security. We could talk more when he arrived in town. I thanked him.

'Don't bother,' he said before hanging up.

So, everything was set.

'You want to go with me?' I asked Ilana while we waited in a lobby outside David's office. 'I can arrange for security. You can stay at the cottage. You don't have to go.'

'No, I want to be with you, John,' she responded. 'Please, do not leave me behind.'

'Okay, but it could get dangerous.'

'No, I want to be with you,' she demanded again, determination in her voice.

Ilana could be very stubborn. I was learning more about her every day. If she wanted to be with me, I would let her. I had tried to keep Monica away because of the danger, but it had not worked. I was determined not to make the same mistake with Ilana.

'Mr. Van Laan,' the receptionist called my name. 'Mr. Dykstra will see you now.'

She escorted us into his office even though I knew the way. David rose from behind his desk when we entered and smiled.

'Well. Do you want to make the call, or should I?'

'What call?' he asked.

'The call to Phillip to tell him I will not be meeting with him tomorrow.'

David smiled as if he had anticipated everything. 'You sure you want to do this?'

I explained it all to David including my call to Charlie, the call which solidified my decision. David smiled occasionally as I talked, like he knew what I would tell him. I assumed he did. I suspected he had orchestrated everything behind my back, putting all the pieces in place, only needing me to make the proper decision. I asked him if he would be willing to drive us to the Muskegon Airport. I suggested we leave through his back entrance. It could get a little dicey, I warned him. A car had followed us into town.

'I'll take you,' he replied without further comment.

From a window in David's office, the car that followed us could be seen parked near my Mercedes. I gave the keys to my Mercedes to David and told him to enjoy. He said he would drive it to the cottage and leave it in my garage.

'Don't bother calling Phillip,' I volunteered. 'I'll make the call as soon as we are on the plane. I want to hear Phillip's voice when I tell him.'

David smiled.

'Look David, I'm going to need your help at some point in all this. I don't have a plan yet. That's why I'm going to Montana to meet with my guys. I promise to call you as soon as I know more.'

'You want me to come with you?' he offered.

'No, but thanks for offering.'

He nodded.

'Let's go, I don't want that guy outside to get nervous. The sooner we are out of here the better. He won't miss us for a while.'

David rose from behind his desk to get his coat as I explained that the plane should be at the Muskegon Airport in about fifteen minutes. It should be waiting for us when we arrive at the airport.

MUSKEGON, MICHIGAN AIRPORT, 2:38 P.M. JOHN

'Would you please put me through to Phillip?' I said to Martha, his secretary, over my cell phone.

Our plane's engines could be heard idling in the background. We were seated inside, waiting for the tower's permission to taxi to the runway. I took the opportunity to call Phillip.

The back door of the building where David worked had been our escape route. His secretary met us around the corner driving David's car. We decided to use David's secretary because we didn't think the guys watching us would suspect a secretary. It was all a bit overly dramatic, but it worked. The drive from Grand Haven to the Muskegon Airport was uneventful. No one tailed us.

Al met us in the airport lounge when we arrived. The plane was outside and ready to fly. I thanked David's secretary and told her to tell David I would call him when I had some news. After climbing the stairs to the plane, I settled into one of the comfortable leather seats. Ilana knew the routine by this time. It looked like we were flying in the same plane which had got us out of Cancun, Mexico. That flight seemed like a lifetime ago, but in fact, it had only been about a month. So much has happened since then. I felt like a different person. In a way, I guessed this was good. I needed to be a different person if I wanted to return to my old job. My beach-bum personality would have to go on vacation for a while. It was time to wake up the work-a-acholic in my brain.

'And who might be calling?' Martha asked as if she was the secretary for some big time, hotshot.

'John Van Laan,' I replied simply.

She had taken a real dislike to me ever since I turned on her boss. That was how she saw it. Fact was I didn't turn on him. I just didn't include him in my plans.

I heard her clunk the phone on her desk and yell at Phillip. 'It's John. Do you want to talk to him?' They worked in a small office complex, only a couple of rooms. Verbal communication was efficient.

'Good afternoon, John,' Phillip said. 'I thought our meeting wasn't until tomorrow. What can I do for you?'

'I need more time, Phillip. I won't be at our meeting tomorrow.'

He didn't reply immediately. I don't think he had anticipated my call. Finally, he responded as I expected. 'John, that is not acceptable. Our offer is a one-time offer, and the alternative is, as we have discussed, not negotiable. You need to be at my office tomorrow as we agreed. Sorry, no more time.'

'Can't make it.'

'Not good enough. Why don't you put David on the phone so I can convince him to help you decide?'

'David is not here.'

'You're in David's office,' he said smugly. 'Don't play games with me.'

'No, actually I'm not.'

'Where are you, John?'

'That's not important, Phillip. Here's the deal. Please inform your partners I will contact you when I'm ready to sign the papers, not before. Until then they will simply have to be patient.'

'Patience is not one of their virtues.'

'Perhaps you should teach them to be patient. Isn't that what you always preached.'

'I think you misunderstand my meaning.'

The tension in his voice rose as our conversation continued. He must have promised my signed papers to his partners by tomorrow afternoon. Now, he would fail, and failure was not something Phillip liked to admit.

'I understand perfectly, Phillip,' I responded.

'John, I'm speaking to you as a friend. Please don't do this.'

'Phillip, we have not been friends for a long time.'

'I can't save you later if you don't sign now. Signing the papers tomorrow is your only hope.'

'Hope for what?'

'I don't have to tell you what. But I will say this. If you thought it was bad before, it will be ten times worse in the future if you don't sign.'

Phillip was too smart to say something on the phone which might be recorded and incriminate him. But the meaning of his words was clear.

'Phillip, this conversation is over.' I abruptly closed my cell phone.

Al came back and asked if we were ready to go.

I looked at Ilana and took her hand with Phillip's warning churning in my gut.

'Yes, we're ready.'

MONTANA, THE WESTERN MOUNTAINS, MONDAY, JUNE 8, 3:35 P.M. JOHN

Pictures of white-capped mountains and crystal clear lakes surrounded by lush green forests entice exasperated exiles of big cities.

They move to Montana's pristine mountain valleys in the summer to live a more contented life. When the first snows of winter hit, they frantically call for snowplow service. It is only then they are unceremoniously informed that most vehicles can't get in or out of these mountain valleys in the winter. Snow piles high and too fast to be removed. A snowmobile is needed if one wishes to travel. And oh, by the way, be sure to wait for a good clear day to make your trip. Otherwise, you might get caught in a blizzard, get lost and your body never found until spring when the snow melts.

The natives know better.

On average, only fifty days a year are completely frost-free in the high mountain country of Montana. Foreigners are advised to pack up and get out while they still can before they freeze to death in the snow. Some do. And some don't, later wishing they had listened. After about a year or two of snow and cold, most retreat back to warmer climates.

Tim was different. He was a native. He was familiar with cold and snow. He lived in a small town in a mountain valley. He once told me when he wants to get away in the summer, he goes up to his father's cabin high in the mountains. When I had laughed at his remark, an incredulous look crossed his face. He asked me what was so funny. I told him where he lived in the mountains was about as far from civilization as most people ever go.

After landing at the airport in Copper Montana, Tim met us at the gate of the airport. A brief discussion led to a decision to use his father's cabin for our meeting. It was as safe a place as existed on this earth according to Tim. He suggested we drive there on Monday after everyone arrived, said it would be a great place to do some planning. Although snow still covered the high mountains, it was melting. He assured me we should be able to make the trip up the mountain in four-wheel drive trucks. He seemed honestly excited to take us.

I didn't say no.

I could have, perhaps. But it is not easy to say no to Tim. He has a natural charm. Comes from his Irish ancestry. He's one of those people who have a wonderful exuberance for life. A tall, handsome man, Tim has black wavy hair and a big, broad smile. And like most other Irish men, he was convinced he was God's gift to women. However, in his case, it was true. His natural animal magnetism seemed to attract them. Lucky for me he was married because he began to work his charm on Ilana as soon as he met her. And much to my discontent, she decided to call him Mr. Tim.

We got an early start Monday morning driving to his father's cabin. After a few hours of driving dry pavement, we turned off the main road onto a two-track weed-covered dirt road, which looked like it went nowhere. Tim said he knew the way. His pickup truck slipped and slid over the gravel road weaving up a mountain through trees and rocks. The road's nonexistent shoulder infrequently fell straight off the mountainside down to rock-strewn valleys below. As we climbed farther up the mountain, I began to wonder if this was a good idea after all.

His four-wheel drive extended cab pickup continued to make steady progress up the mountain; lurching and digging up a road which occasionally appeared to be nothing more than a goat path. Tim was in his element. Pockets of snow began to cover the ground the higher we went. Working the steering wheel, he fought through the snow and mud, the pickup's wheels splashing and sliding through the ruts. I held on, trying not to look down at the valleys below, which appeared miniature the higher we climbed higher.

Clarence rode with us. He had arrived in the morning. He sat in the back seat of Tim's pickup seemingly unconcerned. He lived and worked in the hills of Queensland, Australia. He was the CEO of the Nullamana Mining Company, supervising a number of sapphire mines. Middle-aged, Clarence was a big man with strong hands and shoulders. He was accustomed to being outside in the mountains. I don't think this trip bothered him at all.

Ilana, on the other hand, my warm weather island girl, was accustomed to none of this, not the cold or the high terrain. I had tried to convince her to stay with Sarah, Tim's wife in the valley, but she insisted on coming, despite feeling insecure in constantly changing environments. I couldn't blame her. Few people have ever experienced as many cultural changes in such a short period of time as Ilana was experiencing. For her, it must have felt like she was time-traveling through space. I was amazed she was managing as well as she was. Still, she had not completely adjusted and I think this was why she was happier being with me. I was the one constant in her life.

I had warned her she would be the only woman in the group. This, however, didn't seem to deter her. In fact, I think she rather liked the idea. Ilana liked attention. But as we traveled up the rutted mountain road, I wasn't so sure she thought she had made the right decision, constantly jabbing her fingernails in my arm, holding on tightly each time our pickup jumped and bounced over the rough road. I tried to assure her everything was okay. But the fact was, I cringed each time the road traversed a mountainside which fell off steeply to nothing valleys below. I was, after all, a flatlander from the Midwest. I was not born and raised in the mountains like Tim. Ilana must have sensed my unease and it only made her fears worse.

'See all the white stuff,' I said, trying to take her mind off the perils of the road. 'That's snow. That's the cold stuff I have been telling you about.'

She nodded under a white wool cap, not yet fully aware of how cold it would be where we were headed. She would soon find out.

Truth was, she had succumbed to a minor state of shock from the minute she stepped off the plane in Copper. It was near freezing at the time. The sun had disappeared behind mountains in the distance and a metallic cold wind blew into the valley off snow-covered peaks. The spring jacket she was wearing when she boarded the plane was not nearly warm enough to avoid a chill. Tim drove us directly from the airport to the company's apartment in town. I turned up the thermostat as soon as we arrived. The kitchen had been stocked with food earlier in the day. We ate some cheese and crackers before going directly to bed. Both of us were dead tired. Ilana initially shivered under the covers until I wrapped my arms around her. A down-filled comforter slowly warmed us. After a while, she stopped shivering and went to sleep.

A second pickup followed close behind Tim's truck, carrying Charlie and two CIA agents. Their names were Brad and Steve. Their truck was being driven by one of Tim's men, named Derek. Both trucks carried supplies, enough for a week. I wasn't sure we would be at the cabin this long, but Tim insisted we had enough food and supplies in case the weather turned bad. I didn't argue. He knew these mountains better than I did.

Charlie had arrived Saturday afternoon. He took up lodging in the company's other apartment in town. The mining company had two. The larger of the two apartments was taken by Charlie and his guys.

On Sunday Ilana and I went shopping. Two of Charlie's guys came with us for protection. I didn't fight this arrangement because I knew from previous experience Charlie would insist. Ilana bought every warm piece of clothing she could find in the stores that fit her. I purchased a couple of sweaters, jeans, and a warm jacket along with other necessities. Shopping was something I only did when I had to, and then as efficiently as possible. Ilana, on the other hand, took her time, enjoying the freedom to buy anything she wanted. I had to be patient and it wasn't easy.

That day was relatively peaceful which was good because we needed a break to get our heads together after the mess in Charlottesville and my confrontation with Phillip in Grand Haven. Charlie and I spent some time later in the afternoon, going over everything which happened. He prepared a report for his bosses at Langley, CIA headquarters. He said a portion of the report would be forwarded to the Charlottesville police department from the CIA. It would contain the reasons why I could not return immediately to answer their questions. Everything the police needed to know was in the report. They shouldn't complain, but Charlie said they probably would anyway. He suggested I go to the police station when I returned to Charlottesville and fill out a separate report. This would make everyone happy.

Our discussion, between Charlie and me, was conducted in a very professional manner. But I sensed, as I'm sure he did, that we were not discussing everything. Some old emotional baggage lay hidden under the surface. This was in direct contrast to the conversation we had on the phone not too many days before. I wondered if it was easier to talk from a distance than in person. Face to face, we fell into old habits that limited communication.

However, I did take the opportunity to ask him about Ilana's immigration problems. Charlie said he would handle it. It would take time. Paperwork for something like this was a long process, but he believed he could help her, get her a temporary visa. He said not to worry.

Ilana now sat next to me in Tim's truck dressed in a pink, down-filled jacket, jeans, a black turtle neck, a light blue sweater, wool socks, and hiking boots. She looked like an overstuffed Barbie Doll from a Lands End catalog. She had on a white wool cap and somewhere in her pockets were ear muffs. She was determined to not be cold.

I squeezed her hand.

'Isn't it beautiful here?' I asked as Tim's truck rounded a corner, revealing a broad sweeping valley beneath us. Off in the distance, rows of mountains, some with snow covered peaks rose high into a blue sky. It was a clear sky day and the sun's heat could be felt through the windows of the truck, warm in the thin mountain air.

'We're almost to the cabin,' Tim said as he wrestled the wheel of the pickup truck. 'This is God's country. You are going to love it here, Ilana. We should have a snowball fight when we get to my cabin.'

'I don't like to fight,' she responded.

'It's not a real fight.' Tim laughed and gave her one of his infectious smiles.

Tim's log cabin turned out to be much more than a simple cabin, more like a large hunting lodge built out of logs. Set on an open plateau cut into the mountain overlooking a valley, the place was large enough to hold several families. Tim's father was a doctor in Helena. He obviously had money because the place was grand.

A steep slope of large boulders protected the lodge from northern winds on one side. Off in the distance, a spectacular mountain vista spread out before us on the other side. A small stream fed by spring snow melt flowed around and under ice shelves between the cabin and the rocky slope.

Supplies from the trucks were unloaded after arriving. Tim coordinated everything, including the assignment of bedrooms. The main room in the lodge had a two-story ceiling. Tim called it the great room. It functioned as a sitting room, a dining room and was open to a kitchen. Tall windows overlooked a beautiful mountain vista. I instantly liked the place, reminded me of my apartment in Charlottesville. An interior, second story balcony on two sides was accessed by a staircase. Bedroom doors were spaced evenly along the length of the balcony. Tim gave Ilana and me the master bedroom, smiling mischievously when he assigned the room. A deck outside our bedroom overlooked the stream.

A long porch out front was a great place to sit and view the breathtaking mountain vista without interference. The interior of the lodge was lacquered wood, giving the place the feel of a cabin. Overstuffed armchairs and couches built for comfort had been placed throughout the interior including the bedrooms. Tables were crafted from flat-cut logs with legs made from tree branches. Our bedroom had a natural stone fireplace. Tim said he would bring enough firewood to keep Ilana warm throughout the night.

While we were unloading the trucks, Ilana walked around outside, mesmerized by the snow, feeling it crunch under her boots. It was my job to carry our luggage into the lodge, two new big suitcases full of her clothes along with my smaller suitcase. Traveling with a woman was a new experience for me. I was learning I would have to make some adjustments.

After lugging everything upstairs to the bedroom, I went out on the front porch in time to see Tim show Ilana how to pack a snowball. The sun was shining at the time in the rare mountain air. Even though the temperature was a few degrees below freezing, it didn't feel cold.

Gathering snow off the railing of the porch, I formed a loosely held snowball in my gloves. Underhanded, I arched it neatly towards Tim, who saw it coming at the last second and turned, allowing it to fall harmlessly off his back. He then threw the snowball he had made for Ilana at me with more velocity. I ducked. The snowball hit the cabin, falling on the porch.

Together we eyed Ilana.

Tim smiled and bent down to gather more snow. She sensed immediately what was about to happen and took off running. Tim gave chase quickly closing in with two direct hits to the back of her white wool hat. She stopped running and reached down without bothering to form a snowball and started shoveling the white stuff in his direction as fast as she could. Instantly they were on each other shoveling snow until both of them were covered, rolling on the ground in laughter.

Clarence and Charlie, who had come out on the porch to see what all the fuss was about, smiled amusingly at the two contestants who were acting like a couple of juvenile delinquents.

TUESDAY, JUNE 9, 7:55 A.M. JOHN

Coffee steamed in the rare high mountain air.

Behind distant white-capped mountain peaks, the sun rose, spreading rosy hue across the clear blue sky. Dressed in a warm coat I sat outside on the porch, enjoying the hushed anticipation of a new day in the mountains. Tim was the only other person out of bed at the time. He was inside, busy preparing breakfast.

Even though it was June, the sun did not make its appearance over the mountain tops until late in the morning. And it wasn't especially easy to get out of bed when it was cold and dark outside. I threw a couple of logs on the fire before leaving the bedroom to warm up the room for Ilana. She was still sleeping at the time, her beautiful eyes closed, looking quite content lying on a white pillow under a fluffy warm comforter. Hopefully, she was dreaming of swimming near a reef in Belize. She had to be exhausted, due to the constant change in her life in the last few weeks. On the outside, she seemed to be doing fine, but I wondered. It had to be difficult for her.

The smell of coffee from the kitchen permeated the cabin when I closed the bedroom door. Going downstairs, I grabbed a cup of the hot liquid, saying only a brief good morning to Tim before heading for the porch dressed in my new winter coat.

It was crystal cold outside. Clarence joined me after a while. Yesterday afternoon Tim had taken a couple of wood rocking chairs out of winter storage and placed them on the porch. The chairs were very comfortable and it was Zen-like sitting in the clear mountain air sipping a steaming hot cup of coffee. Neither one of us spoke more than a few words of greeting as the mountain scenery spread before us like God's great work of art.

The wind whispered in the distance as we rested, painting wispy clouds streaking off the tips of distant snow-covered mountain peaks against a deep blue sky. All sense of depth and distance was lost in the vast open space. It seemed as if we could reach out to touch the tops of mountains. But in reality, they were miles of hard travel away.

Except for a few housekeeping chores, we had accomplished almost nothing after arriving at the lodge the previous day; nothing except to get a sense of the place. Tim grilled steaks for dinner. Ilana helped by making a salad that was too spicy for my taste, but all the guys said it was great. I wondered if they were just trying to be nice. We relaxed after dinner, didn't talk business, took the time instead to become reacquainted.

Tim and Clarence were already friends. They communicated regularly comparing mining procedures and machine improvements. Although they technically worked for two independent companies, they often conferred with each other. This was one of the basic platforms of my business strategy: legally independent companies working together under one board, managing a mining, marketing, and distribution network. Case in point; improved mining procedures developed under Clarence and Tim were shared with other sapphire miners all over the world.

Tim's guy, Derek, who drove the second pickup truck, had stayed to help with the chores. He was a nice enough guy, didn't talk much, kind of short and stocky with sandy brown hair which looked unkempt under a blue baseball cap. I assumed he was in the kitchen now helping Tim with breakfast.

The two CIA guys who arrived with Charlie were like Derek in that they didn't talk much. Steve and Brad were their names. One had brown hair and the other had black hair. That was how I kept them apart. Other than this difference, they were almost indistinguishable. Both about six feet tall with closely cropped hair. They mostly stayed to themselves, knew their job and it was to protect us. A satellite communication system was established. They spent their time like a couple of marines doing field reconnaissance. They had to be ex-military, good posture and a look of absolute resolve. They made me feel both secure and nervous at the same time. I'm not comfortable around military types who think guns and force are the answer to most problems. When I asked Charlie about them, he smiled and told me to let them do their jobs.

Charlie was the enigma in the group. Highly educated and yet from a humble background, I always sensed that Charlie was still trying to determine where he fit in. His African American heritage had to make this difficult in a white man's world. Fortunately, it was changing, but not fast enough for Charlie.

Fact was I liked Charlie, and I think he liked me. But despite our mutual respect, we had always seemed to find a way to piss each other off. However, I was determined not to let this happen again. This time we needed to be on the same side. But since our arrival in Montana, our conversations had been limited. Monica's name had not been discussed. And although I thought it would be good for us to talk about her, it hadn't happened.

'So how are you, mate?' Clarence asked, breaking the cold silence on the outdoor porch, speaking with a heavy Australian accent as he sipped his coffee.

The sun felt good on my face after it finally rose over the mountains, warming the cold brisk morning air as I contemplated his question. I didn't really know how to answer. I finally decided to just be honest. 'I think I would rather be in Belize.'

'How was it?'

'Belize is a beautiful place. I think you would like it. Warm blue seas full of marine life, lots of flowers, and friendly people.' I sipped my coffee, imagining a typical morning sitting on the dock by the sea, feeling strangely homesick for someplace that had been my home for only one short year.

'Good place to get away?'

'I needed to go, Clarence. Monica's death was very hard. You remember her?'

'Of course, I remember her. We almost died together in the fire at my lab. You saved my life that day. I'm sure you haven't forgotten.'

'Yes, sorry, of course. So much has happened since then. It all seems like a blur.'

'Was she the one?' he asked in an almost fatherly tone.

I didn't respond.

'I kind of thought she might be,' he continued. 'I remember how you looked at her. It wasn't the same as your other secretaries. She was great, right?'

'Yea, she was,' I admitted. 'But I didn't know how good she was until she was gone when it was too late.'

I sipped my coffee watching receding shadows slowly fill the valley with sunshine. It was a beautiful spring morning in the mountains. An overnight prickly white frost covered the trees and bushes with soft white glitter, slowly evaporating into the thin mountain air.

'I'm glad you're here Clarence,' I said. 'I know it had to be a long trip from Australia.'

'My obligation mate, you remember I was the one who called and asked you to come back. It seemed the least I could do.'

'You know I don't have many friends left in the company. You and Tim are probably my closest allies.'

'I think you underestimate your position, John. The board wants you back. Even if they may not have fully understood what you did for the company before you left, they certainly understand it now.'

'How bad is it?'

'It's bad and getting worse every day. Prices for all grades of sapphire are falling weekly. If the trend continues, my mining company will soon be operating at a loss. As it is now, our lab is the only operation that is keeping us out of bankruptcy. Ask Tim. I know he is considering the possibility of suspending operations at his mine this year. Our costs and his are higher than in developing countries. Lower prices are making it very difficult for us to operate at a profit.'

'How are the Distribution Houses doing?'

'They are still alright. They can cut costs. And because they are buying the finished stones for less, they can sell at lower prices and still make a profit. Bob Anderson's New York Distribution House is making plenty of money. Every time I talk to him about my mine, he simply tells me to cut costs. He either doesn't get it or he doesn't want to admit he understands.'

'And my company, how is my company doing?' I asked.

'I'm not really sure. Doing okay, I guess, but I don't really know.'

'I think I know. Bob and I had a brief conversation before I returned to the States. From what he implied, I have to assume it is in trouble.'

'Have you talked to him since?'

'No. I have purposely put that off. I wanted to talk to you and Tim first.'

'So why did you return?' Clarence finally asked the one question which had been on his mind. 'I thought after I talked to you in Belize, you were determined to stay away.'

'I had no choice,' I replied honestly, telling Clarence about the fire at my house in Belize and my meeting with Phillip. When I was done, our coffee was cold. I suggested we go inside, maybe talk some more later

'So, you really didn't want to return?'

'It was inevitable, Clarence,' I replied. 'Don't feel bad about calling me. I think I always knew I would have to come back someday. The bad guys just made my decision easier.'

'I'm glad you're back, John.'

'Thanks, Clarence.'

'You're welcome.'

'Can I assume we are in this thing together?'

'We are.'

10:10 A.M. JOHN

Derek threw some logs into the big stone fireplace of the great room.

Ilana was upstairs in the master bedroom at the time, when it was warm, sitting huddled under a blanket in a stuffed armchair, reading a magazine near her private roaring fire. No televisions were in the lodge, too far from any coverage. She had to be content with reading travel magazines. Dressed in another one of her new outfits, she wore a white turtleneck, jeans and a new gray and brown wool sweater.

A hearty meal of bacon, eggs, hash browns and toast was prepared by Tim. We gathered around the table after Tim said it was ready. Conversation was friendly and light-hearted. Everyone seemed to be getting comfortable. After breakfast, it was time for work. Clarence and Tim headed to one corner of the great room to talk mining. I decided to try to talk to Charlie; this time in more depth.

The lodge had a library off the great room under the master bedroom overlooking the stream. Shelves of books, including both medical and literary books, lined one wall. A couple of comfortable armchairs looked great for taking a nap. Tim's dad must have used the room as an office when he was at his cabin. A large desk was stacked with medical research journals. A doctor's work is never done, always more to learn.

Charlie stood without saying a word and followed me into the library. I shut the door and motioned for him to sit in one of the armchairs.

'Don't fall asleep now,' I warned him.

'Yea, these chairs look very comfortable,' he smiled.

'So, what has been happening in the real world?' I asked, assuming he knew more than I did. 'I have been pretty isolated in Belize.'

He nodded. 'Not much, really; all the players decided to stay off the radar screen after what happened in New York. I have tried to stay in touch with your case for obvious reasons, but nothing important has happened. The only significant development concerns Phillip. I've been tracking him. It seems he has established a working relationship with his friends in Thailand. He now runs a small business that sells gems from Thailand to U.S. jewelry manufacturers. From all reports, he is doing quite well. His sales are increasing monthly and he is making money. My sources tell me he is looking at new offices, but I don't know why. He doesn't need much room for what he does. All the real work is done in Thailand. His only job is to make sales calls to clients and mail a few small orders. A majority of the gems are sent directly from Thailand to his U.S. clients without going through his office.'

'Strictly a legitimate operation?' I asked.

'Nothing illegal in what he is doing.'

'I assume his contact in Thailand is the same person we met in New York.'

'Yes.'

I nodded.

'And he's the same guy who wants your stock?' Charlie stated for the record.

'Yes. Before I called you, Phillip forced me back into the same situation I was in before, sign over the stock or be killed. Except this time, you weren't outside my door.'

Charlie paused before saying, 'John, you know I'm sorry about what happened in New York. I thought you and Monica were in danger and... well... I guess I thought you needed to be rescued. Now I wonder.'

He was talking about the night that Monica had died in a hail of gunfire in a New York hotel room. The night that now lingers in my memory and nightmares. It was Charlie's CIA agents who started shooting first. They busted down the door to the hotel room, came in firing with a vengeance. That gave them an advantage in the chaos. But despite all their precautions and training, Monica was killed in the gunfire. The operation took only a few minutes, but in retrospect, the sounds of gunfire and screaming seemed to continue forever.

'Charlie, I think it's time we clear the air,' I suggested. 'I don't know what would have happened if you had not come in. And you don't either. It's possible they would have killed us as soon as I signed the papers.'

'I don't think so. I have reviewed the tapes of this night. I'm now convinced you would have walked out of that room alive if I hadn't stormed the room. I made a mistake, John. I'm sorry.'

'You have a tape?' I asked, ignoring his apology for a moment.

'Yes, the telephone call Monica made to me on her cell phone was taped. My phone automatically transfers all my calls to a central recording studio at Langley. The calls are kept for thirty days or longer if they are needed.'

'You have listened to this tape?'

'I have. The audio was technically enhanced so it could be understood.'

I was stunned. Although I had relived this night many times, it was always from memory. I couldn't imagine what it would be like to actually hear what was said.

Charlie read my thoughts. 'I'll never let you hear that tape, John. It wouldn't do you any good.'

'I understand. It's just... the idea of it is unsettling... Let me ask you something. Don't you have Phillip's voice on the tape?'

'Yes and no, he didn't say much and he was too far from where Monica was sitting to be heard clearly.'

'I see. I was just wondering if the tape could implicate him.'

'I understand. We tried, but our technicians could not make his voice clear enough to hold up in court. And since there are no other collaborating witnesses, it would be your word against his.'

I thought about what he said for a moment before letting it pass. Charlie and his guilt needed my attention first.

'Charlie,' I began. 'Real life happens at a fast pace. Decisions can't always wait. You made a decision you thought was right at the time. Remember how you saved me earlier in the day? I never questioned your decision then and I'm not questioning you now about what happened that night. It's over.'

A tear may have formed in his eye as I was talking. I wasn't sure because he quickly looked down and rubbed his eye.

'Charlie, I hope someday we can be friends.'

'I would like that too,' he replied after a pause.

'Okay, let's work on it.'

'Yes,' he agreed. 'But first I need to ask you to forgive me for what happened.'

I was lost for words. 'Charlie, what are you talking about? I already told you I don't question what you did.'

'John, what happened in that hotel room was not right. I was in charge. And it affected you more than it did me. So, I need to ask you to forgive me because I was responsible.'

None of this seemed like something that would come from Charlie. He was always so sure of himself. He must have spent a lot of time thinking about what happened that night. What he was asking was obviously very important to him.

'Stand up,' I demanded.

He did.

'Charlie, I'll forgive you if you will do something for me.'

'Sure,' he said looking me in the eye. 'What is it?'

'Forgive me for having her in that room that night.'

'But you could not have known.'

'Doesn't matter.'

He seemed to understand. He bowed his head. 'Yah... okay, John.'

I gave him a hug.

'I forgive you, Charlie.'

'And I forgive you too.' He returned the hug and we sat down again.

'Charlie, one more thing,' I continued. 'I have never admitted this to anyone... even her. But... I loved her, Charlie... more than I can ever know.'

'I know you did, John.'

'You did?'

'I knew.'

I wondered again why I had been so stupid to ignore something that was so obvious to everyone but me.

11:05 A.M. JOHN

From their viewpoint, behind some boulders high above the cabin, they clearly saw me walk toward one of the trucks.

There was no need to be in a hurry. I was not walking fast and it was a clear day with almost no wind. It was an easy shot. Slowly now, don't pull the trigger, just lightly squeeze. The bullet thudded into the door of the pickup, missing me by inches, making a small round hole in the metal. I heard the shot and saw the hole, but didn't immediately react; more surprised than understanding.

Charlie and I had just finished our meeting. I went outside to retrieve my briefcase which I had inadvertently left in the truck. Some notes I made while in Copper were inside, an agenda for today. I stuck the briefcase behind the passenger seat for the trip up the mountain and forgot to unload it along with our luggage when we arrived.

A second thud dented the pickup, abusing its smooth surface as I dove inside. Several more bullets shattered both the side and rear windows, glass exploding into the air. I closed my eyes as I crouched down behind the door. I didn't feel secure where I was, so I scrambled across the seat, opened the driver's door, and rolled head-first down on the ground in the snow behind the truck.

Charlie must have been watching from a window because I heard him yell. 'Get down and stay down, John. We'll handle this.'

Brad and Steve, Charlie's CIA buddies were already on the move, guns in hand.

A few more shots ricocheted off the gravel near where I lay behind the truck.

Tim and Clarence came outside when they heard Charlie. He immediately started yelling at them to get back inside. Tim grabbed his arm, fell to his knees, the sleeve of his shirt seeping blood. Clarence crawled over to help get Tim back inside the open door.

Brad threw an automatic rifle to Charlie who was standing against a wall behind a corner of the lodge, trying to see where the shots were coming from. When a shot shattered a window near where Charlie stood, he turned away in time to avoid being hit by flying glass. Shooting back in anger, he aimed up the rock hill on the other side of the stream.

'Should we go after them,' Brad asked Charlie, sounding almost calm like this was something he did every day.

'Get going,' Charlie ordered decisively before shooting another round up the hill as incoming bullets continued to thud into the walls of the lodge. A loud explosion blew out a window, wood splinters flying. Everyone ducked behind whatever shelter they could find. Brad and Steve headed for the back of the lodge.

From where I crouched behind the truck, I assumed the shooters were near the top of the hill behind some boulders. They had a perfect spot to view the lodge. The pickup truck shielded me, but I was stuck where I was. I couldn't get back to the lodge without becoming a moving target, and that did not seem like a good option.

A flash of light reflected off a gun barrel up the slope when a man stood up from behind one of the boulders and fired three more shots into my pick-up truck, blowing out one of the tires as I covered my head.

11:15 A.M. BRAD

'Damn,' Brad said to himself. It's not going to be easy to get to those guys.

Using hand signals, Brad silently pointed in the direction he thought the shots were coming from. His buddy Steve nodded in agreement.

If the shooters were pros, Brad thought, they could sit up on those rocks for a long time, taking potshots at the lodge. The rocks offered them not only a great view but also perfect protection from returning fire. Either these guys were good or they had been simply lucky. It was time to find out. Brad knew he would have to take some chances to flush them.

He rested for a moment against the back exterior of the lodge, trying to think through his next moves. Hopefully, he and Steve had more firepower to their advantage. He didn't think the guys in the rocks had seen him yet. That should give him the time he needed to cover a short open distance from the back of the lodge to the nearest boulders at the bottom of the hill. It would not be an easy run in the snow and his route would take him over the ice-covered stream. He wasn't sure the ice would hold him, but the stream didn't look too deep. He guessed he would find out soon enough.

Steve was crouching above him on a deck outside one of the bedrooms.

'You ready?' Brad signaled.

'When you are.' Steve nodded while mouthing the words.

Brad took a deep breath.

Steve fired a heavy volume of lead up the hill as a rifle was raised from behind a rock. Brad immediately dug for the hill, running low and hard, never looking up, hoping to hear nothing but Steve's gun behind him.

Running was harder than he had calculated, the snow deeper, slippery, slushy, difficult to get traction. He breathed and ran, hearing a shot fired from the hill. They must have seen him. Water splashed under his boots as he ran into the stream, slipping on breaking ice, rolling and sliding into the cold, wet water, scraping his knee. He fought to regain his balance. Another shot sounded. He heard Steve firing nonstop behind him. Lead splashed in the snow and ice around him. He had to wade through the stream, water deep, finally getting to the other side without being hit. He lunged the last few yards, sliding in the snow, banging his head as he slid behind a boulder for shelter.

Breathing hard, fearing pain would tell him he had been hit. He had been shot before. It was no fun. It hurt like hell. But he felt nothing except cold and wet. His face was bruised and icy water saturated his now totally soaked clothes to his skin. His knee ached from the fall, but no major pain. He had not been shot. Wiping off his gun, he checked the magazine. He was cold. He was angry. He had almost been killed. He was now more determined than ever to get these guys.

Steve fired another volley as the sound of an automatic rifle came from the direction of the lodge. Brad assumed Charlie was trying to cover him.

Crawling around the boulder, he began a slow climb up the hill, moving from one boulder to another, staying out of the line of fire from the men above him. It was difficult work. The hill was steep. Wet slippery snow made his going rough. Breathing hard, boots sliding and digging for grip, his hands now bleeding from small cuts holding the ice-cold, sharp-edged rocks. Charlie and Steve could be heard firing random volleys to cover his slow progress. Sporadic shots continued to come from above. He found a level spot, halfway up the hill where he could rest for a moment. After firing a few shots just because they were making him mad, he sat down again.

Some yelling could be heard from the guys above him. His knee hurt like hell and climbing didn't make it any better. He was cold and wet from falling in the stream. Okay, he knew he should have dressed warmer, but he hadn't in his haste to get outside. He had just grabbed his gun and ran. Now he shivered even as he sweated from his climb. Time to get this over with; he took another deep breath and continued climbing, holding his gun with one hand, trying to find a grip on the rocks with the other hand to maintain balance. His fingers began to turn red and numb from rock cuts and cold. He dug his boots into the hillside, fighting for each step, worrying less and less about the guys above him and more about not falling.

He was not an experienced climber. He was going too fast for the steep terrain. He made a mistake and started to slip. Reaching for a grip with his bare hand, touching nothing but sheer, hard rock wall, nothing to hold. Fingers pressed against the abrasive rock, hoping for a grip, tearing his flesh; he began to slide down the coarse surface. Fearing he could not stop, an open drop-off loomed below. Screaming inwardly at himself for his stupidity, he should have been more careful. Now he was probably going to die because he had been dumb. Falling, he began to pick up speed with nothing to slow his descent down the steep slope. Hard rocks below waited for him.

His boot caught, dug into a narrow ledge, wavered, knees bent, fingers grasping for a grip, he held on, tipping on the edge of balance, finally resting, body flat against the hard wall, taking deep breaths of relief as a shot bounced off rocks near where his face was pressed against the cold stone.

That was close, too close. He needed to be more careful. Looking up the hill, he selected an alternate route, which would take longer but appeared to offer more shelter and easier footing. Staying low, pressed against the rock wall, he accomplished a controlled slide down the face of the rock to a flat area behind a large boulder. From there, he started up the hill again, his new route taking him around, behind, and above the shooters. Brad made steady progress, ignoring his badly scraped knee, breathing hard in the thin mountain air, he climbed steadily without resting. He knew he was in great shape, but this climb was more difficult than he imagined. He wasn't cold anymore, just mad and sweating from exertion. His gun felt numb in his hand, but he didn't notice, using it sometimes as a crutch.

The guys above him must have lost track of him, because nobody was shooting at him. He climbed carefully now, fully aware he did not want to fall again, each breath, each step bringing him closer to his goal. When he finally thought he was above and behind their position, he glanced slowly around a rock.

Three men were standing on a ledge behind some boulders. They had a perfect view of the lodge. A couple of whiskey bottles lay in the snow at their feet. Occasionally they stood up and fired, then sat down to reload or take another swig of whiskey, laughing, having fun.

Brad checked his gun. Loading a dry magazine in the chamber, he wiped his gun and cleaned his hands on his pants, getting as much dirt and blood off his fingers as possible.

When he was ready, he stood to see one of the men wiring together what appeared to be sticks of dynamite. The man twisted fuses in place as Brad watched in amazement. He couldn't let the guy throw those sticks at the lodge. The dynamite could do some serious damage

Carefully taking aim, he pulled the trigger. Bullets tore holes in the man's plaid shirt when he stood to throw the explosives. Immediately, he fell in agony. His throw aborted, the dynamite exploding harmlessly halfway down the hill while the man thrashed in the snow, slowly bleeding to death.

His buddies watched him die. Wide-eyed, surprised, and confused, they ran.

Brad fired.

A bullet caught a second guy in the back of his knee. He fell hard bouncing off a boulder, gashing his face. Several more bullets quickly slashed into his back and he was dead before he hit the ground. The third man turned to see his buddy fall, raising his gun in surrender as bursts of lead penetrated his body, turning his face into a gruesome death mask of mangled blood and flesh.

Where he fell over on his back, dead in the cold snow, warm red blood stained the clean white, crystals of virgin snow into a soft pink death shroud around the man's brutalized skull.

12:45 P.M. JOHN

A trail of smeared blood tracked across the bed of the pickup truck where the bodies of the shooters had been placed.

Their limbs layed in odd uncomfortable angles to their bodies on the cold hard metal. Their rifles had been placed alongside the bodies as if they were standing at attention. These symbols of their owner's power were now nothing more than a testament to their cause of death. The two who still had eyes were closed; their mouths open, gaping as if they were still screaming. The third body had no eyes, no mouth, no face, just a gruesome red death mask of torn flesh and bone.

I turned away in disgust.

Tim identified two of the men, the two who still had faces. They had both worked for him at the mine off and on. Part-timers he called them. Everyone knew just about everyone else around this part of the country. He thought he had a good idea who the third man was, one of their drinking buddies, but he wasn't sure.

After killing the men, Brad waved to Steve from the top of the hill. Steve was already running for the base of the hill at the time. Hearing the sound of Brad's gun, he immediately ran to back up Brad. He stopped only after Brad signaled it was over.

We waited inside the lodge. Charlie wouldn't let anyone outside until he was positive the crisis had passed. He stood guard by the door with his gun in case more attackers were in the area. When it was determined the danger had passed, he and Tim drove the pickup truck which was not damaged around the backside of the hill, parking the truck next to the shooter's truck. Then both trucks were driven down the hill and parked next to the lodge.

Tim figured someone must have hired the men to attack us. He didn't think they did it on their own accord. I suggested Phillip, but this was a guess, only because Phillip had spent a fair amount of time in Copper. He had friends in town. He may have been told we were here. It was a small town. People talked. Tim thought it was a possibility. Charlie cautioned us; and said we were speculating. He only worked with cold hard facts.

I wondered if these men were hired to kill us or simply harass us; take a few shots, throw some harmless dynamite, and then return to town like a bunch of outlaw cowboys, whooping and drinking. But it didn't matter now. They were dead. Their fatal mistake was not doing their homework. No one told them they were up against a couple of CIA agents with military training. It seemed a waste.

Charlie used his satellite telephone to call Langley. From what I could decipher from his one-sided conversation, Langley agreed to notify the Salt Lake City office of the FBI. Charlie asked for a helicopter to retrieve the bodies so they could be identified.

I went inside the cabin while he was still talking on the phone. I had seen and heard enough. The sunshine and clear mountain air was now spoiled. Everything suddenly looked gray in a haze of frozen death. Disgusted, I wondered if this was worth it. How many more people had to die before this was over? I seemed to be marching in time to a dirge of death. Not knowing when it would happen, just knowing the dreadful music would start playing again soon, signaling death was walking in my footsteps.

Ilana stayed inside the cabin. She didn't want to see the dead men and I couldn't blame her. When I went to find her, she was sitting by the fire in the great room, curled up in a fetal position, softly crying. This was all much too much for her; her first time away from home, then the shooting in Charlottesville, and now this.

Tim entered the room. When he saw Ilana crying, he came over to us.

'I have sedatives in the bathroom,' he suggested. 'My dad always keeps medicine in the cabin. Would you like me to get one for her?'

'Want something to help you calm down?' I asked her quietly.

She looked at us with her big brown eyes; wiped her face with her hand and said, 'No thank you, Tim. I will be fine.' She then turned her back to us and stood by the fire feeling its warmth, not wanting us to see her tears.

Cold mountain air began to creep into every warm corner of the lodge, flowing in through the broken windows. Splinters of wood and glass lay scattered around the interior. A bloodstain could be seen drying on the front porch where Tim had been wounded. Just a minor cut he said.

'You sure you're okay?' I asked Ilana after Tim walked away.

'I'm fine,' she said with conviction.

Charlie covered the bodies and moved the dead men's pickup down the road. Nobody wanted the bodies near the cabin. An FBI helicopter was due late afternoon. Brad was scheduled to go with the helicopter. He would make a full report on the shootings before returning.

Brad and Steve were outside talking and grinning. They were our conquering heroes. I was thankful for their courage. They had protected us. But something was lost in the exchange.

Charlie told us he and Steve would stay with us for protection. The Montana State Police had been called and asked to keep an eye on roads leading to the two-track up to the cabin. Charlie assured us we were safe.

What remained of the morning was spent cleaning and fixing windows with duct tape and plywood Tim found in a storage area. It wasn't pretty, but it kept the cold out. Tim called his office in Copper and asked them to schedule carpenters to replace the broken windows. For now, our make-shift repairs would have to be sufficent.

Speaking of make-shift repairs, Tim refused to go into town to get stitches in his arm. He claimed to have sustained far worse injuries working at his mine. He said, if he went to a hospital every time, he had a minor cut, he would never get anything done. Clarence put a bandage on his arm. The bullet wound was a clean cut which didn't penetrate his arm. Tim put on a different shirt and helped with repairs, only occasionally wincing in pain.

After a late lunch, I pulled Charlie aside.

'I'm not sure I made the right choice,' I said to him.

'Why, because of what happened?' Charlie asked.

'Men are dead, Charlie. Could have been you and me.'

'John, you're in a war. People die in wars.'

'Doesn't have to be. I can sign and the war is over.'

'Give up.'

'Yea, just give up.'

'Walk away, walk away from your friends, your miners, your dead girlfriend.'

'Yea, walk away before somebody else gets killed.'

'And the consequences, what about the consequences?'

'What about them?'

'John, everything has consequences. Your war has plenty- jobs, money, power, control, all the normal consequences. Sure, you can walk away, but you cannot ignore the consequences.'

I paused. 'Charlie, be honest with me. Do you really think you can protect me?'

'I will not lie to you, John. It's going to be difficult. If someone is determined to kill you, there are a thousand ways to do it. It is much easier to kill someone than to keep them alive.'

'Thanks for the optimistic outlook.'

'John, I'm trying to be honest with you.'

'I appreciate that.'

'So, do you want to continue?' He looked me in the eye. 'It's your choice.'

'Not really...but I will.'

'What are your plans?' he asked.

'Let me talk to Tim and Clarence next. You and I can talk again later.'

I paused, reconsidering. 'No, let's all talk together. I think you are as much a part of this now, as they are.

Why don't I get everyone together and let's make some hard decisions?'

10:45 P.M. JOHN

The sun had disappeared hours ago.

It was now pitch black outside the glass windows of the lodge.

Tim, Clarence, Charles, and I spent most of the day planning. In order to revive my company, I needed to regain control which meant becoming the CEO again. Charley was included in every aspect of our talks because security was an integral element of the equation. Charlie was articulate and helpful and told us what we needed to do to stay alive and what we needed to avoid. Our plans were based on his advice.

As we talked, I began to think we could actually make it happen. Of course, none of this mattered if I couldn't get the company back on track. That was step two. Step three was to go after the guys who were trying to kill me.

Step three was what motivated Charlie.

A fire was burning quietly in our bedroom when I entered at the end of the day. Ilana was sitting near the fireplace curled up in a big, overstuffed armchair. A book she had found in the library was in her lap. She looked good. She was fast becoming the one beautiful constant in my eyes. I hoped she was feeling better after the morning's gruesome events, but I didn't know. Unfortunately, my meetings occupied my time well into the evening. Apart from sharing a dinner that she helped prepare, I spent almost no time with her. But from what I observed at dinner, she seemed to be okay.

After pulling an armchair close to her, I took her feet on my lap and began to gently massage them. She put her book down and rested her head on the back of her chair.

'What have you been doing?' she asked.

'Making plans.'

'What are you planning?'

'To get my old job back.'

I assumed she knew what this meant. I had told her many stories from my former life and work. They had helped us pass the time when we were in Belize. She absorbed everything I told her. Occasionally she even corrected me when I made a mistake; some wrong detail in my story, something I had previously told her. She always amazed me with her memory.

'Does this mean we will be returning to Charlottesville?' she asked.

'Yes, I talked to Helen today. My office is being cleaned and repaired. We should be able to return in a few days.

'Will we be safe?'

'I wish I could tell you we will be perfectly safe, Ilana. But I can't. Charlie will assign men to stay with us. They will help, but we will be in danger.'

I continued to rub her feet. 'If you want to return to Belize, I will pay for everything.'

'No, I think I want to be with you, John' she replied without hesitation.

'You sure?'

She gave me the look women sometimes give, the look which begs the question; why are men so stupid?

'How will you get your job back?' she asked.

'I will ask the board to give it to me. It will take a vote to decide. However, I have more stock than anyone else and votes for issues, such as who is going to run the company, are based on stock ownership. Clarence will vote for me and so will Tim. I only need a few other directors to vote for me and I will be the CEO again.'

'Do you think you will get the votes you need?'

'Yes,' I replied, surprised at her question. It was clear she understood. I decided I needed to quit underestimating this woman. She probably understood far more than I realized.

'When will this happen?' she asked.

'The next quarterly board meeting is coming soon. Bob Anderson, the current CEO will call a meeting.'

'Does he know you want his job?'

'No.'

'Will he vote for you?'

'I don't know. It's possible he will. But it is also possible he will want to keep his job. He gets paid to do it, a lot of money. So, I don't really know what he will do. But even if he doesn't vote for me, I'm not sure it will matter. Tim and Clarence think the board will support me.'

'What will you do?'

'You mean after I get my job back?'

'Yes.'

'I will try to make the company healthy again.'

'Can you do that?'

'I don't know. It will be difficult.'

'Do you really want to do this, John?'

'I don't know if I have a choice anymore.'

She pondered my response for a moment before asking, 'Couldn't we just return to Belize?'

'Ilana, my enemies will find us in Belize as they found us here today. And they will try to kill me.'

She sat in silence for a moment. 'So nowhere is safe?'

'Nowhere.'

'What can I do to help?' she asked, acknowledging what we both knew to be true.

'I will need you to be strong and alert to danger.'

She smiled knowingly and asked, 'Are we ever returning to Belize, John?'

'As soon as this is all over, we will go to Belize to live.'

She jumped into my lap and gave me a big hug. It was the best thing that happened all day. As I sat with her in my arms, I hoped I wasn't lying to her. I didn't think I was. I really did want to return to Belize. And just to make it official, I made a mental note to have Helen call the attorney for the estate I had been renting in Belize. I would try to buy the land.

The house had burned, but I could have it rebuilt.

WEDNESDAY, JUNE 10, 5:10 A.M. JOHN

We had decided to leave in the morning.

Collectively we made this decision late last night. No one wanted to stay. The joy was gone. Our time in the mountains was spoiled by an ugly tragedy.

Ilana had slept poorly. No better than I. We both tossed and turned. Early in the morning, I suggested we get out of bed. It was before sunrise. I needed to get up even if she didn't. Every time I closed my eyes, I saw splinters of glass flying through the air or dead uncomfortable bodies lying in the back of a pickup truck with half their faces blown off.

It was about five in the morning.

After I put a few logs on the fire to warm the room, Ilana went into the bathroom to take a shower. I quietly walked down to the kitchen to make some coffee. A couple of bagels were sitting on the counter in a plastic bag. I put one of them in the toaster and I was waiting for it to pop when Tim walked in.

'Couldn't sleep?' he asked.

'No.'

'Me either.'

'Want some coffee?'

'Sure.'

I poured a couple of cups and gave one to Tim. The hot liquid tasted good in the cool morning air.

'So why did you decide to work your mine this year?' I asked him. 'Clarence told me you were going ahead. Won't it be tough to make a profit given current prices for rough.'

'Oh, you know me, John. I'm an optimistic person. Besides, the preliminary borings indicate we will be working in a very productive area of the valley this summer. If the percentage of sapphires per cubic yard turns out to be as high as I hope, we might be able to eke out a profit. That depends, of course, on the prices stabilizing... If they fall, we're in trouble. But it's worth the gamble. A lot of people depend on the mine for their income. I would be letting them down if I didn't try.'

'I see.'

'Besides, you're back.'

'I can't promise you anything. You know that.'

'I know, but I told you, I'm an optimistic person,' he smiled.

I sipped my coffee without comment.

'Say, why don't you come to my office when we get into town?' he suggested. 'The first shipment of rough should be in by the time we return.'

'Why not?' I replied. 'My apartment in Charlottesville won't be ready for a couple of days. There's no need to rush back to Virginia.'

11:20 A.M. JOHN

We packed after breakfast for the drive down the mountain.

Clarence decided to travel to New York as long as he was in the States. Said he had business in the Big Apple. He planned to stop at Bob's office but promised not to mention he had seen me.

Charlie went with Clarence; said he was anxious to get back to work. They took the good truck to catch an early flight out of Copper; the truck which wasn't full of bullet holes. We had to wait for the blown tire on the other truck to be changed and the windows taped. It took time and didn't look too good when Tim was done, but good enough to get us down the mountain. We switched trucks at Tim's house for our drive into Copper.

Charlie' satellite phone was used to make travel arrangements. I told him not to worry about Ilana and me. My apartment wouldn't be ready for a few days, and I wanted to spend time with Tim. Steve was assigned to stay with us as a precaution.

Tim's office sat near the top of a hill overlooking the town. The town of Copper had flourished when copper mining was at its peak. But only a few small mines were operating now, most were shut down. Some of the old mines were environmental super sites, soured by mercury pollutants in the ground water. I don't think anyone really knew what to do with them. A few old timers sat around town, waiting for the mines to reopen, hoping the good old days would reappear. But that probably wasn't going to happen any time soon.

Near the top of the road to Tim's office, our truck turned onto a gravel driveway leading to his building. Previously a copper mining office, the weathered gray corrugated metal on his building looked old and tired, but inside it had been completely renovated with newly painted walls and restored flooring. The top two floors were offices. The bottom floors for used for sorting and shipping rough sapphires. We went immediately to a lower level after arriving. Tim was anxious to see the first stones from the mining season.

A large white walled room with clean vinyl floors greeted our arrival. Rows of tables functioned as workstations. I introduced Ilana to an employee I knew who had been with Tim's company from the beginning. Janice was her name.

After spreading a quantity of rough stones on a clear glass tabletop, 'Look carefully,' Janice said to Ilana. 'Do you see color in any of these stones?'

Bright light from florescent bulbs below the translucent tabletop allowed Ilana to see a hint of color in the dull rough surface of a few stones. She picked up one stone, different from the others which displayed a weak reddish color. Its surface was dull and smooth from years of flowing down mountain streams. Presently it exhibited very little to give away its potential beauty, but when cut and polished its gleaming facets would reflect light in a myriad of flashing colors.

I explained to Ilana that sapphires are naturally occurring crystals. Their color depended on trace elements which were infused in the stones when they were formed deep in the earth. Most sapphires are thought to be blue. But purple, green, yellow, and orange are also common colors found in sapphires. Sapphires which have a deep red color are called rubies.

'You probably have a pink sapphire in your hand,' I said to her. "It will be a beautiful natural gemstone after cutting.'

'You have a good eye,' Janice agreed. 'Would you like to help me for a while?'

Ilana looked at me. 'Can I?'

'Sure, I'll be in Tim's office. Come and find us when you get tired.'

Tim was reading the initial mine reports when I found him in his office.

'How does it look?' I asked.

'Hopeful,' he replied. 'It's too early to know for sure, but I think we might be okay.'

CHARLOTTESVILLE VIRGINIA, FRIDAY, JUNE 12, 1:35 P.M. JOHN

I dragged Ilana's second set of new luggage into my ruined apartment past workers busy filling bullet holes in the walls.

The place smelled of fresh paint and wall plaster and I didn't know how comfortable I would be living with the smell and the mess. But I didn't want to stay in a hotel if I could help it.

We spent the previous day in Copper with Tim and Sarah. It felt good to be with them. Sometime in the morning, I got a call from Helen. She told me about a memorial service for Arny. Said it would be held on Saturday. At first, I wasn't sure I wanted to go, but I knew I owed him. And when Helen said she had postponed the service hoping I could attend, I called Al and asked him if he could fly us to Charlottesville in time. Originally, I had planned to stay in Copper for a few more days, wait for my apartment to be fully repaired, but I didn't want miss Arny's service.

Charlie called and asked if his guys could use Arny's old apartment. He said it was the best place for them while they kept us under twenty-four-hour surveillance, courtesy of the CIA. So, having them in Arny's place was not my idea, but Charlie had asked. And when he reminded me he had promised to take care of me, but only if I was willing to listen to him. If not, he couldn't help me. I agreed even though I knew it was going to be tough having someone besides Arny living next door, but I had no choice. I had to do what Charlie told me to do.

Arny's apartment had been thoroughly cleaned when I went in to inspect it. It looked and smelled sterile, empty rooms and newly painted white walls. All of Arny's memorabilia, like his jazz records and baseball trivia had been hauled away. I didn't like it. I wanted it as it was before. But then, I wanted Arny alive and well. And he wasn't coming back.

It was time to let him go.

SATURDAY, JUNE 13, 2:25 P.M. JOHN

The day of Arny's funeral was a warm, blue, sky day with a light breeze.

I hoped the weather was a good sign, thinking sunshine might make his service feel less depressing. But I knew the weather would have made no difference to Arny. He was never one to let anything get him down. Life for him held too much joy to linger over something as trivial as the color of the sky.

The service was held at a local, predominately black Baptist church. It was his church. The minister was his friend. We drove to the church in the company limo, an old Cadillac which was used primarily to ferry clients from the airport to my office. It had to be washed first because it had been parked in the garage unused for months. It was the last moveable relic from my old company still residing in Charlottesville. Apparently, the car was not fancy enough for New York City. Helen said Bob didn't want it. I personally couldn't remember the last time I sat in it. I think I got it from Bob after he purchased a new one.

Steve multi tasked, chauffeured the car while being our bodyguard. Everyone fit comfortably inside. Ilana, Helen, and Charlie came with me. Helen had insisted on coming despite her assumed relationship with Arny, more a lifelong combatant than a friend. However, apparently their constant bickering was more congenial than it appeared on the surface. She said she would miss him. And she was not the only one. Something I would discover later at his church.

Charlie drove in from Washington for the service. I didn't know why. Charlie didn't really know Arny very well. Yet he said he wanted to go. Probably had something to do with Monica telling him stories about Arny. She and Arny were good friends before her death. Perhaps Charlie came to represent her.

Ilana insisted on driving into town early in the morning to buy a new, demurely colored dress. I assumed she was using his funeral as an excuse to buy one more dress, but I was wrong. The funeral was a much more elaborate affair than I anticipated. She suggested I wear a black suit and a sedately colored tie which she found in my closet. The suit had been purchased for formal occasions and sat in my closet unused ever since. Initially, I resisted wearing it, but finally agreed to make her happy.

Lines of gleaming and freshly washed cars were parked at the church when we arrived, more cars than I expected. As I walked toward the church from the parking lot, I was glad I had listened to my wardrobe expert. It was obvious Ilana knew more about proper funeral attire than did I.

The church was filled with friends of Arny, mostly African Americans. The men were dressed in elegant attire which would have put to shame a gathering of U.S. senators; pinstriped suits, pockets stuffed with silk handkerchiefs and matching-colored ties. The ladies were equally adorned in richly colored flowing dresses and stylish hats.

The church had a white wood exterior with a contrasting black roof and a steeple with a cross. It was a simple structure, typical of southern Baptist churches. It occupied a hill overlooking the town of Charlottesville, located near the University of Virginia. Polished black doors greeted us at its entrance. Inside were rows of red velvet cushions covering glossy hardwood, pews. We found a seat near the rear of the church and waited for the service to begin. I was amazed at how many people continued to stream down the center aisle. I didn't think Arny had this many friends. Some turned and nodded to me as they walked down the aisle. I recognized a few of his poker buddies who had visited his apartment. They knew who I was, but then, that probably wasn't too difficult. Only a few white people were in the church.

All this made me slightly uncomfortable. The story of the shooting had made headlines in the local paper. Helen showed me the articles in the morning. Everyone knew how Arny died. I wondered if any of his friends blamed me for his death.

Sunshine streaked in through the brightly colored, stained-glass windows of the church, shedding a soft light over the proceedings. A simple wood podium adorned with a cross stood in the middle of an elevated red-carpet platform at the front of the church. Choir members in gold robes marched silently into rows of elevated pews directly behind the preacher's podium. The service began with the choir singing a haunting old spiritual as the preacher walked up to the podium. Distinguished by a head of curly white hair and a neatly trimmed beard in stark contrast to his dark skin; the preacher was a tall dominating figure, looming over the podium in a flowing black robe.

I had hoped to make it through Arny's service without showing emotion. I remembered Monica's funeral. I didn't want a repeat of that performance. But as the choir softy sang the old familiar spiritual, I began to break down. Reaching for Ilana's hand for comfort, I hoped Charlie didn't notice my pathetic gesture. He was sitting on the other side of Ilana. Steve sat next to me with Helen on his side.

The preacher began with a simple reading of David's psalm, 'The Lord is my Shepard. I shall not want...' Spoken with a booming bass voice, the words of the Psalm filled every silent corner of the church, followed by the choir softly singing an old spiritual which began with the words, 'Were you there when they nailed him to the cross...'

As I listened, tears formed slowly in the corners of my eyes. I remembered all the good times I had with Arny, and I thanked God for allowing me into this man's life. It was time I did not deserve; a gift I now realized was precious. Problem was, Arny didn't need to die. I asked God why. But then I questioned why I was asking. I was the person who had brought this tragedy to Arny, not God. God didn't need to answer me. I needed to answer to Arny. Bitter silent tears drifted through my anxious mind and down my cheeks as I listened half-heartedly to the preacher recite his expected eulogy, speaking of Arny's devotion to his church and his great faith in the Lord.

I couldn't help wondering as I listened. If ever Arny needed God, he needed Him the day he died, needed His angels looking out for him when bullets headed his way. But they were not there to save him, to shield his fragile body from pain, from being torn apart by hard metal traveling at great speed.

While I sat in his church surrounded by Arny's friends, I thought about the life that most of the people in this church had lived; in a world seemingly devoid of God, a world where lynching was ignored by the local law establishments; a world of forced separation, a world consumed by widespread racial hatred and envy, a world without pity. And yet, Arny and his friends had never lost their faith. They attended this church despite their problems, attended almost every Sunday. So, what was I missing? What did these people know which I did not?

I never had to ask Arny where he went on Sunday morning because he always made a point of telling me, often joking he was off to meet his Maker. When he suggested I should join him, I told him I wasn't quite ready to meet my Maker, not just yet.

Arny was gone now to meet his Maker. And I imagined God smiling, sharing a joke with Arny in heaven. Was it wrong to think of Arny joking with God? I didn't think so. Heaven would not be heaven for Arny without a joke.

When the preacher finished his eulogy, he opened the podium to anyone who wanted say a few words about their friend Arny. Slowly and in an orderly fashion, one after another, men and women told stories of how Arny had touched their lives. I listened amazed at how many people had known and loved this man. Some told funny stories and the congregation laughed. Others told sad stories in silence. Almost everyone from the poorest to the best dressed in the church had a story to tell. As I listened, I wondered how many people would attend my funeral. Probably not more than a handful, maybe no one. And what would people say about me at my funeral? Would they say something flattering, or would they simply be silent, sit in the pews and say nothing.

Ilana poked me in the side. 'Aren't you going to get up and say something?' she whispered in my ear.

I didn't know how to tell her that self-conscious Dutchmen do not go in for public displays of emotion. We are more likely to sit and silently stew in our self-absorbed soup of guilty emotions.

She poked me again.

Then Charlie turned and glanced at me.

I assumed Charlie, who was black, also understood the culture of this church. He too expected me to say something.

The church became awkwardly silent as I stewed. The preacher's eyes searched the room for anyone else who wanted to contribute. I tried to hide, but finally stood up, not really knowing what I was going to say, just knowing I had to say something. Walking the long aisle in the middle of the church, the congregation turned to me as I looked straight ahead as if I was in a trance, which I was.

The preacher stepped aside, leaving the podium empty for me.

A sea of black faces turned expectantly to me when I looked around, hesitating... unsure... Finally, turning to the choir director who was sitting behind me, I asked. 'Could you have the choir softly sing 'Amazing Grace?'

The director nodded.

I then turned to the audience, speaking into the microphone. 'Words alone cannot tell you how much this man meant to me. So instead of listening to me talk about my friend Arny, please allow the words and melody of this song express the essence of his life. He loved this old song. I often heard it whisper on the wind from his apartment at night. As you listen, please take a moment to remember this man in his life, not his death. He lived a good life, a life filled with laughter and song... He was my friend and my time with him was a gift.... I can't tell you how sorry I am that his life ended prematurely... And I am truly sorry for the part I played in his death... For that... please forgive me.'

Then I shut up.

The director whispered the name of the song to the choir and the organist. Slowly, almost mournfully the choir began to sing. 'A-maz-ing Grace... how sweet...the sound... that saved a wretch... like me...'

I stood at the podium for a moment, listening to the choir sing behind me, before slowly walking the middle aisle while the sweet melody of the Arny's song filled the church. I didn't stop, didn't return to my pew. Continued walking until I got to the door at the rear of the church and went outside. I couldn't stay in his church any longer.

A hot sun beat on my black suit as I waited alone in the parking lot, leaning against the limo, becoming uncomfortably warm.

I was only vaguely aware of the elements of my existence, too absorbed in a tangle of conflicting emotions whirling through my mind. I couldn't help but wonder. Do we all have times in our lives when we do not have a clue about what to do? Is being alive in this complex world so overwhelming at times, so crushing that we can become temporarily paralyzed? Even someone like me, someone who attempts to carefully craft every single move in life. Even for me, moments exist when not one rational thought crosses my mind.

After few minutes, Charlie arrived and stood beside me without saying a word.

While we waited by the limo for the others to return, a procession of Arny's friends came to shake my hand. Some of his buddies held my hand for a moment, then smiled and walked away without saying a word.

I struggled to hold my tears inside.

7:15 P.M. JOHN

Light faded in the still evening, casting shadows of tall oaks over a small, seldomly used deck outside my den; visibly sheltering it from the outside world.

I felt comfortable and secure behind the trees in the dimming sunlight even though I knew Charlie wouldn't like it. I didn't care. I needed to be away from the clatter of people in Arny's old apartment.

It had been a long day.

Arny's funeral service was difficult. A dull headache throbbed in my temples ever since returning to my apartment, accompanied by a sad swathe of memories hiding in the corners of my mind. I could feel them waiting like a cat in a forest, waiting for a chance to strike, sink its teeth into the veins of my neck, spread the scent of death through my mind, reeling into a deep depression. I didn't need that, couldn't afford it. I had a job to do.

I had to get away from Arny's apartment, away from everything which reminded me of him. I chose the deck because it was one of only a few places in my apartment which wasn't a mess.

The work of rebuilding was still in progress. Bullet holes had been filled. New glass installed in some of the windows and the kitchen flooring replaced where it was impossible to remove blood stains. Cabinets and appliances were scheduled to be delivered on Monday. Most of my old furniture had been hauled away, too brutalized to be repaired. It was decided to start over. Anything still useable had been shoved off to one side and covered with sheets. The rest went to the dump. Ilana and I had to sleep in the guest bedroom. It was one of only a few rooms in the apartment which had not been damaged.

Charlie bought Chinese for dinner, set up in Arny's apartment. Being there was difficult for me. Everything seemed oddly uncomfortable, out of place. I kept expecting to see Arny's smiling face walk in the door at any time. But he was absent, and I missed him. There is no other way to say it. I missed him. I wanted him back. I wanted to see his smile. I wanted to hear his stupid jokes. I wanted my friend.

Some of his relatives introduced themselves to me after his funeral. It was the first time I had ever met them. To my knowledge he had not been in contact with them for a very long time. Perhaps his family was not on the best of terms. They didn't say, but the truth was they were very friendly. They thanked me for being a good friend to Arny. Inheritance was not mentioned. I assumed they thought it was unlikely. Helen thankfully intervened after a couple of minutes; took them to one side and told them they could have his possessions if they wanted. Late in the afternoon after his funeral, they came and took everything.

I kept only one item from his apartment which I instructed Helen to save for me. It was a picture of an old Indian Chief in full headdress. Arny had purchased it at an art gallery in town. I wanted it because the old chief in the painting reminded me of him in a way, defiant and undefeated by life.

His picture and some of my artwork were currently in storage in the main office vault. Actually, it would be more accurate to say the vault contained only the artwork which had not been trashed in the shooting. All the other artworks had been discarded along with the rest of the junk.

His vast record collection had been given to his club along with half of his savings as an endowment. The other half of his money went to The United Negro College Fund. It was a cause he supported in the past. Everything was done as his will stipulated.

Arny's place looked completely different now. New furniture and other household items had been purchased. This was so Charlie's men would have a place to live. I should have been grateful to Charlie for offering to help. I knew it made Ilana feel more secure. But having CIA guys living next door made me uncomfortable. I wondered if I would ever have my old life back. Or at a minimum, an existence which approximated a normal life.

I sipped wine while watching the sun retreat behind the oak trees. Ilana found me eventually. We didn't talk at first, just sat and listened to sounds in the woods. It was as if both of us were trying to find a way to adjust to our new existence.

'You okay?' I finally asked her.

'Yes, I'm okay. You will see. I am a strong woman.' She smiled at me.

In a way I didn't doubt her. She seemed more resilient than me. She had laughed and joked with Charlie and the others at dinner while I had been a mute observer. Helen also ate with us. She had done most of the work preparing for the funeral. It seemed only right to have her share a meal with us. She and Ilana were becoming friends. This was not true with Monica. I think because Helen was always a little resentful of Monica. I didn't sense the same attitude towards Ilana. Helen was taking an interest in her, more like a mother than as a friend. Helen must have realized Ilana needed someone in her life, someone other than me. During dinner I overheard Helen giving Ilana some helpful suggestions, such as dining protocol. Ilana seemed grateful, eager to learn. I made a mental note to arrange time when they could be together. I thought it would be good for both of them.

'And you, John? Are you okay?' she asked, looking at me with her big brown beautiful eyes.

I couldn't help but smile. She looked so good in the soft light of the evening. I wondered how I would cope with all this if she wasn't with me.

'Yes, I will be okay.'

'What do we do now?' she asked, assuming her old habit of quizzing me in the evenings as in Belize.

I was grateful for her question. It was as if she was re-establishing our routine, something we had shared in the past, something we could do now. Life goes on.

I decided I wouldn't exclude her from any part of my world, not like I had done with Monica. We would do this together. I answered her question. Began by describing what was required to make the company healthy again, return it to the predominant supplier of sapphire in the world. I didn't use any big words which she would not understand. I didn't need to because most seemingly complicated business strategies are really quite simple when reduced to their basic elements. Marketing for instance is only a matter of knowing what the buyer wants and making sure they know you have it. After that, the job is to manufacture a good product and deliver it to the customer when promised for a reasonable price. It always amazes me how often big businesses seems to forget these basic principles and fail miserably as a result.

I warned her. There are people in Thailand who won't be happy when they discover I am active in my company again.

She said she understood. She had heard the stories about what happened the past.

I told her not to worry. Charlie had been Monica's friend. He wanted to bring the people to justice who had killed her and Arny. He had promised to protect us, but I also told her I couldn't promise her we would be completely safe. I asked her again if she wanted to stay.

'This is going to be dangerous,' I said. 'If you ever feel you have had enough, I'll understand. You don't have to stay.'

She thought for a moment. 'I did not know Arny well, but I liked him, John. And I never knew your friend, Monica, but I think I would have liked her too. And I have told you. The man who hired me in Belize, he is not a nice man. He tried to kill you and he burned your house. I too could have been dead in your house. If I had died, this man would have had no pity for me. You know this is true.'

I nodded.

'These men, they should not be doing what they are doing,' she continued. 'It is not right. And you know that bad man told me he would kill me if I talked to you. So, I am in danger also. I need protection just like you.'

'I understand.'

'I like you Mr. John...Please forgive me for calling you this name. Sometimes it seems good to say the words again.'

'It's okay.'

'Do you like me too, Mr. John?'

'I like you Ms. Ilana.'

I picked her up. Her body resting in my arms felt good. She laughed when I carried her into the guest bedroom, knowing what would happen next.

As I lay in bed with Ilana sleeping beside me, I began to feel like I had returned from the dead. As close to being mentally where I was before the night when Monica died; as close I had felt for a long time. I also knew I couldn't change the past and the memories of Monica's death would always haunt me, but it was time to move on.

I rested comfortably and eventually slept without nightmares.

FRIDAY, JULY 10, 2:35 P.M. JOHN

Drawn eggshell-white curtains created a visual barrier over the windows, concealing an expansive view the valley outside my office.

The depressing translucent cloth shielded the sun from spreading light over newly purchased furniture. Everything inside my office looked coldly institutional in the artificial light.

I missed my old office.

My new office felt unfamiliar now, smelling of new leather and fresh paint. Only the base of my old coffee table had survived the sniper's attack. The half inch, plate glass top had to be replaced, but the same old hunk of driftwood base I had pulled from the shores of Lake Michigan was still useful, even though a few newly inserted bullets holes now marred its water-sculpted, rustic form.

The gray holes were a constant reminder for me to be constantly vigil. I was no longer free to take long lonely walks to the top of my mountain. I could not go outside unless one of Charlie's guys accompanied me. And these post military manikins were now in charge of when and where I could go, not me. They were a pain, but I had to listen. I didn't have a choice. Not if I wanted to stay alive. Or so Charlie explained to me in uncontested detail.

'Listen, John,' he said. 'You have been lucky so far, but now you need to rely on something besides luck. Do what Brad and Steve say, nothing more. Okay?'

'Okay, Charlie.'

My drapes had been closed for almost a month now. No snipers could see inside. And I also could not look outside. My apartment and my office were beginning to feel like cages, and I was the caged animal; a secure and well feed animal, but an animal without freedom.

Charlie was happy. I was not.

Ilana came into my office that afternoon like most days. She didn't bother me, didn't say a word, just curled up on one of the couches and read a magazine.

I didn't mind. I enjoyed seeing her while I worked.

In the weeks since we had been in Charlottesville, she had seldom strayed far from me; except for time spent with Helen. They had become good friends. Helen was teaching her about modern day life in the United States. This was good. But Ilana was starting to concern me. She no longer seemed to be the free-spirited woman I met in Belize. Our confinement was bending her mind even more than mine. She was becoming introverted and quiet. And from time to time, I thought I saw sadness in her eyes.

I could not help her. She was a prisoner of my life now. It was a choice she had made. Or was it a choice made for her when she took money from a man in the Mayan jewelry shop.

I tried to cheer her by reminiscing about our life in Belize. We spent evenings after dinner mostly talking about her island. To stay busy, she cooked our meals. Because, as she explained, it was the only way she could eat good food; food prepared as she liked it. However, she constantly complained about my choice of beer.

She could find nothing in stores to replace the Belican Beer she had in Belize. I suggested having Al fly to Belize on a beer run. I told her she could go with him, help him buy the beer and go for a swim. She asked me how much that would cost. When I gave her an approximate figure, she had refused. Said she didn't like spending money unnecessarily.

I ate almost everything she cooked although I don't normally like spicy foods. Thankfully, she knew my tastes and cooked my food separate from hers.

Charlie's guys also ate her cooking. They never complained. I guess they thought it was better than fast food hamburgers and fried chicken which was their other options. Or at least I never heard them complaining. So, I guess they liked her food.

She smiled when I looked at her.

I had been working on a speech for the board meeting, making notes. My legs were starting to cramp. My body was no longer capable of sitting behind a desk all day. I stood to stretch my legs.

The new computers on my desk were silent and dark, no incoming data from around the world on their screens, no mining reports or sales reports from the three distribution houses in New York, Hong Kong and London. And no reports of new cut stones from Sri Lanka or reports from Australia of the number of carats of color enhanced stones coming out of their lab. Hopefully, all this would change after the board meeting.

I was getting anxious.

Time was close.

I took a few calls, not many, mostly from Clarence and Tim. We spent time comparing notes for the board meeting. Clarence said he would wait until the morning of the meeting before telling Bob I was coming. Apparently, Bob had been bugging him, wondering what I was doing. Clarence told him he didn't know. Bob called my office several times after discovering I was in Charlottesville. I refused his calls, told Helen to tell him I wasn't taking any calls, not yet. She used Arny's death and the attack on my office as an excuse. Bob didn't sound too happy when she explained the situation, but said he understood.

Helen had been coming to work every day. She knew the plan. With my permission she allowed some calls from board members and employees to go to me. Only calls from people she knew had been loyal to me in the past. I was respectfully vague with them, saying I was getting settled, no decisions until later.

Charlie called daily.

He was tracking Phillip's movements. It seemed Mr. Phillip Palmer had flown to Thailand shortly after I left Grand Haven. He attended several conferences in the company of highly placed Thai officials. This unfortunately was as much as Charlie knew, but it was more than enough to make us concerned. Events were still swirling out of control. And like before. I saw no pattern in any of it, only a series of random tragedies which could never have been imagined.

I couldn't help but wonder if I had made the right decision.

JULY 12, 3:30 A.M. JOHN

The windows in my bedroom were open a crack.

Charlie wouldn't be happy if he knew. He didn't like anything open for obvious reasons. Or should I say, reasons obvious to him, not me. Personally, I missed the sounds of waves breaking on the shores of the Caribbean or the Big Lake. And since I couldn't have these when I was in Charlottesville, I needed something else to fill that void. I needed to be able to listen to the forest outside my bedroom as I drifted to sleep, the crickets, the tree frogs, the whisper of wind through leaves.

However, sleep was illusive that night even with my windows open. Finally, I got out of bed. Too many anxious thoughts were swirling around in my brain. After locating my bathrobe in the dark, I tiptoed out of the bedroom so I wouldn't disturb Ilana.

Sitting at my office desk with a small desk light lighting a tally sheet of stock ownership, the board meeting was on my mind. I was concerned about the vote. If I wanted to be CEO again, I needed a minimum of fifty-one percent of the stock to vote for me.

Stock ownership in the company originally had been distributed based on alliances established when the company was first incorporated. It all seemed so logical then, but now it was a mess, too many deaths.

I still owned twenty-five percent of the stock.

Although... I assumed Phillip and his Thai buddies might have a problem with that. They probably thought they owned my stock. And one thing was true, they had paid for the shares. I had their money. And normally this would have given them what they wanted. But I never signed the stock over to them. So, in reality, they had nothing they could take to a court of law. Plus, I didn't believe the Thai would be eager to go to court. Secret offshore bank accounts, assaults and murders stood in their way, things they would not want a court of law to review.

So, we were in a standoff. Too many mitigating factors like the death of Monica and the attack on my apartment stood in the way of my ever signing the stock over to them. As long as I was willing to live the fear of dying, the stock belonged to me.

Bob Anderson, the current chairman of the board and CEO, also owned stock. He was the head of our New York Distribution House. By virtue of this fact, he had been granted fifteen percent of the stock when the company was formed. Even though I didn't know for sure, I thought of Bob as my opposition. It wouldn't be easy for him to give up control. Too many perks came with the job of CEO, private jets, a large salary, big bonuses. I assumed Bob would not go away easily. His nature was to be a control freak who always attempted to dominate meetings. He assumed he was smarter than anyone in the room, always spouting off about something. When I ran the board meeting, I had to ignore his rambling because I didn't really want to get rid of him. He was good at his job; running the New York Distribution House. He understood the business. And like a good soldier he followed orders even when he disagreed. He had been a good partner and good friend. But things change when power is involved. Power and money are never easy to give up.

Arthur Wilson, who had been the head of the London Distribution House, also received fifteen percent when the company was formed. Arthur was dead now; killed on the streets of New York in a drive-by shooting. Phillip had inferred that Mr.

Nue's Thailand group was responsible for Arthur's death, but this was never proved. I assumed Arthur's stock was in his estate and its ownership transferred to his wife Elizabeth by his will. Regrettably, I had not talked to her since his death, but before his death, Arthur and Bob had allied against me. So, it was possible Bob would have Elizabeth's support. But again, I didn't know this for a fact.

Lin was another fifteen percent stockholder by virtue of the fact that he had been chosen to run the Hong Kong Distribution House. He came highly recommended by one of our original investment banking partners located in Hong Kong. They made his employment a condition of their investment. I didn't disagree. I liked Lin. But he too was dead, killed on the same night and in the same room as Monica; killed like her by a stray bullet. I knew nothing of his family background. So effectively Lin's stock ownership was a mystery. According to Clarence, who is the board secretary, no one had claimed his stock to date. This was unsettling because on the night he was killed, he had confessed to working for the Thai. Therefore, it was probable the Thai now controlled his stock.

Vidu was another dead stockowner. He had been appointed to our board and given five percent of the stock due to the company's relationship with his business. His factories in Sri Lanka did most of the cutting and polishing of company's rough sapphire. Vidu had been poisoned by a needle thrust into his back as he waited for a cab on a street corner in Chicago. I attributed his death to the Thai, but again, I couldn't prove it. Vidu had willed his stock to his brother before his death. His brother replaced Vidu on the board, and this meant his brother controlled five percent of the stock. I assumed his brother would follow Vidu's lead and support me.

Tim and Clarence controlled five percent individually. The companies they represented owned the stock, but they voted for it and I knew I could count on them.

Because Lin's stock was a mystery, I needed the support of one other stockholder if I hoped to regain my old job at the next meeting. The only other major stockholder was Tom Rice. He represented Accent Investment Inc., a New York investment banking firm. His company had been one of my initial investors, helping to financially get my company off the ground. He had never sold his shares which his company received by virtue of their investment in the company's private stock offering. In fact, he had bought out the other two investment banking firms who initially helped my company. They sold their stock to him at a very good profit I might add. They, along with Tom, were the guys who believed me when the company was only wishful thinking. Without these investors' money, my company would not exist today. But after what happened last year, I had to believe Tom Rice wished he had sold his stock like the others. It had to be almost worthless now given the condition of the company. However, as far as I knew, he still sat on the board and controlled fifteen percent of the stock.

The other board members were not stockholders. Their membership rotated on a yearly basis. They were men and women who represented mining interests from around the world. I didn't know the names of the current board members because it had been a year since I last attended a meeting. However, they would not be included in the vote. Our bylaws stipulated that in the case of disputes which pertained to the election of officers, these matters would be referred to the shareholders for a vote.

I had not contacted Vidu's brother or Tom Rice to date. I didn't want to put them in an awkward position if they happened to be talking to Bob before the meeting. I felt I could rely on Vidu's brother, but Tom Rice was a wild card. If I counted my shares along the shares of Tim and Clarence, I had thirty-five percent of the votes. If I added Vidu's brother, the total was forty percent. That meant the decision to reinstate me would depend on how Tom voted.

There was one other possibility: Arthur's wife, Elizabeth. I could call her and ask for her support, but this would be a difficult conversation, especially after her husband's death. He had turned on me, became an ally of the Thai. Still, it was possible she would side with me despite what her husband did. I knew her well. She could be a very independent woman.

So, truth was, I had two opportunities to become CEO - Tom and Elizabeth.

I briefly wondered how Elizabeth was doing. She had a difficult marriage with Arthur. They lead separate lives. I made a mental note to call her soon regardless of how the board meeting went. I owed her a call. It was something I had neglected too long. But I decided to wait until after the meeting. It would appear to be too self-serving to call her now before going to New York.

After rechecking the figures in my head one more time, trying to visualize how the meeting might go, thinking through all the possible scenarios which might occur, preparing, hoping nothing would go wrong... eventually, I lay down on one of the couches and fell asleep with only the small light on my desk softly illuminating the far corners of my office.

NEW YORK CITY, NY, WEDNESDAY, JULY 15, 7:35 A.M. PHILLIP

Phillip entered the restaurant, slowly scanning the room.

When he determined Mr. Nue was not there, he selected a booth near a window and sat down to wait.

Outside the restaurant, New Yorkers scurried across the sidewalks, their heads bent against a wind accelerating through the imposing canyons of tall skyscrapers. A storm was moving up the eastern seaboard, a nor'easter swirling off the coast, driving rain inland from the ocean. The storm mattered not to Phillip. He had more important things on his mind. He had waited a long time for this moment, and now that it had finally come. He needed to concentrate. Nue would be here shortly. Final preparations were required.

A waiter arrived at his table. Phillip asked for coffee while explaining to the waiter that he was waiting for a friend. He wasn't ready to order breakfast. When his coffee came, Phillip sipped it slowly, enjoying the warmth and aroma; his mind actively going over his agenda. He wondered again what was the best way to proceed. In Thailand he had argued endlessly with Nue about what approach to take and it was Nue, who had made the final decision, not Phillip.

He didn't care for Nue's decisions. In fact, Phillip never liked the man. Nue was always ignoring Phillip's recommendations. And this was a problem for Phillip because Phillip liked being in control. Phillip had to find a way to make Mr. Nue understand how he, Phillip, could make Nue's family rich again, if only they would listen to him. For now, he would need to be patient.

Patience was a virtue. Put a plan in place and let it work. Time was not a factor. This was what he had learned while traveling the world. It was a lesson few Americans understood.   Only ultimate success is required. Everything else is unimportant including time. He would just have to be more patient and smarter than all of them. If he could do this, he was confident he would eventually win.

It started to rain outside his window. Slowly at first, then the rain came down hard driven by a fierce wind. Sidewalks quickly cleared. Early morning New Yorkers ran to avoid the downpour.

The door to the restaurant opened.

Nue walked in and closed the door quickly; but not before another man followed him inside, a man Phillip had never met.

7:40 A.M. BOB

Bob Anderson absentmindedly looked out his window as streams of water distorted his expensive view of the New York City skyline.

Mesmerized by the ferocity of the storm, he congratulated himself again on having the foresight to come to his office early, not waiting for a morning traffic jam to disrupt his already tight schedule. He had briefly considered staying in town last night just to be certain he wasn't late for the meeting. But sleeping in his bed at home took precedence. Instead, he came into town early. Now he was happy he had been so smart. From what he could see of the miniature vehicles on the streets far below his office windows. Traffic was quickly becoming gridlocked by the storm.

He sipped his morning coffee in quiet contentment. The quarterly meeting of the board of directors would be held in his office. There was no need for him to go outside in the traffic and rain. And no more expensive board meetings at the Club. In so many ways, the company was now being run far more efficiently than before.

Good because sales and profits were down.

Quickly discarding this disquieting detail from his mind, he wandered down a hall to check on preparations for the meeting one more time.

The caterer was busy at work. Everything was progressing. A long table in his conference room had been placed against a wall covered by a white table cloth. Silver coffee makers were steaming, filling the room with the fresh aroma of hot coffee. Pitchers of fruit juice neatly lined up next to small clean glasses placed on the table. Trays of bagels and muffins, knives and forks, a continental breakfast for the board members; everything was in order, everything as it should be.

Emily was in charge. Bob's executive secretary could be seen scurrying around, tidying the tiniest negligent flaws in the immaculately prepared conference room. Only the distorted view of the city, water streaming down the windows, disturbed her desired order. Emily hoped the weather would break before the meeting. Everything needed to be perfect.

Tasteful artwork, modern framed abstracts graced the walls, complimenting the colors in the carpet. Brown leather armchairs circled the conference table. Booklets and binders placed in front of each chair containing the latest financial reports and other pertinent information, printed materials purposely produced to present a positive spin for a company that was, in reality, going downhill fast. Sales charts, which would have shown descending lines indicating declining growth, had been purposely excluded from the materials. Instead, a P.R. firm was hired to write positive copy such as: 'In the current economic conditions, the company has made excellent progress in maintaining ...'

Bob complimented Emily on her work.

She smiled and continued her attention to detail, straightening material prepared for each board member. Ten members would be attending the quarterly meeting. This was an unusually low number for a meeting. Many had called to say they were sorry they would be unable to attend, pressing matters, family circumstances, unavoidable travel delays; so sorry. Such unforeseen absences were never a cause for concern in the past, but today, they worried Bob. However, it was possible the board members were busy as they indicated. It didn't have to mean anything. It didn't necessarily indicate the company was becoming, as he feared, less relevant.

He sighed inwardly. Their absence wasn't that important. What was important was the two new members who would be in attendance. They would more than cover for the excused gaps at the table.

No one besides Bob knew they were coming.

After calling to say they would attend the meeting, they had faxed him copies of documents establishing their stock ownership for his verification. Bob had checked the documents and concluded they were indeed stockowners.

And since his due diligence validating their ownership had only recently been authenticated; he decided it would be prudent to wait until the meeting to announce their presence to the other members.

7:45 A.M. JOHN

In the past, Mike was my regular driver whenever I was in New York.

I had given him a job working for my company shortly before I resigned. It was a reward for his saving my life. But apparently, he and Bob did not get along. Mike quit shortly after I left the country and returned to driving a big dark blue Buick for hire like so many other chauffeured cars in New York City. Helen told me what happened.

I called Mike as soon as I knew we were headed for New York. His Buick now waited outside our hotel entrance, its motor running, windshield wipers working at the maximum speed in a driving rainstorm. He pulled under the sheltered hotel canopy and quickly got out to open the back door when he saw me come out of the rotating entrance doors following a short, dark-haired woman who looked very cute in a pale-yellow raincoat. Ilana smiled at him with big brown eyes, and he was in love again, a natural reaction for a healthy Italian like Mike.

I watched all this in amusement, thinking some things never change. Ilana slid into the back seat with Mike totally mesmerized by her every move. I had to give him a small shove in the back to get his attention.

'Great to see you again, Mike.' I said.

'Oh... good to see ya too, Mr. Van Laan,' Mike shook my hand.

'John to you, Mike.' I replied.

'Ya, John, it is.' He grinned.

'Where to today, boss?' he asked after settling behind the steering wheel of his Buick.

'How about some breakfast so we can catch up? You hungry?'

'I'm Italian. I'm always hungry.'

'You're always something else,' I laughed. 'May I introduce Ilana to you? She will be coming with us today.'

He turned and nodded to her.

'Nice to meet you, Mike,' she said.

'By the way, see that dark brown Ford behind us.' I pointed to a car which sat idling in the rain behind us. 'That car will be following us. Try not to lose them, okay. That will not make them happy. They are CIA.'

'Okay, but please tell them those guys they have to keep up. I can't be waiting for them all day,' he laughed.

'Duly noted. Now, let's go. I'm hungry.'

7:48 A.M. CLARENCE

Clarence combed the few remaining hairs on the top of his big bald head while standing in front of the bathroom mirror in his hotel.

Oh well, he thought, only so much he could do to make his old mug look good. He paused for a moment to listen to the rain pelt against the hotel windows with a monotonous rhythm. Silently cursing, he spent enough time outside in the wind and rain while working in Australia. When away from the mines, he liked the weather to be nice so he could dress up and not have to worry about the rain messing with his last remaining curls. Back home at the mines, he wore an old red hat that covered his head so he didn't have to think about how his hair looked. But here, well... He briefly wondered if all men were this vain. Or was he the only big old Australian lug who still cared about how he looked?

A white shirt and tie had been packed by his wife Shirley. She took charge of all his preparations for traveling. He was no good at buying suits and ties. He missed her now. Sometimes, she came with him on business trips. It gave them time together. When he was working the mines, he was mostly gone from home. Looking after five mines in different parts of Western Australia was a big job. She understood. She was a great lady. He knew he was lucky to have her.

He tried to straighten his tie, finally giving up after tying it one more time. He couldn't do it any better. It was almost eight o'clock. He wondered if Bob was in his office. From experience, he knew that Bob seldom came into work early. But perhaps he had made an exception today, came early because of the board meeting.

He could try to call him now.

So where, he wondered, had he put Bob's telephone number? Quickly remembering, he had laid his personal telephone directory on the desk in his hotel room last night because he didn't want to have to search for it in the morning; his call to Bob was too important. It was a detail he wanted out of the way before breakfast, if possible.

'Yes... Bob Anderson, please... This is Clarence Aldridge...Yes, I will wait.'

Bob was in, good. Clarence sat down at his desk, tapping a pen. 'Bob, yes, it's Clarence... Yes, I will be coming as I promised... Yes...' he listened to Bob rattle on about preparations for the meeting, waiting for an opening so he could tell Bob that John had decided to come to the meeting today.

That was as much information as he was prepared to communicate.

7:55 A.M. JOHN

The restaurant smelled of frying bacon, complimented by the sweet aroma of coffee.

The hostess gave Mike a hug. She was obviously a friend. And like Mike, she was Italian with lots of thick black hair tied loosely in a bun. Her big movie-star eyes were heavily lined with black mascara and years of anxious troubles. She must have been a beauty in her youth before too many servings of pasta had rounded out a fine full figure. Still, she was beautiful when she smiled and her walk was full of grace.

Mike found a table in the back covered with a red and white checkered cloth. The restaurant was warm and friendly on a cold, stormy morning. Patrons talked loudly in animated language filled with Italian expletives. It reminded me of Rome; never a dull moment. Italians always seem to find a way to make the most mundane occasion a celebration.

'So, Mike, how's life?' I asked after ordering.

'Life is good, my friend.'

Mike and I had a history. He had been my driver the last time I was in New York. He had saved my ass when we were being chased by some guys on motorcycles, seemingly intent on putting a bullet in my brain. But that was a story from another day. And I was purposely trying not to think about it. I wanted to stay calm and be prepared for the Board Meeting. But truth was, I wasn't doing a very good job. It was hard not to think about what happened the last time I was in New York. I was uptight. It was difficult not to be. The streets and tall buildings of this city held too many memories of screeching tires and loud gunshots, all returning to me in mental flashbacks.

Our breakfast came while we talked, mostly about current politics and sports, Mike's favorite subjects. He was helping me relax. I had no desire to talk about the past and I certainly didn't want to talk about it in front of Ilana. She was having enough trouble adjusting to one more new environment, especially this one: the big, crowded city streets of New York. At one point in the morning, as we were preparing to go to the lobby, Ilana had asked me if Mike was the guy who was my driver in the stories; I told her about this city.

I didn't lie. I told her the truth. So, she knew about Mike. I turned to see her eating her breakfast in quiet solitude, adding nothing to our conversation. That wasn't like her.

My cell phone rang. I assumed it was Clarence. He had promised to call after talking to Bob. But the call wasn't from Clarence; Charlie was on the line instead.

'I have some news,' he said.

'Go ahead.'

'Phillip is in town. I thought you would want to know.'

'Interesting.'

'That's it... just interesting. Any thoughts about why he's in New York?' Charlie asked.

'No, could be lots of reasons. I assume it's a coincidence.'

'You're probably right. Any news on your side?'

'Nothing really, just waiting for Clarence to call. Unless he tells me something unexpected, I will be attending the board meeting.'

'Keep me informed?'

'I'll call you after the meeting.'

'Good, are my guys with you?'

'They are sitting at the table next to us. Don't worry.'

'It's my job to worry,' he replied.

8:10 A.M. BOB

Bob put down his phone.

He had just received the one call he had been dreading for a month.

As time closed in on the board meeting, he began to think it would not come, and he quit worrying about it. But now, at the last minute, it came, and he was forced to face it.

And it was the one problem he did not want to face this morning of all mornings.

Damn, he said to himself. Why now? Why wait until now? Why didn't he return my calls? Why did John have his buddy Clarence call me instead?

Bob turned his office chair around to face the windows. The storm wasn't slowing. If anything, it was getting worse, raining so hard; he could not see the buildings across the street. A distorted colorless haze greeted him through rain splattered windows. The storm was unsettling, offering nothing to calm his nerves.

Despite the bad news he had just received, he smiled unconsciously. After getting a fresh cup of coffee, he took a small silver flask from his desk and poured some whiskey into his cup to calm his nerves. He took a sip, now anxious for the meeting to begin.

It didn't take a genius to understand something was up. John was not coming to make his life easy, he mused.

Well, I have a surprise for you too, Mr. John Van Laan.

9:55 A.M. ILANA

Watching without really seeing the flashing images or listening to the talking heads on the TV screen; Ilana was preoccupied.

Why, she wondered, why was it always so cold and rainy in this country? She never minded the rain in Belize. The warm rain on her island made the flowers grow. And rainwater was collected from rooftops and held in cisterns for cleaning and other chores. Rain in Belize was a blessing. But here it was always raining, and the rain was cold and damp rain, not like the warm rain on her island, which brought relief from the heat. This cold, wet rain was full of sadness, and it did not go away like at home. Here, the rain could last for days. She did not like this cold, depressing rain.

But more than disliking the rain, she disliked being away from John, being alone in a hotel room in this New York City, a big, busy city full of so many people. She had just begun to become accustomed to living in Charlottesville. John's apartment was beautiful; so many pretty things to see and touch. It had been fun. And Helen, her new friend, was helping her and she was trying to learn. But sometimes it was very difficult living there. She didn't like being inside for hours; no time to run and swim, no time to see the clear blue sky. This was hard.

But she liked being with John. He made up for what was bad. And she wanted to be good for him. She wanted to keep her spirits high. But this was not always easy. Sometimes, she missed the beach and the water, mostly the warm breezes. But she was trying to adjust to her new circumstances. If she and John were to make a life together, she knew she had to try.

He was patient.

Although sometimes he looked annoyed; sometimes when she was complaining, he would scowl. She knew the look. But then he would smile and give her a kiss. He would say not to worry about whatever it was that was bothering her. Or he would take time to help her, explain how some new gadget worked. Things she had never seen in Belize. She wondered why Americans needed so many gadgets. Did these gadgets make their life better or just more complicated?

He had told her she could not come with him this morning. She had to return to their hotel after breakfast. His meeting was important. He needed to concentrate. He did not have time for her this morning.

She said she understood, but she did not like it. This place was so strange. She understood very little of what she was to do here. She wished she could talk to Helen. She had so many questions to ask Helen. But she would have to wait until she returned to Charlottesville. Then she would ask Helen. Perhaps it would be good to make a list of questions; something to fill her time.

A desk in their studio hotel room contained some stationary and a pen. She sat down and began to write, telling herself everything would be okay.

But she did not feel okay.

10:10 A.M. JOHN

Phillip Palmer's smug mug overpowered my field of vision.

No other person sitting at the board of directors meeting drew my attention like he did. Not Bob who was standing at the head of the conference table making opening remarks, droning on innocuously about nothing important. Not Clarence or Tim; I did not take the time to exchange a smile or a simple nod with them as I had intended. Not Tom Rice, who I hoped would shore up my support. I had no opportunity to see if he smiled or frowned when I walked into the room, a clue that would tell me if he might vote for or against me when I was nominated to be the Chairman of the Board and CEO. That was important because I needed to know what he was thinking. But I had ignored him completely because my eyes were strangely captivated by one person alone, one face in a sea of dull faces around a long conference table: Phillip Palmer sitting at the table in all his overstated grandeur- curly brown hair neatly combed, tied in a ponytail, long narrow nose, and those eyes, those beady black eyes. I was only drawn to those eyes.

I was not sure I showed it, but inside I knew I lost my cool. Except for the fact that those beady black eyes looked as equally shocked to see me, as I was to see him. Except for this, I think I would have completely lost it. He, however, was able to change the expression on his face quickly. Like a trained character actor, his face went blank.

I wasn't so fortunate. Not because I had not given any thought to how I wanted to appear when I walked into the meeting. I had been mentally preparing myself to walk into the room quietly and take a chair at the conference table with nothing more than a nod to the board members, a look of unconcern as if nothing unusual was in the air. Act calm, I told myself, show no tension, and give nothing away that might indicate my real purpose for being at this meeting. But Phillip Palmer spoiled my grand entrance because I was so surprised when I saw him. A look of obvious astonishment crossed my face, and to add to my growing confusion, he was seated at the conference table in a chair normally reserved only for board members.

What the hell did that mean?

I had waited until the last minute to come to the meeting. Not because I was looking for a grand entrance but because if I had come in earlier, I might have been asked questions I did not want to answer. The meeting was scheduled to begin at ten. However, most meetings don't start on time. I estimated if I arrived ten minutes late, I could sit down with a minimum of commotion. But apparently, I had miscalculated. The meeting was well underway when I entered the room. Bob halted his opening remarks when he saw me, asked if I would like to sit in an empty chair next to him at the head of the table, a chair which, apparently, he had reserved for me. I nodded in agreement, even though I would have preferred to sit at the other end of the table, away from him. But I thought it would have been discourteous to ignore him. As I proceeded to my designated chair, I felt their eyes on me, the board members following my every move in the unnaturally silent room.

'John,' Bob shook my hand before I could sit. 'So good to see you again. We were just getting started. Why don't you take a seat so we can continue?'

I think I stumbled slightly when sitting, more nervous than I intended, thanks to Phillip of course. My name was handwritten on a nameplate on the table in front of my chair. Bob, as always, was efficient, if nothing else. He continued his welcoming speech as I listened, his precise public speaking voice a bit overbearing as usual. But then he always talked like this. Even in casual conversation, he spoke like he was delivering a speech.

Fortunately, my seat at the head of the table wasn't near Phillip. He was sitting farther down and across the long conference table. After a few minutes when it became obvious Bob was determined to rattle on for a while, I decided to get a cup of coffee and a poppy seed cupcake from the table near the wall, something to calm my nerves. When I returned to my seat, Phillip's chiseled profile; his protruding nose once again drew my attention even though I tried to avoid looking at him. As usual, he was immaculately dressed for his role, wearing an expensive-looking black, pinstriped suit, white shirt, and flashy red tie. Tall and handsome in an odd sort of way, he had a thin face and angular frame. I could feel his beady black eyes on me, and I sensed he was enjoying my discomfort.

Next to Phillip sat an Oriental gentleman with an enigmatic expression on a face common to his race. Small, thin eyes and mouth gave him a genetic advantage. Thousand years of breeding had created a face so completely void of expression it was as if Orientals lacked the ability to portray emotion. Their normally impenetrable demeanor made it difficult to see inside their souls, to know what they were thinking; making them a daunting foe when negotiating.

Hearing my name forced me back to reality.

'I'm sure you all know John Van Laan. He is attending this meeting after a long absence,' Bob said in a distinctly dour tone of voice, lacking enthusiasm, which suggested he might finish his sentence by saying, 'for reasons only he knows.' But he didn't say that.

He continued, 'John owns considerable stock in the company. Of course, he is always welcome at our board meetings. However, as some of you know, he resigned his position as an officer and a board member. His place at this table today is, therefore, unofficial.'

I thought this was an interesting position to take. Bob was informing me I had no vote on the board.

He asked if I had anything I wanted to say.

I could have disagreed with his assessment of my privileges, but I didn't want to alarm him at this time. Instead, I thanked him for inviting me to sit at the table and suggested I would be happy to sit in an observer's chair if he preferred.

He said I was welcome at the table.

With his welcome speech concluded Bob continued to the first item on his agenda. 'I would like to take this opportunity to introduce two new stockholders to the board. Shortly, I will make a motion to have them elected. But first, allow me to clarify their qualifications.'

Clarence, sitting across and down a few seats from me, gave me a look which told me he knew nothing about this action. Clarence was the Board Secretary. He should have been informed. This was an obvious breach of board etiquette by Bob.

'Mr. Phillip Palmer comes to us because he has purchased stock from the estate of the late Arthur Wilson,' Bob explained. 'I have checked the authenticity of his claim and found it to be true.'

Although I tried, it was difficult to look unconcerned when I heard this news. Truth was, I was shocked, my mind racing. It meant Phillip owned fifteen percent of the company, the stock I assumed was still being held by Elizabeth, Arthur's widow. She must have sold it to him. That made no sense. As far as I knew, Elizabeth never liked Phillip. So how was it possible he had convinced her to sell him the stock?

Bob continued, 'Mr. Lee Van, sitting next to Mr. Palmer, comes to us from Hong Kong. He is the recipient of his brother's stock through his brother's will. I think all of you knew his brother, Lin, before his untimely death.' He paused. 'Mr. Van and Mr. Palmer have both worked diligently with our lawyers to validate their stock. After proper due diligence, I have informed them their claims are accepted.'

Bob paused again before continuing. 'They have requested a seat on our board, given they are major stockholders. In addition, they have demonstrated to me they are knowledgeable in our business. Each of them has extensive experience in dealing in the colored gemstone business. In your board materials, you will find resumes outlining the careers of these gentlemen. Also, you will see I have included a memorandum detailing the legal due diligence that I conducted on your behalf to validate their claims. Perhaps now would be a good time to take a break so you can read over this material. My apologies for not getting it to you prior to the meeting, but my office only recently completed this work. And since the next scheduled board meeting is not for three months, I thought it prudent to call for their election today... Any questions before we take a break?'

No one spoke, least of all me.

'All right, fifteen minutes for coffee, and then we will vote.' Bob stood promptly to go to the coffee table.

It may not have been true, but to me, Bob looked like the cat who had just eaten a proverbial canary. A smirk covered his face. I imagined him thinking: okay, John Van Laan, you thought you could waltz in here on a whim. Well, take that John Van Laan.

Bob, of course, knew my history with Phillip because some of it was his history. He knew about Phillip, about Phillip's complicity in the crimes committed against me. Nothing which could be proved, nothing but my word against his. I thought this should have been enough to prevent Phillip from ever receiving a seat on the board. But obviously I was wrong because there was Phillip in real life, sitting at the table.

Most of the other board members, with the exception of recent appointees, were also well aware of my feelings towards Phillip. They had to know I didn't want anything to do with this man. However, according to Bob, I was powerless to stop Bob's motion. I didn't have a vote. I could do nothing but sit and watch a disaster in the making.

I took a deep breath. It was time to accomplish something productive. I stood up to greet some old friends, shaking hands and smiling. Thankfully, most of the members made small talk, avoiding questions about my reasons for being at the meeting. Out of the corner of my eye, I spotted Tom Rice, our investment banker, pushing his way through the crowd. He grabbed my arm as soon as he got near and led me unceremoniously out of the room and into the hall, seemingly unconcerned that everyone was watching him. Tom was a big-time mover and shaker in the world of high finance. Apparently, appearances didn't matter to him.

'John,' he said, not bothering to lower his voice. 'I guess I should be asking you what you are doing here, but we don't have time for that because I need to ask you what the heck are we going to do about these guys?'

Tom knew and disliked Phillip as much as I did. His aversion went back to Phillip's involvement in a previous investment. Tom's firm had lost a considerable amount of money in that fiasco. Tom always suspected Phillip played a part in his losses.

'Tom, good to see you too,' I said, keenly aware others were listening.

Clarence and Tim joined us in the hall. I shook hands with them as if this was the first time I had seen them in a long time. Then I leaned over and whispered to Tom. 'Let them play their hand for now. I will need your support shortly.'

He looked me in the eye and nodded, confirming what I hoped. He would be on my side when the chips were down. We casually chatted about nothing important for a few minutes before returning inside.

I could feel Bob's stare when I reentered the room. I studiously ignored him, sat at the conference table, and read the legal papers concerning Phillip and Lee's stock.

Phillip had purchased his stock indirectly from Arthur's estate. Apparently, a middleman was involved. It was possible Elizabeth never knew where her stock was headed. I wondered how much money she received for her stock. And now as I thought of it, I wondered where Phillip found the money to buy her stock. He was not a rich man. Nothing made sense.

As for Lee Tran, apparently he was the designated recipient of stock through the will of his brother Lin. I wondered if that was true. Was he really was a relative. It all seemed a bit wrong. Lin had never mentioned a brother to me. But then, we never talked about family, just business. Shortly before he died, the truth came out. I discovered Lin had been working for the Thai from the beginning. So, if this man was Lin's brother, then he probably also had ties to the Thai. Meaning the Thai controlled his stock.

Between Phillip and Lee, they controlled thirty percent of the stock in the company. It didn't take much in the way of calculations to realize my position had suddenly become more tenuous. I assumed the ultimate goal of the Thai group was to gain control of the company from the inside, which is why they wanted my stock. That would give them fifty-five percent, a majority. Game over.

I sipped my coffee and tried to remain calm while the other board members slowly gathered around the long conference table.

Bob called the meeting to order. 'Gentlemen,' he began. 'As you know, the company has been experiencing some difficult problems, but we now have an opportunity to change that. It is my judgment we can put these issues behind us by joining forces with our competitors, thereby creating a unified direction dedicated to succeed on a global ...' he rambled on.

Bob always liked to hear himself talk. His normal manner of speaking was to speak loudly with the clear voice of a drillmaster, head erect. Thinking perhaps if he said something loud enough and long enough, it might become true. However, in this case, Bob was deluded. He was suggesting an alliance through Phillip's and Lin's known association with the Thai. A CIA report given to the board after Monica's death detailed their relationship with the Thai. My guess was Bob thought electing Phillip and Lee to the board was what the Thai wanted. He hoped this would usher in a new era of cooperation between our company and the Thai.

He was wrong. I knew the Thai, and they had only one thought in mind, and it was not cooperation. It was control. Their goal was to take over our company one way or the other. They were not interested in joining forces. No, only one of us would control the international market in sapphires. We would not be working together. This was a winner-take-all game. The ongoing violence in our relationship was a clear indication that compromise was not an alternative.

'I believe having Mr. Phillip Palmer and Mr. Lee Tran join our board is a first step in creating a better future,' Bob concluded. 'Therefore, I would like to make a motion to this effect. Do I have a second?'

I winced at hearing Phillip's name, but I could do nothing to stop the motion. And apparently, no other board member was prepared to take a stand. After a brief discussion, a vote was taken while I sat silently stewing. The motion carried on a voice vote. Afterwards, the meeting proceeded with traditional verbal presentations by members of the board. I never really liked this part of the meetings, even when I was the chairman. The information contained in these reports had previously been made available in written form mailed to the board members prior to the meeting. It didn't need a formal verbal presentation. I tolerated these presentations mainly because they allowed our partners in the company an opportunity to be heard. It was a courtesy.

Clarence had mailed me the materials before the meeting. The reports appeared on the surface to be nothing out of the ordinary. But if you read between the lines, the company was in trouble. Still profitable but on a downward spiral. The numbers may have justified Bob's salary and perks, which I presumed was his ultimate goal, but underneath, the company was failing. Apparently, everyone was hiding behind a veil of statistics. No one had the guts to acknowledge the situation.

This was for later. I had more pressing issues. I wondered if I had missed anything in my preparations for the next session of the meeting. It would be more difficult now, with Phillip and Lin's brother in attendance. But it couldn't be helped. I waited and listened impatiently, my mind racing. Finally, mercifully, Bob called for a lunch break. The morning session was over.

I had no appetite. Instead of eating, I decided to call Ilana. We had spent very little time apart since leaving Belize. It felt oddly strange to be away from her for a whole morning. I wondered briefly if I was mentally prepared to run the company. Did I really have it in me to do it again? Before, I would have never considered calling my girlfriend in the middle of a board meeting. I was all business. Not now, now I desperately needed to hear her voice.

Standing in the hall, alone with my cell phone to my ear. 'Ilana, you okay?' I asked.

'Yes,' she replied. 'How is your meeting?'

We talked, small talk, nothing important. I was content to simply listen to the sweet, melodic rhythm of her words. I said goodbye after only a few minutes when a panicked desire to be anywhere but at this board meeting suddenly overwhelmed me.

I badly wanted to be on my sailboat, white water flowing over its rails, the sun shining with Ilana at my side.

2:35 P.M.

'Mr. Chairman,' Clarence stood and addressed the board immediately after the last presentation was completed.

I, of course, knew what was coming next.

'Yes, Mr. Aldridge,' Bob responded.

'Mr. Chairman and members of the board,' Clarence began. 'Sales figures indicate the company has sustained a serious decline over the last year. The effect on my Australian mining operations has been devastating. Our sales are down thirty-five percent and ...'

'Mr. Aldridge, may I ask what this is concerning?' Bob interrupted immediately.

'You may ask, and I will explain.'

'Mr. Aldridge,' Bob interrupted again, addressing Clarence by his formal name. 'We have an agenda. Could you please wait until new business to make your proposal?'

Bob was predictable, if nothing else. We assumed he would ask Clarence to wait. But we knew waiting until the end of the meeting might not work. It would be too easy to simply call for adjournment at that time. I had done this in the past when I was Chairman. Therefore, it was decided we should make our case immediately after the last presentation.

'The action I'm about to propose cannot wait,' Clarence responded honestly.

Bob now had to assume something was coming, something he probably wouldn't like. Responding like a colonel in the Army, he spoke with authority, 'I think not, Mr. Aldridge. We will follow the agenda. Our next order of business is...'

'Let the gentleman speak,' stated Mr. Chi, head of the Vietnamese Department of Mining.

His voice was unexpected. Although, I was happy he intervened. But his interruption didn't seem to make any difference to Bob. I don't think Bob ever liked the man. Bob's resentment to him probably went back to the Vietnamese War. He and Chi had been combatants at the time, enemies. But Vietnam had become an important source of rubies and sapphires in recent years. This was the reason Mr. Chi currently occupied a seat on our board, as did other representatives of sapphire mines from around the globe.

'Mr. Chi,' Bob said. 'You are a new board member. Please try to understand that we have a protocol that we follow on this board. This is not the time for new business.'

'Mr. Chairman,' Chi argued. 'I am now in America. And I have been told in America every man is free to speak. I assume this rule applies in a business meeting.' He stared at Bob as if he would have preferred to challenge him with an AK 47 in his hands.

'For God's sake, let the man speak,' Tom Rice piped in, sounding bored with this whole exchange.

This was not a good start. The atmosphere was poisoned early.

Phillip predictably jumped into the discussion, assuming anything my friend Clarence was going to propose was not in his interest, and his instincts were correct. Using his best oratorical voice, he announced, 'Mr. Chairman, all companies have an order to their proceedings. I assume this company is no different. This is not a freedom of speech issue. It is simply a matter of protocol. Now, Mr. Chairman, can we kindly proceed with the agenda?'

'Mr. Chairman, I nominate John Van Laan to be the Chairman of this Board and the Chief Executive Officer.' Clarence ignored Phillip, immediately making his motion without bothering with introductory remarks.

'And I second the motion,' Tim chimed in on cue.

Clarence continued before Bob could interrupt him. 'Since I expect the motion to be opposed on the board, I request an immediate vote of the shareholders of the company to confirm this election as provided by our by-laws.'

'Now Clarence,' Bob said. 'I don't think this motion is in order.'

'It is in perfect order.' Clarence responded. 'This company is failing, and it is time for new leadership. In the past, we have experienced the leadership Mr. Van Laan brings to the table. It is time we put him in control again.'

Bob looked at me. I nodded, acknowledging I was a party to the motion. Lin's brother sat placidly through the whole exchange. Phillip stood ready to give another verbal blast. But Bob brought the gavel down hard and called for order before anyone could speak.

I did not expect his response. I thought he would try harder to put off the motion. But instead, he said. 'We have an important motion on the table and it requires a vote. Obviously, my leadership is being questioned and I need to know I have the support of a majority of my fellow stockholders. I believe this matter needs clarification before we can proceed. Mr. Van Laan, as you can see, is at this meeting for the sole purpose of assuming his former position in the company.' He looked around the room. 'Conveniently, all current stockholders are in attendance today. So, the time to vote is now before conducting any further business... May I suggest the board appoint two of our independent members to form a committee for the purpose of tallying the votes? Then we shall proceed immediately to a vote.'

'May I speak, Mr. Chairman?' Phillip piped in.

'No, Phillip. I think the time for speaking is after the vote,' Bob countered.

'Mr. Chairman...'

'Sit down, Phillip,' Bob said with authority.

Phillip sat.

I said nothing through this whole exchange. It wasn't my place to plead my case.

Bob quickly appointed a committee to tally the vote. He then asked the stockholders to vote their shares, support for or against the motion to appoint Mr. John Van Laan as the new chairman and CEO, a simple yes or no vote would do. Mark your vote on a plain piece of paper, sign the paper along with the number of shares you control.

I voted yes, along with the number of shares I owned. Carefully folding the paper, I gave it to Bob's executive assistant, Emily, who collected the votes from the shareholders. The appointed committee walked from the room to tally the votes while the rest of us waited in strained silence.

Turning to Bob, speaking as quietly as possible. 'We need to talk no matter how this turns out.'

Bob ignored me.

10:10 P.M. JOHN

A half-empty glass of wine sat on the coffee table.

Somewhere in the background, the TV droned, ignored by me, but watched by Ilana, who was sitting on a couch in our hotel suite.

The board meeting and the post-meeting dinner were thankfully over. I was physically exhausted and mentally drained. Getting off the couch in a semi-trance to mindlessly look out a window, the expansive skyline of New York at night greeted my half-hearted viewing. Thousands of flickering white windows dotting a dark sky set in a forest of profanely tall buildings... silhouettes in shades of gray. Streams of red and white lights crawled below in opposite directions on the streets, cars caught in games of stop and go, crammed together in long lines between invisible fences. Flashing blue and red emergency vehicles swerved in and out of the congested traffic, a crisis never far away. Calm is not a word used to describe New York. Pulsing, cursing, flows of aggressive behavior... abandoned... lost... isolated humans; these words are far better suited to define the anxiety which grips this city. Millions of our species jammed together like trapped animals on a small confining island, a place where you can't walk ten feet without encountering another annoying human being... and yet, a place where you never feel more alone.

Central Park loomed below in the semi-darkness, a void in the middle of a city of lights. The park was designed to be a retreat from the intensity of the city. But it held its own versions of terror. Rapes and muggings were not uncommon occurrences, especially at night... murder never far removed.

Don't get me wrong; I love New York, the vibrant energy of the city, the theater, the art, the great beauty of its buildings, and its resilient people. But never distant from these images is another side, a darker side. Like the night I saw a man lying dead on a sidewalk in the village. Blood oozed from a wound in his side, forming a crimson puddle on a cold gray sidewalk under stark white streetlights. Only an hour before, I had observed the man alive, doing his job, screening incoming patrons outside a bar. He was an energetic man in life. In death, he was motionless. A small crowd gathered around his fallen body. Most New Yorkers simply walked around this crowd, ignoring the dead man. It was something they had seen too many times. No need to stop and gawk. They continued with the energy and isolation of the city driving them ever forward.

Unable to relax, I slipped away from the restless energy which existed on the other side of the glass window and retreated to the couch next to Ilana. She ignored me, seemingly content to watch her TV program. I rested for a moment, allowing the din from the TV to neutralize the overactive noise in my brain, listening, yet unaware of what was being said by the talking heads on the screen. Turning to Ilana without thought, I leaned over and kissed the gentle curve of her neck, brushing my lips past her ear. She instinctively moved away, her ear tingling. I then lowered my attention to another area of her sumptuous body, smothering my face in the round sensuality that lived beneath the soft texture of her sweater.

'John,' she scolded.

I retreated, leaning my head on the couch and closing my eyes.

She sighed, switched off the TV with the remote.

'Ilana, I'm...' I began a half-hearted apology.

'Don't talk, John.' She crawled over me on the couch and slipped her sweater over her head. Naked from the waist up, she leaned her warm breasts into my face and kissed the top of my head.

'Is this what you were looking for?' She smiled.

'Indeed.'

I unbuckled her jeans, rolled her over on the couch, slipped off her pants and panties. Kissing her belly button and running my hands up her naked thighs. She reached down and pressed my hand against her wet bottom. Unbuttoning my shirt and then my pants, she assisted me until I, too, was anxious and naked. We lay on the couch, enjoying a slow embrace. In time we made love, softly, confidently, fully.

Afterwards, I carried her to bed and covered her with warm blankets. She smiled and immediately closed her eyes in sleep. Jealous of her ability to fall to sleep so easily, I rested beside her, awake, not able to sleep, not this night. Instead, I lay in the bed, wondering if I would ever sleep again.

My day had gone nothing like I thought. Mostly, it had been very troubling. Although I didn't expect it to be easy, I never considered how hard it would be. And even though I achieved what I wanted, I was once more the CEO and Chairman of the Board, my success did not come without challenging consequences. If I needed any evidence to prove this point, all I had to do was relive the traditional evening dinner in my mind. It had been a real letdown. Instead of a celebration as I had hoped, the dinner was attended by only a few of the members. It was all too obvious the board was now hopelessly divided into camps.

My camp talked quietly about nothing in particular. We knew the task ahead would be impossibly hard. We didn't want to spoil a good dinner by discussing the company's problems. After dinner, we said a reserved goodbye and quietly slipped into the night, each of us buried in our individual thoughts.

As I lay in bed, I tried to somehow purge the problems of the company from my mind by thinking about something else. I chose Belize, wondered again if I had made a mistake. Would it have been better to simply return to Belize and take my chances? Perhaps the Thai would leave me alone this time. Perhaps they wouldn't try to kill me if I demonstrated no interest in trying to resuscitate the company, signifying I was willing to let it die. Did I have a better chance of staying alive in Belize than here? Truth was, I didn't know, couldn't know, too many variables.

Despite my best efforts to think about something else, thoughts from the past continued to surface through my brain. Just returning to New York City for the first time since the night when everything had gone so terribly wrong, the night when Monica had died in my arms, was troubling.

I couldn't stop thinking about her. I was afraid to sleep, afraid my dreams would again force me to relive that terrible night.

CHARLOTTESVILLE, FRIDAY, AUGUST 21, 5:50 P.M. JOHN

The computers on my desk were alive with incoming data. In only a month, the constant blinking activity choreographed across the screens had become a mundane constant again.

A new advertising campaign was in the works. Bob had not altered the company's material during his tenure as CEO. It was good, but it had grown old and stale with use. He had not wanted to spend money to develop a new campaign. And he also slowly reduced expenditures for media time; saving a considerable amount of funds in the process. But, the company had lost considerable market share as a result, due to ignoring the obvious correlation between advertising and sales.

Our advertising agency responded brilliantly. I immediately liked the new look, more upbeat than the previous campaign, full of bright artistic images set to high tempo music in quick rhythmic displays of colorful gemstones across the screen. I hoped it would attract younger buyers.

But everything takes time.

I had to constantly remind myself to be patient. However, despite my impatience, we were making progress... sluggish progress.

I had been concentrating on projects that could be accomplished from my office in Charlottesville. It would soon be time to hit the road. Clients and suppliers needed to be convinced. Face-to-face meetings were required. Some work can't be accomplished over a phone. It wasn't going to be easy. We had competition now. Our friends from Thailand were gaining market share every week. It was different than before I resigned. Then, we held a virtual monopoly. That was no longer true.

My job was mostly a mind game; a kind puzzle if you like. I had to convince certain influential people in the business that my company was their best option. Now that may sound easy, but the execution was complex. And if I was to succeed, I needed a visible proof statement. I hoped our new advertising campaign would be this proof, more than anything else, proof that we were serious once again about doing business at a high level.

Another piece of the puzzle was to beef up our foundation. On my order, the company made a special one-time gift to the foundation of twenty million dollars. That was a huge risk because it seriously depleted our already limited cash reserves. But I felt it had to be done. The main beneficiaries of our foundation were third-world mining communities. If we were to succeed, we needed their cooperation. And to get it, we had to demonstrate to them we were once again serious about helping them.

Bob had cut the program dramatically. He had saved money doing so, but he had also sent a clear message to our miners. He didn't say it. He didn't need to. They got the message. They immediately assumed we were no longer interested in them. This had to change, because the miners were the first stop in our supply chain.

The foundation gave money through non-profit organizations helping mining communities all over the world. It financed schools and medical clinics. It gave college scholarships to promising children of the miners. It paid for a vaccination program. It built community centers and libraries. It changed lives.

I was still a member of the board of the foundation. I did not resign from this post when I left town. Even though I had not attended a meeting for a year, I knew what was happening in the foundation. The minutes from all the meetings were mailed to me. So, I knew the foundation badly needed new funding. If I was going to convince the miners to sell exclusively to my company again, I would have to prove to them we were interested in helping them as before. And that's why the first stop on my scheduled travel plans was to attend the next session of the foundation board.

I took a breather after reviewing the advertising materials one more time. The drapes across the expanse of windows in my office were closed at the time. This was constant mental nuisance. Occasionally I opened the drapes and looked outside just to prove to myself the valley beyond my windows really existed. But I was a target. I knew I was a target and that's why the drapes needed to be closed even though the isolation was getting to me.

The executive functions of the company had been moved back to Charlottesville from New York. Although, some tasks, such as accounting, remained in New York under Bob's supervision. I hoped this would encourage him. Plus, it was more efficient for now than spending a lot of money to relocate. However, the gesture seemed to make no difference to Bob. He was not a happy camper. My friend Bob was bitter.   He declined my calls. All communication between our offices was currently being handled by second level personnel in our organizations.

Jason, my previous young whiz-kid, numbers assistant, returned to Charlottesville to work for me. He told me he never liked working for Bob. He was happy to be with me again. The rest of executive staff was thin. They were instructed to work closely with New York. It wasn't ideal, but I was currently satisfied the arrangement was working.

The most disappointing outcome of my short tenure as CEO was the second half of the board meeting. It had been a disaster, still a sour taste in my mouth every time I thought about it. Things quickly degenerated after the vote. Phillip, that impertinent prick, took over. He called the vote an outrage and raised several points of order, all of which I duly ignored. But his complains had an effect- the atmosphere poisoned. Lee Tran, Lin's brother, was his accomplice. Lee calmly supported Phillip's every move throughout our discussion. The independent board members remained neutral. They were too smart to get involved. The meeting quickly degenerated into a verbal contest between me and Phillip. Finally, I called for an early adjournment to shut Phillip up and the board quickly agreed, happy to be gone.

Since the meeting, I have called a few board members on the phone. They listened but without much enthusiasm, giving me minimum lip service. Promises were just promises, nothing more. Only actions would convince them. And the more I talked to them, the more obvious it became. Bob had allowed the company to decline farther than I imagined. In many ways, it was almost gone, flat-lined.

I had only a narrow window of opportunity to find a heartbeat before it was dead.

GRAND HAVEN, MICHIGAN, FRIDAY, AUGUST 28, 11:10 A.M.
JOHN

'So, Phillip is in town?' I stated for the record.

'Yes, saw him at his favorite restaurant this morning.' David said over his phone. 'First time in over a month.'

'I know. Charlie has been tracking him. He's been traveling, Thailand, Vietnam, India, and Hong Kong. Probably up to no good.'

'Just thought you would want to know he's here now.'

'Thanks. What's your advice?'

David, my friend and legal advisor spoke calmly and with intelligence. It was easy to understand why his clients liked him. He was not only a good lawyer, but he was also a good man. His common sense suggestions were normally right on the mark. But today I didn't like his advice. He told me I should talk to Phillip. Phillip was a force in my company now, on the board of directors. He said I could not ignore him.

I thanked David and said I would think about it.

David knew I wouldn't call Phillip, but he had told me to do so anyway, just to make me think about Phillip in a different light. Typical of David.

I sat in my deck chair and took a sip of coffee.

Lake Michigan spread out before me like the Caribbean Sea, except these waters were cool and not as blue. Still, it was a beautiful morning, the lake a rolling surface of cobalt green glass. Small waves washed up a flawless, storm-swept beach below my deck. The intense contrast of the soft beige sand compared to the glassy water of the lake was a delight to my eye. I sipped my coffee, listening to Ilana hum in the kitchen. She was a happy person again. This was not her Belize, but she liked being liberated from the closed-draped office in Charlottesville. Living on the shoreline of a large body of water made her feel more at home.

Truth was, we both needed a break.

I had worked intensely since the board meeting, put in long hours in a closed office which did nothing to improve my attitude. Ilana had not been faring any better than me. She seemed to be slowly falling into a depression. Her usual cheery attitude had disappeared. She was trying to act happy, but I knew it was forced, doing it for me. Occasionally, I found her sitting in a room alone, soft tears falling from her cheeks. She would look up when I entered and quickly dry her eyes with her hand and smile. If I asked her what was wrong, she would say nothing. I would beg her to talk to me, but she would brush me off. I couldn't break through her defenses. I knew she was trying to be upbeat for me, but it was having the opposite effect. Her all-too-obvious cover-up only caused me to worry about her more. I encouraged her to spend time with me in my office, hoping this would help. She did in the beginning. But before we left town, she had been mostly absent. When I could, I spent time with her, but not often enough, too much work to do.

I discovered I couldn't work as hard as before. I wanted to, and I was getting better at it, but only through mental discipline. It didn't come naturally like before. I was starting to wear down. I was becoming increasingly irritated, even at the smallest things. In addition, the road was beckoning. I had people to see and places to go. But I sensed Ilana and I both needed a break first if we were to survive our time on the road.

Michigan is a great place in the summer. We decided to visit my cottage on the shores of Lake Michigan for a few relaxing days. After our cottage visit, we were scheduled to fly to a foundation board meeting in California. From there to Hong Kong. Bob had hired a replacement for Lin to run our Hong Kong Distribution House. I needed to meet him and this could only be done properly face to face.

After Hong Kong, it was off to old London town to visit Arthur's replacement for the same reason. Face time with both gentlemen was required before the next scheduled quarterly board meeting. Already a month and a half had passed since the last meeting. My trip required immediate attention.

David's call lay heavy on my mind, his advice to talk to Phillip. But I had no desire to confront Phillip. Any meeting with that imbecile did not fall under the category of a vacation; probably just the opposite. Besides, Charlie wouldn't want me anywhere near Phillip. Truth was, he had not been crazy about my idea of going to Michigan in the first place. He was only happy when he had me safely entombed in the cocoon he had created out of my Charlottesville office. That place was wired for security, CIA style. Whatever that meant, he wouldn't tell me, said the technology was classified. His guys lived next door in Arny's old apartment. Replacements rotated in and out of Charlottesville from Langley. It was all very neat and orderly. Very safe, but I felt trapped.

My cottage presented a completely different challenge for Charlie and his guys. I had politely informed them I was not going to live behind closed drapes when I was at the lake. Ilana and I needed sunshine and fresh air. I would take my chances. Charlie had initially said no, but I overruled him.

His guys were staying in the guest bedrooms. They roamed around the cottage, day and night, in shorts and t-shirts, shoulder harnesses with guns. It was a joke really. Ever try to hide a gun under a t-shirt? Not possible. They looked ridiculous in the recreational setting of my cottage. I laughed and told them to enjoy themselves, but they were nervous. And just when they started to relax, Charlie called and they got all up-tight again, walking around like the Secret Service on patrol. I told them I was not the President of the United States and the world would not care if I died. So, relax and have some fun. They said this was fine with them, but Charlie would kick their collective asses if something happened to me.

After a few days of sun and fresh air, my spirits began to improve. But David's suggestion I talk to Phillip was messing with my mind. I needed to think about something else, like going for a swim. The weather forecast promised temperatures close to ninety degrees in the afternoon.

'Hey you,' I poked my head inside after opening the screen door. 'Want to go for a swim?'

'No, that water is cold.' Ilana replied.

She liked being at the cottage, but she was having a difficult time understanding why the water in the big lake wasn't eighty degrees like the tropical waters off her island in Belize.

The water temperature that day was closer to seventy-four degrees, warm for Lake Michigan but not warm enough for my tropical island lady. She was content to sunbathe in her bikini and occasionally splash around in the water near the shore to cool off, but this was the extent of her enjoyment of the lake. Still, I saw a marked improvement in her mood.

I knew I had made the right decision coming to Michigan.

1:15 P.M. JOHN

The intense summer sun beat down, turning the beach into a sizzling desert.

Running quickly across the hot sandy surface to cool my burning feet at the water's edge while thinking I should have gone swimming in the morning as I had earlier planned when it wasn't so hot, but my phone had kept me busy and I couldn't get away until after lunch.

Steve, my CIA bodyguard, followed close behind carrying a gun under a towel. I had earlier suggested bringing a big gun with him because the seagulls could be vicious. He grumbled when he put his foot in the water. He was a Florida boy and like Ilana, he didn't like the cool lake.

To me the clear cool water was refreshing. Without hesitation I dove in, having learned as a boy there was no easy way to adjust to cold water. It's best to let it hit you all at once. Your body will adjust quickly. Then it's great. Going slow only prolongs the agony.

With no chop and the wind-down, gentle swells rolled lazily across the glassy surface of the lake, making swimming easy. I fell into a rhythmic stroke, my muscles warming as I exercised. For whole moments, I forgot about Phillip and all my other troubles. The water took me to another world. Swimming at the easy pace of a long-distance swimmer was relaxing. I had done very little in the way of exercise since the board meeting. Enjoying the simple physical exertion of gliding through the water was pure luxury.

Sound travels exceptionally well in water. The low, faint noise of something mechanical was the first evidence of a boat. I could hear it coming from a distance, but I continued swimming, not overly concerned. Boats running parallel to the shore are a common occurrence in August. But eventually, the noise became louder, more difficult to ignore. The high-pitched tension of a boat's propeller broke my exercise adrenaline high and I stopped to take a look, paddling lazily on the surface of the water. The big white bow of a boat was still a long distance away. I didn't think I needed to be worried. However, I did notice I had swum farther from shore than I originally intended and it is not easy for a boater to see the head of a swimmer bobbing above the surface of the water in the lake and therefore, probably prudent to head towards shore.

I was only vaguely aware of Steve yelling at me at the time. Mostly, I was embarrassed. I knew from experience that motorboats often travel at high speeds, enamored with their free-flowing love affair with velocity, they are not necessarily concerned about swimmers. I needed to quickly get out of the boat's path to avoid a problem. The sound of the boat's propellers increased in my ears as I swam, causing me to pick up the pace of my arms and double my kick.

Stopping to take another quick look, I paddled in an upright position, hoping to see the boat traveling on a course away from me. I was only about a hundred yards from shore at the time and most boats travel farther from shore. The boat should not have been a problem, but there it was, its big white bow not veering away, closing in, coming towards me in a hurry.

I swam hard for the shore, assuming the pace of a short-distance swimmer, listening to the roar of the engine in my ears. Turning my head to take a breath, I could see the boat close in, white water spraying off its big white bow, breaking the glassy surface, disturbing the water's gentle tranquility. Taking a quick breath of air in one of those crystal clear, split-second decisions when adrenalin kicks your body into high gear, I dove in panicked desperation, stroking hard down into the cold black water. My breathing was already exhausted from furious swimming. I had to fight the urge to surface for air, my lungs tightening in rebellion. Pulling hard with my arms, kicking wildly, hoping to dive far enough, fast enough, stroking deeper, fighting to stay down, my lungs screaming for air as the boat splashed the calm liquid surface above me into a gassy white confusion, causing a wave of displaced water to curl my body into a ball, the boat's wake mercilessly tossing me uncontrollably beneath the surface. Lungs now completely exhausted, no longer able to succumb to discipline, I was frantic for air. I stroked for the surface, rising up, head finally breaking free, filling my starved lungs with life giving oxygen, coughing in the disturbed white-water wake behind the boat.

I couldn't be absolutely certain in the watery confusion which surrounded me, but I thought I saw a man standing in the stern of the boat who appeared to be looking at me. It was hard to identify him through distorted wet vision, but I imagined a smile on his face and he looked a lot like Phillip Palmer, tall, narrow build, hawkish nose.

I silently cursed, thinking it was probably my rage, which made me think he was Phillip.

11:55 A.M. JOHN

Visions of puffy white clouds wandered lazily across the sky as I lay on the sand.

With Steve's help, I had crawled up on the beach and rolled over on my back, panting, out of breath, half dead. Misty white apparitions flowing high above me appeared to be dancing to the song of a distant drummer who knew nothing about the panicked, untamed breathing that was still tormenting my adrenaline-stimulated body. I was having a difficult time trying to slow my heartbeat, still breathing in great, panicked gulps of air like a man who was taking the last breaths of his sorry life. Fortunately, the sight of the clouds helped calm me down; offering some assurance of normality, some evidence all was not lost. Like maybe my life was not just one mad dash after another to escape death.

After a few more long, deep breaths, filling my body with life-giving oxygen, my heart rate began to slow, and I could actually think clearly again. Steve was standing over me at the time like a scolding school teacher. I knew what he was thinking.

'Look, Steve,' I sat up, 'I don't know if the guy in the boat saw me. It was really my fault. I should not have been swimming out that far into the lake.'

'Yea, well, from my angle, it sure looked like the bastard turned directly into you.'

'We will never know, will we?' I replied.

Steve was probably right, but I didn't want to admit it. When my shaky legs felt like they could bear my weight again, I stood up. The quiet waters of the lake were no longer a friendly place, and even though my feet burned in the hot sand, I slowly walked up the beach toward the stairs, ignoring the pain because I was too weak to move any faster.

Truth was I was mad as hell and getting madder. Escape from a constant stream of violent threats seemed to be all but elusive, just a dream from a former life. Still, I was not willing to give in, not yet anyway...

After washing the beach sand off my feet and body with water from a hose on the deck, I entered the cottage without bothering to dry off, water dripping from my body, leaving a trail of dark stains across the carpet as I headed towards my bedroom, not caring. Ilana watched as I passed her in a silent rage. Slamming the bedroom door in frustration, I threw my wet bathing suit against a wall and dried off with a towel. While putting on clean shorts and a polo shirt, an errant thought began to circulate in my overstressed brain, an irrational idea growing out of the fertile soil of my anger. If I had to talk to that bastard, now was as good a time as any.

My briefcase containing a personal phone book was in the cottage somewhere. Phillip's number was in that book, but I didn't really need it. I knew his phone number by heart.

The call was a mistake and of course. I knew this. I should have waited until I was rational, but I dialed Phillip's number anyway.

For some odd reason, he answered the call himself, not his secretary. Maybe because Martha, his witch in residence, was out flying on her broomstick somewhere. Or perhaps because he was still standing in the back of a boat with his cell phone. It didn't matter why.

'Hel lo,' he said, dividing the word in two distinct syllables, sounding nonsensically overly dramatic, which was normal for him.

I almost laughed out loud, but the grating sound of his voice stopped me cold. Just hearing his voice irritated my damaged nerves like a fingernail raked across a chalkboard.

'Phillip, this is John. We need to talk.'

'Oh, so now you want to talk. Why now?' he asked.

'I don't know... just thought maybe we should talk before I die.'

'Well, in that case, the answer is no, I don't want to talk to you.' he replied. 'It can wait until after your funeral.'

'Look, Phillip,' I said, ignoring his meager attempt at humor. 'I'm not in the mood to play word games. Here's the deal. I didn't ask you to buy Arthur's stock, but you did. So now you're a stockholder in my company and member of my board. Therefore, we need to be able to talk from time to time.'

'John, we have nothing to discuss that can't be brought up at the next board meeting. And any conversations we could have had before are now pointless. Remember, I offered you one last chance to go on with your life... No... let me say this in terms even you can understand. I was instructed to give you one more opportunity. It was not my idea, but I did it anyway. I tried to make you listen to reason. But you did as I expected. You ignored me... So okay; you've had your last chance to talk to me. It's gone. And just so you clearly understand, my partners have instructed me to withdraw the offer. We have nothing more to discuss.'

'What partners, Phillip.'

'I'm not going to answer that. Do you think I'm stupid? You're probably recording this conversation.'

I realized he was right. I had never discussed it with Charlie, but it was possible either Phillip's or my phone was being bugged by the CIA.

'Okay, let's talk in town, at your restaurant if you like,' I suggested. 'Where no one can tape us.'

'No. The time for talking is over.'

'What are you getting out of this, Phillip?' I couldn't believe he would just ignore me. 'Is it money, Phillip? Is money your goal? Is it a lot of money? Is it enough money you are willing to be an accomplice to murder, my murder? Is the money really that important to you?'

He didn't respond.

I continued my tirade. 'Do you know what happened to me today, Phillip? Someone tried to run over me with a motorboat!'

He didn't say anything.

'So, tell me, Phillip, did you have anything to do with that?'

Again, no answer, nothing, silence.

'Are you trying to kill me?'

'That's nonsense, John,' he calmly replied.

I should have shut up at this point. I knew he would eventually retreat into his self-made world of lies. He always did. But I continued anyway, trying to get to him, force him to face reality, my reality, my pain. Or maybe I did it just because it felt good to yell at him.

'My best friend is in his grave,' I exclaimed. 'His body is a distorted mess of bullet holes. That's not nonsense, Phillip. That's real. And Vidu, who was a friend of yours at one time. He's also dead, poisoned while waiting for a cab in Chicago. And my girlfriend, the woman you met in New York. Dead, just like the others. Their deaths are not nonsense. They are all too real. And you are an accomplice to the murder of all of them,' I fairly screamed at him.

He responded as I expected, as I knew he would as if nothing I said mattered. 'You had your chance,' he replied. 'And you didn't take it.'

I wondered how he could do it. How he could wrap a mask of lies so tightly around his skull that nothing could get through.

'Did you really think I could walk away? Did you, Phillip?' I shouted in exasperation. 'Did you think I could let you and your friends win after what happened? Did you think I could do that?'

'It might have been wise.'

'Wisdom had nothing to do with it. This is about murder and greed... And you...you are in deep.'

He didn't answer, and his silence made me even more furious. He was tuning me out like he always did, retreating once again into his world of lies.

'Phillip, your friends killed my girlfriend. And with her, they killed the life I wanted. She is gone now. And I don't care about my life anymore. Don't you understand? I will fight you and your friends even if it means my death.

Nothing else matters,' I screamed and slammed down the phone.

9:20 P.M. JOHN

Sunsets over the lake can be as ethereal as music.

Azure blues and soft pinks streaked across the evening sky, colors flowing through clouds near the horizon set on a canvas shaded at the edges by the soft grays of an invading night.

I was alone on the deck at the time.

This was not normal. Usually, Ilana sat with me. Tonight, she was content to watch TV sitting inside the cottage. I didn't blame her. I had not been acting very well. Only a few words had escaped my lips since my deadly encounter with the boat, and most of those were yelled at Phillip. Everyone had heard me scream from behind the closed doors of my bedroom. My cottage is not that big, and the walls are not soundproof.

I was embarrassed. I pride myself on maintaining control. I had failed. I made two mistakes that day, one after another, first the swim and second the call.

A glass of whiskey was in my hand. I had taken the liquid warmth out on the deck to calm my jagged nerves. I didn't really like the guy I saw in the mirror that evening. As a result, I was staying mostly to myself while everyone else was maintaining a comfortable distance from me, as if I had some kind of disease to be avoided, like the plague.

Although... we did eat dinner together, and some small talk accompanied our meal, but I had contributed almost nothing to the conversation.

Again, not normal.

Normally, I liked to kid the CIA guys about their gung-ho, narrow-minded view of the world, their 'me versus the enemy' viewpoint, their black-and-white picture of history. I would ask them questions that made them think about America's role in the world and their particular part in it as CIA guys. Kinda like a devil's advocate, I pricked their conscious. It made for lively discussions. And Ilana's perspective, coming from a small country in Central America, supplied fuel to our conversation. But this night was different. Tonight, we ate our food in a subdued silence.

Despite everything, the weather was beautiful, with sunshine and gentle, warm breezes off the lake. Yet I was having difficulty getting out from underneath a dread funk caused by my conversation with Phillip. I had tried, did some work earlier to take my mind off him, checking inventory figures and lowering our purchase price for ruby out of Myanmar, hoping to gain control of these gemstones. But my mind was not really into the work. I simply couldn't stop thinking about that idiot, Phillip.

As I took a sip of whiskey, allowing the smooth liquid comfort to ease down my throat, the sun broke from behind a low cloud above the horizon, casting a bright orange glare over the lake. I had to look away. It was too bright. In a few minutes, the bright orb would fall below the water's surface, and then the real light show would begin, reflecting off distant waters in a kaleidoscope of colors.

I closed my eyes to the glare and tried to rest, allowing the gentle, rhythmic lapping of waves to calm my fragile nerves. The whiskey was working its magic, helping me to retreat into its mind-numbing, alcohol-induced semi-coma; not having to think about anything about Phillip, about Monica, about my disastrous life in general. When the sun finally set below the horizon and I could open my eyes again, I was mindlessly attracted to a seagull floating lazily over the lake. The bird settled gently on the water near shore before letting out several uninterrupted squawks. Like scratches on a record, the squawking bird broke the calm serenity of the shoreline, burrowing into my mind like a sharp knife, forcing me to once again face my problems.

One problem in particular was bothering me more than all the others, and it was a problem I had been trying to avoid thinking about. Because it was probably the biggest mistake I had made that day, bigger than my swim in the lake, bigger than the phone call to Philip.

It concerned Ilana. She had heard my diatribe when I was talking to Phillip. She heard me say distinctly with a loud voice that I didn't care about life anymore, not after Monica died.

Not good.

Having her hear what I said was a mistake. It must have hurt her. Caused her to think I did not care about her, care about my life with her. Okay, I was angry when I said it, but this was no excuse. It was a mistake, another mistake, a big mistake, one mistake after another. This day had been a disaster. While it should have been a good, beautiful day on the beach, a time to relax; it had instead turned into a bitter, ugly mess.

I took another sip of warm whiskey, listening to gently rolling waves break over the shore as I tried to relax. I couldn't. I had to talk to her first.

She was watching television when I went inside to find her.

'Ilana, would you please join me on the deck.'

Her big brown eyes looked at me and I knew at that moment I did not want to lose this woman. Wearing a yellow t-shirt and white short-shorts, which showed off her long brown legs, she got off the couch with the flowing confident motion of an athlete. I loved being near her, seeing her move with a free and easy grace which always gave me a lift.

The sky filled with color as we settled onto lounge chairs on the deck. Soft pinks reflected off the water, instantly coloring the underside of wind-brushed clouds against a darkening sky.

'Ilana, I said some words in anger earlier this afternoon I did not mean. I know you heard them, and I need you to know that what I said is not true. I do care about living. And the reason I care is you.'

'John, you don't have....'

'No, please listen,' I paused.

Getting up, I went around behind her lounge chair and got down on one knee to wrap my arms around her, kissing her jet-black hair, feeling its glistening texture, soft and luxurious, on my lips.

'Ilana,' I whispered into her ear.

She was listening. I knew she was listening. I could feel her rigid body waiting.

'I don't know where I would be today if you had not come into my life, but I don't think it would be a good place.'

She pulled away and turned so she could look into my eyes. 'Do you still love her, John? Do you still love the girl who died in that hotel room?'

'Yes, of course, I still love her. But she is dead.'

Ilana looked hurt, her eyes sad.

'I can't bring her back to life, Ilana,' I pleaded. 'She's gone, and you are now the woman in my life.'

'John, you know I want to be with you, but only if you want me. If not, then I will go away.'

'Please stop. I'm sorry for what I said on the phone; I was mad and...'

'I can't be the girl in the hotel room. I can only be me,' she continued, ignoring my weak excuse.

'I know.'

'Do you want me? Do you want me to stay?'

'Of course, I do, more than ever.'

She looked at me long and hard. Finally, I felt her body relax. I had passed a test in her mind. Not because I deserved to pass but because she had accepted my words.

'It's going to be difficult and dangerous,' I continued.

'Can we go back home when we are done?' she asked timidly.

'You know I want to return to Belize when this is done.'

A smile formed on her face. 'I want to swim in the warm waters by the reef again. Would you like that too, John?'

'Yes, I would like to swim with you.'

I held her close as deep orange rays of light, the last traces of the sun, dissolved into a black night sky. The sunset was glorious. But as the beauty of the sunset transformed the physical world around us into a better place, a bitter question kept whirling through my mind.

I wondered... Was I telling the truth when I was talking to Ilana?

Or was I closer to the truth when I was screaming at Phillip?

PEBBLE BEACH GOLF CLUB, CARMEL, CALIFORNIA, TUESDAY, SEPTEMBER 8, 11:55 A.M. JOHN

Make a slow full turn, left shoulder under my chin, right leg stiff to prevent a tendency to fall back.

Now hesitate at the top, allowing my hands to fully cock, then left hip begins to turn downward towards the ball, upper body follows, uncoiling, accelerating, releasing my wrists. The club face contacted the ball with the whip of its shaft, and rose high in a lazy hook over a rise of green grass, disappearing out of sight. Satisfied a minor miracle had occurred, meaning my golf ball was actually traveling somewhat close to its intended path, I turned nonchalantly and gave my driver to my caddy as if this was an everyday occurrence. It was not. Caddy knew better. Lou was his name, and this was the eighth hole.

'Nice shot,' Steve said as Lou put a headcover on the club before placing it in my bag.

'Do you think it's dry?' I asked Steve. He was my CIA sentry on duty that day. Gun in his shoulder-holster, always vigilant in case trouble showed up. Either Steve or Brad was with me whenever I went outside. Not intrusive, in the background, but always present, I was learning to live with their constant irritating presence.

'Should be fine,' Steve answered.

I wondered. He could be optimistic. I would just have to wait and see.

A gentle breeze was blowing cool off the Pacific Ocean. The sun shone brightly over the green grass hills of the golf course. Only a few wispy clouds marred an otherwise flawless blue sky. It was a perfect day for golf and I was playing one of the great courses in the world, Pebble Beach.

Who said some days aren't better than others?

Gary, my playing partner, pushed his tee into the ground. He was older and could no longer make as full a turn as in his younger days. Still, he had a great swing, which rarely, if ever, got him into trouble. He drove his ball low with a fade, disappearing over the rise and falling right of where I thought my ball had landed. I knew he was safely on the fairway. I wasn't so sure about my ball. A rise of grass in front of the tee blocked our view of the fairway. I could only hope my ball was still on the course and not somewhere in the great Pacific Ocean. If it was too far, it might be in the sea.

Toby and Bill took their turns next to the tee. They were a couple of strangers who had joined us for the round. Their games were no match for ours, but they were having a good time, laughing while making mostly double bogies. I enjoyed their company. They used a golf cart to get around the course. Taking a cart required them to stay on the cart path because the course was wet. Gary and I had a caddy, which allowed us to walk the fairways. As a result, we were seldom near Toby and Bill except at the tee or near the green. That suited me fine. I enjoyed the solitude of the game without constant social interruptions. There is something Zen about golf, something about becoming totally immersed in the simple exercise of hitting a small white ball surrounded by mother nature. Watching it fly with the wind: green grass, rolling landscape, and a vast ocean; just you and the elements.

My caddy's name was Lou. He was an old hippy from San Francisco who had settled for making a living as a caddy. This was as good as it got for him: lots of fresh air and exercise. I wondered if his attitude towards life wasn't better than mine. He seemed to be happy most of the time and he came with a natural gift of gab. Lou was doubling today, which meant he carried both my bag and Gary's.

'Someone has to play this hole today,' Gary quipped as we headed up the rise at an easy walking pace. 'It might as well be us, don't you think?'

I smiled. An interesting way to look at it, and yes, why not us? The sun was warm. An offshore breeze moderated the air temperature, and the golf course was in great shape. So, yes, why not us?

The blue Pacific appeared beyond the green fairway ahead and to the right. Silent, long swells of rolling dark green water marched endlessly towards high, rock-walled cliffs. I immediately began to search for my ball as soon as I was over the rise, hoping to see a white speck on dry ground.

'That must be your ball,' Lou said to my relief, pointing as he trudged a step or two behind. He was happy to have two clients who mostly kept their balls in the fairway, never too far from each other. This made his job of carrying our two bags easier.

'Thanks,' I replied.

My shot had run closer to the cliffs than I intended. In one respect, this was good because it meant my next shot to the eighth green would not be too long, given that the shortest distance to the green was over water.

Gary's ball was about twenty-five yards right and behind mine. His next shot was about thirty yards farther from the green and over a semi-circular cavern of vertical rock walls falling into the Pacific Ocean. The odds of his hitting the green were long; it was too far. If he tried, chances were high, his ball would get wet. It would be far wiser and safer to go for the fairway, short and left of the green. From this position, he would have an easy pitch. One putt could still get him a par.

Toby and Bill had already driven their cart at break-neck speed to where it was only a short walk to their balls. They hit their second shot before us. Bill's shot landed on the fairway well back of the green on the left. Toby went foolishly for the green, lofting a shot high in the air only to watch it fight an off-ocean breeze, slicing mightily to the right before splashing into the ocean and disappearing into the depths, gone forever to the golf ball graveyard in the sea.

Gary hit short left, as I expected, with a nicely controlled shot.

I was next. It was about one eighty-five over water to the middle of the green from where I stood. Anything short would land in the ocean. The hole was below where I stood on a plateau, looking over the cliff. This made the shot shorter than the actual yardage. I selected a four iron which would flight the ball down and out of the wind, giving it a better chance of making the green.

'That's the right stick,' Lou said confidently, stepping back. 'You don't need to kill it. Just a smooth swing will do the job.'

I smiled, knowing this was easy to say but hard to do. I tried, but at the last instant, I jerked the shot protectively left. The Pacific Ocean was too great a mental hazard to avoid a small adjustment in my swing. I cursed myself inwardly, knowing I would not have many opportunities in my lifetime to play this shot. So why not go for the green? What would be so terrible about hitting it into the water?

My ball flew high and long, but as soon as I hit it, I knew it was destined to hook with the wind and miss the green to the left. It landed in the left bunker and took a small hop before settling down a slope in the sand. Oh well, I thought, the eighth hole is one of the hardest holes on this course. I would have to try to get up and down from the sand.

Lou took my club without a comment, wiped it off with a towel before hefting my bag up on his shoulder and heading toward the hole. We had an easy walk to the green around the cliff where the ocean had cut a notch in the land by relentlessly pounding at the rock face.

Toby and Bill were already in their cart and driving to their next shots. We didn't need to rush. It would be some time before our playing companions completed their next shots. I only hoped they would hit their balls somewhere near the green. I hated waiting on a golf course. But hey, it was a beautiful day, and this was one of the great golf courses in the world. I had no reason to be in a hurry. Still, it wasn't my nature to be patient. I'm always in a hurry, even when I try to relax.

I deliberately took a moment to feel the breeze in my face and watch the waves below curl into long green walls of water. However, even with all this natural beauty surrounding me, I was still finding it difficult to stay focused. My mind kept wandering, thinking about events which were bothering me; such as a recent meeting with Charlie and David which crept into my consciousness like an unwanted guest.

The meeting had been bothering me for some time. Charlie and I had argued, as was our nature. David attempted to mediate, as was his nature, but without much success.

I didn't want to argue with Charlie. I knew I needed him on my side. But my resolve didn't seem to be enough to keep us from our natural tendency to disagree. We once again found ourselves at cross purposes as in the past.

The meeting took place a few days after the incident with the boat. I was finally feeling relaxed at the time. The big lake was working its magic, warm and calm for days. Even Ilana eventually found the water almost acceptable. I coaxed her into the lake a few times, and she actually enjoyed it. Charles's guys stayed close when we were on the beach and fortunately, we experienced no more dangerous incidents.

The meeting took place the day before I left for California. Charlie had flown into Grand Haven from Washington. He had called ahead and said he had a plan, and it would be easier to discuss in person. I was reluctant, nor wanting to relinquish the last day of my vacation, but I finally agreed to meet with him. Including David in our discussions had been my idea. I told Charlie that David was a man whose judgment I trusted. I wanted him to hear what Charlie said.

We met in David's air-conditioned office. I spent most of my time staring out the window like a young kid wishing I was outside playing. I didn't want to be in an office on a nice day, and I'm sure that didn't help the situation.

Toby's awkward swing brought me back to reality. He chunked his next shot short into a green-side bunker, which mercifully saved his ball from going in the Pacific. Bill thinned a low-pitch shot, which ran through the green and into the fringe on the other side of the hole. Gary hit a nice high-pitch shot which checked up on the green about ten feet from the hole, giving him a good chance to make par.

Lou walked over to where I was surveying my shot from the bunker, handing me my sand wedge. The green flowed down from the bunker's edge towards the hole. The pin was cut in the center. To get close, I needed to land the ball on the near edge of the green and hope it would run down the slope and stop near the hole.

Toby was up next. He took a couple of mighty swings from the bunker on the other side of the green, scattering sand into the air with each swing. Fortunately, his second attempt actually landed his ball on the green. He smiled at his accomplishment.

Now was my turn. I opened the blade of my wedge, hoping to drive the club under the ball, forcing sand to lift the ball up quickly and drop it softly onto the green while trying to avoid a skulled shot where the club bounces off the sand into the middle of the ball, sending it flying over the green into the ocean. My concern caused me to drive the club too deep into the sand with just enough force to clear the bunker but not enough to avoid having the ball land in the long grass on the fringe of the green, slowed it significantly, stopping well short of the hole by about seven feet. Stew raked the sand as I surveyed my putt. The botched bunker shot left me a tricky downhill putt with about two feet of break.

As I was waiting at the edge of the green for the other players to putt, I became momentarily mesmerized by the vast Pacific Ocean reaching out to Hawaii. And even though I wasn't trying to think about Charlie, his plan kept interrupting my thoughts. He described a sting operation, luring Phillip and his Thai friends into a conversation about their complicity or direct involvement in the New York incident where Arthur had been killed. Charlie described the elaborate surveillance equipment he had at his disposal, suggesting that the conversation could be recorded on tape and used as evidence to put Phillip on trial. As for the Thai group, the incriminating tape might not get them indicted. They had diplomatic immunity, but at a minimum, the evidence could ban them from ever doing business in the U.S. again.

I liked the end results of Charlie's plan, but it didn't fit my vision of what needed to be accomplished. I had two goals in mind when I decided to return to my company. My first goal was to revitalize the company. The second one was to deal with Phillip and the Thai. I argued we really couldn't set up an effective sting operation as long as my company was weak. The Thai needed a reason to meet with me. And as long as they knew the company was in serious trouble, they didn't need to do anything but give it time to die, which was exactly what they had been doing. With Phillip and Lin's relative on the board, the Thai were in a perfect position to monitor and stall any efforts to revitalize the company. They had the situation well under control. But what they had not bargained for was my return to work. However, until I demonstrated to them that I could make a difference, they had no reason to be worried. So why meet with me? I asked Charlie. Why discuss the past? Their strategy was to be patient and wait for the company to fail. Take it over when that could be accomplished with little expense.

I argued we needed to rebuild the company first. Then go after the bad guys.

Charlie asked if I was up to the task.

I had to tell him the truth... I didn't know.

So why not set up the sting now, he demanded.

Because I wasn't ready, I protested. Sure, I wanted to get Phillip and the Thai as bad he did. But I wanted to get them when we were in a position of strength, not weakness.

Charlie thought that was stupid. Let's get on with the job, he had argued.

David, as usual, patiently tried to mediate. But when our discussion quickly degenerated into a test of wills, David was good, but he wasn't good enough to deal with Charlie and me. Logic got lost in the middle of our discussion. Egos took over.

David finally gave up and invited us to lunch, hoping, I guess, that we would cool off. But he didn't know our history.

Lunch turned out to be a pretty tense affair.

'It's your turn to putt,' Gary brought me out of my musing. He had already missed his ten-footer, but because he had a higher handicap than me; I had to give him a stroke on the hole. Meaning his score was five for a net four and, I needed to make my putt for a four or lose the hole. I lined up the ball about two feet left of the hole and attempted to stroke it smoothly but watched helplessly as the ball rolled through the break, coming to rest three feet past the hole. I made the come-back putt, but my chance for a par was gone. I had lost the hole to Gary.

Mentally, I blamed Charlie for the missed putt, rationalizing that he had been on my mind, inhibiting my ability to concentrate and causing me to miss the putt. This was pure bullshit, of course, but a scapegoat sometimes comes in handy in the game of golf.

Charlie flew to Washington directly after lunch. And I had felt dissatisfied ever since. I called him a few days later, hoping to clear the air. But it was pretty obvious he was still mad, and the phone call accomplished nothing.

The ninth hole at Pebble Beach is a long par four with the Pacific Ocean running the full length of the hole on the right side. It isn't as spectacular as the eighth hole, but the dramatic views of the ocean hazard play on your mind. It demands a long, straight drive, hoping to avoid a slice that would end up in the water. The rough on the safe side, the left side of the fairway from the ocean, is up a gentle hillside. Predictably, I missed my drive to the left into the left rough to avoid the ocean. And I blamed the bad drive on the fact I had missed my putt which I blamed Charlie for messing with my concentration. All of this was a lame blame game, I knew. I was responsible, not Charlie. As I walked the fairway to my ball, I was determined to get my concentration back before my next shot.

A session of the Company's foundation board was scheduled for later in the day. This was the reason we were in California. The afternoon session was principally devoted to a special disbursement of the twenty million dollars recently donated by my company. I came to California to urge the board to distribute the money quickly.

Gary Hartman, my playing partner, was the current chairman of the foundation. He had asked for and received a morning recess so we could play the course. He was a retired executive who had run a large venture capital fund in New York. His company had approached me several years before, suggesting I consider using money from his firm for my company's expansion in return for a stake. He liked what he saw, mostly the work we did with third-world miners. His investment bank had funded other companies which had a positive impact on the communities where they were operating. I turned him down. I told him I didn't need the money. However, our conversations gave me an opportunity to become acquainted with Gary. When a vacancy on our foundation board became available, I suggested he consider taking a seat on the board. He accepted, and eventually, he became the chairman.

Gary was an avid golfer. He didn't wish to miss the opportunity to play Pebble Beach. In fact, I think he chose this site for the foundation board meeting so he could play the course.

Some of the other board members were also playing in foursomes behind us. I wasn't sure how we happened to be playing with Toby and Bill. They were not members of the board, but it didn't matter. I was enjoying my match with Gary. We were having a good time. Our bet was two dollars four ways: two on the front nine, two on the back nine, two for the eighteen, and an automatic press on the back. It wasn't the money that mattered. It was the symbolic exchange of funds indicating a win or a loss that counted. It was really about pride, which was a lot more important than money. Gary knew this. It made for good competition.

We were staying at the Lodge. Gary had insisted Ilana and I take the best room. Waking up in the morning I raised my head from my pillow to a view of the Pacific Ocean. One window on the other side of our suit looked down the eighteenth hole of Pebble Beach Golf Course. Otters played off the rocks in Stillwater Cove while I drank my first cup of coffee that morning.

Ilana liked the room. I think she was having fun, although she thought the golf course was a waste of good land. Why not trees and a park for children to play? She suggested planting flowers, building walking paths to the beach below. I didn't argue with her. She could never understand golf with her background. I imagined her now enjoying a room service lunch while watching cable news.

Lou waited patiently while I stood behind my ball in the rough. 'What do you think?' I asked him.

'About two ten to the center,' he said, meaning two hundred and ten yards to the center of the green. He had walked off the distance from a marker. 'How about your seven wood?' he suggested.

It was a long way to the green because I had lost yardage by bending my tee shot left into the hill away from the ocean. A straight drive would have traveled farther, but I had bailed out to be safe. Fortunately, the hole was playing slightly downwind. That would help, but the ball was lying on the side of a hill below my feet, making it easy to lose it to the right. And too far right meant going into the ocean.

I selected a five-wood, ignoring Lou's advice. I hoped taking an easy swing which would give me more control. With luck, I would be able to run the ball up on the green.

'You sure you want that much club?' Stew asked.

I gave him my head cover. 'Smooth swing, Lou, gives me a better chance of keeping the ball on dry ground.'

He stepped back.

I had tried to control the shot, but it had a mind of its own, sailing high in the blue sky in a slow fade to the right, heading dangerously towards the ocean before the off-ocean breeze pushed back and dropped it softly on the fairway, rolling to about ten yards short of the green. Not where I wanted it, but not a terrible shot.

Gary had a stroke on this hole as well. I had lost the last hole when I missed my putt. We were even for the match. I couldn't afford to lose another hole. This was the ninth and last hole on the front side. Two dollars of pride were on the line. Gary's drive had found the short grass of the fairway and rolled. His drive was longer than mine. He was smiling when he walked past my ball. He lofted his second shot towards the green using a wood with a good swing, but probably because he was worried about losing his ball in the water, or perhaps because he forgot to take into consideration the wind coming from his right, his ball sailed high, got caught in the breeze and drifted slowly into the left bunker.

We headed for the green with Toby and Bill racing ahead of us for their third shots. Lou followed behind, carrying our bags.

I thought about the afternoon session of the foundation as we walked. Decisions on the board were not mine alone to make. The foundation was an independent organization, but since the money came principally from my company, the board usually gave me some latitude regarding its use. I wanted the bulk of the money to be given to miners in the Far East and Africa. These workers had been largely ignored by Bob. And as a result, they were currently selling most of their gems to someone else. And I presumed this 'someone else' was a representative of the Thai family dynasty.

Bill and Toby both made nice third shots to the green. I complimented them and headed for my ball. My next shot was an easy pitch to the green down slightly to the hole which was cut in the front left.

'It's going to break about a foot to the right,' Lou warned me.

I settled over the shot and swung slowly, directing the club principally with my right hand. It landed on the green and drifted towards the hole just as Lou had predicted, ending up about two feet short and below the hole, an easy putt for par.

Gary stepped into the bunker. He had a difficult shot, but he also had a stroke on this hole. If he could hit his sand shot close and make the putt, he would win the hole, four net three. The best I could do was a par for a four. If Gary won the hole, he would win the front-side bet. I waited while he surveyed his shot. I knew he was a good bunker player. The odds of him making par were excellent.

The afternoon foundation board meeting drifted into my thoughts. Gemstones from the Far East and Africa were pivotal in our effort to regain control of the market. We didn't have control anymore, and we were not doing anywhere near the volume as in the past. It was struggle. Success revolved around control and volume more than anything. Our current circumstances were not a catastrophe yet, as Bob had indicated. The company was still profitable, but not nearly as profitable as it had been.

But in reality, our situation was far worse. What Bob failed to recognize was the business was slowly failing. We were losing margin every month. Our competitors in Thailand were steadily lowering prices. We had no choice but to match them. And if this trend continued, we would be squeezed out of the market completely in no time. Their advantage was that they had better financial resources and lower costs; they could out-wait us. I needed to regain the upper hand quickly if my company was to survive. A long, protracted fight would not work in my favor.

Gary swung. Sand flew on the green followed nicely by his ball which landed short rolling downhill and stopping about fifteen feet from the hole. A make-able putt, but not easy. Bill and Toby were up next.

I thought about how to get the miners on my side again as I watched Bill and Toby. It would not be easy, and I would have to call in some IOUs. But first I had to convince them I was serious about revitalizing the benefit programs for their communities. The twenty million dollars given to the foundation was necessary. It was a do-or-die gesture. Either the money succeeded, or my company would fail. I had used most of our cash reserves to make the donation. No second chance was available. It was a big gamble, and I didn't have the luxury of waiting long for their reaction. We needed to regain control of the supply side of the market almost immediately if we were to survive.

Gary missed his putt. His score was five for a net four. I tapped in for a four, meaning our match was halved on the front side. He smiled weakly, knowing he had lost a golden opportunity.

I was not too disappointed. Nine more holes of great golf lay in front of us with the eighteenth hole of Pebble Beach as the grand final hole. However, somewhere on the back nine, my mind went absent without leave, absorbed in my problems, thinking about everything but golf.

And regrettably, I lost the match.

HONG KONG, FRIDAY, SEPTEMBER 11, 8:15 A.M. JOHN

Ilana did not like Hong Kong.

She made this completely clear from the day we landed. She said she was happy to be on this trip with me, but too many people lived in this city. She did not like this crowded city.

Island, I corrected her.

Well, it didn't feel like an island to her, not like her island home. 'Where did all these people come from?' She demanded. If it had not been for hotel room service, I think she would have left on the first plane home. Instead, she stated emphatically she would be staying in our hotel room for the duration of our time in Hong Kong.

This was fine with Ben, her assigned CIA bodyguard for our trip. It meant he would not have to wander through the city with her, making certain she was safe. He grew up on a farm in Kansas. He didn't like the crowded streets of Hong Kong any more than Ilana did.

I, however, decided Ilana should come with me to my meeting with the head of the Hong Kong Distribution House. Despite her stated goal of never leaving our hotel, I thought it would be good for her to experience the city. It made no sense to travel thousands of miles to Hong Kong and stay in a hotel room the whole time.

Surprisingly, she did not complain. In fact, she seemed almost happy when I asked her. It made me wonder if she was staying in the hotel so I wouldn't have to worry about her. The woman could be a mystery sometimes. Ben, on the other hand, was not happy.

I was not concerned Ilana would be a problem at the meeting. In fact, I thought she could help. The central reason for my coming to Hong Kong was to become acquainted with the man who ran our Hong Kong Distribution House. It was responsible for approximately one-third of our sales. Ilana's perspective of him could prove to be helpful. More and more it was becoming obvious she was a very intelligent woman. I was curious to hear what she would say about this man.

If the meeting began to drag or our discussion was boring, I had a backup plan. I would have Ilana return to our hotel with Ben. She didn't need to stay. However, I was not overly concerned. I didn't expect the meeting to take long. If the guy was cordial, friendly, and helpful, we could move quickly through my agenda. But if not, I might have to probe deeper, and our meeting might take longer.

An early morning meeting had been requested. I didn't want to make this a two-day affair. But apparently my request did not meet with my host's approval. Helen reported that when she called his office to tell him the day and time of my arrival, he was not pleased. He asked for a postponement. Said he was busy. But in the end, he agreed. Not because he wanted to, but because Helen didn't give him a choice. She could be a very persuasive woman when she wished to be. I knew this from first-hand experience.

My initial reaction to his behavior bordered on his being unprofessional. His uncooperative attitude was not expected. It was not a good start to our relationship. I hoped it didn't mean I would have to spend all day with him, but I was prepared to do so if necessary.

Located in the heart of the business district, the home of the Hong Kong Distribution House was a tall modern building caught in the shadows of surrounding high-rises. Multi-colored fluorescent signs at the street level expressed the energetic whirl and intense activity of the city. A kaleidoscope of blinking lights reflecting off the smooth glass exterior of the building greeted us as we approached the entrance. The main floor lobby had walls of glass and stone. A self-perpetuating waterfall located in the center fell into a tranquil pool of water from an upper floor down a sculptured stone wall.

Ilana was momentarily mesmerized by the elegant surroundings. After pausing to look around, we headed to the express elevator for the executive offices. Steve and Ben, our bodyguards for the trip, waited patiently behind us as the elevator took us high into the Hong Kong skyline. Stainless steel doors opened on the top floor to a spotless reception room. A wall of windows on one side of the room offered a view of the restless miniature activity at the street level, many floors below. I immediately noticed a new glass wall had been installed around the receptionist's desk. It was an addition since the last time I was in this building. Four uniformed security guards were stationed at ready in each corner of the room. An automatic door made of heavy metal and activated by a palm print reader was located at one end of the room. Employees entering the interior sections of the offices were required to place their hands on the reader near the door. Once their handprint was recognized, the door automatically opened. A security guard, standing beside the door, allowed only one employee to walk through this procedure at a time.

A different procedure was required for visitors. Phones had been placed conveniently on tables in the lobby. Signs written in several languages directed visitors to please call the receptionist and state clearly their name and the reason for their visit. After the receptionist approved the authenticity of a visitor's request, she instructed them by phone to approach a second security door, again, one person at a time. She would nod to the guard, who pushed a button that opened a door. The visitor was escorted by a separate guard down an interior hall to a specified conference room. No physical contact with the receptionist was allowed under the new system.

All this was very different from the last time I visited, shortly after the Distribution House had been robbed. Broken glass, dried blood, and yellow police tape had decorated the lobby at that time. A majority of the inventory had been stolen. Millions of dollars of valuable gemstones disappeared in a couple of hours. That robbery was the reason for the new security. Similar measures had been instituted at the other two Distributions Houses in New York and London. Bob had made this one of his first tasks when he became CEO. Another robbery similar to the one in Hong Kong would have bankrupted the company.

Lin Tran was in charge of the Hong Kong House at the time of the robbery. He had been one of my closest allies. Or so I thought at the time. But in the end, I learned he had been betraying me all along. This was extremely difficult for me to understand. I wondered how he could have been working for my enemies at the same time he was telling me he was on my side. I had wanted to ask him this question, but he died before I could talk to him. I couldn't help thinking about him as I called the receptionist to tell her who I was and the reason for my visit. She politely told me to please take a seat while she contacted my host, Mr. Bingyu.

Her instructions surprised me. Normally, I did not have to wait in the lobby of my Distribution Houses. I was ushered inside immediately. Not this time, but I didn't object. The receptionist looked at me while she made her call. I was sure she knew who I was. She had probably been alerted to my arrival. Still, I was treated as any other common visitor.

My table phone buzzed after a few long minutes, and the receptionist instructed me to approach the security door. I informed her a friend would be accompanying me. She said this was fine. My friend should go through the security door first. I told her no. I would go first and wait for her on the other side of the door. She paused and nodded her head, said Mr. Bingyu would meet with me shortly. I thanked her.

Ilana looked nervous, uncomfortable with all the security protocol. I put my arm around her waist, told her not to worry.

Conference room A was our destination. A guard directed us to the room. After entering, I immediately thought someone had made a mistake. Conference room A looked more like a room normally reserved for interviewing prospective employees or traveling salesmen. It was windowless for one thing. Only one pathetic painting decorated its otherwise stark white walls. About four or five well-worn stackable plastic chairs were scattered around the room surrounding a metal conference table. A gray, coffee-stained carpet covered the floor.

Ilana looked surprised, asked me what we were doing here.

I was immediately sorry I had insisted she come with me. And unfortunately, Steve and Ben were no help. They were waiting in the lobby. I had convinced them; they had no reason to worry. The tightly controlled interior of this office was safe. I had never had a problem when visiting this office in the past. Now I wished I had brought them with me. I reluctantly began to mentally prepare for a long day.

Mr. Guo Bingyu arrived after a short wait, which I presumed was designed to demonstrate his independence from my authority.

This was true. He was independent. He did not work directly for me, and I could not fire him. The Hong Kong Distribution House, which he supervised, was legally independent from my company. But I could literally close it down anytime I chose. I simply had to withdraw product. All the gemstones sold from this distributor came from my company and they were sold at prices I dictated. This indirectly made me his boss. Still, it was clear from his reaction to my visit that he intended to test the strength of his independence. I was very disappointed in his reaction, but at the same time, I knew it would be difficult to replace him or his facility, especially now when so much needed to be accomplished in a short period of time. Plus, my company held the mortgage on this building, and it was a complication I could not afford to ignore. An interruption in the mortgage payment would have severe consequences for my bottom line. Therefore, I did not wish to replace him, but I also knew I had to immediately establish my authority. If I didn't, I would have problems in the future.

Guo was taller than most of his Chinese countrymen and younger than I anticipated. A handsome man, he had a full head of shiny black hair which was neatly combed in a modern hairstyle. He wore a conservative, dark gray suit accented with thin gold pinstripes, accessorized with a gold and red striped silk tie. I knew from his resume he had worked as Lin's right-hand man from the beginning. As such he was the most experienced employee we had in Hong Kong. Still, I now had to wonder if he was the right person for the job.

He extended his hand.

I smiled.

As I expected, he looked surprised to see a woman with me. He attempted to hide his reaction, but his thin oriental eyes, darting back and forth between Ilana and me, gave him away. It was obvious she made him uncomfortable.

He bowed to Ilana.

I watched, amused, as she attempted to bow in return while looking at me and smiling weakly.

'Please have a seat. Would you like coffee or tea?' he asked, speaking fluent English with a pronounced British accent, making it obvious he had been born and raised on this island, as his resume stated.

I didn't expect him to offer us refreshments. I thought he would immediately move us to a more comfortable environment before continuing. The room where we were felt like a police shake-down cell.

'Mr. Bingyu, may I call you by your first name?' I asked.

I knew from experience it was not polite to proceed immediately to a first name relationship with a Chinese. However, I decided to test him early. I didn't have time for convention. It was crunch time. I had only a few hours.

He looked surprised, obviously displeased with my request. He knew he had two choices and he didn't like either one.

'Of course, please call me Guo,' he finally replied.

'Good, you may call me John, and this is Ilana. Now, may I request we move to another room. I think we would be more productive in one of the other larger conference rooms.'

'I agree, Mr. Van Laan,' he replied, quickly failing my request to use first names. 'Certainly, it would be better to have our meeting in another room, but unfortunately, all the other rooms are occupied.'

Speaking very slowly and with what I hoped he would interpret as clear intention. 'Guo, I gave you two weeks' notice of my arrival and my intentions for this trip. Now, I know, from having been involved in almost every aspect of the design and construction of this building, you have many other conference rooms. I insist we move immediately to a more pleasant room. I don't care who you have to move to accommodate us, but I insist we go now. If not, I will leave.'

He took his time answering me and he did not respond with a statement. Instead, he opened a door. I assumed his action meant we were moving. However, before we could take a step, three muscular oriental gentlemen dressed in black silk suits entered the room.

'Mr. Van Laan,' Guo said, standing by the door. 'Your reputation for being direct is obviously well founded. And because you have requested it, we will immediately move to another room. Let us do so without further discussion. But before we do, please allow me to tell you I had hoped to broach this subject with more diplomacy. However, you have given me neither the time nor the inclination to do so. Please follow me, sir.'

'Do I have a choice?' I asked, looking at the men surrounding us.

'No Sir, you do not. Your choices this morning have been greatly diminished,' he said calmly.

'May my friend return to the lobby?' I asked.

'No, she must come with us. I'm sorry; I know this may be unfortunate for her, but it cannot be helped.'

GRAND HAVEN, MICHIGAN, THURSDAY, SEPTEMBER 10, 8:35 P.M. DAVID

David packed the last of his cottage attire, throwing his clothes hastily into a suitcase.

He was tired. All he really wanted was a drink and a good night's sleep in his bed. He had been on the road too long. Plus, a delayed flight home after an extended business trip in which he was the lead trial lawyer in cooperation with another law firm only added to his exhaustion. The good news was that they had won a big court case. A large judgment was involved, and his share was considerable. The defendant had been guilty as sin. The guy had illegally taken millions from his clients. David had no sympathy for him.

Yet, the case had taken too much of his time. He had worked day and night on the case through the summer before traveling out of town for the trial. Court time had been intense. Now, finally he was home where he could relax. But first he had promises to keep, obligations made during the time he had been away. Mary and the kids had been promised a long weekend at John's cottage. It was their reward for putting up with his extended absences.

He reluctantly finished packing his clothes.

He had suggested that Mary go without him, but Mary argued John was his friend, not hers. She never felt comfortable at John's cottage without David, even though she knew John and David had an agreement. If David looked after the cottage during John's absence, his family could use it whenever they liked. Still, Mary was not comfortable at the cottage alone. Some day, she said they should buy a place of their own on the water. Then David could come and go as he pleased.

David gave in, just happy he never had to argue against Mary in a court of law. He knew it would be a losing proposition.

The kids were excited. John's cottage was always a treat for them. They didn't have school the next day. It was some sort of professional day for the teachers or something. It meant they had a free day to roam the beach when the weather was still good.

It was time to go.

He grabbed his suitcase in one hand and his tennis shoes in the other, hurrying down a hall. It was past eight-thirty in the evening. If they were to have any opportunity to get their kids into bed at a decent hour, they needed to go now.

He wondered what John was doing this evening, or was it the morning of the next day where John was. David knew John had an overseas trip somewhere in the Far East. He also knew the dangers John faced.

He said a prayer in his heart for his friend, John, and headed out his door.

HONG KONG SEPTEMBER 12, 9:10 A.M. JOHN

There was nothing I could do. I had to follow Guo's instructions.

He waited patiently for me with his three black suited goons standing behind him observing our standoff. I assumed they were there to enforce his wishes. I suppose I could have tested this theory, but I sensed it would be a futile exercise.

I was trying to look unconcerned, not wanting Ilana to sense the rising panic that was creeping into my heart, but I was beginning to understand the depth of the mistake I had made. Steve and Ben were no help. They were stuck behind an impenetrable security door, which mattered little because it would probably be hours before they became concerned. I had told them I didn't know how long my meeting would take, perhaps all afternoon. Just relax.

And it was dumb to have taken Ilana with me, putting her in danger. The only real emotion I felt initially was total stupidity. Real fear would come later.

I took Ilana's hand, trying to remain calm, but I was anything but calm as our entourage traveled down a hall. Memories of blueprints of the building passed through my mind, thinking maybe I could find an escape route. But if my memory was right, there was no way out except for a couple of service elevators down a hall, and they were blocked by the three large goons who were escorting us. Whether I liked it or not, I was going to find out what Guo had in mind for us. I fully expected it to be unpleasant, something like being ushered into one of the back rooms, tied up, shot dead and carted off to be dumped in the harbor.

Strangely, Ilana didn't appear frightened. She strolled beside me as if nothing was out of the ordinary. I suspected it was an act. She was too smart not to see our predicament for what it was. After passing the conference rooms, which is where I thought we were headed, I became even more concerned. Apparently, Guo's intentions were not casual conversation, and this only made me worry even more.

At the end of a hall, Guo stopped and pressed his hand on a palm reader. A door to a back hallway opened. One of the three black-suited goons pushed through in front of us and waited for us to enter, effectively cutting off any escape. It didn't matter. I couldn't abandon Ilana even if I wanted to run.

We were ushered unceremoniously down several more halls. Finally, we arrived at a room that I did not remember seeing on any previous visits. It was a large room with a grand view of the Hong Kong skyline. Sparely furnished with one highly polished wood table placed in the center, surrounded by several ornate, expensive-looking chairs made of dark mahogany and upholstered in deeply colored maroon cloth. Sculpted, gold-framed paintings adorned the walls. The pictures depicted country settings that looked Chinese but reminded me of another country. A small elegant ceramic tea set sat on a dark wood table in one corner.

However, the room's real surprise came in the form of a gentleman who was sitting tranquilly in one of the chairs surrounding the table. His face was very familiar. It lived in my nightmares. I involuntarily shivered at the sight of him, even though it was not cold in the room.

When we entered the room, he briefly looked up, interrupting his work. No surprise registered on his face. He simply returned to working on some papers which were spread in front of the him, ignoring us as we filed inside. The three goons quickly assumed ominous positions in the room like sentries. Two stood by the door and one behind the gentleman who continued to study his papers.

'Please sit,' the gentleman finally said without looking up.

I held a chair for Ilana, inwardly seething in cold anger.

Before she sat down, Ilana spoke in a voice filled with calm intensity. 'I don't know your name sir,' she said. 'But where I come from, it is not courteous to remain seated when a lady enters the room.'

When he did not immediately respond to her first broadside, she asked indignantly. 'May I please know your name?'

The man smiled and slowly rose to his feet. 'Forgive me my lack of manners,' he said. 'My name is Mr. Nue. And may I ask who you are?'

Guo looked like he wanted to speak, but Ilana answered before he could say a word.

'I am Ilana Maria Rodriguez Emula,' she said with dignity.

Now, I was surprised. I had never before heard her full formal name.

Mr. Nue bowed to her. Ilana bowed in return. She was catching on fast.

'Mr. Van Laan knows who I am,' Nue said, turning to me with a slight bow.

Nue was a small man with delicate features. He didn't look Thai, although that was his nationality. To me, he appeared to be more Chinese, with narrow eyes and closely cropped black hair. And he was right. I knew him. I had first met him the night Monica died. He was the head of the Thai delegation who had shoved their way into Lin's hotel room. It was the night I could not forget. Mr. Nue had been untouched by the bullets that flew through the room that night, killing Monica and Lin. According to Charlie, he sat calmly through the shooting, simply waiting for it to end. And because he possessed a diplomatic passport, he had been allowed to walk away a free man several days later. When it became apparent he would not answer their questions, the CIA had no choice but to let him go.

This was the one and only time I had ever seen the man. But the memory of his face was deeply ingrained in my brain. More than any other man, I hated him.

I held him personally responsible for the death of Monica.

UPPER NEW YORK STATE, SEPTEMBER 11, 9:25 P.M. GARY

Gary Hartman closed the door to his home office.

He had work to do and he wanted to do it in peace and quiet. Even though it was late in the evening, he decided to get his work done tonight. He had a golf game scheduled for the morning. He didn't have to think about his what he had to do while he was playing. The weather report for tomorrow was good. It was forecast to be beautiful, gentle breezes and not too hot; a great day for golf.

He closed his mind to the outside world. The letters he was about to write the relief agencies needed to implicitly underscore the importance of spending the money they received from his foundation quickly. If not, the money would be withdrawn and allocated to a different agency.

The foundation Gary headed did not spend money directly. They didn't have the resources. Instead, they selected non-profit agencies to manage programs the foundation financially supported. Unfortunately, some of these service agencies were infamous for moving slowly. They had no sense of urgency like a normal business, seemingly oblivious to the demands of time.

At the recent meeting of the foundation board, members spent considerable time discussing on how to coerce agencies to move quickly in dispersing the allocations which had been donated by John's company. Existing programs were identified which could act fast. Funds were sent, specifically for the purpose of making these programs more productive. It was hoped this would move the money into the field without delay.

John hoped the miners who received these funds would respond by selling their rough gemstones exclusively to his company. However, this message was never stated in formal correspondence. Gary had no problem with this. Everyone benefited.

Point was, the letters were important. And for that reason, Gary decided to write them himself. He had time and he knew how important they were to John. Problem was, he had been putting the task off. Now the letters needed to be mailed.

Then, he would be free to enjoy his golf game in the morning in peace.

HONG KONG, 9:16 A.M. JOHN

Nue smiled. 'Now that we have been properly introduced, perhaps we can discuss matters which are important to both of us.'

The three stone-faced men in black silk suits continued standing against the wall behind Nue like apartment store manikins, looking straight ahead, never wavering. I hated them. I hated what they represented. I was their prisoner. I wanted them gone, but I doubted they would agree.

Strangely, when I should have been thinking about more pressing matters, I became captivated by these three black-suited enforcers. Something about their serene faces, dressed in expensive suits and highly polished shoes, captured my attention. I wondered what they were thinking. Did they fully understand their function, which was to apply violence when violence was required? Was their job simple? Kill when it was required. No gray areas. No need to analyze the depth of a man's soul to determine if he was worthy of life or death. No need to decide who died and who did not. Someone made their decisions for them. They simply followed orders.

I wondered if they had any regrets. Or did they like their job? The only downside I could think of was an occasional threat of danger, but since they normally worked from a position of strength, having great firepower at their disposal, perhaps they didn't need to worry. In the simplicity of their work environment, they looked content.

For a brief moment, I toyed with the idea of standing up and joining these simple-minded purveyors of cold violence. Perhaps I should stand against the wall next to them and ignore Mr. Nue.

I did not.

'Mr. Van Laan,' Mr. Nue interrupted my misguided musing. 'I thought this would be a good time to renew our acquaintance.'

Something about this man made me admire him even as I hated him. His demeanor was tranquil, as if nothing in this world bothered him. He appeared to have great self-control. I wondered if he ever got frustrated. I badly wanted to test him.

'Mr. Nue,' I responded. 'I did not travel thousands of miles to talk to you. I came here to see Guo. Had I known you wished to meet with me, I would have agreed, but only if our meeting occurred under different circumstances.'

He smiled but did not comment.

'However, in one respect, I have made some progress today.' I continued. 'Seeing you here has answered certain questions I had about Guo. I now know I cannot trust him.'

Mr. Nue smiled again. 'I'm pleased you see clearly. It was never my intention to deceive you.'

'Oh, I think it has always been your intention to deceive me. You have deceived me as Lin deceived me for years. I cannot disagree with you more.'

'I'm sorry you feel this way. Perhaps it's time we put our relationship in clearer waters.'

'I'm not sure this is possible after what has happened in the past.'

'All things are possible, Mr. Van Laan. You only have to open your mind.'

'Perhaps you are right. Perhaps we can clear the air. But if you are serious about having a conversation, I demand we reschedule for a time and at a place where we can both be comfortable.'

Mr. Nue paused before he responded. 'Let me apologize for your discomfort,' he began. 'But I must disagree with you. It is important we continue now. We need to come to an understanding. Only then can we meet under the conditions you describe.'

'Does this mean you will not allow us to leave?'

'This meeting will continue until I decide it's over,' he said without emotion.

I slumped in my chair even though I was trying not to give anything away. I was starting to panic, and I was afraid I was showing it. Too much about this meeting reminded me of my last meeting with Mr. Nue, the one which ended in death.

Ilana looked at me. I hoped she did not fully understand how bad our situation was.

No one spoke for a moment. Finally, I found my voice again. 'I'm sorry, but I have to disagree again,' I said. 'It is obvious you can hold us for as long as you wish. But you do not control me, Mr. Nue. And it is not my desire to talk with you under these circumstances... As far as I'm concerned, this meeting is over.'

He stared at me for a long time, his eyes never wavering, face expressionless, nothing I could read. I knew I had made a bad mistake in coming here, and I was going to pay for my poor judgment, most likely die as a result. But all I felt was anger. Truth was, I was willing to meet with Mr. Nue... more than willing to meet with him. In fact, this was the meeting Charlie wanted. Only Phillip was not present to make it perfect. And Charlie did not have the room wired.

But not like this. This felt like the first painful seconds after an automobile accident. You are hurt. You know you are hurt, but all you can think about is desperately wishing you could turn back the clock, just thirty seconds, so you can do it all over again. Stop, go back, anything to avoid what just happened. But unfortunately, this was not possible. I knew I couldn't turn back the clock. But I didn't have to cooperate with Mr. Nue, not if I didn't want to. I was mad as hell at him for putting me in this situation, and I was determined he would not get what he wanted, no matter what it cost me.

'Mr. Van Laan,' he said as if he was reading my mind. 'I understand your anger, but perhaps you will change your mind after you have heard what I have to offer.'

'I only want to hear that I'm free to go.' I responded.

He ignored what I said and continued. 'Your company has cost me and my people much sadness,' he began, sounding like he was giving a well-rehearsed speech. 'You have taken my time and my thoughts. And I have given you a large sum of money to solve my problem, but I did not get what I need from you.'

I interrupted him. 'Do you really think your money can compensate me for what you have taken from me? I would gladly give back every bloody cent if you could return to me what you have taken. Do you think you can do that? Can you bring my friends back to life?' I said, looking him in the eye.

He bowed his head without looking up. 'Please allow me to continue...' he paused. 'I had planned to speak with you about these deaths. They were regrettable, and I wish to offer you my sincere apology for the death of the woman. I am sorry. But I cannot undo what has been done. I assume you blame me for her death, and in a way, you are right. But in another way, we are all a product of our time and our destiny. There is no guilt, only truth.'

I looked at him, wondering where this man came from and what made him tick. He was not like any man I had ever met. Certainly, he was my enemy, but he was more than a simple label could explain.

'Perhaps this is a good time to stop for some refreshments,' he offered.

Guo immediately stood without a word of instruction and left the room.

'May I stand?' I asked.

'Certainly,' Nue replied.

Ilana followed me to the one side of the room. The guards moved, offering us some privacy in a corner by a window.

I whispered to Ilana, 'You okay?'

'Yes,' she replied simply.

The city outside the window moved restlessly far below. I felt like a jailed prisoner observing an outside world I could not visit. Shortly Guo returned, followed by two very beautiful girls dressed in traditional silk dresses. They carried several place settings for tea and some small treats that resembled cookies. After setting the refreshments on the table, they bowed and left the room without a word.

'Please eat and drink,' Mr. Nue said. 'Then we will talk.'

'Go ahead,' I said to Ilana. 'I'm not hungry.'

LANGLEY, VIRGINIA, 7:35 P.M.
CHARLIE

Charlie leaned into his desk chair.

He needed a break. It was late on a Friday evening, and he was a workaholic by nature, still in his CIA office, analyzing confidential field reports and writing memos to his superiors.

A recent promotion was his current problem, the reason for his late nights in the office. Paperwork and more paperwork came with his new job. The additional work was getting old, real fast. Fieldwork never looked so good. He wondered how he could spend more time in the field without giving up his promotion and, more importantly, an increase in pay. However, no easy solution loomed on his horizon. He would need to improvise if he was to succeed, invent excuses to get out of the office. Being tied to a desk sucked. The sting operation he had outlined to John Van Laan was one potential solution. But John had turned him down, and this did not make Charlie happy.

Monica's death slipped into his mind as it always did at times like this. His heart ached again, remembering the sight of her lifeless body lying on the floor in that hotel room. It was a picture he would never forget. He had gone over the events of that night so many times in his head that he had become almost delirious thinking about it. He always came away with the same answer. He had to get into their room. What was happening inside it was unacceptable. John was being coerced into giving up his stock under the threat of death. And even if John had signed over his stock, Charlie wasn't a hundred percent sure the Thai would have let him and Monica walk out unharmed. It was highly possible they would have been killed immediately after John signed.

Regardless of his justifications, the events of that night had turned into a complete fiasco. Not his fault, perhaps; he knew Monica's death was an accident. Still, he couldn't help feeling responsible. Perhaps he had been wrong. Perhaps he should have stayed outside the hotel room and waited.

This thought had continuously haunted his sleepless nights. Wondering if John and Monica could have walked away if he had waited and she would be alive today?

He didn't know. He couldn't ever know. And as badly as he wanted to stop thinking about it, he couldn't. Her death was too devastating, too hurtful to ever forget.

They had been friends, he and Monica, good friends. But secretly, he had wanted more. He was in love with her. He, a poor black student from the inner city on a minority scholarship, was in love with her, a smart, rich white girl from an upper-middle-class family. He knew it wouldn't work. He had nothing to offer. Someday, maybe, someday, he could look her in the eye as an equal. And this thought had motivated him to work hard. After graduating from law school, they remained friends, both of them pursuing their careers. They had a few dates, but as friends after long hours of work. Then, when his career gained momentum, when he began to feel more confident, thinking maybe he would tell her how he really felt, John Van Laan appeared on the scene. And it was clear from the beginning she was madly in love with John.

He had stepped away as he should. He didn't interfere.

He had waited too long.

HONG KONG, 9:45 A.M. JOHN

'Now that you and your friend Miss Emula have been refreshed, may we continue?' asked Mr. Nue.

'Thank you for your hospitality, but we really must go.' I responded, knowing it was a futile request.

Ignoring me completely, he continued. 'Mr. Van Laan, we have both made mistakes in the past. I believe it is time to put these mistakes behind us and do what we should have done in the beginning.'

I was not interested in anything he was proposing. I simply wanted to hate this man, not negotiate with him. 'Mr. Nue, please listen to me. I do not want to talk to you. I only want to leave. Do you understand?'

'I am listening to you. It is you who is not listening. Look around you. If I wanted to end your life today, I could have done so by now. Nothing prevents me. It was foolish of you to come here. Didn't it occur to you that Lin's immediate subordinate would be in our employment? In many ways, you have acted wisely, but in this, you have been foolish.'

He spoke politely as if he were a professor giving a lecture to a student. The problem was that he was right. I had made a horrible mistake. Still, I didn't need to have my mistake thrown in my face, and not by him of all people. I started to say something, but he continued to lecture me like I was a schoolboy who was not allowed to speak without raising my hand first.

'However, instead of making you pay for your mistake,' he continued, 'I want to offer you an apology. And in return, I would like an opportunity to start over. I know it may be difficult for you to forget the past, but nothing good can come from continuing as we have,' he paused. 'What I am suggesting, Mr. Van Laan, is to move forward together now on a path that will be productive for both of us.'

I replied, speaking as calmly as I could under the circumstances. But I could hear my voice getting louder, not believing he had the guts to say the words he was saying. 'Why do you think that's possible,' I asked. 'Don't you understand why I want to have nothing to do with you? Every time I think about you, all I see is the dead eyes of my girlfriend, her sad, dead eyes looking at me, asking me why she had to die. Don't you get that? Don't you understand why I don't want to have anything to do with you,' I continued, trying to control my anger. 'And this apology of yours, I don't want an apology... All I want is to get out of here.'

'I understand,' he said. 'But you need to listen. I offered you an apology because it needed to be said. Because we can't go on without it.'

'What do you want from me?' I finally asked in exasperation. I was getting nowhere with the man, and it was becoming increasingly frustrating. 'You say you want to start over. Okay, how about this? You go your way, and I'll go my way. And I don't ever want to see your face again. That is my peace offering. I will walk away and pray I never have to deal with you again. This is as much as I can give.'

He waited in silence. It was as if he was offering me a chance to vent my anger because he knew I needed it. He was right. But his being smart, his reading my mind, it only made me madder. I didn't like it. I didn't like being manipulated. The problem was I was continuing to play into his hands. I couldn't help it. I was angry.

'No, I take it back. I can't... I can't offer you anything,' I replied. 'Because the only thing I want... really want...' I paused... because I knew I should be shutting up, but I was too angry. I couldn't stop myself. 'I want to see your dead body lying in a wood casket like all my dead friends.' I glared at him.

He sat for a moment with his head bowed.

I waited in silence. I was so mad I could feel my hands shaking under the table.

Finally, he spoke. 'I understand, but what good would come from my death? Please consider this for a moment.'

'Go to hell,' I spat.

He sat silently as I seethed in anger. No one moved. It became deathly quiet.

Anticipation cut through the air like a sharp knife, desperate anticipation. Everyone knew something horrible was about to happen, but a moment of silence needed to be offered first: time to bow our heads and say a prayer. Then, wait for an act of awful proportion, something so ugly it required its own time, its own space. It was too terrible to exist in ordinary times.

Nue turned to one of the bodyguards and asked for a gun. The bodyguard complied, taking his gun from his shoulder holster. Nue took the weapon in his hand and looked at it long and hard.

I stared at him in disbelief. Although I knew this might happen- him killing me. I never actually believed it would happen. I didn't think I would die, not today, here in this place, dead forever. However, as I stared at him, I became more and more convinced this was the end. I was going to die. No way out now. I gripped Ilana's hand under the table and stared a Nue, unwilling to show fear.

He opened the magazine and showed me the bullets.

'This gun is real,' he said. 'And the bullets are deadly. I am not playing a game, Mr. Van Laan. I understand your feelings... It is time to deal with you.'

My heart dropped. I had made one last mistake, became angry when I should have been pleading for my life.

He did not look up when he spoke. 'If it is my time to die today, then it is my time,' he said softly.

What?

I was confused. What was he saying? What the hell was he talking about? His time to die? Is that what he said? I thought I was the one who was going to die, not him.

He turned to Guo and spoke clearly. 'Guo, after Mr. Van Laan kills me, you will escort him and his lady friend to the elevators so they can leave in peace. You will personally be responsible for their safety. If he is harmed in any way, my men will dispose of you. Do you understand?'

Guo bowed in response.

Nue then turned to his bodyguards and to a man they also bowed, acknowledging his orders. He slid the magazine into the handle of the gun with a click and gave it to his bodyguard. Nue then motioned for the man to give the gun to me. The bodyguard nodded, bowed, and handed me the gun.

The gun... It felt cold and heavy in my hand... I was too shocked to know how to react. My hand was shaking. I couldn't hold the gun steady.

Ilana instinctively moved away from me and the gun.

Nue spoke, 'It is time to put the past behind us, Mr. Van Laan. It seems you leave me no other alternative to accomplish this task except one. If you wish to kill me, if this is what it takes for you to move on with your life, then do it now. You have my word you will not be harmed. You will be allowed to go safely after you have killed me.'

I held the gun without speaking, unable to look at it, at him, at Nue, my enemy, the man I wanted dead. My mind became confused in a whirl of detached thoughts. Nothing made sense... Somehow, I knew he was speaking the truth. This was his world. His word was law. His people would do as he asked, which meant I could kill him with a simple action: point the gun and pull the trigger. It would be easy. Or was it? I held the gun, trying urgently to decide what to do.

'You cannot kill this man,' Ilana interrupted my tortured thoughts.

I looked at her without really seeing her and slowly laid the gun on the table. She was right. I could not kill Nue. I could never do it in cold blood. It was not in me, and Nue was right. It would accomplish nothing.

'I see you have chosen not to kill me today.' Mr. Nue stated. 'For this, I thank you. Please accept this gun as a sign of my sincere apology for everything that has happened. If you ever have any doubts about my true intentions after you leave this room, please check the gun. You will see it is loaded with real bullets. I did not lie to you.'

'May we leave now?' I asked Nue weakly.

'In one minute, please.'

I didn't respond, sitting in a blind stupor, trying to make sense out of what just happened.

He continued. 'My people need jobs. If you and I can find a path to work together to help my people, then may we seek this path. I have prepared a proposal which I believe would be good for your company and also help the people of my country. We can talk about this proposal after you have had time to read it. In the meantime, I will not harm you. I promise. You have my word.'

He waited quietly, expecting me to respond.

I was too shaken to answer.

He continued, 'I'm asking only one thing from you today. Will you read my proposal? If you agree, then I would like to talk to you in the future,' he paused. 'It is your choice. I need to know. Tell me if you will consider my proposal. If not, if you have no desire to consider my proposal, then tell me now and I will not send it to you. And... we will continue as we have to this day.'

He paused again before saying. 'I think you know what that means, and I don't think it would be good for either of us.'

I looked at him in disbelief. He was asking me to consider changing everything: the way I thought about him, about his country, his family, all the pain he had caused me and others, everything... I needed time... The decision was huge. My mind raced with possibilities.

'May I have your answer?' he asked in a quiet voice.

Through a fog of indecision, I heard Ilana speak.

'We will consider your proposal,' she said as if she was always the one who made decisions for us.

Nue looked confused. He did not expect my lady friend to answer for me. In a way I was glad. She put him off balance for the first time.

'Is it over?' I asked him.

'Is what over?' he answered.

'Is all the pain over? Can I safely assume you won't try to kill me anymore if I agree to your proposal?

He nodded. 'If we can come to an agreement, you will be safe.'

'Then we will consider your proposal,' I said, using the plural pronoun, as did Ilana. 'Now, may we go?'

Nue stood and motioned to a bodyguard to open the door.

The gun lay on the table.

I walked towards the door holding Ilana's hand, praying no one would prevent us from leaving.

'Stop, Mr. Van Laan,' Nue said before I could reach the door.

My heart sank.

'You must take the gun with you,' he said. 'I don't want you to ever question the truth of my gesture. It is very important you take the gun.'

The hard metal shape of the gun lay on the table, beautiful in its simplicity. Compact power, life, and death resided in this small machine, something so small you could hold it in your hand, point, and pull the smooth trigger, a simple act, nothing complicated, nothing to learn; just hold tightly and let this wonderful instrument of death do its worst, end another person's life forever.

I picked up the gun while looking directly at him. My finger instinctively released the safety without thought.

Seeing something in my eyes, he stepped back, perhaps afraid for the first time.

Monica, sweet Monica, I saw her in my mind, her head weeping blood, blood-red tears which tasted sweet on my lips. I again felt her; the weight of her body, heavy on my chest where we lay on the floor of the hotel room, her dead weight, a weight which offered no relief, a weight which could not rise from my embrace. And her eyes, her blank eyes, her dead blank eyes, stared at me again.

The heavy gun fit in my hand like it had been made for me, made for this moment in time. Pull the trigger; a simple act really. One movement of my finger and all the hate I had for this man would be erased forever.

Nue's eyes narrowed to a slit, squinting to see inside my soul. What he saw, he did not like.

For one moment, one moment lost in time... for one fleeting second, I held the gun in my hand with my finger on the trigger... not for long... just long enough to turn towards him.

He stepped back, unsure, wondering if he had made a mistake and was going to die.

Ilana touched my shoulder.

I turned to her.

She held out her hand.

I gave her the gun.

She clicked off the safety, put the gun in her purse, and, without saying a word, walked slowly towards the door.

10:05 A.M. JOHN

The second my shoes touched the sidewalk outside the door of the Hong Kong Distribution House, I stopped and closed my eyes, allowing the warmth of the sun to rest against my face.

Hong Kong whirled around me in all its intense excitement. People pushed, stopped, cursed, rushed around a strange white man and a brown-skinned woman who were standing very still in the middle of the sidewalk, encased by a mass of humanity intent on action, anxious to be in motion, always wanting to go somewhere.

I had no concern for them.

I simply stood very still, luxuriating in the fact I was alive; happy my body was not slowly cooling, sinking to the bottom of the Hong Kong Harbor. I had escaped from the prison upstairs in that strange room. My death sentence had been commuted. I was a free man.

Ilana stood beside me wondering, I suppose, if I had finally gone completely mad.

Our two CIA bodyguards set up a perimeter around us, shielding us from the pedestrian traffic, keeping the masses at bay.

But I did not want to be shielded.

I wanted to be part of the crowd, just another man walking the sidewalk like them, not a man who was constantly fearing death. A cloud had lifted. I was a free man again. Nue had promised me it was over. I took Ilana's hand and began to walk towards our hotel, falling into an easy pace with the crowd.

Monica smiled. In my mind's eye, I saw her smile at me, her sweet smile. A tear formed in my eye as I thought about her, but I did not raise my hand to wipe it away.

I simply let the tear fall to the pavement.

THE END

Below see excerpts from Book 4, PRESUMPTION OF SANITY

BANGKOK, THAILAND, NUE

While sipping tea at his favorite restaurant, Nue read a report that had arrived on his desk from Hong Kong that morning.

An unoccupied, empty chair on the other side of the table was his only companion that day. Nue liked it this way. He valued his time alone, his solitude. There was plenty of time during the day to talk. Lunch was his time to think, to plan. When he was home in Bangkok, he always ate lunch in this restaurant, at this table specially reserved for him. Made from the finest deep-grain mahogany and polished to a glossy dark finish, the table was set flawlessly with expensive hand-painted china and heavy silverware. This was no ordinary restaurant. Only the very rich ate here.

In the middle of the restaurant was an immaculately landscaped rock garden beside a quiet pool filled with brightly colored, delicate flowers and lush flora, creating a visually contrasting natural scene for the pleasure of the patrons inside the restaurant. Occasionally, Nue looked up from reading to take a moment to enjoy its beauty. After a short time, a waiter arrived and respectfully waited for Nue to remove his papers before placing plates of steaming food on the table.

'Are you in need of anything else, sir?' the waiter asked.

'No, that will be all,' Nue replied.

The waiter moved away with a bow.

Nue frowned to himself as he ate, unhappy with what he had been reading in the report from Hong Kong. Obviously, the tall, red-haired young American who had been appointed by John to manage the Hong Kong Distribution House was on to something. It was possible he was attempting to trace the gems which were being siphoned off and sent to Phillip. If this was true, it was not good. But it was not yet clear the young man had discovered what was happening.

Nue still had time before he would have to deal with the young man.

SOMETIME LATER, IN THE INTERIOR OF THAILAND, JOHN

I felt it first before hearing it.

A vibration in the air passing through my body followed by a low rumble which sounded like the resonance of distant thunderstorm. I couldn't identify it. It seemed to hang in the air so low that it was almost easier to feel it in my bones than hear it.

Tim looked puzzled. 'An avalanche?' he questioned calmly from his experience in the mountains of Montana.

'See any snow?' I laughed.

'I know, but it sounds like an avalanche.'

The low rumble quickly gained in intensity coming from the direction of the village. We were initially blinded to the commotion, behind a bend in the river and blocked by a forest of tall trees which began to sway, wind rushing through their upper branches in a clear blue sky, a sky with no clouds, no reason for wind or the threat of severe weather.

No reason for a sudden disturbance...